ON THE TRAIL OF EVIL

So close were the two canoes that Kaviri had only an opportunity to note the white face of Tarzan in the bow of the oncoming craft before his men were upon their feet, yelling like mad devils and thrusting their long spears at the occupants of the other canoe.

But a moment later Kaviri would have given all that he possessed to have been safely within his distant village. From the bottom of the apeman's canoe rose the frightful apes of Akut, growling and barking, with long, hairy arms outstretched to grasp the menacing spears. As the canoes touched, Tarzan spoke a few low words to Sheeta and Akut.

With a blood-freezing scream, a huge panther sprang upon them, wreaking fearful havoc with his mighty talons and long, sharp fangs, while Akut buried his yellow canines in the necks of those that came within his reach . . .

By Edgar Rice Burroughs
Published by Ballantine Books:

THE TARZAN SERIES
Tarzan of the Apes (#1)
The Return of Tarzan (#2)
The Beasts of Tarzan (#3)
The Son of Tarzan (#4)
Tarzan and the Jewels of Opar (#5)
Jungle Tales of Tarzan (#6)
Tarzan the Untamed (#7)
Tarzan the Terrible (#8)
Tarzan and the Golden Lion (#9)
Tarzan and the Ant Men (#10)
Tarzan, Lord of the Jungle (#11)
Tarzan and the Lost Empire (#12)
Tarzan at the Earth's Core (#13)
Tarzan the Invincible (#14)
Tarzan Triumphant (#15)
Tarzan and the City of Gold (#16)
Tarzan and the Lion Man (#17)
Tarzan and the Leopard Men (#18)
Tarzan's Quest (#19)
Tarzan and the Forbidden City (#20)
Tarzan the Magnificent (#21)
Tarzan and the Foreign Legion (#22)
Tarzan and the Madman (#23)
Tarzan and the Castaways (#24)

COMPLETE AND UNABRIDGED!

And be sure to look for all 11 books of the *Mars* series and all 6 books of the *Pellucidar* series, also published by Ballantine!

THE BEASTS OF TARZAN

Edgar Rice Burroughs

THE SON OF TARZAN

A Del Rey® Book

BALLANTINE BOOKS • NEW YORK

A Del Rey® Book
Published by Ballantine Books

This Edgar Rice Burroughs, Inc., Authorized Edition published in the United States by Ballantine Books, a division of Random House, Inc., New York, and simultaneously in Canada by Random House of Canada Limited, Toronto. "The Beasts of Tarzan" was originally published in *All-Story Cavalier Weekly Magazine* in 1914. "The Son of Tarzan" was originally published in *All-Story Weekly Magazine* in 1915–16.

http://www.randomhouse.com

Library of Congress Catalog Card Number: 96-96599

ISBN 0-345-40830-6

This authorized edition published by arrangement with Edgar Rice Burroughs, Inc.

Manufactured in the United States of America

First Edition: November 1996

10 9 8 7 6 5 4 3 2

Contents

THE BEASTS
OF TARZAN

To
JOAN BURROUGHS

Contents

1

Kidnapped

"THE ENTIRE AFFAIR is shrouded in mystery," said D'Arnot. "I have it on the best of authority that neither the police nor the special agents of the general staff have the faintest conception of how it was accomplished. All they know, all that anyone knows, is that Nikolas Rokoff has escaped."

John Clayton, Lord Greystoke—he who had been "Tarzan of the Apes"—sat in silence in the apartments of his friend, Lieutenant Paul D'Arnot, in Paris, gazing meditatively at the toe of his immaculate boot.

His mind revolved many memories, recalled by the escape of his arch-enemy from the French military prison to which he had been sentenced for life upon the testimony of the ape-man.

He thought of the lengths to which Rokoff had once gone to compass his death, and he realized that what the man had already done would doubtless be as nothing by comparison with what he would wish and plot to do now that he was again free.

Tarzan had recently brought his wife and infant son to London to escape the discomforts and dangers of the rainy season upon their vast estate in Uziri—the land of the savage Waziri warriors whose broad African domains the ape-man had once ruled.

He had run across the Channel for a brief visit with his old friend, but the news of the Russian's escape had already cast a shadow upon his outing, so that though he had but just arrived he was already contemplating an immediate return to London.

"It is not that I fear for myself, Paul," he said at last. "Many times in the past have I thwarted Rokoff's designs upon my life; but now there are others to consider. Unless I misjudge the man, he would more quickly strike at me through my wife or son than directly at me, for he doubtless realizes that in no other way could he inflict greater anguish upon me. I must go back to them at once, and remain with them until Rokoff is recaptured—or dead."

As these two talked in Paris, two other men were talking together in a little cottage upon the outskirts of London. Both were dark, sinister-looking men.

One was bearded, but the other, whose face wore the pallor of long confinement within doors, had but a few days' growth of black beard upon his face. It was he who was speaking.

"You must needs shave off that beard of yours, Alexis," he said to his companion. "With it he would recognize you on the instant. We must separate here in the hour, and when we meet again upon the deck of the *Kincaid*, let us hope that we shall have with us two honored guests who little anticipate the pleasant voyage we have planned for them.

"In two hours I should be upon my way to Dover with one of them, and by tomorrow night, if you follow my instructions carefully, you should arrive with the other, provided, of course, that he returns to London as quickly as I presume he will.

"There should be both profit and pleasure as well as other good things to reward our efforts, my dear Alexis. Thanks to the stupidity of the French, they have gone to such lengths to conceal the fact of my escape for these many days that I have had ample opportunity to work out every detail of our little adventure so carefully that there is little chance of the slightest hitch occurring to mar our prospects. And now good-bye, and good luck!"

Three hours later a messenger mounted the steps to the apartment of Lieutenant Paul D'Arnot.

"A telegram for Lord Greystoke," he said to the servant who answered his summons. "Is he here?"

The man answered in the affirmative, and, signing for the message, carried it within to Tarzan, who was already preparing to depart for London.

Tarzan tore open the envelope, and as he read his face went white.

"Read it, Paul," he said, handing the slip of paper to D'Arnot. "It has come already."

The Frenchman took the telegram and read:

"Jack stolen from the garden through complicity of new servant. Come at once.—JANE."

As Tarzan leaped from the roadster that had met him at the station and ran up the steps to his London town house he was met at the door by a dry-eyed but almost frantic woman.

Quickly Jane Porter Clayton narrated all that she had been able to learn of the theft of the boy.

The baby's nurse had been wheeling him in the sunshine on the walk before the house when a closed taxicab drew up at the corner of the street. The woman had paid but passing attention to the vehicle, merely noting that it discharged no passenger, but stood at the curb with the motor running as though waiting for a fare from the residence before which it had stopped.

Almost immediately the new houseman, Carl, had come running from the Greystoke house, saying that the girl's mistress wished to speak with her for a moment, and that she was to leave little Jack in his care until she returned.

The woman said that she entertained not the slightest suspicion of the man's motives until she had reached the doorway of the house, when it occurred to her to warn him not to turn the carriage so as to permit the sun to shine in the baby's eyes.

As she turned about to call this to him she was somewhat surprised to see that he was wheeling the carriage rapidly toward the corner, and at the same time she saw the door of the taxicab open and a swarthy face framed for a moment in the aperture.

Intuitively, the danger to the child flashed upon her, and with a shriek she dashed down the steps and up the walk toward the taxicab, into which Carl was now handing the baby to the swarthy one within.

Just before she reached the vehicle, Carl leaped in beside his confederate, slamming the door behind him. At the same time the chauffeur attempted to start his machine, but it was evident that something had gone wrong, as though the gears refused to mesh, and the delay caused by this, while he pushed the lever into reverse and backed the car a few inches before again attempting to go ahead, gave the nurse time to reach the side of the taxicab.

Leaping to the running-board, she had attempted to snatch the baby from the arms of the stranger, and here, screaming and fighting, she had clung to her position even after the taxicab had got under way; nor was it until the machine had passed the Greystoke residence at good speed that Carl, with a heavy blow to her face, had succeeded in knocking her to the pavement.

Her screams had attracted servants and members of the families from residences near by, as well as from the Greystoke home. Lady Greystoke had witnessed the girl's brave battle, and had herself tried to reach the rapidly passing vehicle, but had been too late.

That was all that anyone knew, nor did Lady Greystoke dream of the possible identity of the man at the bottom of the plot until her husband told her of the escape of Nikolas Rokoff from the French prison where they had hoped he was permanently confined.

As Tarzan and his wife stood planning the wisest course to pursue, the telephone bell rang in the library at their right. Tarzan quickly answered the call in person.

"Lord Greystoke?" asked a man's voice at the other end of the line.

"Yes."

"Your son has been stolen," continued the voice, "and I alone may help you to recover him. I am conversant with the plot of those who took him. In fact, I was a party to it, and was to share in the reward, but now they are trying to ditch me, and to be quits with them I will aid you to recover him on condition that you will not prosecute me for my part in the crime. What do you say?"

"If you lead me to where my son is hidden," replied the ape-man, "you need fear nothing from me."

"Good," replied the other. "But you must come alone to meet me, for it is enough that I must trust you. I cannot take the chance of permitting others to learn my identity."

"Where and when may I meet you?" asked Tarzan.

The other gave the name and location of a public-house on the waterfront at Dover—a place frequented by sailors.

"Come," he concluded, "about ten o'clock tonight. It would do no good to arrive earlier. Your son will be safe enough in the meantime, and I can then lead you secretly to where he is hidden. But be sure to come alone, and under no circumstances notify Scotland Yard, for I know you well and shall be watching for you.

"Should any other accompany you, or should I see suspicious characters who might be agents of the police, I shall not meet you, and your last chance of recovering your son will be gone."

Without more words the man rang off.

Tarzan repeated the gist of the conversation to his wife. She begged to be allowed to accompany him, but he insisted that it might result in the man's carrying out his threat of refusing to aid them if Tarzan did not come alone, and so they parted, he to hasten to Dover, and she, ostensibly, to wait at home until he should notify her of the outcome of his mission.

Little did either dream of what both were destined to pass

through before they should meet again, or the far distant—but why anticipate?

For ten minutes after the ape-man had left her Jane Clayton walked restlessly back and forth across the silken rugs of the library. Her mother heart ached, bereft of its firstborn. Her mind was in an anguish of hopes and fears.

Though her judgment told her that all would be well were her Tarzan to go alone in accordance with the mysterious stranger's summons, her intuition would not permit her to lay aside suspicion of the gravest dangers to both her husband and her son.

The more she thought of the matter, the more convinced she became that the recent telephone message might be but a ruse to keep them inactive until the boy was safely hidden away or spirited out of England. Or it might be that it had been simply a bait to lure Tarzan into the hands of the implacable Rokoff.

With the lodgment of this thought she stopped in wide-eyed terror. Instantly it became a conviction. She glanced at the great clock ticking the minutes in the corner of the library.

It was too late to catch the Dover train that Tarzan was to take. There was another, later, however, that would bring her to the Channel port in time to reach the address the stranger had given her husband before the appointed hour.

Summoning her maid and chauffeur, she issued instructions rapidly. Ten minutes later she was being whisked through the crowded streets toward the railway station.

It was nine-forty-five that night that Tarzan entered the squalid "pub" on the waterfront in Dover. As he passed into the evil-smelling room a muffled figure brushed past him toward the street.

"Come, my lord!" whispered the stranger.

The ape-man wheeled about and followed the other into the ill-lit alley, which custom had dignified with the title of thoroughfare. Once outside, the fellow led the way into the darkness, nearer a wharf, where high-piled bales, boxes, and casks cast dense shadows. Here he halted.

"Where is the boy?" asked Greystoke.

"On that small steamer whose lights you can just see yonder," replied the other.

In the gloom Tarzan was trying to peer into the features of his companion, but he did not recognize the man as one whom he had ever before seen. Had he guessed that his guide was Alexis Paul-vitch he would have realized that naught but treachery lay in the man's heart, and that danger lurked in the path of every move.

"He is unguarded now," continued the Russian. "Those who took him feel perfectly safe from detection, and with the exception of a couple of members of the crew, whom I have furnished with enough gin to silence them effectually for hours, there is none aboard the *Kincaid*. We can go aboard, get the child, and return without the slightest fear."

Tarzan nodded.

"Let's be about it, then," he said.

His guide led him to a small boat moored alongside the wharf. The two men entered, and Paulvitch pulled rapidly toward the steamer. The black smoke issuing from her funnel did not at the time make any suggestion to Tarzan's mind. All his thoughts were occupied with the hope that in a few moments he would again have his little son in his arms.

At the steamer's side they found a monkey-ladder dangling close above them, and up this the two men crept stealthily. Once on deck they hastened aft to where the Russian pointed to a hatch.

"The boy is hidden there," he said. "You had better go down after him, as there is less chance that he will cry in fright than should he find himself in the arms of a stranger. I will stand on guard here."

So anxious was Tarzan to rescue the child that he gave not the slightest thought to the strangeness of all the conditions surrounding the *Kincaid*. That her deck was deserted, though she had steam up, and from the volume of smoke pouring from her funnel was all ready to get under way made no impression upon him.

With the thought that in another instant he would fold that precious little bundle of humanity in his arms, the ape-man swung down into the darkness below. Scarcely had he released his hold upon the edge of the hatch than the heavy covering fell clattering above him.

Instantly he knew that he was the victim of a plot, and that far from rescuing his son he had himself fallen into the hands of his enemies. Though he immediately endeavoured to reach the hatch and lift the cover, he was unable to do so.

Striking a match, he explored his surroundings, finding that a little compartment had been partitioned off from the main hold, with the hatch above his head the only means of ingress or egress. It was evident that the room had been prepared for the very purpose of serving as a cell for himself.

There was nothing in the compartment, and no other occupant. If the child was on board the *Kincaid* he was confined elsewhere.

For over twenty years, from infancy to manhood, the ape-man

had roamed his savage jungle haunts without human companion-ship of any nature. He had learned at the most impressionable period of his life to take his pleasures and his sorrows as the beasts take theirs.

So it was that he neither raved nor stormed against fate, but instead waited patiently for what might next befall him, though not by any means without an eye to doing the utmost to succour himself. To this end he examined his prison carefully, tested the heavy planking that formed its walls, and measured the distance of the hatch above him.

And while he was thus occupied there came suddenly to him the vibration of machinery and the throbbing of the propeller.

The ship was moving! Where to and to what fate was it car-rying him?

And even as these thoughts passed through his mind there came to his ears above the din of the engines that which caused him to go cold with apprehension.

Clear and shrill from the deck above him rang the scream of a frightened woman.

2

Marooned

As TARZAN AND his guide had disappeared into the shadows upon the dark wharf the figure of a heavily veiled woman had hur-ried down the narrow alley to the entrance of the drinking place the two men had just quitted.

Here she paused and looked about, and then as though satisfied that she had at last reached the place she sought, she pushed bravely into the interior of the vile den.

A score of half-drunken sailors and wharf-rats looked up at the unaccustomed sight of a richly gowned woman in their midst. Rapidly she approached the slovenly barmaid who stared half in envy, half in hate, at her more fortunate sister.

"Have you seen a tall, well-dressed man here, but a minute since," she asked, "who met another and went away with him?"

The girl answered in the affirmative, but could not tell which way the two had gone. A sailor who had approached to listen to the conversation vouchsafed the information that a moment before as he had been about to enter the "pub" he had seen two men leaving it who walked toward the wharf.

"Show me the direction they went," cried the woman, slipping a coin into the man's hand.

The fellow led her from the place, and together they walked quickly toward the wharf and along it until across the water they saw a small boat just pulling into the shadows of a nearby steamer.

"There they be," whispered the man.

"Ten pounds if you will find a boat and row me to that steamer," cried the woman.

"Quick, then," he replied, "for we gotta go it if we're goin' to catch the *Kincaid* afore she sails. She's had steam up for three hours an' jest been a-waitin' fer that one passenger. I was a-talkin' to one of her crew 'arf an hour ago."

As he spoke he led the way to the end of the wharf where he knew another boat lay moored, and, lowering the woman into it, he jumped in after and pushed off. The two were soon scudding over the water.

At the steamer's side the man demanded his pay and, without waiting to count out the exact amount, the woman thrust a handful of banknotes into his outstretched hand. A single glance at them convinced the fellow that he had been more than well paid. Then he assisted her up the ladder, holding his skiff close to the ship's side against the chance that this profitable passenger might wish to be taken ashore later.

But presently the sound of the donkey engine and the rattle of a steel cable on the hoisting-drum proclaimed the fact that the *Kincaid*'s anchor was being raised, and a moment later the sailor heard the propellers revolving, and slowly the little steamer moved away from him out into the channel.

As he turned to row back to shore he heard a woman's shriek from the ship's deck.

"That's wot I calls rotten luck," he soliloquized. "I might jest as well of 'ad the whole bloomin' wad."

* * *

When Jane Clayton climbed to the deck of the *Kincaid* she found the ship apparently deserted. There was no sign of those she sought nor of any other aboard, and so she went about her search for her husband and the child she hoped against hope to find there without interruption.

Quickly she hastened to the cabin, which was half above and half below deck. As she hurried down the short companion-ladder into the main cabin, on either side of which were the smaller rooms occupied by the officers, she failed to note the quick closing of one of the doors before her. She passed the full length of the main room, and then retracing her steps stopped before each door to listen, furtively trying each latch.

All was silence, utter silence there, in which the throbbing of her own frightened heart seemed to her overwrought imagination to fill the ship with its thunderous alarm.

One by one the doors opened before her touch, only to reveal empty interiors. In her absorption she did not note the sudden activity upon the vessel, the purring of the engines, the throbbing of the propeller. She had reached the last door upon the right now, and as she pushed it open she was seized from within by a powerful, dark-visaged man, and drawn hastily into the stuffy, ill-smelling interior.

The sudden shock of fright which the unexpected attack had upon her drew a single piercing scream from her throat; then the man clapped a hand roughly over the mouth.

"Not until we are farther from land, my dear," he said. "Then you may yell your pretty head off."

Lady Greystoke turned to look into the leering, bearded face so close to hers. The man relaxed the pressure of his fingers upon her lips, and with a little moan of terror as she recognized him the girl shrank away from her captor.

"Nikolas Rokoff! M. Thuran!" she exclaimed.

"Your devoted admirer," replied the Russian, with a low bow.

"My little boy," she said next, ignoring the terms of endearment—"where is he? Let me have him. How could you be so cruel—even as you—Nikolas Rokoff—cannot be entirely devoid of mercy and compassion? Tell me where he is. Is he aboard this ship? Oh, please, if such a thing as a heart beats within your breast, take me to my baby!"

"If you do as you are bid no harm will befall him," replied Rokoff. "But remember that it is your own fault that you are here. You came aboard voluntarily, and you may take the consequences. I little thought," he added to himself, "that any such good luck as this would come to me."

He went on deck then, locking the cabin door upon his prisoner, and for several days she did not see him. The truth of the matter being that Nikolas Rokoff was so poor a sailor that the heavy seas the *Kincaid* encountered from the very beginning of her voyage sent the Russian to his berth with a bad attack of sea-sickness.

During this time her only visitor was an uncouth Swede, the *Kincaid*'s unsavoury cook, who brought her meals to her. His name was Sven Anderssen, his one pride being that his patronymic was spelt with a double "s."

The man was tall and raw-boned, with a long yellow moustache, an unwholesome complexion, and filthy nails. The very sight of him with one grimy thumb buried deep in the lukewarm stew, that seemed, from the frequency of its repetition, to constitute the pride of his culinary art, was sufficient to take away the girl's appetite.

His small, blue, close-set eyes never met hers squarely. There was a shiftiness of his whole appearance that even found expression in the cat-like manner of his gait, and to it all a sinister suggestion was added by the long slim knife that always rested at his waist, slipped through the greasy cord that supported his soiled apron. Ostensibly it was but an implement of his calling; but the girl could never free herself of the conviction that it would require less provocation to witness it put to other and less harmless uses.

His manner toward her was surly, yet she never failed to meet him with a pleasant smile and a word of thanks when he brought her food to her, though more often than not she hurled the bulk of it through the tiny cabin port the moment that the door closed behind him.

During the days of anguish that followed Jane Clayton's imprisonment, but two questions were uppermost in her mind—the whereabouts of her husband and her son. She fully believed that the baby was aboard the *Kincaid*, provided that he still lived, but whether Tarzan had been permitted to live after having been lured aboard the evil craft she could not guess.

She knew, of course, the deep hatred that the Russian felt for the Englishman, and she could think of but one reason for having him brought aboard the ship—to dispatch him in comparative safety in revenge for his having thwarted Rokoff's pet schemes, and for having been at last the means of landing him in a French prison.

* * *

Tarzan, on his part, lay in the darkness of his cell, ignorant of the fact that his wife was a prisoner in the cabin almost above his head.

The same Swede that served Jane brought his meals to him, but, though on several occasions Tarzan had tried to draw the man into conversation, he had been unsuccessful.

He had hoped to learn through this fellow whether his little son was aboard the *Kincaid*, but to every question upon this or kindred subjects the fellow returned but one reply, "Ay tank it blow purty soon purty hard." So after several attempts Tarzan gave it up.

For weeks that seemed months to the two prisoners the little steamer forged on they knew not where. Once the *Kincaid* stopped to coal, only immediately to take up the seemingly interminable voyage.

Rokoff had visited Jane Clayton but once since he had locked her in the tiny cabin. He had come gaunt and hollow-eyed from a long siege of seasickness. The object of his visit was to obtain from her her personal check for a large sum in return for a guarantee of her personal safety and return to England.

"When you set me down safely in any civilized port, together with my son and my husband," she replied, "I will pay you in gold twice the amount you ask; but until then you shall not have a cent, nor the promise of a cent under any other conditions."

"You will give me the check I ask," he replied with a snarl, "or neither you nor your child nor your husband will ever again set foot within any port, civilized or otherwise."

"I would not trust you," she replied. "What guarantee have I that you would not take my money and then do as you pleased with me and mine regardless of your promise?"

"I think you will do as I bid," he said, turning to leave the cabin. "Remember that I have your son—if you chance to hear the ago-nized wail of a tortured child it may console you to reflect that it is because of your stubbornness that the baby suffers—and that it is your baby."

"You would not do it!" cried the girl. "You would not—could not be so fiendishly cruel!"

"It is not I that am cruel, but you," he returned, "for you permit a paltry sum of money to stand between your baby and immunity from suffering."

The end of it was that Jane Clayton wrote out a check of large denomination and handed it to Nikolas Rokoff, who left her cabin with a grin of satisfaction upon his lips.

The following day the hatch was removed from Tarzan's cell,

and as he looked up he saw Paulvitch's head framed in the square of light above him.

"Come up," commanded the Russian. "But bear in mind that you will be shot if you make a single move to attack me or any other aboard the ship."

The ape-man swung himself lightly to the deck. About him, but at a respectful distance, stood a half-dozen sailors armed with rifles and revolvers. Facing him was Paulvitch.

Tarzan looked about for Rokoff, who he felt sure must be aboard, but there was no sign of him.

"Lord Greystoke," commenced the Russian, "by your continued and wanton interference with M. Rokoff and his plans you have at last brought yourself and your family to this unfortunate extremity. You have only yourself to thank. As you may imagine, it has cost M. Rokoff a large amount of money to finance this expedition, and, as you are the sole cause of it, he naturally looks to you for reimbursement.

"Further, I may say that only by meeting M. Rokoff's just demands may you avert the most unpleasant consequences to your wife and child, and at the same time retain your own life and regain your liberty."

"What is the amount?" asked Tarzan. "And what assurance have I that you will live up to your end of the agreement? I have little reason to trust two such scoundrels as you and Rokoff, you know."

The Russian flushed.

"You are in no position to deliver insults," he said. "You have no assurance that we will live up to our agreement other than my word, but you have before you the assurance that we can make short work of you if you do not write out the check we demand.

"Unless you are a greater fool than I imagine, you should know that there is nothing that would give us greater pleasure than to order these men to fire. That we do not is because we have other plans for punishing you that would be entirely upset by your death."

"Answer one question," said Tarzan. "Is my son on board this ship?"

"No," replied Alexis Paulvitch, "your son is quite safe elsewhere; nor will he be killed until you refuse to accede to our fair demands. If it becomes necessary to kill you, there will be no reason for not killing the child, since with you gone the one whom we wish to punish through the boy will be gone, and he will then be to us only a constant source of danger and embarrassment. You see, therefore, that you may only save the life of your son by saving your own, and you can only save your own by giving us the check we ask."

"Very well," replied Tarzan, for he knew that he could trust them to carry out any sinister threat that Paulvitch had made, and there was a bare chance that by conceding their demands he might save the boy.

That they would permit him to live after he had appended his name to the cheque never occurred to him as being within the realms of probability. But he was determined to give them such a battle as they would never forget, and possibly to take Paulvitch with him into eternity. He was only sorry that it was not Rokoff.

He took his pocket checkbook and fountain pen from his pocket.

"What is the amount?" he asked.

Paulvitch named an enormous sum. Tarzan could scarce restrain a smile.

Their very cupidity was to prove the means of their undoing, in the matter of the ransom at least. Purposely he hesitated and haggled over the amount, but Paulvitch was obdurate. Finally the ape-man wrote out his check for a larger sum than stood to his credit at the bank.

As he turned to hand the worthless slip of paper to the Russian his glance chanced to pass across the starboard bow of the *Kincaid*. To his surprise he saw that the ship lay within a few hundred yards of land. Almost down to the water's edge ran a dense tropical jungle, and behind was higher land clothed in forest.

Paulvitch noted the direction of his gaze.

"You are to be set at liberty here," he said.

Tarzan's plan for immediate physical revenge upon the Russian vanished. He thought the land before him the mainland of Africa, and he knew that should they liberate him here he could doubtless find his way to civilization with comparative ease.

Paulvitch took the check.

"Remove your clothing," he said to the ape-man. "Here you will not need it."

Tarzan demurred.

Paulvitch pointed to the armed sailors. Then the Englishman slowly divested himself of his clothing.

A boat was lowered, and, still heavily guarded, the ape-man was rowed ashore. Half an hour later the sailors had returned to the *Kincaid*, and the steamer was slowly getting under way.

As Tarzan stood upon the narrow strip of beach watching the

departure of the vessel he saw a figure appear at the rail and call aloud to attract his attention.

The ape-man had been about to read a note that one of the sailors had handed him as the small boat that bore him to the shore was on the point of returning to the steamer, but at the hail from the vessel's deck he looked up.

He saw a black-bearded man who laughed at him in derision as he held high above his head the figure of a little child. Tarzan half started as though to rush through the surf and strike out for the already moving steamer; but realizing the futility of so rash an act he halted at the water's edge.

Thus he stood, his gaze riveted upon the *Kincaid* until it disappeared beyond a projecting promontory of the coast.

From the jungle at his back fierce bloodshot eyes glared from beneath shaggy overhanging brows upon him.

Little monkeys in the treetops chattered and scolded, and from the distance of the inland forest came the scream of a leopard.

But still John Clayton, Lord Greystoke, stood deaf and unseeing, suffering the pangs of keen regret for the opportunity that he had wasted because he had been so gullible as to place credence in a single statement of the first lieutenant of his archenemy.

"I have at least," he thought, "one consolation—the knowledge that Jane is safe in London. Thank Heaven she, too, did not fall into the clutches of those villains."

Behind him the hairy thing whose evil eyes had been watching his as a cat watches a mouse was creeping stealthily toward him.

Where were the trained senses of the savage ape-man?

Where the acute hearing?

Where the uncanny sense of scent?

3

Beasts at Bay

SLOWLY TARZAN UNFOLDED the note the sailor had thrust into his hand, and read it. At first it made little impression on his sorrow-numbed senses, but finally the full purport of the hideous plot of revenge unfolded itself before his imagination.

"This will explain to you" [the note read] "the exact nature of my intentions relative to your offspring and to you.

"You were born an ape. You lived naked in the jungles—to your own we have returned you; but your son shall rise a step above his sire. It is the immutable law of evolution.

"The father was a beast, but the son shall be a man—he shall take the next ascending step in the scale of progress. He shall be no naked beast of the jungle, but shall wear a loincloth and copper anklets, and, perchance, a ring in his nose, for he is to be reared by men—a tribe of savage cannibals.

"I might have killed you, but that would have curtailed the full measure of the punishment you have earned at my hands.

"Dead, you could not have suffered in the knowledge of your son's plight; but living and in a place from which you may not escape to seek or succour your child, you shall suffer worse than death for all the years of your life in contemplation of the horrors of your son's existence.

"This, then, is to be a part of your punishment for having dared to pit yourself against   N.R.

"P.S.—The balance of your punishment has to do with what shall presently befall your wife—that I shall leave to your imagination."

19

As he finished reading, a slight sound behind him brought him back with a start to the world of present realities.

Instantly his senses awoke, and he was again Tarzan of the Apes.

As he wheeled about, it was a beast at bay, vibrant with the instinct of self-preservation, that faced a huge bull-ape that was already charging down upon him.

The two years that had elapsed since Tarzan had come out of the savage forest with his rescued mate had witnessed slight diminution of the mighty powers that had made him the invincible lord of the jungle. His great estates in Uziri had claimed much of his time and attention, and there he had found ample field for the practical use and retention of his almost superhuman powers; but naked and unarmed to do battle with the shaggy, bull-necked beast that now confronted him was a test that the ape-man would scarce have welcomed at any period of his wild existence.

But there was no alternative other than to meet the rage-maddened creature with the weapons with which nature had endowed him.

Over the bull's shoulder Tarzan could see now the heads and shoulders of perhaps a dozen more of these mighty forerunners of primitive man.

He knew, however, that there was little chance that they would attack him, since it is not within the reasoning powers of the anthropoid to be able to weigh or appreciate the value of concentrated action against an enemy—otherwise they would long since have become the dominant creatures of their haunts, so tremendous a power of destruction lies in their mighty thews and savage fangs.

With a low snarl the beast now hurled himself at Tarzan, but the ape-man had found, among other things in the haunts of civilized man, certain methods of scientific warfare that are unknown to the jungle folk.

Whereas, a few years since, he would have met the brute rush with brute force, he now sidestepped his antagonist's headlong charge, and as the brute hurtled past him swung a mighty right to the pit of the ape's stomach.

With a howl of mingled rage and anguish the great anthropoid bent double and sank to the ground, though almost instantly he was again struggling to his feet.

Before he could regain them, however, his white-skinned foe had wheeled and pounced upon him, and in the act there dropped from the shoulders of the English lord the last shred of his superficial mantle of civilization.

Once again he was the jungle beast revelling in bloody conflict with his kind. Once again he was Tarzan, son of Kala the she-ape.

His strong, white teeth sank into the hairy throat of his enemy as he sought the pulsing jugular.

Powerful fingers held the mighty fangs from his own flesh, or clenched and beat with the power of a steam-hammer upon the snarling, foam-flecked face of his adversary.

In a circle about them the balance of the tribe of apes stood watching and enjoying the struggle. They muttered low gutturals of approval as bits of white hide or hairy bloodstained skin were torn from one contestant or the other. But they were silent in amazement and expectation when they saw the mighty white ape wriggle upon the back of their king, and, with steel muscles tensed beneath the armpits of his antagonist, bear down mightily with his open palms upon the back of the thick bullneck, so that the king ape could but shriek in agony and flounder helplessly about upon the thick mat of jungle grass.

As Tarzan had overcome the huge Terkoz that time years before when he had been about to set out upon his quest for human beings of his own kind and colour, so now he overcame this other great ape with the same wrestling hold upon which he had stumbled by accident during that other combat.

The little audience of fierce anthropoids heard the creaking of their king's neck mingling with his agonized shrieks and hideous roaring.

Then there came a sudden crack, like the breaking of a stout limb before the fury of the wind. The bullet-head crumpled forward upon its flaccid neck against the great hairy chest—the roaring and the shrieking ceased.

The little pig-eyes of the onlookers wandered from the still form of their leader to that of the white ape that was rising to its feet beside the vanquished, then back to their king as though in wonder that he did not arise and slay this presumptuous stranger.

They saw the newcomer place a foot upon the neck of the quiet figure at his feet and, throwing back his head, give vent to the wild, uncanny challenge of the bull-ape that has made a kill. Then they knew that their king was dead.

Across the jungle rolled the horrid notes of the victory cry. The little monkeys in the treetops ceased their chattering. The harsh-voiced, brilliant-plumed birds were still. From afar came the answering wail of a leopard and the deep roar of a lion.

It was the old Tarzan who turned questioning eyes upon the little knot of apes before him. It was the old Tarzan who shook his head as though to toss back a heavy mane that had fallen before his face—an old habit dating from the days that his great shock of thick, black hair had fallen about his shoulders, and often tumbled before his eyes when it had meant life or death to him to have his vision unobstructed.

The ape-man knew that he might expect an immediate attack on the part of that particular surviving bull-ape who felt himself best fitted to contend for the kingship of the tribe. Among his own apes he knew that it was not unusual for an entire stranger to enter a community and, after having dispatched the king, assume the leadership of the tribe himself, together with the fallen monarch's mates.

On the other hand, if he made no attempt to follow them, they might move slowly away from him, later to fight among themselves for the supremacy. That he could be king of them, if he so chose, he was confident; but he was not sure he cared to assume the sometimes irksome duties of that position, for he could see no particular advantage to be gained thereby.

One of the younger apes, a huge, splendidly muscled brute, was edging threateningly closer to the ape-man. Through his bared fighting fangs there issued a low, sullen growl.

Tarzan watched his every move, standing rigid as a statue. To have fallen back a step would have been to precipitate an immediate charge; to have rushed forward to meet the other might have had the same result, or it might have put the bellicose one to flight—it all depended upon the young bull's stock of courage.

To stand perfectly still, waiting, was the middle course. In this event the bull would, according to custom, approach quite close to the object of his attention, growling hideously and baring slavering fangs. Slowly he would circle about the other, as though with a chip upon his shoulder; and this he did, even as Tarzan had foreseen.

It might be a bluff royal, or, on the other hand, so unstable is the mind of an ape, a passing impulse might hurl the hairy mass, tearing and rending, upon the man without an instant's warning.

As the brute circled him Tarzan turned slowly, keeping his eyes ever upon the eyes of his antagonist. He had appraised the young bull as one who had never quite felt equal to the task of overthrowing his former king, but who one day would have done so. Tarzan saw that the beast was of wondrous proportions, standing over seven feet upon his short, bowed legs.

His great, hairy arms reached almost to the ground even when he stood erect, and his fighting fangs, now quite close to Tarzan's face, were exceptionally long and sharp. Like the others of his tribe, he differed in several minor essentials from the apes of Tarzan's boyhood.

At first the ape-man had experienced a thrill of hope at sight of the shaggy bodies of the anthropoids—a hope that by some strange freak of fate he had been again returned to his own tribe; but a closer inspection had convinced him that these were another species.

As the threatening bull continued his stiff and jerky circling of the ape-man, much after the manner that you have noted among dogs when a strange canine comes among them, it occurred to Tarzan to discover if the language of his own tribe was identical with that of this other family, and so he addressed the brute in the language of the tribe of Kerchak.

"Who are you," he asked, "who threatens Tarzan of the Apes?"

The hairy brute looked his surprise.

"I am Akut," replied the other in the same simple, primal tongue which is so low in the scale of spoken languages that, as Tarzan had surmised, it was identical with that of the tribe in which the first twenty years of his life had been spent.

"I am Akut," said the ape. "Molak is dead. I am king. Go away or I shall kill you!"

"You saw how easily I killed Molak," replied Tarzan. "So could I kill you if I cared to be king. But Tarzan of the Apes would not be king of the tribe of Akut. All he wishes is to live in peace in this country. Let us be friends. Tarzan of the Apes can help you, and you can help Tarzan of the Apes."

"You cannot kill Akut," replied the other. "None is so great as Akut. Had you not killed Molak, Akut would have done so, for Akut was ready to be king."

For answer the ape-man hurled himself upon the great brute who during the conversation had slightly relaxed his vigilance.

In the twinkling of an eye the man had seized the wrist of the great ape, and before the other could grapple with him had whirled him about and leaped upon his broad back.

Down they went together, but so well had Tarzan's plan worked out that before ever they touched the ground he had gained the same hold upon Akut that had broken Molak's neck.

Slowly he brought the pressure to bear, and then as in days gone by he had given Kerchak the chance to surrender and live, so now he gave to Akut—in whom he saw a possible ally of great strength and resource—the option of living in amity with him or dying as he had just seen his savage and heretofore invincible king die.

"*Ka-goda?*" whispered Tarzan to the ape beneath him.

It was the same question that he had whispered to Kerchak, and in the language of the apes it means, broadly, "Do you surrender?"

Akut thought of the creaking sound he had heard just before Molak's thick neck had snapped, and he shuddered.

He hated to give up the kingship, though, so again he struggled to free himself; but a sudden torturing pressure upon his vertebra brought an agonized "*ka-goda!*" from his lips.

Tarzan relaxed his grip a trifle.

"You may still be king, Akut," he said. "Tarzan told you that he did not wish to be king. If any question your right, Tarzan of the Apes will help you in your battles."

The ape-man rose, and Akut came slowly to his feet. Shaking his bullet head and growling angrily, he waddled toward his tribe, looking first at one and then at another of the larger bulls who might be expected to challenge his leadership.

But none did so; instead, they drew away as he approached, and presently the whole pack moved off into the jungle, and Tarzan was left alone once more upon the beach.

The ape-man was sore from the wounds that Molak had inflicted upon him, but he was inured to physical suffering and endured it with the calm and fortitude of the wild beasts that had taught him to lead the jungle life after the manner of all those that are born to it.

His first need, he realized, was for weapons of offence and defence, for his encounter with the apes, and the distant notes of the savage voices of Numa the lion, and Sheeta, the panther, warned him that his was to be no life of indolent ease and security.

It was but a return to the old existence of constant bloodshed and danger—to the hunting and the being hunted. Grim beasts would stalk him, as they had stalked him in the past, and never would there be a moment, by savage day or by cruel night, that he might not have instant need of such crude weapons as he could fashion from the materials at hand.

Upon the shore he found an out-cropping of brittle, igneous rock. By dint of much labour he managed to chip off a narrow sliver some twelve inches long by a quarter of an inch thick. One edge was quite thin for a few inches near the tip. It was the rudiment of a knife.

With it he went into the jungle, searching until he found a fallen tree of a certain species of hardwood with which he was familiar.

From this he cut a small straight branch, which he pointed at one end.

Then he scooped a small, round hole in the surface of the prostrate trunk. Into this he crumbled a few bits of dry bark, minutely shredded, after which he inserted the tip of his pointed stick, and, sitting astride the bole of the tree, spun the slender rod rapidly between his palms.

After a time a thin smoke rose from the little mass of tinder, and a moment later the whole broke into flame. Heaping some larger twigs and sticks upon the tiny fire, Tarzan soon had quite a respectable blaze roaring in the enlarging cavity of the dead tree.

Into this he thrust the blade of his stone knife, and as it became superheated he would withdraw it, touching a spot near the thin edge with a drop of moisture. Beneath the wetted area a little flake of the glassy material would crack and scale away.

Thus, very slowly, the ape-man commenced the tedious operation of putting a thin edge upon his primitive hunting knife.

He did not attempt to accomplish the feat all in one sitting. At first he was content to achieve a cutting edge of a couple of inches, with which he cut a long, pliable bow, a handle for his knife, a stout cudgel, and a goodly supply of arrows.

These he cached in a tall tree beside a little stream, and here also he constructed a platform with a roof of palm leaves above it.

When all these things had been finished it was growing dusk, and Tarzan felt a strong desire to eat.

He had noted during the brief incursion he had made into the forest that a short distance upstream from his tree there was a much-used watering place, where, from the trampled mud of either bank, it was evident beasts of all sorts and in great numbers came to drink. To this spot the hungry ape-man made his silent way.

Through the upper terrace of the treetops he swung with the grace and ease of a monkey. But for the heavy burden upon his heart he would have been happy in this return to the old free life of his boyhood.

Yet even with that burden he fell into the little habits and manners of his early life that were in reality more a part of him than the thin veneer of civilization that the past three years of his association with the white men of the outer world had spread lightly over him—a veneer that only hid the crudities of the beast that Tarzan of the Apes had been.

Could his fellow peers of the House of Lords have seen him then they would have held up their noble hands in holy horror.

Silently he crouched in the lower branches of a great forest giant that overhung the trail, his keen eyes and sensitive ears strained into the distant jungle, from which he knew his dinner would presently emerge.

Nor had he long to wait.

Scarce had he settled himself to a comfortable position, his lithe, muscular legs drawn well up beneath him as the panther draws his hindquarters in preparation for the spring, than Bara, the deer, came daintily down to drink.

But more than Bara was coming. Behind the graceful buck came another which the deer could neither see nor scent, but whose movements were apparent to Tarzan of the Apes because of the elevated position of the ape-man's ambush.

He knew not yet exactly the nature of the thing that moved so stealthily through the jungle a few hundred yards behind the deer; but he was convinced that it was some great beast of prey stalking Bara for the selfsame purpose as that which prompted him to await the fleet animal. Numa, perhaps, or Sheeta, the panther.

In any event, Tarzan could see his repast slipping from his grasp unless Bara moved more rapidly toward the ford than at present.

Even as these thoughts passed through his mind some noise of the stalker in his rear must have come to the buck, for with a sudden start he paused for an instant, trembling, in his tracks, and then with a swift bound dashed straight for the river and Tarzan. It was his intention to flee through the shallow ford and escape upon the opposite side of the river.

Not a hundred yards behind him came Numa.

Tarzan could see him quite plainly now. Below the ape-man Bara was about to pass. Could he do it? But even as he asked himself the question the hungry man launched himself from his perch full upon the back of the startled buck.

In another instant Numa would be upon them both, so if the ape-man were to dine that night, or ever again, he must act quickly.

Scarcely had he touched the sleek hide of the deer with a momentum that sent the animal to its knees than he had grasped a horn in either hand, and with a single quick wrench twisted the animal's neck completely round, until he felt the vertebrae snap beneath his grip.

The lion was roaring in rage close behind him as he swung the deer across his shoulder, and, grasping a foreleg between his strong teeth, leaped for the nearest of the lower branches that swung above his head.

With both hands he grasped the limb, and, at the instant that Numa sprang, drew himself and his prey out of reach of the animal's cruel talons.

There was a thud below him as the baffled cat fell back to earth, and then Tarzan of the Apes, drawing his dinner farther up to the safety of a higher limb, looked down with grinning face into the gleaming yellow eyes of the other wild beast that glared up at him from beneath, and with taunting insults flaunted the tender carcass of his kill in the face of him whom he had cheated of it.

With his crude stone knife he cut a juicy steak from the hindquarters, and while the great lion paced, growling, back and forth below him, Lord Greystoke filled his savage belly, nor ever in the choicest of his exclusive London clubs had a meal tasted more palatable.

The warm blood of his kill smeared his hands and face and filled his nostrils with the scent that the savage carnivora love best.

And when he had finished he left the balance of the carcass in a high fork of the tree where he had dined, and with Numa trailing below him, still keen for revenge, he made his way back to his treetop shelter, where he slept until the sun was high the following morning.

4

Sheeta

THE NEXT FEW days were occupied by Tarzan in completing his weapons and exploring the jungle. He strung his bow with tendons from the buck upon which he had dined his first evening upon the new shore, and though he would have preferred the gut of Sheeta for the purpose, he was content to wait until opportunity permitted him to kill one of the great cats.

He also braided a long grass rope—such a rope as he had used so many years before to tantalize the ill-natured Tublat, and which later had developed into a wondrous effective weapon in the practised hands of the little ape-boy.

A sheath and handle for his hunting-knife he fashioned, and a quiver for arrows, and from the hide of Bara a belt and loincloth. Then he set out to learn something of the strange land in which he found himself. That it was not his old familiar west coast of the African continent he knew from the fact that it faced east—the rising sun came up out of the sea before the threshold of the jungle.

But that it was not the east coast of Africa he was equally positive, for he felt satisfied that the *Kincaid* had not passed through the Mediterranean, the Suez Canal, and the Red Sea, nor had she had time to round the Cape of Good Hope. So he was quite at a loss to know where he might be.

Sometimes he wondered if the ship had crossed the broad Atlantic to deposit him upon some wild South American shore; but the presence of Numa, the lion, decided him that such could not be the case.

As Tarzan made his lonely way through the jungle paralleling the shore, he felt strong upon him a desire for companionship, so that gradually he commenced to regret that he had not cast his lot with the apes. He had seen nothing of them since that first day, when the influences of civilization were still paramount within him.

Now he was more nearly returned to the Tarzan of old, and though he appreciated the fact that there could be little in common between himself and the great anthropoids, still they were better than no company at all.

Moving leisurely, sometimes upon the ground and again among the lower branches of the trees, gathering an occasional fruit or turning over a fallen log in search of the larger bugs, which he still found as palatable as of old, Tarzan had covered a mile or more when his attention was attracted by the scent of Sheeta upwind ahead of him.

Now Sheeta, the panther, was one whom Tarzan was exceptionally glad to fall in with, for he had it in mind not only to utilize the great cat's strong gut for his bow, but also to fashion a new quiver and loincloth from pieces of his hide. So, whereas the apeman had gone carelessly before, he now became the personification of noiseless stealth.

Swiftly and silently he glided through the forest in the wake of the savage cat, nor was the pursuer, for all his noble birth, one whit less savage than the wild, fierce thing he stalked.

As he came closer to Sheeta he became aware that the panther on his part was stalking game of his own, and even as he realized this fact there came to his nostrils, wafted from his right by a vagrant breeze, the strong odour of a company of great apes.

The panther had taken to a large tree as Tarzan came within sight of him, and beyond and below him Tarzan saw the tribe of Akut lolling in a little, natural clearing. Some of them were dozing against the boles of trees, while others roamed about turning over bits of bark from beneath which they transferred the luscious grubs and beetles to their mouths.

Akut was the closest to Sheeta.

The great cat lay crouched upon a thick limb, hidden from the ape's view by dense foliage, waiting patiently until the anthropoid should come within range of his spring.

Tarzan cautiously gained a position in the same tree with the panther and a little above him. In his left hand he grasped his slim stone blade. He would have preferred to use his noose, but the foliage surrounding the huge cat precluded the possibility of an accurate throw with the rope.

Akut had now wandered quite close beneath the tree wherein lay the waiting death. Sheeta slowly edged his hind paws along the branch still further beneath him, and then with a hideous shriek he launched himself toward the great ape. The barest fraction of a second before his spring another beast of prey above him leaped, its weird and savage cry mingling with his.

As the startled Akut looked up he saw the panther almost above him, and already upon the panther's back the white ape that had bested him that day near the great water.

The teeth of the ape-man were buried in the back of Sheeta's neck and his right arm was round the fierce throat, while the left hand, grasping a slender piece of stone, rose and fell in mighty blows upon the panther's side behind the left shoulder.

Akut had just time to leap to one side to avoid being pinioned beneath these battling monsters of the jungle.

With a crash they came to earth at his feet. Sheeta was screaming, snarling, and roaring horribly; but the white ape clung tenaciously and in silence to the thrashing body of his quarry.

Steadily and remorselessly the stone knife was driven home through the glossy hide—time and again it drank deep, until with a final agonized lunge and shriek the great feline rolled over upon its side and, save for the spasmodic jerking of its muscles, lay quiet and still in death.

Then the ape-man raised his head, as he stood over the carcass of his kill, and once again through the jungle rang his wild and savage victory challenge.

Akut and the apes of Akut stood looking in startled wonder at the dead body of Sheeta and the lithe, straight figure of the man who had slain him.

Tarzan was the first to speak.

He had saved Akut's life for a purpose, and, knowing the limitations of the ape intellect, he also knew that he must make this purpose plain to the anthropoid if it were to serve him in the way he hoped.

"I am Tarzan of the Apes," he said, "Mighty hunter. Mighty fighter. By the great water I spared Akut's life when I might have taken it and become king of the tribe of Akut. Now I have saved Akut from death beneath the rending fangs of Sheeta.

"When Akut or the tribe of Akut is in danger, let them call to Tarzan thus"—and the ape-man raised the hideous cry with which the tribe of Kerchak had been wont to summon its absent members in times of peril.

"And," he continued, "when they hear Tarzan call to them, let them remember what he has done for Akut and come to him with great speed. Shall it be as Tarzan says?"

"Huh!" assented Akut, and from the members of his tribe there rose a unanimous *"Huh."*

Then, presently, they went to feeding again as though nothing had happened, and with them fed John Clayton, Lord Greystoke.

He noticed, however, that Akut kept always close to him, and was often looking at him with a strange wonder in his little bloodshot eyes, and once he did a thing that Tarzan during all his long years among the apes had never before seen an ape do—he found a particularly tender morsel and handed it to Tarzan.

As the tribe hunted, the glistening body of the ape-man mingled with the brown, shaggy hides of his companions. Oftentimes they brushed together in passing, but the apes had already taken his presence for granted, so that he was as much one of them as Akut himself.

If he came too close to a she with a young baby, the former would bare her great fighting fangs and growl ominously, and occasionally a truculent young bull would snarl a warning if Tarzan approached while the former was eating. But in these things the treatment was no different from that which they accorded any other member of the tribe.

Tarzan on his part felt very much at home with these fierce, hairy progenitors of primitive man. He skipped nimbly out of reach of each threatening female—for such is the way of apes, if they be not in one of their occasional fits of bestial rage—and he growled back at the truculent young bulls, baring his canine teeth even as they. Thus easily he fell back into the way of his early life, nor did it seem that he had ever tasted association with creatures of his own kind.

For the better part of a week he roamed the jungle with his new friends, partly because of a desire for companionship and partially through a well-laid plan to impress himself indelibly upon their memories, which at best are none too long; for Tarzan from past experience knew that it might serve him in good stead to have a tribe of these powerful and terrible beasts at his call.

When he was convinced that he had succeeded to some extent in fixing his identity upon them he decided to again take up his exploration. To this end he set out toward the north early one day, and, keeping parallel with the shore, traveled rapidly until almost nightfall.

When the sun rose the next morning he saw that it lay almost directly to his right as he stood upon the beach instead of straight out across the water as heretofore, and so he reasoned that the shore line had trended toward the west. All the second day he continued his rapid course, and when Tarzan of the Apes sought speed, he passed through the middle terrace of the forest with the rapidity of a squirrel.

That night the sun set straight out across the water opposite the land, and then the ape-man guessed at last the truth that he had been suspecting.

Rokoff had set him ashore upon an island.

He might have known it! If there was any plan that would render his position more harrowing he should have known that such would be the one adopted by the Russian, and what could be more terrible than to leave him to a lifetime of suspense upon an uninhabited island?

Rokoff doubtless had sailed directly to the mainland, where it would be a comparatively easy thing for him to find the means of delivering the infant Jack into the hands of the cruel and savage foster parents, who, as his note had threatened, would have the upbringing of the child.

Tarzan shuddered as he thought of the cruel suffering the little one must endure in such a life, even though he might fall into the hands of individuals whose intentions toward him were of the kindest. The ape-man had had sufficient experience with the lower savages of Africa to know that even there may be found the cruder virtues of charity and humanity; but their lives were at best but a series of terrible privations, dangers, and sufferings.

Then there was the horrid after-fate that awaited the child as he grew to manhood. The horrible practices that would form a part of his life training would alone be sufficient to bar him forever from association with those of his own race and station in life.

A cannibal! His little boy a savage man-eater! It was too horrible to contemplate.

The filed teeth, the slit nose, the little face painted hideously.

Tarzan groaned. Could he but feel the throat of the Russ fiend beneath his steel fingers!

And Jane!

What tortures of doubt and fear and uncertainty she must be suffering. He felt that his position was infinitely less terrible than hers, for he at least knew that one of his loved ones was safe at home, while she had no idea of the whereabouts of either her husband or her son.

It is well for Tarzan that he did not guess the truth, for the knowledge would have but added a hundredfold to his suffering.

As he moved slowly through the jungle, his mind absorbed by his gloomy thoughts, there presently came to his ears a strange scratching sound which he could not translate.

Cautiously he moved in the direction from which it emanated, presently coming upon a huge panther pinned beneath a fallen tree.

As Tarzan approached, the beast turned, snarling, toward him, struggling to extricate itself; but one great limb across its back and the smaller entangling branches pinioning its legs prevented it from moving but a few inches in any direction.

The ape-man stood before the helpless cat fitting an arrow to his bow that he might dispatch the beast that otherwise must die of starvation; but even as he drew back the shaft a sudden whim stayed his hand.

Why rob the poor creature of life and liberty, when it would be so easy a thing to restore both to it! He was sure from the fact that the panther moved all its limbs in its futile struggle for freedom that its spine was uninjured, and for the same reason he knew that none of its limbs were broken.

Relaxing his bowstring, he returned the arrow to the quiver and, throwing the bow about his shoulder, stepped closer to the pinioned beast.

On his lips was the soothing, purring sound that the great cats themselves made when contented and happy. It was the nearest approach to a friendly advance that Tarzan could make in the language of Sheeta.

The panther ceased his snarling and eyed the ape-man closely. To lift the tree's great weight from the animal it was necessary to come within reach of those long, strong talons, and when the tree had been removed the man would be totally at the mercy of the savage beast; but to Tarzan of the Apes fear was a thing unknown.

Having decided, he acted promptly.

Unhesitatingly, he stepped into the tangle of branches close to the panther's side, still voicing his friendly and conciliatory purr. The cat turned his head toward the man, eyeing him steadily— questioningly. The long fangs were bared, but more in preparedness than threat.

Tarzan put a broad shoulder beneath the bole of the tree, and as he did so his bare leg pressed against the cat's silken side, so close was the man to the great beast.

Slowly Tarzan extended his giant thews.

The great tree with its entangling branches rose gradually from the panther, who, feeling the encumbering weight diminish, quickly crawled from beneath. Tarzan let the tree fall back to earth, and the two beasts turned to look upon one another.

A grim smile lay upon the ape-man's lips, for he knew that he had taken his life in his hands to free this savage jungle fellow; nor would it have surprised him had the cat sprung upon him the instant that it had been released.

But it did not do so. Instead, it stood a few paces from the tree watching the ape-man clamber out of the maze of fallen branches.

Once outside, Tarzan was not three paces from the panther. He might have taken to the higher branches of the trees upon the opposite side, for Sheeta cannot climb to the heights to which the ape-man can go; but something, a spirit of bravado perhaps, prompted him to approach the panther as though to discover if any feeling of gratitude would prompt the beast to friendliness.

As he approached the mighty cat the creature stepped warily to one side, and the ape-man brushed past him within a foot of the dripping jaws, and as he continued on through the forest the panther followed on behind him, as a hound follows at heel.

For a long time Tarzan could not tell whether the beast was following out of friendly feelings or merely stalking him against the time he should be hungry; but finally he was forced to believe that the former incentive it was that prompted the animal's action.

Later in the day the scent of a deer sent Tarzan into the trees, and when he had dropped his noose about the animal's neck he called to Sheeta, using a purr similar to that which he had utilized to pacify the brute's suspicions earlier in the day, but a trifle louder and more shrill.

It was similar to that which he had heard panthers use after a kill when they had been hunting in pairs.

Almost immediately there was a crashing of the underbrush close at hand, and the long, lithe body of his strange companion broke into view.

At sight of the body of Bara and the smell of blood the panther gave forth a shrill scream, and a moment later two beasts were feeding side by side upon the tender meat of the deer.

For several days this strangely assorted pair roamed the jungle together.

When one made a kill he called the other, and thus they fed well and often.

On one occasion as they were dining upon the carcass of a boar that Sheeta had dispatched, Numa, the lion, grim and terrible, broke through the tangled grasses close beside them.

With an angry, warning roar he sprang forward to chase them from their kill. Sheeta bounded into a nearby thicket, while Tarzan took to the low branches of an overhanging tree.

Here the ape-man unloosed his grass rope from about his neck, and as Numa stood above the body of the boar, challenging head erect, he dropped the sinuous noose about the maned neck, drawing the stout strands taut with a sudden jerk. At the same time he called shrilly to Sheeta, as he drew the struggling lion upward until only his hind feet touched the ground.

Quickly he made the rope fast to a stout branch, and as the panther, in answer to his summons, leaped into sight, Tarzan dropped to the earth beside the struggling and infuriated Numa, and with a long, sharp knife sprang upon him at one side even as Sheeta did upon the other.

The panther tore and rent Numa upon the right, while the ape-man struck home with his stone knife upon the other, so that before the mighty clawing of the king of beasts had succeeded in parting the rope he hung quite dead and harmless in the noose.

And then upon the jungle air there rose in unison from two savage throats the victory cry of the bull-ape and the panther, blended into one frightful and uncanny scream.

As the last notes died away in a long-drawn, fearsome wail, a score of painted warriors, drawing their long war-canoe upon the beach, halted to stare in the direction of the jungle and to listen.

5

Mugambi

BY THE TIME that Tarzan had travelled entirely about the coast of the island, and made several trips inland from various points, he was sure that he was the only human being upon it.

Nowhere had he found any sign that men had stopped even temporarily upon this shore, though, of course, he knew that so quickly does the rank vegetation of the tropics erase all but the most permanent of human monuments that he might be in error in his deductions.

The day following the killing of Numa, Tarzan and Sheeta came upon the tribe of Akut. At sight of the panther the great apes took to flight, but after a time Tarzan succeeded in recalling them.

It had occurred to him that it would be at least an interesting experiment to attempt to reconcile these hereditary enemies. He welcomed anything that would occupy his time and his mind beyond the filling of his belly and the gloomy thoughts to which he fell prey the moment that he became idle.

To communicate his plan to the apes was not a particularly difficult matter, though their narrow and limited vocabulary was strained in the effort; but to impress upon the little, wicked brain of Sheeta that he was to hunt with and not for his legitimate prey proved a task almost beyond the powers of the ape-man.

Tarzan, among his other weapons, possessed a long, stout cudgel, and after fastening his rope about the panther's neck he used this instrument freely upon the snarling beast, endeavouring in this way to impress upon its memory that it must not attack the great, shaggy, manlike creatures that had approached more closely once they had seen the purpose of the rope about Sheeta's neck.

That the cat did not turn and rend Tarzan is something of a miracle which may possibly be accounted for by the fact that twice when it turned growling upon the ape-man he had rapped it sharply upon its sensitive nose, inculcating in its mind thereby a most wholesome fear of the cudgel and the ape-beasts behind it.

It is a question if the original cause of his attachment for Tarzan was still at all clear in the mind of the panther, though doubtless some subconscious suggestion, superinduced by this primary reason and aided and abetted by the habit of the past few days, did much to compel the beast to tolerate treatment at his hands that would have sent it at the throat of any other creature.

Then, too, there was the compelling force of the manmind exerting its powerful influence over this creature of a lower order, and, after all, it may have been this that proved the most potent factor in Tarzan's supremacy over Sheeta and the other beasts of the jungle that had from time to time fallen under his domination.

Be that as it may, for days the man, the panther, and the great apes roamed their savage haunts side by side, making their kills together and sharing them with one another, and of all the fierce and savage band none was more terrible than the smooth-skinned, powerful beast that had been but a few short months before a familiar figure in many a London drawing room.

Sometimes the beasts separated to follow their own inclinations for an hour or a day, and it was upon one of these occasions when the ape-man had wandered through the treetops toward the beach, and was stretched in the hot sun upon the sand, that from the low summit of a nearby promontory a pair of keen eyes discovered him.

For a moment the owner of the eyes looked in astonishment at the figure of the savage white man basking in the rays of that hot, tropic sun; then he turned, making a sign to someone behind him. Presently another pair of eyes were looking down upon the ape-man, and then another and another, until a full score of hideously trapped, savage warriors were lying upon their bellies along the crest of the ridge watching the white-skinned stranger.

They were down wind from Tarzan, and so their scent was not carried to him, and as his back was turned half toward them he did not see their cautious advance over the edge of the promontory and down through the rank grass toward the sandy beach where he lay.

Big fellows they were, all of them, their barbaric headdresses and grotesquely painted faces, together with their many metal ornaments and gorgeously coloured feathers, adding to their wild, fierce appearance.

Once at the foot of the ridge, they came cautiously to their feet, and, bent half-double, advanced silently upon the unconscious white man, their heavy war-clubs swinging menacingly in their brawny hands.

The mental suffering that Tarzan's sorrowful thoughts induced had the effect of numbing his keen, perceptive faculties, so that the advancing savages were almost upon him before he became aware that he was no longer alone upon the beach.

So quickly, though, were his mind and muscles wont to react in unison to the slightest alarm that he was upon his feet and facing his enemies, even as he realized that something was behind him. As he sprang to his feet the warriors leaped toward him with raised clubs and savage yells, but the foremost went down to sudden death beneath the long, stout stick of the ape-man, and then the lithe, sinewy figure was among them, striking right and left with a fury, power, and precision that brought panic to the ranks of the blacks.

For a moment they withdrew, those that were left of them, and consulted together at a short distance from the ape-man, who stood with folded arms, a half-smile upon his handsome face, watching them. Presently they advanced upon him once more, this time wielding their heavy war-spears. They were between Tarzan and the jungle, in a little semicircle that closed in upon him as they advanced.

There seemed to the ape-man but slight chance to escape the final charge when all the great spears should be hurled simultaneously at him; but if he had desired to escape there was no way other than through the ranks of the savages except the open sea behind him.

His predicament was indeed most serious when an idea occurred to him that altered his smile to a broad grin. The warriors were still some little distance away, advancing slowly, making, after the manner of their kind, a frightful din with their savage yells and the pounding of their naked feet upon the ground as they leaped up and down in a fantastic war dance.

Then it was that the ape-man lifted his voice in a series of wild, weird screams that brought the blacks to a sudden, perplexed halt. They looked at one another questioningly, for here was a sound so hideous that their own frightful din faded into insignificance beside it. No human throat could have formed those bestial notes, they were sure, and yet with their own eyes they had seen this white man open his mouth to pour forth his awful cry.

But only for a moment they hesitated, and then with one accord they again took up their fantastic advance upon their prey; but even then a sudden crashing in the jungle behind them brought them once more to a halt, and as they turned to look in the direction of this new noise there broke upon their startled visions a sight that may well have frozen the blood of braver men than the Wagambi.

Leaping from the tangled vegetation of the jungle's rim came a huge panther, with blazing eyes and bared fangs, and in his wake a score of mighty, shaggy apes lumbering rapidly toward them, half erect upon their short, bowed legs, and with their long arms reaching to the ground, where their horny knuckles bore the weight of their ponderous bodies as they lurched from side to side in their grotesque advance.

The beasts of Tarzan had come in answer to his call.

Before the Wagambi could recover from their astonishment the frightful horde was upon them from one side and Tarzan of the Apes from the other. Heavy spears were hurled and mighty war-clubs wielded, and though apes went down never to rise, so, too, went down the men of Ugambi.

Sheeta's cruel fangs and tearing talons ripped and tore at the black hides. Akut's mighty yellow tusks found the jugular of more than one sleek-skinned savage, and Tarzan of the Apes was here and there and everywhere, urging on his fierce allies and taking a heavy toll with his long, slim knife.

In a moment the blacks had scattered for their lives, but of the score that had crept down the grassy sides of the promontory only a single warrior managed to escape the horde that had overwhelmed his people.

This one was Mugambi, chief of the Wagambi of Ugambi, and as he disappeared in the tangled luxuriousness of the rank growth upon the ridge's summit only the keen eyes of the ape-man saw the direction of his flight.

Leaving his pack to eat their fill upon the flesh of their victims—flesh that he could not touch—Tarzan of the Apes pursued the single survivor of the bloody fray. Just beyond the ridge he came within sight of the fleeing black, making with headlong leaps for a long war-canoe that was drawn well up upon the beach above the high tide surf.

Noiseless as the fellow's shadow, the ape-man raced after the terror-stricken black. In the white man's mind was a new plan, awakened by sight of the war-canoe. If these men had come to his island from another, or from the mainland, why not utilize their craft to make his way to the country from which they had come? Evidently it was an inhabited country, and no doubt had occasional intercourse with the mainland, if it were not itself upon the continent of Africa.

A heavy hand fell upon the shoulder of the escaping Mugambi before he was aware that he was being pursued, and as he turned to do battle with his assailant giant fingers closed about his wrists and he was hurled to earth with a giant astride him before he could strike a blow in his own defence.

In the language of the West Coast, Tarzan spoke to the prostrate man beneath him.

"Who are you?" he asked.

"Mugambi, chief of the Wagambi," replied the black.

"I will spare your life," said Tarzan, "if you will promise to help me to leave this island. What do you answer?"

"I will help you," replied Mugambi. "But now that you have killed all my warriors, I do not know that I even can leave your country, for there will be none to wield the paddles, and without paddlers we cannot cross the water."

Tarzan rose and allowed his prisoner to come to his feet. The fellow was a magnificent specimen of manhood—a black counterpart in physique of the splendid white man whom he faced.

"Come!" said the ape-man, and started back in the direction from which they could hear the snarling and growling of the feasting pack. Mugambi drew back.

"They will kill us," he said.

"I think not," replied Tarzan. "They are mine."

Still the black hesitated, fearful of the consequences of approaching the terrible creatures that were dining upon the bodies of his warriors; but Tarzan forced him to accompany him, and presently the two emerged from the jungle in full view of the grisly spectacle upon the beach. At sight of the men the beasts looked up with menacing growls, but Tarzan strode in among them, dragging the trembling Wagambi with him.

As he had taught the apes to accept Sheeta, so he taught them to adopt Mugambi as well, and much more easily; but Sheeta seemed quite unable to understand that though he had been called upon to devour Mugambi's warriors he was not to be allowed to proceed after the same fashion with Mugambi. However, being well filled, he contented himself with walking round the terror-stricken savage, emitting low, menacing growls while he kept his flaming, baleful eyes riveted upon the black.

Mugambi, on his part, clung closely to Tarzan, so that the ape-man could scarce control his laughter at the pitiable condition to which the chief's fear had reduced him; but at length the white took the great cat by the scruff of the neck and, dragging it quite close to the Wagambi, slapped it sharply upon the nose each time that it growled at the stranger.

At the sight of the thing—a man mauling with his bare hands one of the most relentless and fierce of the jungle carnivora—Mugambi's eyes bulged from their sockets, and from entertaining a sullen respect for the giant white man who had made him prisoner, the black felt an almost worshipping awe of Tarzan.

The education of Sheeta progressed so well that in a short time Mugambi ceased to be the object of his hungry attention, and the black felt a degree more of safety in his society.

To say that Mugambi was entirely happy or at ease in his new environment would not be to adhere strictly to the truth. His eyes were constantly rolling apprehensively from side to side as now one and now another of the fierce pack chanced to wander near him, so that for the most of the time it was principally the whites that showed.

Together Tarzan and Mugambi, with Sheeta and Akut, lay in wait at the ford for a deer, and when at a word from the ape-man the four of them leaped out upon the affrighted animal the black was sure that the poor creature died of fright before ever one of the great beasts touched it.

Mugambi built a fire and cooked his portion of the kill; but Tarzan, Sheeta, and Akut tore theirs, raw, with their sharp teeth, growling among themselves when one ventured to encroach upon the share of another.

It was not, after all, strange that the white man's ways should have been so much more nearly related to those of the beasts than were the savage blacks. We are, all of us, creatures of habit, and when the seeming necessity for schooling ourselves in new ways ceases to exist, we fall naturally and easily into the manners and customs which long usage has implanted ineradicably within us.

Mugambi from childhood had eaten no meat until it had been cooked, while Tarzan, on the other hand, had never tasted cooked food of any sort until he had grown almost to manhood, and only within the past three or four years had he eaten cooked meat. Not only did the habit of a lifetime prompt him to eat it raw, but the craving of his palate as well; for to him cooked flesh was spoiled flesh when compared with the rich and juicy meat of a fresh, hot kill.

That he could, with relish, eat raw meat that had been buried by himself weeks before, and enjoy small rodents and disgusting grubs, seems to us who have been always "civilized" a revolting fact; but had we learned in childhood to eat these things, and had we seen all those about us eat them, they would seem no more sickening to us now than do many of our greatest dainties, at which a savage African cannibal would look with repugnance and turn up his nose.

For instance, there is a tribe in the vicinity of Lake Rudolph that will eat no sheep or cattle, though its next neighbours do so. Near by is another tribe that eats donkey-meat—a custom most revolting to the surrounding tribes that do not eat donkey. So who may say that it is nice to eat snails and frogs' legs and oysters, but disgusting to feed upon grubs and beetles, or that a raw oyster, hoof, horns, and tail, is less revolting than the sweet, clean meat of a fresh-killed buck?

The next few days Tarzan devoted to the weaving of a bark-cloth sail with which to equip the canoe, for he despaired of being able to teach the apes to wield the paddles, though he did manage to get several of them to embark in the frail craft which he and Mugambi paddled about inside the reef where the water was quite smooth.

During these trips he had placed paddles in their hands, when they attempted to imitate the movements of him and Mugambi, but so difficult is it for them long to concentrate upon a thing that he soon saw that it would require weeks of patient training before they would be able to make any effective use of these new implements, if, in fact, they should ever do so.

There was one exception, however, and he was Akut. Almost from the first he showed an interest in this new sport that revealed a much higher plane of intelligence than that attained by any of his tribe. He seemed to grasp the purpose of the paddles, and when Tarzan saw that this was so he took much pains to explain in the meagre language of the anthropoid how they might be used to the best advantage.

From Mugambi Tarzan learned that the mainland lay but a short distance from the island. It seemed that the Wagambi warriors had ventured too far out in their frail craft, and when caught by a heavy tide and a high wind from offshore they had been driven out of sight of land. After paddling for a whole night, thinking that they were headed for home, they had seen this land at sunrise, and, still taking it for the mainland, had hailed it with joy, nor had Mugambi been aware that it was an island until Tarzan had told him that this was the fact.

The Wagambi chief was quite dubious as to the sail, for he had never seen such a contrivance used. His country lay far up the broad Ugambi River, and this was the first occasion that any of his people had found their way to the ocean.

Tarzan, however, was confident that with a good west wind he could navigate the little craft to the mainland. At any rate, he decided, it would be preferable to perish on the way than to remain indefinitely upon this evidently uncharted island to which no ships might ever be expected to come.

And so it was that when the first fair wind rose he embarked upon his cruise, and with him he took as strange and fearsome a crew as ever sailed under a savage master.

Mugambi and Akut went with him, and Sheeta, the panther, and a dozen great males of the tribe of Akut.

6

A Hideous Crew

THE WAR-CANOE WITH its savage load moved slowly toward the break in the reef through which it must pass to gain the open sea. Tarzan, Mugambi, and Akut wielded the paddles, for the shore kept the west wind from the little sail.

Sheeta crouched in the bow at the ape-man's feet, for it had seemed best to Tarzan always to keep the wicked beast as far from the other members of the party as possible, since it would require little or no provocation to send him at the throat of any than the white man, whom he evidently now looked upon as his master.

In the stern was Mugambi, and just in front of him squatted

Akut, while between Akut and Tarzan the twelve hairy apes sat upon their haunches, blinking dubiously this way and that, and now and then turning their eyes longingly back toward shore.

All went well until the canoe had passed beyond the reef. Here the breeze struck the sail, sending the rude craft lunging among the waves that ran higher and higher as they drew away from the shore.

With the tossing of the boat the apes became panic-stricken. They first moved uneasily about, and then commenced grumbling and whining. With difficulty Akut kept them in hand for a time; but when a particularly large wave struck the dugout simultaneously with a little squall of wind their terror broke all bounds, and, leaping to their feet, they all but overturned the boat before Akut and Tarzan together could quiet them. At last calm was restored, and eventually the apes became accustomed to the strange antics of their craft, after which no more trouble was experienced with them.

The trip was uneventful, the wind held, and after ten hours' steady sailing the black shadows of the coast loomed close before the straining eyes of the ape-man in the bow. It was far too dark to distinguish whether they had approached close to the mouth of the Ugambi or not, so Tarzan ran in through the surf at the closest point to await the dawn.

The dugout turned broadside the instant that its nose touched the sand, and immediately it rolled over, with all its crew scrambling madly for the shore. The next breaker rolled them over and over, but eventually they all succeeded in crawling to safety, and in a moment more their ungainly craft had been washed up beside them.

The balance of the night the apes sat huddled close to one another for warmth; while Mugambi built a fire close to them over which he crouched. Tarzan and Sheeta, however, were of a different mind, for neither of them feared the jungle night, and the insistent craving of their hunger sent them off into the Stygian blackness of the forest in search of prey.

Side by side they walked where there was room for two abreast. At other times in single file, first one and then the other in advance. It was Tarzan who first caught the scent of meat—a bull buffalo— and presently the two came stealthily upon the sleeping beast in the midst of a dense jungle of reeds close to a river.

Closer and closer they crept toward the unsuspecting beast, Sheeta upon his right side and Tarzan upon his left nearest the great heart. They had hunted together now for some time, so that they worked in unison, with only low, purring sounds as signals.

For a moment they lay quite silent near their prey, and then at a sign from the ape-man Sheeta sprang upon the great back, burying his strong teeth in the bull's neck. Instantly the brute sprang to his feet with a bellow of pain and rage, and at the same instant Tarzan rushed in upon his left side with the stone knife, striking repeatedly behind the shoulder.

One of the ape-man's hands clutched the thick mane, and as the bull raced madly through the reeds the thing striking at his life was dragged beside him. Sheeta but clung tenaciously to his hold upon the neck and back, biting deep in an effort to reach the spine.

For several hundred yards the bellowing bull carried his two savage antagonists, until at last the blade found his heart, when with a final bellow that was half-scream he plunged headlong to the earth. Then Tarzan and Sheeta feasted to repletion.

After the meal the two curled up together in a thicket, the man's black head pillowed upon the tawny side of the panther. Shortly after dawn they awoke and ate again, and then returned to the beach that Tarzan might lead the balance of the pack to the kill.

When the meal was done the brutes were for curling up to sleep, so Tarzan and Mugambi set off in search of the Ugambi River. They had proceeded scarce a hundred yards when they came suddenly upon a broad stream, which the Negro instantly recognized as that down which he and his warriors had paddled to the sea upon their ill-starred expedition.

The two now followed the stream down to the ocean, finding that it emptied into a bay not over a mile from the point upon the beach at which the canoe had been thrown the night before.

Tarzan was much elated by the discovery, as he knew that in the vicinity of a large watercourse he should find natives, and from some of these he had little doubt but that he should obtain news of Rokoff and the child, for he felt reasonably certain that the Russian would rid himself of the baby as quickly as possible after having disposed of Tarzan.

He and Mugambi now righted and launched the dugout, though it was a most difficult feat in the face of the surf which rolled continuously in upon the beach; but at last they were successful, and soon after were paddling up the coast toward the mouth of the Ugambi. Here they experienced considerable difficulty in making an entrance against the combined current and ebb tide, but by taking advantage of eddies close in to shore they came about dusk to a point nearly opposite the spot where they had left the pack asleep.

Making the craft fast to an overhanging bough, the two made their way into the jungle, presently coming upon some of the apes feeding upon fruit a little beyond the reeds where the buffalo had fallen. Sheeta was not anywhere to be seen, nor did he return that night, so that Tarzan came to believe that he had wandered away in search of his own kind.

Early the next morning the ape-man led his band down to the river, and as he walked he gave vent to a series of shrill cries. Presently from a great distance and faintly there came an answering scream, and a half-hour later the lithe form of Sheeta bounded into view where the others of the pack were clambering gingerly into the canoe.

The great beast, with arched back and purring like a contented tabby, rubbed his sides against the ape-man, and then at a word from the latter sprang lightly to his former place in the bow of the dugout.

When all were in place it was discovered that two of the apes of Akut were missing, and though both the king ape and Tarzan called to them for the better part of an hour, there was no response, and finally the boat put off without them. As it happened that the two missing ones were the very same who had evinced the least desire to accompany the expedition from the island, and had suffered the most from fright during the voyage, Tarzan was quite sure that they had absented themselves purposely rather than again enter the canoe.

As the party were putting in for the shore shortly after noon to search for food a slender, naked savage watched them for a moment from behind the dense screen of verdure which lined the river's bank, then he melted away upstream before any of those in the canoe discovered him.

Like a deer he bounded along the narrow trail until, filled with the excitement of his news, he burst into a native village several miles above the point at which Tarzan and his pack had stopped to hunt.

"Another white man is coming!" he cried to the chief who squatted before the entrance to his circular hut. "Another white man, and with him are many warriors. They come in a great war-canoe to kill and rob as did the black-bearded one who has just left us."

Kaviri leaped to his feet. He had but recently had a taste of the white man's medicine, and his savage heart was filled with bitterness and hate. In another moment the rumble of the war-drums rose from the village, calling in the hunters from the forest and the tillers from the fields.

Seven war-canoes were launched and manned by paint-daubed, befeathered warriors. Long spears bristled from the rude battleships, as they slid noiselessly over the bosom of the water, propelled by giant muscles rolling beneath glistening, ebony hides.

There was no beating of tom-toms now, nor blare of native horn, for Kaviri was a crafty warrior, and it was in his mind to take no chances, if they could be avoided. He would swoop noiselessly down with his seven canoes upon the single one of the white man, and before the guns of the latter could inflict much damage upon his people he would have overwhelmed the enemy by force of numbers.

Kaviri's own canoe went in advance of the others a short distance, and as it rounded a sharp bend in the river where the swift current bore it rapidly on its way it came suddenly upon the thing that Kaviri sought.

So close were the two canoes to one another that the black had only an opportunity to note the white face in the bow of the oncoming craft before the two touched and his own men were upon their feet, yelling like mad devils and thrusting their long spears at the occupants of the other canoe.

But a moment later, when Kaviri was able to realize the nature of the crew that manned the white man's dugout, he would have given all the beads and iron wire that he possessed to have been safely within his distant village. Scarcely had the two craft come together than the frightful apes of Akut rose, growling and barking, from the bottom of the canoe, and, with long, hairy arms far outstretched, grasped the menacing spears from the hands of Kaviri's warriors.

The blacks were overcome with terror, but there was nothing to do other than to fight. Now came the other war-canoes rapidly down upon the two craft. Their occupants were eager to join the battle, for they thought that their foes were white men and their native porters.

They swarmed about Tarzan's craft; but when they saw the nature of the enemy all but one turned and paddled swiftly upriver. That one came too close to the ape-man's craft before its occupants realized that their fellows were pitted against demons instead of men. As it touched Tarzan spoke a few low words to Sheeta and Akut, so that before the attacking warriors could draw away there sprang upon them with a blood-freezing scream a huge panther, and into the other end of their canoe clambered a great ape.

At one end the panther wrought fearful havoc with his mighty talons and long, sharp fangs, while Akut at the other buried his yellow canines in the necks of those that came within his reach, hurling the terror-stricken blacks overboard as he made his way toward the centre of the canoe.

Kaviri was so busily engaged with the demons that had entered his own craft that he could offer no assistance to his warriors in the other. A giant of a white devil had wrested his spear from him as though he, the mighty Kaviri, had been but a newborn babe. Hairy monsters were overcoming his fighting men, and a black chieftain like himself was fighting shoulder to shoulder with the hideous pack that opposed him.

Kaviri battled bravely against his antagonist, for he felt that death had already claimed him, and so the least that he could do would be to sell his life as dearly as possible; but it was soon evident that his best was quite futile when pitted against the super-human brawn and agility of the creature that at last found his throat and bent him back into the bottom of the canoe.

Presently Kaviri's head began to whirl—objects became confused and dim before his eyes—there was a great pain in his chest as he struggled for the breath of life that the thing upon him was shutting off for ever. Then he lost consciousness.

When he opened his eyes once more he found, much to his surprise, that he was not dead. He lay, securely bound, in the bottom of his own canoe. A great panther sat upon its haunches, looking down upon him.

Kaviri shuddered and closed his eyes again, waiting for the ferocious creature to spring upon him and put him out of his misery of terror.

After a moment, no rending fangs having buried themselves in his trembling body, he again ventured to open his eyes. Beyond the panther kneeled the white giant who had overcome him.

The man was wielding a paddle, while directly behind him Kaviri saw some of his own warriors similarly engaged. Back of them again squatted several of the hairy apes.

Tarzan, seeing that the chief had regained consciousness, addressed him.

"Your warriors tell me that you are the chief of a numerous people, and that your name is Kaviri," he said.

"Yes," replied the black.

"Why did you attack me? I came in peace."

"Another white man 'came in peace' three moons ago," replied Kaviri, "and after we had brought him presents of a goat and cassava and milk, he set upon us with his guns and killed many of my people, and then went on his way, taking all of our goats and many of our young men and women."

"I am not as this other white man," replied Tarzan. "I should not have harmed you had you not set upon me. Tell me, what was the face of this bad white man like? I am searching for one who has wronged me. Possibly this may be the very one."

"He was a man with a bad face, covered with a great, black beard, and he was very, very wicked—yes, very wicked indeed."

"Was there a little white child with him?" asked Tarzan, his heart almost stopped as he awaited the black's answer.

"No, *bwana*," replied Kaviri, "the white child was not with this man's party—it was with the other party."

"Other party!" exclaimed Tarzan. "What other party?"

"With the party that the very bad white man was pursuing. There was a white man, woman, and the child, with six Mosula porters. They passed up the river three days ahead of the very bad white man. I think that they were running away from him."

A white man, woman, and child! Tarzan was puzzled. The child must be his little Jack; but who could the woman be—and the man? Was it possible that one of Rokoff's confederates had conspired with some woman—who had accompanied the Russian—to steal the baby from him?

If this was the case, they had doubtless purposed returning the child to civilization and there either claiming a reward or holding the little prisoner for ransom.

But now that Rokoff had succeeded in chasing them far inland, up the savage river, there could be little doubt but that he would eventually overhaul them, unless, as was still more probable, they should be captured and killed by the very cannibals farther up the Ugambi, to whom, Tarzan was now convinced, it had been Rokoff's intention to deliver the baby.

As he talked to Kaviri the canoes had been moving steadily upriver toward the chief's village. Kaviri's warriors plied the paddles in the three canoes, casting sidelong, terrified glances at their hideous passengers. Three of the apes of Akut had been killed in the encounter, but there were, with Akut, eight of the frightful beasts remaining, and there was Sheeta, the panther, and Tarzan and Mugambi.

Kaviri's warriors thought that they had never seen so terrible a crew in all their lives. Momentarily they expected to be pounced upon and torn asunder by some of their captors; and, in fact, it was all that Tarzan and Mugambi and Akut could do to keep the snarling, ill-natured brutes from snapping at the glistening, naked bodies that brushed against them now and then with the movements of the paddlers, whose very fear added incitement to the beasts.

At Kaviri's camp Tarzan paused only long enough to eat the food that the blacks furnished, and arrange with the chief for a dozen men to man the paddles of his canoe.

Kaviri was only too glad to comply with any demands that the ape-man might make if only such compliance would hasten the departure of the horrid pack; but it was easier, he discovered, to promise men than to furnish them, for when his people learned his intentions those that had not already fled into the jungle proceeded to do so without loss of time, so that when Kaviri turned to point out those who were to accompany Tarzan, he discovered that he was the only member of his tribe left within the village.

Tarzan could not repress a smile.

"They do not seem anxious to accompany us," he said, "but just remain quietly here, Kaviri, and presently you shall see your people flocking to your side."

Then the ape-man rose, and, calling his pack about him, commanded that Mugambi remain with Kaviri, and disappeared in the jungle with Sheeta and the apes at his heels.

For half an hour the silence of the grim forest was broken only by the ordinary sounds of the teeming life that but adds to its lowering loneliness. Kaviri and Mugambi sat alone in the palisaded village, waiting.

Presently from a great distance came a hideous sound. Mugambi recognized the weird challenge of the ape-man. Immediately from different points of the compass rose a horrid semicircle of similar shrieks and screams, punctuated now and again by the blood-curdling cry of a hungry panther.

7

Betrayed

THE TWO SAVAGES, Kaviri and Mugambi, squatting before the entrance to Kaviri's hut, looked at one another— Kaviri with ill-concealed alarm.

"What is it?" he whispered.

"It is Bwana Tarzan and his people," replied Mugambi. "But what they are doing I know not, unless it be that they are devouring your people who ran away."

Kaviri shuddered and rolled his eyes fearfully toward the jungle. In all his long life in the savage forest he had never heard such an awful, fearsome din.

Closer and closer came the sounds, and now with them were mingled the terrified shrieks of women and children and of men. For twenty long minutes the bloodcurdling cries continued, until they seemed but a stone's throw from the palisade. Kaviri rose to flee, but Mugambi seized and held him, for such had been the command of Tarzan.

A moment later a horde of terrified natives burst from the jungle, racing toward the shelter of their huts. Like frightened sheep they ran, and behind them, driving them as sheep might be driven, came Tarzan and Sheeta and the hideous apes of Akut.

Presently Tarzan stood before Kaviri, the old, quiet smile upon his lips.

"Your people have returned, my brother," he said, "and now you may select those who are to accompany me and paddle my canoe."

Tremblingly Kaviri tottered to his feet, calling to his people to come from their huts; but none responded to his summons.

"Tell them," suggested Tarzan, "that if they do not come I shall send my people in after them."

Kaviri did as he was bid, and in an instant the entire population of the village came forth, their wide and frightened eyes rolling from one to another of the savage creatures that wandered about the village street.

Quickly Kaviri designated a dozen warriors to accompany Tarzan. The poor fellows went almost white with terror at the prospect of close contact with the panther and the apes in the narrow confines of the canoes; but when Kaviri explained to them that there was no escape—that Bwana Tarzan would pursue them with his grim horde should they attempt to run away from the duty—they finally went gloomily down to the river and took their places in the canoe.

It was with a sigh of relief that their chieftain saw the party disappear about a headland a short distance upriver.

For three days the strange company continued farther and farther into the heart of the savage country that lies on either side of the almost unexplored Ugambi. Three of the twelve warriors deserted during that time; but as several of the apes had finally learned the secret of the paddles, Tarzan felt no dismay because of the loss.

As a matter of fact, he could have traveled much more rapidly on shore, but he believed that he could hold his own wild crew together to better advantage by keeping them to the boat as much as possible. Twice a day they landed to hunt and feed, and at night they slept upon the bank of the mainland or on one of the numerous little islands that dotted the river.

Before them the natives fled in alarm, so that they found only deserted villages in their path as they proceeded. Tarzan was anxious to get in touch with some of the savages who dwelt upon the river's banks, but so far he had been unable to do so.

Finally he decided to take to the land himself, leaving his company to follow after him by boat. He explained to Mugambi the thing that he had in mind, and told Akut to follow the directions of the black.

"I will join you again in a few days," he said. "Now I go ahead to learn what has become of the very bad white man whom I seek."

At the next halt Tarzan took to the shore, and was soon lost to the view of his people.

The first few villages he came to were deserted, showing that news of the coming of his pack had traveled rapidly; but toward evening he came upon a distant cluster of thatched huts surrounded by a rude palisade, within which were a couple of hundred natives.

The women were preparing the evening meal as Tarzan of the Apes poised above them in the branches of a giant tree which overhung the palisade at one point.

The ape-man was at a loss as to how he might enter into communication with these people without either frightening them or arousing their savage love of battle. He had no desire to fight now, for he was upon a much more important mission than that of battling with every chance tribe that he should happen to meet with.

At last he hit upon a plan, and after seeing that he was concealed from the view of those below, he gave a few hoarse grunts in imitation of a panther. All eyes immediately turned upward toward the foliage above.

It was growing dark, and they could not penetrate the leafy screen which shielded the ape-man from their view. The moment that he had won their attention he raised his voice in the shriller and more hideous scream of the beast he personated, and then, scarce stirring a leaf in his descent, dropped to the ground once again outside the palisade, and, with the speed of a deer, ran quickly round to the village gate.

Here he beat upon the fibre-bound saplings of which the barrier was constructed, shouting to the natives in their own tongue that he was a friend who wished food and shelter for the night.

Tarzan knew well the nature of the black man. He was aware that the grunting and screaming of Sheeta in the tree above them would set their nerves on edge, and that his pounding upon their gate after dark would still further add to their terror.

That they did not reply to his hail was no surprise, for natives are fearful of any voice that comes out of the night from beyond their palisades, attributing it always to some demon or other ghostly visitor; but still he continued to call.

"Let me in, my friends!" he cried. "I am a white man pursuing the very bad white man who passed this way a few days ago. I follow to punish him for the sins he has committed against you and me.

"If you doubt my friendship, I will prove it to you by going into the tree above your village and driving Sheeta back into the jungle before he leaps among you. If you will not promise to take me in and treat me as a friend I shall let Sheeta stay and devour you."

For a moment there was silence. Then the voice of an old man came out of the quiet of the village street.

"If you are indeed a white man and a friend, we will let you come in; but first you must drive Sheeta away."

"Very well," replied Tarzan. "Listen, and you shall hear Sheeta fleeing before me."

The ape-man returned quickly to the tree, and this time he made a great noise as he entered the branches, at the same time growling ominously after the manner of the panther, so that those below would believe that the great beast was still there.

When he reached a point well above the village street he made a great commotion, shaking the tree violently, crying aloud to the panther to flee or be killed, and punctuating his own voice with the screams and mouthings of an angry beast.

Presently he raced toward the opposite side of the tree and off into the jungle, pounding loudly against the boles of trees as he went, and voicing the panther's diminishing growls as he drew farther and farther away from the village.

A few minutes later he returned to the village gate, calling to the natives within.

"I have driven Sheeta away," he said. "Now come and admit me as you promised."

For a time there was the sound of excited discussion within the palisade, but at length a half-dozen warriors came and opened the gates, peering anxiously out in evident trepidation as to the nature of the creature which they should find waiting there. They were not much relieved at sight of an almost naked white man; but when Tarzan had reassured them in quiet tones, protesting his friendship for them, they opened the barrier a trifle farther and admitted him.

When the gates had been once more secured the self-confidence of the savages returned, and as Tarzan walked up the village street toward the chief's hut he was surrounded by a host of curious men, women, and children.

From the chief he learned that Rokoff had passed up the river a week previous, and that he had horns growing from his forehead, and was accompanied by a thousand devils. Later the chief said that the very bad white man had remained a month in his village.

Though none of these statements agreed with Kaviri's, that the Russian was but three days gone from the chieftain's village and that his following was much smaller than now stated, Tarzan was in no manner surprised at the discrepancies, for he was quite familiar with the savage mind's strange manner of functioning.

What he was most interested in knowing was that he was upon

the right trail, and that it led toward the interior. In this circumstance he knew that Rokoff could never escape him.

After several hours of questioning and cross-questioning the
ape-man learned that another party had preceded the Russian by
several days—three whites—a man, a woman, and a little man-
child, with several Mosulas.

Tarzan explained to the chief that his people would follow him
in a canoe, probably the next day, and that though he might go on
ahead of them the chief was to receive them kindly and have no
fear of them, for Mugambi would see that they did not harm the
chief's people, if they were accorded a friendly reception.

"And now," he concluded, "I shall lie down beneath this tree
and sleep. I am very tired. Permit no one to disturb me."

The chief offered him a hut, but Tarzan, from past experience
of native dwellings, preferred the open air, and, further, he had
plans of his own that could be better carried out if he remained
beneath the tree. He gave as his reason a desire to be close at hand
should Sheeta return, and after this explanation the chief was very
glad to permit him to sleep beneath the tree.

Tarzan had always found that it stood him in good stead to
leave with natives the impression that he was to some extent possessed of more or less miraculous powers. He might easily have
entered their village without recourse to the gates, but he believed
that a sudden and unaccountable disappearance when he was
ready to leave them would result in a more lasting impression
upon their childlike minds, and so as soon as the village was quiet
in sleep he rose, and, leaping into the branches of the tree above
him, faded silently into the black mystery of the jungle night.

All the balance of that night the ape-man swung rapidly
through the upper and middle terraces of the forest. When the
going was good there he preferred the upper branches of the giant
trees, for then his way was better lighted by the moon; but so
accustomed were all his senses to the grim world of his birth
that it was possible for him, even in the dense, black shadows
near the ground, to move with ease and rapidity. You or I walking beneath the arcs of Main Street, or Broadway, or State Street,
could not have moved more surely or with a tenth the speed of the
agile ape-man through the gloomy mazes that would have baffled
us entirely.

At dawn he stopped to feed, and then he slept for several hours,
taking up the pursuit again toward noon.

Twice he came upon natives, and, though he had considerable
difficulty in approaching them, he succeeded in each instance in

quieting both their fears and bellicose intentions toward him, and learned from them that he was upon the trail of the Russian.

Two days later, still following up the Ugambi, he came upon a large village. The chief, a wicked-looking fellow with the sharp-filed teeth that often denote the cannibal, received him with apparent friendliness.

The ape-man was now thoroughly fatigued, and had determined to rest for eight or ten hours that he might be fresh and strong when he caught up with Rokoff, as he was sure he must do within a very short time.

The chief told him that the bearded white man had left his village only the morning before, and that doubtless he would be able to overtake him in a short time. The other party the chief had not seen or heard of, so he said.

Tarzan did not like the appearance or manner of the fellow, who seemed, though friendly enough, to harbour a certain contempt for this half-naked white man who came with no followers and offered no presents; but he needed the rest and food that the village would afford him with less effort than the jungle, and so, as he knew no fear of man, beast, or devil, he curled himself up in the shadow of a hut and was soon asleep.

Scarcely had he left the chief than the latter called two of his warriors, to whom he whispered a few instructions. A moment later the sleek, black bodies were racing along the river path, up-stream, toward the east.

In the village the chief maintained perfect quiet. He would permit no one to approach the sleeping visitor, nor any singing, nor loud talking. He was remarkably solicitous lest his guest be disturbed.

Three hours later several canoes came silently into view from up the Ugambi. They were being pushed ahead rapidly by the brawny muscles of their black crews. Upon the bank before the river stood the chief, his spear raised in a horizontal position above his head, as though in some manner of predetermined signal to those within the boats.

And such indeed was the purpose of his attitude—which meant that the white stranger within his village still slept peacefully.

In the bows of two of the canoes were the runners that the chief had sent forth three hours earlier. It was evident that they had been dispatched to follow and bring back this party, and that the signal from the bank was one that had been determined upon before they left the village.

In a few moments the dugouts drew up to the verdure-clad bank.

The native warriors filed out, and with them a half-dozen white men. Sullen, ugly-looking customers they were, and none more so than the evil-faced, black-bearded man who commanded them.

"Where is the white man your messengers report to be with you?" he asked of the chief.

"This way, *bwana*," replied the native. "Carefully have I kept silence in the village that he might be still asleep when you returned. I do not know that he is one who seeks you to do you harm, but he questioned me closely about your coming and your going, and his appearance is as that of the one you described, but whom you believed safe in the country which you called Jungle Island.

"Had you not told me this tale I should not have recognized him, and then he might have gone after and slain you. If he is a friend and no enemy, then no harm has been done, *bwana*; but if he proves to be an enemy, I should like very much to have a rifle and some ammunition."

"You have done well," replied the white man, "and you shall have the rifle and ammunition whether he be a friend or enemy, provided that you stand with me."

"I shall stand with you, *bwana*," said the chief, "and now come and look upon the stranger, who sleeps within my village."

So saying, he turned and led the way toward the hut, in the shadow of which the unconscious Tarzan slept peacefully.

Behind the two men came the remaining whites and a score of warriors; but the raised forefingers of the chief and his companion held them all to perfect silence.

As they turned the corner of the hut, cautiously and upon tiptoe, an ugly smile touched the lips of the white as his eyes fell upon the giant figure of the sleeping ape-man.

The chief looked at the other inquiringly. The latter nodded his head, to signify that the chief had made no mistake in his suspicions. Then he turned to those behind him and, pointing to the sleeping man, motioned for them to seize and bind him.

A moment later a dozen brutes had leaped upon the surprised Tarzan, and so quickly did they work that he was securely bound before he could make half an effort to escape.

Then they threw him down upon his back, and as his eyes turned toward the crowd that stood near, they fell upon the malign face of Nikolas Rokoff.

A sneer curled the Russian's lips. He stepped quite close to Tarzan.

"Pig!" he cried. "Have you not yet learned sufficient wisdom to keep away from Nikolas Rokoff?"

Then he kicked the prostrate man full in the face.

"That for your welcome," he said.

"Tonight, before my Ethiop friends eat you, I shall tell you what has already befallen your wife and child, and what further plans I have for their futures."

8

The Dance of Death

THROUGH THE LUXURIANT, tangled vegetation of the Stygian jungle night a great lithe body made its way sinuously and in utter silence upon its soft padded feet. Only two blazing points of yellow-green flame shone occasionally with the reflected light of the equatorial moon that now and again pierced the softly sighing roof rustling in the night wind.

Occasionally the beast would stop with high-held nose, sniffing searchingly. At other times a quick, brief incursion into the branches above delayed it momentarily in its steady journey toward the east. To its sensitive nostrils came the subtle unseen spoor of many a tender four-footed creature, bringing the slaver of hunger to the cruel, drooping jowl.

But steadfastly it kept on its way, strangely ignoring the cravings of appetite that at another time would have sent the rolling, fur-clad muscles flying at some soft throat.

All that night the creature pursued its lonely way, and the next day it halted only to make a single kill, which it tore to fragments and devoured with sullen, grumbling rumbles as though half famished for lack of food.

It was dusk when it approached the palisade that surrounded a large native village. Like the shadow of a swift and silent death it circled the village, nose to ground, halting at last close to the palisade, where it almost touched the backs of several huts. Here the beast sniffed for a moment, and then, turning its head upon one side, listened with up-pricked ears.

What it heard was no sound by the standards of human ears, yet to the highly attuned and delicate organs of the beast a message seemed to be borne to the savage brain. A wondrous transformation was wrought in the motionless mass of statuesque bone and muscle that had an instant before stood as though carved out of living bronze.

As if it had been poised upon steel springs, suddenly released, it rose quickly and silently to the top of the palisade, disappearing, stealthily and catlike, into the dark space between the wall and the back of an adjacent hut.

In the village street beyond women were preparing many little fires and fetching cooking-pots filled with water, for a great feast was to be celebrated ere the night was many hours older. About a stout stake near the centre of the circling fires a little knot of black warriors stood conversing, their bodies smeared with white and blue and ochre in broad and grotesque bands. Great circles of color were drawn about their eyes and lips, their breasts and abdomens, and from their clay-plastered coiffures rose gay feathers and bits of long, straight wire.

The village was preparing for the feast, while in a hut at one side of the scene of the coming orgy the bound victim of their bestial appetites lay waiting for the end. And such an end!

Tarzan of the Apes, tensing his mighty muscles, strained at the bonds that pinioned him; but they had been re-enforced many times at the instigation of the Russian, so that not even the ape-man's giant brawn could budge them.

Death!

Tarzan had looked the Hideous Hunter in the face many a time, and smiled. And he would smile again tonight when he knew the end was coming quickly; but now his thoughts were not of himself, but of those others—the dear ones who must suffer most because of his passing.

Jane would never know the manner of it. For that he thanked Heaven; and he was thankful also that she at least was safe in the heart of the world's greatest city. Safe among kind and loving friends who would do their best to lighten her misery.

But the boy!

Tarzan writhed at the thought of him. His son! And now he—

the mighty Lord of the Jungle—he, Tarzan, King of the Apes, the only one in all the world fitted to find and save the child from the horrors that Rokoff's evil mind had planned—had been trapped like a silly, dumb creature. He was to die in a few hours, and with him would go the child's last chance of succour.

Rokoff had been in to see and revile and abuse him several times during the afternoon; but he had been able to wring no word of remonstrance or murmur of pain from the lips of the giant captive.

So at last he had given up, reserving his particular bit of exquisite mental torture for the last moment, when, just before the savage spears of the cannibals should forever make the object of his hatred immune to further suffering, the Russian planned to reveal to his enemy the true whereabouts of his wife whom he thought safe in England.

Dusk had fallen upon the village, and the ape-man could hear the preparations going forward for the torture and the feast. The dance of death he could picture in his mind's eye—for he had seen the thing many times in the past. Now he was to be the central figure, bound to the stake.

The torture of the slow death as the circling warriors cut him to bits with the fiendish skill, that mutilated without bringing unconsciousness, had no terrors for him. He was inured to suffering and to the sight of blood and to cruel death; but the desire to live was no less strong within him, and until the last spark of life should flicker and go out, his whole being would remain quick with hope and determination. Let them relax their watchfulness but for an instant, he knew that his cunning mind and giant muscles would find a way to escape—escape and revenge.

As he lay, thinking furiously on every possibility of self-salvation, there came to his sensitive nostrils a faint and a familiar scent. Instantly every faculty of his mind was upon the alert. Presently his trained ears caught the sound of the soundless presence without—behind the hut wherein he lay.

His lips moved, and though no sound came forth that might have been appreciable to a human ear beyond the walls of his prison, yet he realized that the one beyond would hear. Already he knew who that one was, for his nostrils had told him as plainly as your eyes or mine tell us of the identity of an old friend whom we come upon in broad daylight.

An instant later he heard the soft sound of a fur-clad body and padded feet scaling the outer wall behind the hut and then a tearing at the poles which formed the wall. Presently through the hole thus made slunk a great beast, pressing its cold muzzle close to his neck.

It was Sheeta, the panther.

The beast snuffed round the prostrate man, whining a little. There was a limit to the interchange of ideas which could take place between these two, and so Tarzan could not be sure that Sheeta understood all that he attempted to communicate to him. That the man was tied and helpless Sheeta could, of course, see; but that to the mind of the panther this would carry any suggestion of harm in so far as his master was concerned, Tarzan could not guess.

What had brought the beast to him? The fact that he had come augured well for what he might accomplish; but when Tarzan tried to get Sheeta to gnaw his bonds asunder the great animal could not seem to understand what was expected of him, and, instead, but licked the wrists and arms of the prisoner.

Presently there came an interruption. Someone was approaching the hut. Sheeta gave a low growl and slunk into the blackness of a far corner. Evidently the visitor did not hear the warning sound, for almost immediately he entered the hut—a tall, naked, savage warrior.

He came to Tarzan's side and pricked him with a spear. From the lips of the ape-man came a weird, uncanny sound, and in answer to it there leaped from the blackness of the hut's farthermost corner a bolt of fur-clad death. Full upon the breast of the painted savage the great beast struck, burying sharp talons in the black flesh and sinking great yellow fangs in the ebon throat.

There was a fearful scream of anguish and terror from the black, and mingled with it was the hideous challenge of the killing panther. Then came silence—silence except for the rending of bloody flesh and the crunching of human bones between mighty jaws.

The noise had brought sudden quiet to the village without. Then there came the sound of voices in consultation.

High-pitched, fear-filled voices, and deep, low tones of authority, as the chief spoke. Tarzan and the panther heard the approaching footsteps of many men, and then, to Tarzan's surprise, the great cat rose from across the body of its kill, and slunk noiselessly from the hut through the aperture through which it had entered.

The man heard the soft scraping of the body as it passed over the top of the palisade, and then silence. From the opposite side of the hut he heard the savages approaching to investigate.

He had little hope that Sheeta would return, for had the great cat intended to defend him against all comers it would have remained by his side as it heard the approaching savages without.

Tarzan knew how strange were the workings of the brains of the mighty carnivora of the jungle—how fiendishly fearless they might be in the face of certain death, and again how timid upon the slightest provocation. There was doubt in his mind that some note of the approaching blacks vibrating with fear had struck an answering chord in the nervous system of the panther, sending him slinking through the jungle, his tail between his legs.

The man shrugged. Well, what of it? He had expected to die, and, after all, what might Sheeta have done for him other than to maul a couple of his enemies before a rifle in the hands of one of the whites should have dispatched him!

If the cat could have released him! Ah! that would have resulted in a very different story; but it had proved beyond the understanding of Sheeta, and now the beast was gone and Tarzan must definitely abandon hope.

The natives were at the entrance to the hut now, peering fearfully into the dark interior. Two in advance held lighted torches in their left hands and ready spears in their right. They held back timorously against those behind, who were pushing them forward.

The shrieks of the panther's victim, mingled with those of the great cat, had wrought mightily upon their poor nerves, and now the awful silence of the dark interior seemed even more terribly ominous than had the frightful screaming.

Presently one of those who was being forced unwillingly within hit upon a happy scheme for learning first the precise nature of the danger which menaced him from the silent interior. With a quick movement he flung his lighted torch into the center of the hut. Instantly all within was illuminated for a brief second before the burning brand was dashed out against the earth floor.

There was the figure of the white prisoner still securely bound as they had last seen him, and in the center of the hut another figure equally as motionless, its throat and breasts horribly torn and mangled.

The sight that met the eyes of the foremost savages inspired more terror within their superstitious breasts than would the presence of Sheeta, for they saw only the result of a ferocious attack upon one of their fellows.

Not seeing the cause, their fear-ridden minds were free to attribute the ghastly work to supernatural causes, and with the thought they turned, screaming, from the hut, bowling over those who stood directly behind them in the exuberance of their terror.

For an hour Tarzan heard only the murmur of excited voices from the far end of the village. Evidently the savages were once more attempting to work up their flickering courage to a point that would permit them to make another invasion of the hut, for now and then came a savage yell, such as the warriors give to bolster up their bravery upon the field of battle.

But in the end it was two of the whites who first entered, carrying torches and guns. Tarzan was not surprised to discover that neither of them was Rokoff. He would have wagered his soul that no power on earth could have tempted that great coward to face the unknown menace of the hut.

When the natives saw that the white men were not attacked they, too, crowded into the interior, their voices hushed with terror as they looked upon the mutilated corpse of their comrade. The whites tried in vain to elicit an explanation from Tarzan; but to all their queries he but shook his head, a grim and knowing smile curving his lips.

At last Rokoff came.

His face grew very white as his eyes rested upon the bloody thing grinning up at him from the floor, the face set in a death mask of excruciating horror.

"Come!" he said to the chief. "Let us get to work and finish this demon before he has an opportunity to repeat this thing upon more of your people."

The chief gave orders that Tarzan should be lifted and carried to the stake; but it was several minutes before he could prevail upon any of his men to touch the prisoner.

At last, however, four of the younger warriors dragged Tarzan roughly from the hut, and once outside the pall of terror seemed lifted from the savage hearts.

A score of howling blacks pushed and buffeted the prisoner down the village street and bound him to the post in the centre of the circle of little fires and boiling cooking-pots.

When at last he was made fast and seemed quite helpless and beyond the faintest hope of succour, Rokoff's shrivelled wart of courage swelled to its usual proportions when danger was not present.

He stepped close to the ape-man, and, seizing a spear from the hands of one of the savages, was the first to prod the helpless victim. A little stream of blood trickled down the giant's smooth skin from the wound in his side; but no murmur of pain passed his lips.

The smile of contempt upon his face seemed to infuriate the Russian. With a volley of oaths he leaped at the helpless captive, beating him upon the face with his clenched fists and kicking him mercilessly about the legs.

Then he raised the heavy spear to drive it through the mighty heart, and still Tarzan of the Apes smiled contemptuously upon him.

Before Rokoff could drive the weapon home the chief sprang upon him and dragged him away from his intended victim.

"Stop, white man!" he cried. "Rob us of this prisoner and our death-dance, and you yourself may have to take his place."

The threat proved most effective in keeping the Russian from further assaults upon the prisoner, though he continued to stand a little apart and hurl taunts at his enemy. He told Tarzan that he himself was going to eat the ape-man's heart. He enlarged upon the horrors of the future life of Tarzan's son, and intimated that his vengeance would reach as well to Jane Clayton.

"You think your wife safe in England," said Rokoff. "Poor fool! She is even now in the hands of one not even of decent birth, and far from the safety of London and the protection of her friends. I had not meant to tell you this until I could bring to you upon Jungle Island proof of her fate.

"Now that you are about to die the most unthinkably horrid death that it is given a white man to die—let this word of the plight of your wife add to the torments that you must suffer before the last savage spear-thrust releases you from your torture."

The dance had commenced now, and the yells of the circling warriors drowned Rokoff's further attempts to distress his victim.

The leaping savages, the flickering firelight playing upon their painted bodies, circled about the victim at the stake.

To Tarzan's memory came a similar scene, when he had rescued D'Arnot from a like predicament at the last moment before the final spear-thrust should have ended his sufferings. Who was there now to rescue him? In all the world there was none able to save him from the torture and the death.

The thought that these human fiends would devour him when the dance was done caused him not a single qualm of horror or disgust. It did not add to his sufferings as it would have to those of an ordinary white man, for all his life Tarzan had seen the beasts of the jungle devour the flesh of their kills.

Had he not himself battled for the grisly forearm of a great ape at that long-gone Dum-Dum, when he had slain the fierce Tublat and won his niche in the respect of the Apes of Kerchak?

The dancers were leaping more closely to him now. The spears were commencing to find his body in the first torturing pricks that prefaced the more serious thrusts.

It would not be long now. The ape-man longed for the last savage lunge that would end his misery.

And then, far out in the mazes of the weird jungle, rose a shrill scream.

For an instant the dancers paused, and in the silence of the interval there rose from the lips of the fast-bound white man an answering shriek, more fearsome and more terrible than that of the jungle-beast that had roused it.

For several minutes the blacks hesitated; then, at the urging of Rokoff and their chief, they leaped in to finish the dance and the victim; but ere ever another spear touched the brown hide a tawny streak of green-eyed hate and ferocity bounded from the door of the hut in which Tarzan had been imprisoned, and Sheeta, the panther, stood snarling beside his master.

For an instant the blacks and the whites stood transfixed with terror. Their eyes were riveted upon the bared fangs of the jungle cat.

Only Tarzan of the Apes saw what else there was emerging from the dark interior of the hut.

9

Chivalry or Villainy

FROM HER CABIN port upon the *Kincaid*, Jane Clayton had seen her husband rowed to the verdure-clad shore of Jungle Island, and then the ship once more proceeded upon its way.

For several days she saw no one other than Sven Anderssen, the *Kincaid's* taciturn and repellent cook. She asked him the name of the shore upon which her husband had been set.

"Ay tank it blow purty soon purty hard," replied the Swede, and that was all that she could get out of him.

She had come to the conclusion that he spoke no other English, and so she ceased to importune him for information; but never did she forget to greet him pleasantly or to thank him for the hideous, nauseating meals he brought her.

Three days from the spot where Tarzan had been marooned the *Kincaid* came to anchor in the mouth of a great river, and presently Rokoff came to Jane Clayton's cabin.

"We have arrived, my dear," he said, with a sickening leer. "I have come to offer you safety, liberty, and ease. My heart has been softened toward you in your suffering, and I would make amends as best I may.

"Your husband was a brute—you know that best who found him naked in his native jungle, roaming wild with the savage beasts that were his fellows. Now I am a gentleman, not only born of noble blood, but raised gently as befits a man of quality.

"To you, dear Jane, I offer the love of a cultured man and association with one of culture and refinement, which you must have sorely missed in your relations with the poor ape that through your girlish infatuation you married so thoughtlessly. I love you, Jane. You have but to say the word and no further sorrows shall afflict you—even your baby shall be returned to you unharmed."

Outside the door Sven Anderssen paused with the noonday meal he had been carrying to Lady Greystoke. Upon the end of his long, stringy neck his little head was cocked to one side, his close-set eyes were half closed, his ears, so expressive was his whole attitude of stealthy eavesdropping, seemed truly to be cocked forward—even his long, yellow, straggly moustache appeared to assume a sly droop.

As Rokoff closed his appeal, awaiting the reply he invited, the look of surprise upon Jane Clayton's face turned to one of disgust. She fairly shuddered in the fellow's face.

"I would not have been surprised, M. Rokoff," she said, "had you attempted to force me to submit to your evil desires, but that you should be so fatuous as to believe that I, wife of John Clayton, would come to you willingly, even to save my life, I should never have imagined. I have known you for a scoundrel, M. Rokoff; but until now I had not taken you for a fool."

Rokoff's eyes narrowed, and the red of mortification flushed out the pallor of his face. He took a step toward the girl, threateningly.

"We shall see who is the fool at last," he hissed, "when I have broken you to my will and your plebeian Yankee stubbornness has cost you all that you hold dear—even the life of your baby—for, by the bones of St. Peter, I'll forego all that I had planned for the brat and cut its heart out before your very eyes. You'll learn what it means to insult Nikolas Rokoff."

Jane Clayton turned wearily away.

"What is the use," she said, "of expatiating upon the depths to which your vengeful nature can sink? You cannot move me either by threats or deeds. My baby cannot judge yet for himself, but I, his mother, can foresee that should it have been given him to survive to man's estate he would willingly sacrifice his life for the honour of his mother. Love him as I do, I would not purchase his life at such a price. Did I, he would execrate my memory to the day of his death."

Rokoff was now thoroughly angered because of his failure to reduce the girl to terror. He felt only hate for her, but it had come to his diseased mind that if he could force her to accede to his demands as the price of her life and her child's, the cup of his revenge would be filled to brimming when he could flaunt the wife of Lord Greystoke in the capitals of Europe as his mistress.

Again he stepped closer to her. His evil face was convulsed with rage and desire. Like a wild beast he sprang upon her, and with his strong fingers at her throat forced her backward upon the berth.

At the same instant the door of the cabin opened noisily. Rokoff leaped to his feet, and, turning, faced the Swede cook.

Into the fellow's usually foxy eyes had come an expression of utter stupidity. His lower jaw drooped in vacuous harmony. He busied himself in arranging Lady Greystoke's meal upon the tiny table at one side of her cabin.

The Russian glared at him.

"What do you mean," he cried, "by entering here without permission? Get out!"

The cook turned his watery blue eyes upon Rokoff and smiled vacuously.

"Ay tank it blow purty soon purty hard," he said, and then he began rearranging the few dishes upon the little table.

"Get out of here, or I'll throw you out, you miserable blockhead!" roared Rokoff, taking a threatening step toward the Swede.

Anderssen continued to smile foolishly in his direction, but one harm-like paw slid stealthily to the handle of the long, slim knife that protruded from the greasy cord supporting his soiled apron.

Rokoff saw the move and stopped short in his advance. Then he turned toward Jane Clayton.

"I will give you until tomorrow," he said, "to reconsider your answer to my offer. All will be sent ashore upon one pretext or another except you and the child, Paulvitch and myself. Then without interruption you will be able to witness the death of the baby."

He spoke in French that the cook might not understand the sinister portent of his words. When he had done he banged out of the cabin without another look at the man who had interrupted him in his sorry work.

When he had gone, Sven Anderssen turned toward Lady Greystoke—the idiotic expression that had masked his thoughts had fallen away, and in its place was one of craft and cunning.

"Hay tank Ay ban a fool," he said. "Hay ban the fool. Ay savvy Franch."

Jane Clayton looked at him in surprise.

"You understood all that he said, then?"

Anderssen grinned.

"You bat," he said.

"And you heard what was going on in here and came to protect me?"

"You bane good to me," explained the Swede. "Hay treat me like darty dog. Ay help you, lady. You yust vait—Ay help you. Ay ban Vast Coast lots times."

"But how can you help me, Sven," she asked, "when all these men will be against us?"

"Ay tank," said Sven Anderssen, "it blow purty soon purty hard," and then he turned and left the cabin.

Though Jane Clayton doubted the cook's ability to be of any material service to her, she was nevertheless deeply grateful to him for what he already had done. The feeling that among these enemies she had one friend brought the first ray of comfort that had come to lighten the burden of her miserable apprehensions throughout the long voyage of the *Kincaid*.

She saw no more of Rokoff that day, nor of any other until Sven came with her evening meal. She tried to draw him into conversation relative to his plans to aid her, but all that she could get from him was his stereotyped prophecy as to the future state of the wind. He seemed suddenly to have relapsed into his wonted state of dense stupidity.

However, when he was leaving her cabin a little later with the empty dishes he whispered very low, "Leave on your clothes an' roll up your blankets. Ay come back after you purty soon."

He would have slipped from the room at once, but Jane laid her hand upon his sleeve.

"My baby?" she asked. "I cannot go without him."

"You do wot Ay tal you," said Anderssen, scowling. "Ay ban halpin' you, so don't you gat too fonny."

When he had gone Jane Clayton sank down upon her berth in utter bewilderment. What was she to do? Suspicions as to the intentions of the Swede swarmed her brain. Might she not be infinitely worse off if she gave herself into his power than she already was?

No, she could be no worse off in company with the devil himself than with Nikolas Rokoff, for the devil at least bore the reputation of being a gentleman.

She swore a dozen times that she would not leave the *Kincaid* without her baby, and yet she remained clothed long past her usual hour for retiring, and her blankets were neatly rolled and bound with stout cord, when about midnight there came a stealthy scratching upon the panels of her door.

Swiftly she crossed the room and drew the bolt. Softly the door swung open to admit the muffled figure of the Swede. On one arm he carried a bundle, evidently his blankets. His other hand was raised in a gesture commanding silence, a grimy forefinger upon his lips.

He came quite close to her.

"Carry this," he said. "Do not make some noise when you see it. It ban you kid."

Quick hands snatched the bundle from the cook, and hungry mother arms folded the sleeping infant to her breast, while hot tears of joy ran down her cheeks and her whole frame shook with the emotion of the moment.

"Come!" said Anderssen. "We got no time to vaste."

He snatched up her bundle of blankets, and outside the cabin door his own as well. Then he led her to the ship's side, steadied her descent of the monkey-ladder, holding the child for her as she climbed to the waiting boat below. A moment later he had cut the rope that held the small boat to the steamer's side, and, bending silently to the muffled oars, was pulling toward the black shadows up the Ugambi River.

Anderssen rowed on as though quite sure of his ground, and when after half an hour the moon broke through the clouds there was revealed upon their left the mouth of a tributary running into the Ugambi. Up this narrow channel the Swede turned the prow of the small boat.

Jane Clayton wondered if the man knew where he was bound. She did not know that in his capacity as cook he had that day been rowed up this very stream to a little village where he had bartered with the natives for such provisions as they had for sale, and that he had there arranged the details of his plan for the adventure upon which they were now setting forth.

Even though the moon was full, the surface of the small river was quite dark. The giant trees overhung its narrow banks, meeting in a great arch above the centre of the river. Spanish moss dropped from the gracefully bending limbs, and enormous creepers clambered in riotous profusion from the ground to the loftiest branch, falling in curving loops almost to the water's placid breast.

Now and then the river's surface would be suddenly broken ahead of them by a huge crocodile, startled by the splashing of the oars, or, snorting and blowing, a family of hippos would dive from a sandy bar to the cool, safe depths of the bottom.

From the dense jungles upon either side came the weird night cries of the carnivora—the maniacal voice of the hyena, the coughing grunt of the panther, the deep and awful roar of the lion. And with them strange, uncanny notes that the girl could not ascribe to any particular night prowler—more terrible because of their mystery.

Huddled in the stern of the boat she sat with her baby strained close to her bosom, and because of that little tender, helpless thing she was happier tonight than she had been for many a sorrow-ridden day.

Even though she knew not to what fate she was going, or how soon that fate might overtake her, still was she happy and thankful for the moment, however brief, that she might press her baby tightly in her arms. She could scarce wait for the coming of the day that she might look again upon the bright face of her little, black-eyed Jack.

Again and again she tried to strain her eyes through the blackness of the jungle night to have but a tiny peep at those beloved features, but only the dim outline of the baby face rewarded her efforts. Then once more she would cuddle the warm, little bundle close to her throbbing heart.

It must have been close to three o'clock in the morning that Anderssen brought the boat's nose to the shore before a clearing where could be dimly seen in the waning moonlight a cluster of native huts encircled by a thorn *boma*.

The Swede called out a number of times before he could obtain a reply from the village, and then only because he had been expected, so fearful are the natives of voices out of the darkness of the night. He helped Jane Clayton ashore with the baby, tied the boat to a small bush, and, picking up their blankets, led her toward the *boma*.

At the village gate they were admitted by a native woman, the wife of the chief whom Anderssen had paid to assist him. She took them to the chief's hut, but Anderssen said that they would sleep without upon the ground, and so, her duty having been completed, she left them to their own devices.

The Swede, after explaining in his gruff way that the huts were doubtless filthy and vermin-ridden, spread Jane's blankets on the ground for her, and at a little distance unrolled his own and lay down to sleep.

It was some time before the girl could find a comfortable position upon the hard ground, but at last, the baby in the hollow of her arm, she dropped asleep from utter exhaustion.

When she awoke it was broad daylight.

About her were clustered a score of curious natives—mostly men, for among the aborigines it is the male who owns this characteristic in its most exaggerated form. Instinctively Jane Clayton drew the baby more closely to her, though she soon saw that the blacks were far from intending her or the child any harm.

In fact, one of them offered her a gourd of milk—a filthy, smoke-begrimed gourd, with the ancient rind of long-curdled milk caked in layers within its neck; but the spirit of the giver touched her deeply, and her face lightened for a moment with one of those almost forgotten smiles of radiance that had helped to make her beauty famous both in Baltimore and London.

She took the gourd in one hand, and rather than cause the giver pain raised it to her lips, though for the life of her she could scarce restrain the qualm of nausea that surged through her as the malodorous thing approached her nostrils.

It was Anderssen who came to her rescue, and taking the gourd from her, drank a portion himself, and then returned it to the native with a gift of blue beads.

The sun was shining brightly now, and though the baby still slept, Jane could scarce restrain her impatient desire to have at least a brief glance at the beloved face. The natives had withdrawn at a command from their chief, who now stood talking with Anderssen, a little apart from her.

As she debated the wisdom of risking disturbing the child's slumber by lifting the blanket that now protected its face from the sun, she noted that the cook conversed with the chief in the language of the Negro.

What a remarkable man the fellow was, indeed! She had thought him ignorant and stupid but a short day before, and now, within the past twenty-four hours, she had learned that he spoke not only English but French as well, and the primitive dialect of the West Coast.

She had thought him shifty, cruel, and untrustworthy, yet in so far as she had reason to believe he had proved himself in every way the contrary since the day before. It scarce seemed credible that he could be serving her from motives purely chivalrous. There must be something deeper in his intentions and plans than he had yet disclosed.

She wondered, and when she looked at him—at his close-set, shifty eyes and repulsive features, she shuddered, for she was convinced that no lofty characteristics could be hid behind so foul an exterior.

As she was thinking of these things the while she debated the wisdom of uncovering the baby's face, there came a little grunt from the wee bundle in her lap, and then a gurgling coo that set her heart in raptures.

The baby was awake! Now she might feast her eyes upon him.

Quickly she snatched the blanket from before the infant's face; Anderssen was looking at her as she did so.

He saw her stagger to her feet, holding the baby at arm's length from her, her eyes glued in horror upon the little chubby face and twinkling eyes.

Then he heard her piteous cry as her knees gave beneath her, and she sank to the ground in a swoon.

10

The Swede

As THE WARRIORS, clustered thick about Tarzan and Sheeta, realized that it was a flesh-and-blood panther that had interrupted their dance of death, they took heart a trifle, for in the face of all those circling spears even the mighty Sheeta would be doomed.

Rokoff was urging the chief to have his spearmen launch their missiles, and the black was upon the instant of issuing the command, when his eyes strayed beyond Tarzan, following the gaze of the ape-man.

With a yell of terror the chief turned and fled toward the village gate, and as his people looked to see the cause of his fright, they too took to their heels—for there, lumbering down upon them, their huge forms exaggerated by the play of moonlight and camp fire, came the hideous apes of Akut.

The instant the natives turned to flee the ape-man's savage cry rang out above the shrieks of the blacks, and in answer to it Sheeta and the apes leaped growling after the fugitives. Some of the warriors turned to battle with their enraged antagonists, but before the fiendish ferocity of the fierce beasts they went down to bloody death.

Others were dragged down in their flight, and it was not until the village was empty and the last of the blacks had disappeared into the bush that Tarzan was able to recall his savage pack to his side. Then it was that he discovered to his chagrin that he could not make one of them, not even the comparatively intelligent Akut, understand that he wished to be freed from the bonds that held him to the stake.

In time, of course, the idea would filter through their thick skulls, but in the meanwhile many things might happen—the

72

blacks might return in force to regain their village; the whites might readily pick them all off with their rifles from the surrounding trees; he might even starve to death before the dull-witted apes realized that he wished them to gnaw through his bonds.

As for Sheeta—the great cat understood even less than the apes; but yet Tarzan could not but marvel at the remarkable characteristics this beast had evidenced. That it felt real affection for him there seemed little doubt, for now that the blacks were disposed of, it walked slowly back and forth about the stake, rubbing its sides against the ape-man's legs and purring like a contented tabby. That it had gone of its own volition to bring the balance of the pack to his rescue, Tarzan could not doubt. His Sheeta was indeed a jewel among beasts.

Mugambi's absence worried the ape-man not a little. He attempted to learn from Akut what had become of the black, fearing that the beasts, freed from the restraint of Tarzan's presence, might have fallen upon the man and devoured him; but to all his questions the great ape but pointed back in the direction from which they had come out of the jungle.

The night passed with Tarzan still fast bound to the stake, and shortly after dawn his fears were realized in the discovery of naked black figures moving stealthily just within the edge of the jungle about the village. The blacks were returning.

With daylight their courage would be equal to the demands of a charge upon the handful of beasts that had routed them from their rightful abodes. The result of the encounter seemed foregone if the savages could curb their superstitious terror, for against their overwhelming numbers, their long spears and poisoned arrows, the panther and the apes could not be expected to survive a really determined attack.

That the blacks were preparing for a charge became apparent a few moments later, when they commenced to show themselves in force upon the edge of the clearing, dancing and jumping about as they waved their spears and shouted taunts and fierce warcries toward the village.

These manoeuvres Tarzan knew would continue until the blacks had worked themselves into a state of hysterical courage sufficient to sustain them for a short charge toward the village, and even though he doubted that they would reach it at the first attempt, he believed that at the second or the third they would swarm through the gateway, when the outcome could not be aught

than the extermination of Tarzan's bold, but unarmed and undis-
ciplined, defenders.

Even as he had guessed, the first charge carried the howling
warriors but a short distance into the open—a shrill, weird challenge from the ape-man being all that was necessary to send them
scurrying back to the bush. For half an hour they pranced and
yelled their courage to the sticking-point, and again essayed a
charge.

This time they came quite to the village gate, but when Sheeta
and the hideous apes leaped among them they turned screaming in
terror, and again fled to the jungle.

Again was the dancing and shouting repeated. This time Tarzan
felt no doubt they would enter the village and complete the work
that a handful of determined white men would have carried to a
successful conclusion at the first attempt.

To have rescue come so close only to be thwarted because he
could not make his poor, savage friends understand precisely what
he wanted of them was most irritating, but he could not find it in
his heart to place blame upon them. They had done their best, and
now he was sure they would doubtless remain to die with him in a
fruitless effort to defend him.

The blacks were already preparing for the charge. A few individuals had advanced a short distance toward the village and were
exhorting the others to follow them. In a moment the whole
savage horde would be racing across the clearing.

Tarzan thought only of the little child somewhere in this cruel,
relentless wilderness. His heart ached for the son that he might no
longer seek to save—that and the realization of Jane's suffering
were all that weighed upon his brave spirit in these that he thought
his last moments of life. Succour, all that he could hope for, had
come to him in the instant of his extremity—and failed. There was
nothing further for which to hope.

The blacks were half-way across the clearing when Tarzan's
attention was attracted by the actions of one of the apes. The beast
was glaring toward one of the huts. Tarzan followed his gaze. To
his infinite relief and delight he saw the stalwart form of Mugambi
racing toward him.

The huge black was panting heavily as though from strenuous
physical exertion and nervous excitement. He rushed to Tarzan's
side, and as the first of the savages reached the village gate the
native's knife severed the last of the cords that bound Tarzan to the
stake.

In the street lay the corpses of the savages that had fallen before the pack the night before. From one of these Tarzan seized a spear and knob stick, and with Mugambi at his side and the snarling pack about him, he met the natives as they poured through the gate.

Fierce and terrible was the battle that ensued, but at last the savages were routed, more by terror, perhaps, at sight of a black man and a white fighting in company with a panther and the huge fierce apes of Akut, than because of their inability to overcome the relatively small force that opposed them.

One prisoner fell into the hands of Tarzan, and him the ape-man questioned in an effort to learn what had become of Rokoff and his party. Promised his liberty in return for the information, the black told all he knew concerning the movements of the Russian.

It seemed that early in the morning their chief had attempted to prevail upon the whites to return with him to the village and with their guns destroy the ferocious pack that had taken possession of it, but Rokoff appeared to entertain even more fears of the giant white man and his strange companions than even the blacks themselves.

Upon no conditions would he consent to returning even within sight of the village. Instead, he took his party hurriedly to the river, where they stole a number of canoes the blacks had hidden there. The last that had been seen of them they had been paddling strongly upstream, their porters from Kaviri's village wielding the blades.

So once more Tarzan of the Apes with his hideous pack took up his search for the ape-man's son and the pursuit of his abductor.

For weary days they followed through an almost uninhabited country, only to learn at last that they were upon the wrong trail. The little band had been reduced by three, for three of Akut's apes had fallen in the fighting at the village. Now, with Akut, there were five great apes, and Sheeta was there—and Mugambi and Tarzan.

The ape-man no longer heard rumors even of the three who had preceded Rokoff—the white man and woman and the child. Who the man and woman were he could not guess, but that the child was his was enough to keep him hot upon the trail. He was sure that Rokoff would be following this trio, and so he felt confident that so long as he could keep upon the Russian's trail he would be winning so much nearer to the time he might snatch his son from the dangers and horrors that menaced him.

In retracing their way after losing Rokoff's trail Tarzan picked it up again at a point where the Russian had left the river and taken to the brush in a northerly direction. He could only account for this change on the ground that the child had been carried away from the river by the two who now had possession of it.

Nowhere along the way, however, could he gain definite information that might assure him positively that the child was ahead of him. Not a single native they questioned had seen or heard of this other party, though nearly all had had direct experience with the Russian or had talked with others who had.

It was with difficulty that Tarzan could find means to communicate with the natives, as the moment their eyes fell upon his companions they fled precipitately into the bush. His only alternative was to go ahead of his pack and waylay an occasional warrior whom he found alone in the jungle.

One day as he was thus engaged, tracking an unsuspecting savage, he came upon the fellow in the act of hurling a spear at a wounded white man who crouched in a clump of bush at the trail's side. The white was one whom Tarzan had often seen, and whom he recognized at once.

Deep in his memory was implanted those repulsive features—the close-set eyes, the shifty expression, the drooping yellow moustache.

Instantly it occurred to the ape-man that this fellow had not been among those who had accompanied Rokoff at the village where Tarzan had been a prisoner. He had seen them all, and this fellow had not been there. There could be but one explanation—he it was who had fled ahead of the Russian with the woman and the child—and the woman had been Jane Clayton. He was sure now of the meaning of Rokoff's words.

The ape-man's face went white as he looked upon the pasty, vice-marked countenance of the Swede. Across Tarzan's forehead stood out the broad band of scarlet that marked the scar where, years before, Terkoz had torn a great strip of the ape-man's scalp from his skull in the fierce battle in which Tarzan had sustained his fitness to the kingship of the apes of Kerchak.

The man was his prey—the black should not have him, and with the thought he leaped upon the warrior, striking down the spear before it could reach its mark. The black, whipping out his knife, turned to do battle with this new enemy, while the Swede, lying in the bush, witnessed a duel, the like of which he had never dreamed to see—a half-naked white man battling with a half-naked black, hand to hand with the crude weapons of primeval man at first, and then with hands and teeth like the primordial brutes from whose loins their forebears sprung.

For a time Anderssen did not recognize the white, and when at last it dawned upon him that he had seen this giant before, his eyes went wide in surprise that this growling, rending beast could ever have been the well-groomed English gentleman who had been a prisoner aboard the *Kincaid*.

An English nobleman! He had learned the identity of the *Kincaid*'s prisoners from Lady Greystoke during their flight up the Ugambi. Before, in common with the other members of the crew of the steamer, he had not known who the two might be.

The fight was over. Tarzan had been compelled to kill his antagonist, as the fellow would not surrender.

The Swede saw the white man leap to his feet beside the corpse of his foe, and placing one foot upon the broken neck lift his voice in the hideous challenge of the victorious bull-ape.

Anderssen shuddered. Then Tarzan turned toward him. His face was cold and cruel, and in the grey eyes the Swede read murder.

"Where is my wife?" growled the ape-man. "Where is the child?"

Anderssen tried to reply, but a sudden fit of coughing choked him. There was an arrow entirely through his chest, and as he coughed the blood from his wounded lung poured suddenly from his mouth and nostrils.

Tarzan stood waiting for the paroxysm to pass. Like a bronze image—cold, hard, and relentless—he stood over the helpless man, waiting to wring such information from him as he needed, and then to kill.

Presently the coughing and haemorrhage ceased, and again the wounded man tried to speak. Tarzan knelt near the faintly moving lips.

"The wife and child!" he repeated. "Where are they?"

Anderssen pointed up the trail.

"The Russian—he got them," he whispered.

"How did you come here?" continued Tarzan. "Why are you not with Rokoff?"

"They catch us," replied Anderssen, in a voice so low that the ape-man could just distinguish the words. "They catch us. Ay fight, but my men they all run avay. Then they get me when Ay ban vounded. Rokoff he say leave me here for the hyenas. That vas vorse than to kill. He tak your vife and kid."

"What were you doing with them—where were you taking them?" asked Tarzan, and then fiercely, leaping close to the fellow with fierce eyes blazing with the passion of hate and vengeance that he had with difficulty controlled, "What harm did you do to my wife or child? Speak quick before I kill you! Make your peace with God! Tell me the worst, or I will tear you to pieces with my hands and teeth. You have seen that I can do it!"

A look of wide-eyed surprise overspread Anderssen's face.

"Why," he whispered, "Ay did not hurt them. Ay tried to save them from that Russian. Your vife was kind to me on the *Kincaid*, and Ay hear that little baby cry sometimes. Ay got a vife an' kid for my own by Christiania an' Ay couldn't bear for to see them separated an' in Rokoff's hands any more. That vas all. Do Ay look like Ay ban here to hurt them?" he continued after a pause, pointing to the arrow protruding from his breast.

There was something in the man's tone and expression that convinced Tarzan of the truth of his assertions. More weighty than anything else was the fact that Anderssen evidently seemed more hurt than frightened. He knew he was going to die, so Tarzan's threats had little effect upon him; but it was quite apparent that he wished the Englishman to know the truth and not to wrong him by harboring the belief that his words and manner indicated that he had entertained.

The ape-man instantly dropped to his knees beside the Swede.

"I am sorry," he said very simply. "I had looked for none but knaves in company with Rokoff. I see that I was wrong. That is past now, and we will drop it for the more important matter of getting you to a place of comfort and looking after your wounds. We must have you on your feet again as soon as possible."

The Swede, smiling, shook his head.

"You go on an' look for the vife an' kid," he said. "Ay ban as gude as dead already; but"—he hesitated—"Ay hate to think of the hyenas. Von't you finish up this job?"

Tarzan shuddered. A moment ago he had been upon the point of killing this man. Now he could no more have taken his life than he could have taken the life of any of his best friends.

He lifted the Swede's head in his arms to change and ease his position.

Again came a fit of coughing and the terrible haemorrhage. After it was over Anderssen lay with closed eyes.

Tarzan thought that he was dead, until he suddenly raised his eyes to those of the ape-man, sighed, and spoke—in a very low, weak whisper:

"Ay tank it blow purty soon purty hard!" he said, and died.

11

Tambudza

TARZAN SCOOPED A shallow grave for the *Kincaid*'s cook, beneath whose repulsive exterior had beaten the heart of a chivalrous gentleman. That was all he could do in the cruel jungle for the man who had given his life in the service of his little son and his wife.

Then Tarzan took up again the pursuit of Rokoff. Now that he was positive that the woman ahead of him was indeed Jane, and that she had again fallen into the hands of the Russian, it seemed that with all the incredible speed of his fleet and agile muscles he moved at but a snail's pace.

It was with difficulty that he kept the trail, for there were many paths through the jungle at this point—crossing and crisscrossing, forking and branching in all directions, and over them all had passed natives innumerable, coming and going. The spoor of the white men was obliterated by that of the native carriers who had followed them, and over all was the spoor of other natives and of wild beasts.

It was most perplexing; yet Tarzan kept on assiduously, checking his sense of sight against his sense of smell, that he might more surely keep to the right trail. But, with all his care, night found him at a point where he was positive that he was on the wrong trail entirely.

He knew that the pack would follow his spoor, and so he had been careful to make it as distinct as possible, brushing often against the vines and creepers that walled the jungle-path, and in other ways leaving his scent-spoor plainly discernible.

As darkness settled a heavy rain set in, and there was nothing for the baffled ape-man to do but wait in the partial shelter of a huge tree until morning; but the coming of dawn brought no cessation of the torrential downpour.

For a week the sun was obscured by heavy clouds, while violent rain and wind storms obliterated the last remnants of the spoor Tarzan constantly though vainly sought.

During all this time he saw no signs of natives, nor of his own pack, the members of which he feared had lost his trail during the terrific storm. As the country was strange to him, he had been unable to judge his course accurately, since he had had neither sun by day nor moon nor stars by night to guide him.

When the sun at last broke through the clouds in the forenoon of the seventh day, it looked down upon an almost frantic ape-man.

For the first time in his life, Tarzan of the Apes had been lost in the jungle. That the experience should have befallen him at such a time seemed cruel beyond expression. Somewhere in this savage land his wife and son lay in the clutches of the arch-fiend Rokoff.

What hideous trails might they not have undergone during those seven awful days that nature had thwarted him in his endeavours to locate them? Tarzan knew the Russian, in whose power they were, so well that he could not doubt but that the man, filled with rage that Jane had once escaped him, and knowing that Tarzan might be close upon his trail, would wreak without further loss of time whatever vengeance his polluted mind might be able to conceive.

But now that the sun shone once more, the ape-man was still at a loss as to what direction to take. He knew that Rokoff had left the river in pursuit of Anderssen, but whether he would continue inland or return to the Ugambi was a question.

The ape-man had seen that the river at the point he had left it was growing narrow and swift, so that he judged that it could not be navigable even for canoes to any great distance farther toward its source. However, if Rokoff had not returned to the river, in what direction had he proceeded?

From the direction of Anderssen's flight with Jane and the child Tarzan was convinced that the man had purposed attempting the tremendous feat of crossing the continent to Zanzibar; but whether Rokoff would dare so dangerous a journey or not was a question.

Fear might drive him to the attempt now that he knew the manner of horrible pack that was upon his trail, and that Tarzan of the Apes was following him to wreak upon him the vengeance that he deserved.

At last the ape-man determined to continue toward the northeast in the general direction of German East Africa until he came upon natives from whom he might gain information as to Rokoff's whereabouts.

The second day following the cessation of the rain Tarzan came upon a native village the inhabitants of which fled into the bush the instant their eyes fell upon him. Tarzan, not to be thwarted in any such manner as this, pursued them, and after a brief chase caught up with a young warrior. The fellow was so badly frightened that he was unable to defend himself, dropping his weapons and falling upon the ground, wide-eyed and screaming as he gazed on his captor.

It was with considerable difficulty that the ape-man quieted the fellow's fears sufficiently to obtain a coherent statement from him as to the cause of his uncalled-for terror.

From him Tarzan learned, by dint of much coaxing, that a party of whites had passed through the village several days before. These men had told them of a terrible white devil that pursued them, warning the natives against it and the frightful pack of demons that accompanied it.

The black had recognized Tarzan as the white devil from the descriptions given by the whites and their black servants. Behind him he had expected to see a horde of demons disguised as apes and panthers.

In this Tarzan saw the cunning hand of Rokoff. The Russian was attempting to make travel as difficult as possible for him by turning the natives against him in superstitious fear.

The native further told Tarzan that the white man who had led the recent expedition had promised them a fabulous reward if they would kill the white devil. This they had fully intended doing should the opportunity present itself; but the moment they had seen Tarzan their blood had turned to water, as the porters of the white men had told them would be the case.

Finding the ape-man made no attempt to harm him, the native at last recovered his grasp upon his courage, and, at Tarzan's suggestion, accompanied the white devil back to the village, calling as he went for his fellows to return also, as "the white devil has promised to do you no harm if you come back right away and answer his questions."

One by one the blacks straggled into the village, but that their fears were not entirely allayed was evident from the amount of white that showed about the eyes of the majority of them as they cast constant and apprehensive sidelong glances at the ape-man.

The chief was among the first to return to the village, and as it was he that Tarzan was most anxious to interview, he lost no time in entering into a palaver with the black.

The fellow was short and stout, with an unusually low and degraded countenance and apelike arms. His whole expression denoted deceitfulness.

Only the superstitious terror engendered in him by the stories poured into his ears by the whites and blacks of the Russian's party kept him from leaping upon Tarzan with his warriors and slaying him forthwith, for he and his people were inveterate maneaters. But the fear that he might indeed be a devil, and that out there in the jungle behind him his fierce demons waited to do his bidding, kept M'ganwazam from putting his desires into action.

Tarzan questioned the fellow closely, and by comparing his statements with those of the young warrior he had first talked with he learned that Rokoff and his *safari* were in terror-stricken retreat in the direction of the far East Coast.

Many of the Russian's porters had already deserted him. In that very village he had hanged five for theft and attempted desertion. Judging, however, from what the Waganwazam had learned from those of the Russian's blacks who were not too far gone in terror of the brutal Rokoff to fear even to speak of their plans, it was apparent that he would not travel any great distance before the last of his porters, cooks, tent-boys, gun-bearers, *askari*, and even his headman, would have turned back into the bush, leaving him to the mercy of the merciless jungle.

M'ganwazam denied that there had been any white woman or child with the party of whites; but even as he spoke Tarzan was convinced that he lied. Several times the ape-man approached the subject from different angles, but never was he successful in surprising the wily cannibal into a direct contradiction of his original statement that there had been no women or children with the party.

Tarzan demanded food of the chief, and after considerable haggling on the part of the monarch succeeded in obtaining a meal. He then tried to draw out others of the tribe, especially the young man whom he had captured in the bush, but M'ganwazam's presence sealed their lips.

At last, convinced that these people knew a great deal more than they had told him concerning the whereabouts of the Russian and the fate of Jane and the child, Tarzan determined to remain overnight among them in the hope of discovering something further of importance.

When he had stated his decision to the chief he was rather surprised to note the sudden change in the fellow's attitude toward him. From apparent dislike and suspicion M'ganwazam became a most eager and solicitous host.

Nothing would do but that the ape-man should occupy the best hut in the village, from which M'ganwazam's oldest wife was forthwith summarily ejected, while the chief took up his temporary abode in the hut of one of his younger consorts.

Had Tarzan chanced to recall the fact that a princely reward had been offered the blacks if they should succeed in killing him, he might have more quickly interpreted M'ganwazam's sudden change in front.

To have the white giant sleeping peacefully in one of his own huts would greatly facilitate the matter of earning the reward, and so the chief was urgent in his suggestions that Tarzan, doubtless being very much fatigued after his travels, should retire early to the comforts of the anything but inviting palace.

As much as the ape-man detested the thought of sleeping within a native hut, he had determined to do so this night, on the chance that he might be able to induce one of the younger men to sit and chat with him before the fire that burned in the center of the smoke-filled dwelling, and from him draw the truths he sought. So Tarzan accepted the invitation of old M'ganwazam, insisting, however, that he much preferred sharing a hut with some of the younger men rather than driving the chief's old wife out in the cold.

The toothless old hag grinned her appreciation of this suggestion, and as the plan still better suited the chief's scheme, in that it would permit him to surround Tarzan with a gang of picked assassins, he readily assented, so that presently Tarzan had been installed in a hut close to the village gate.

As there was to be a dance that night in honor of a band of recently returned hunters, Tarzan was left alone in the hut, the young men, as M'ganwazam explained, having to take part in the festivities.

As soon as the ape-man was safely installed in the trap, M'ganwazam called about him the young warriors whom he had selected to spend the night with the white devil!

None of them was overly enthusiastic about the plan, since deep in their superstitious hearts lay an exaggerated fear of the strange white giant; but the word of M'ganwazam was law among his people, so not one dared refuse the duty he was called upon to perform.

As M'ganwazam unfolded his plan in whispers to the savages

squatting about him the old, toothless hag, to whom Tarzan had saved her hut for the night, hovered about the conspirators ostensibly to replenish the supply of firewood for the blaze about which the men sat, but really to drink in as much of their conversation as possible.

Tarzan had slept for perhaps an hour or two despite the savage din of the revelers when his keen senses came suddenly alert to a suspiciously stealthy movement in the hut in which he lay. The fire had died down to a little heap of glowing embers, which accentuated rather than relieved the darkness that shrouded the interior of the evil-smelling dwelling, yet the trained senses of the ape-man warned him of another presence creeping almost silently toward him through the gloom.

He doubted that it was one of his hut mates returning from the festivities, for he still heard the wild cries of the dancers and the din of the tom-toms in the village street without. Who could it be that took such pains to conceal his approach?

As the presence came within reach of him the ape-man bounded lightly to the opposite side of the hut, his spear poised ready at his side.

"Who is it," he asked, "that creeps upon Tarzan of the Apes, like a hungry lion out of the darkness?"

"Silence, *bwana*!" replied an old cracked voice. "It is Tambudza—she whose hut you would not take, and thus drive an old woman out into the cold night."

"What does Tambudza want of Tarzan of the Apes?" asked the ape-man.

"You were kind to me to whom none is now kind, and I have come to warn you in payment of your kindness," answered the old hag.

"Warn me of what?"

"M'ganwazam has chosen the young men who are to sleep in the hut with you," replied Tambudza. "I was near as he talked with them, and heard him issuing his instructions to them. When the dance is run well into the morning they are to come to the hut.

"If you are awake they are to pretend that they have come to sleep, but if you sleep it is M'ganwazam's command that you be killed. If you are not then asleep they will wait quietly beside you until you do sleep, and then they will all fall upon you together and slay you. M'ganwazam is determined to win the reward the white man has offered."

"I had forgotten the reward," said Tarzan, half to himself, and then he added, "How may M'ganwazam hope to collect the reward now that the white men who are my enemies have left his country and gone he knows not where?"

"Oh, they have not gone far," replied Tambudza. "M'ganwazam knows where they camp. His runners could quickly overtake them—they move slowly."

"Where are they?" asked Tarzan.

"Do you wish to come to them?" asked Tambudza in way of reply.

Tarzan nodded.

"I cannot tell you where they lie so that you could come to the place yourself, but I could lead you to them, *bwana*."

In their interest in the conversation neither of the speakers had noticed the little figure which crept into the darkness of the hut behind them, nor did they see it when it slunk noiselessly out again.

It was little Buulaoo, the chief's son by one of his younger wives—a vindictive, degenerate little rascal who hated Tambudza, and was ever seeking opportunities to spy upon her and report her slightest breach of custom to his father.

"Come, then," said Tarzan quickly, "let us be on our way."

This Buulaoo did not hear, for he was already legging it up the village street to where his hideous sire guzzled native beer, and watched the evolutions of the frantic dancers leaping high in the air and cavorting wildly in their hysterical capers.

So it happened that as Tarzan and Tambudza sneaked warily from the village and melted into the Stygian darkness of the jungle, two lithe runners took their way in the same direction, though by another trail.

When they had come sufficiently far from the village to make it safe for them to speak above a whisper, Tarzan asked the old woman if she had seen aught of a white woman and a little child.

"Yes, *bwana*," replied Tambudza, "there was a woman with them and a little child—a little white piccaninny. It died here in our village of the fever and they buried it!"

12

A Black Scoundrel

WHEN JANE CLAYTON regained consciousness she saw Anderssen standing over her, holding the baby in his arms. As her eyes rested upon them an expression of misery and horror overspread her countenance.

"What is the matter?" he asked. "You ban sick?"

"Where is my baby?" she cried, ignoring his questions.

Anderssen held out the chubby infant, but she shook her head.

"It is not mine," she said. "You knew that it was not mine. You are a devil like the Russian."

Anderssen's blue eyes stretched in surprise.

"Not yours!" he exclaimed. "You tole me the kid aboard the *Kincaid* ban your kid."

"Not this one," replied Jane dully. "The other. Where is the other? There must have been two. I did not know about this one."

"There vasn't no other kid. Ay tank this ban yours. Ay am very sorry."

Anderssen fidgeted about, standing first on one foot and then upon the other. It was perfectly evident to Jane that he was honest in his protestations of ignorance of the true identity of the child.

Presently the baby commenced to crow, and bounce up and down in the Swede's arms, at the same time leaning forward with little hands outreaching toward the young woman.

She could not withstand the appeal, and with a low cry she sprang to her feet and gathered the baby to her breast.

For a few minutes she wept silently, her face buried in the baby's soiled little dress. The first shock of disappointment that the tiny thing had not been her beloved Jack was giving way to a great hope that after all some miracle had occurred to snatch her baby from Rokoff's hands at the last instant before the *Kincaid* sailed from England.

Then, too, there was the mute appeal of this wee waif alone and unloved in the midst of the horrors of the savage jungle. It was this thought more than any other that had sent her mother's heart out to the innocent babe, while still she suffered from disappointment that she had been deceived in its identity.

"Have you no idea whose child this is?" she asked Anderssen. The man shook his head.

"Not now," he said. "If he ain't ban your kid, Ay don' know whose kid he do ban. Rokoff said it was yours. Ay tank he tank so, too.

"What do we do with it now? Ay can't go back to the *Kincaid*. Rokoff would have me shot; but you can go back. Ay take you to the sea, and then some of these black men they take you to the ship—eh?"

"No! no!" cried Jane. "Not for the world. I would rather die than fall into the hands of that man again. No, let us go on and take this poor little creature with us. If God is willing we shall be saved in one way or another."

So they again took up their flight through the wilderness, taking with them a half-dozen of the Mosulas to carry provisions and the tents that Anderssen had smuggled aboard the small boat in preparation for the attempted escape.

The days and nights of torture that the young woman suffered were so merged into one long, unbroken nightmare of hideousness that she soon lost all track of time. Whether they had been wandering for days or years she could not tell. The one bright spot in that eternity of fear and suffering was the little child whose tiny hands had long since fastened their softly groping fingers firmly about her heart.

In a way the little thing took the place and filled the aching void that the theft of her own baby had left. It could never be the same, of course, but yet, day by day, she found her mother-love, enveloping the waif more closely until she sometimes sat with closed eyes lost in the sweet imagining that the little bundle of humanity at her breast was truly her own.

For some time their progress inland was extremely slow. Word came to them from time to time through natives passing from the coast on hunting excursions that Rokoff had not yet guessed the direction of their flight. This, and the desire to make the journey as light as possible for the gently bred woman, kept Anderssen to a slow advance of short and easy marches with many rests.

The Swede insisted upon carrying the child while they traveled, and in countless other ways did what he could to help Jane Clayton conserve her strength. He had been terribly chagrined on discovering the mistake he had made in the identity of the baby, but once the young woman became convinced that his motives were truly chivalrous she would not permit him longer to upbraid himself for the error that he could not by any means have avoided.

At the close of each day's march Anderssen saw to the erection of a comfortable shelter for Jane and the child. Her tent was always pitched in the most favorable location. The thorn *boma* round it was the strongest and most impregnable that the Mosula could construct.

Her food was the best that their limited stores and the rifle of the Swede could provide, but the thing that touched her heart the closest was the gentle consideration and courtesy which the man always accorded her.

That such nobility of character could lie beneath so repulsive an exterior never ceased to be a source of wonder and amazement to her, until at last the innate chivalry of the man, and his unfailing kindliness and sympathy transformed his appearance in so far as Jane was concerned until she saw only the sweetness of his character mirrored in his countenance.

They had commenced to make a little better progress when word reached them that Rokoff was but a few marches behind them, and that he had at last discovered the direction of their flight. It was then that Anderssen took to the river, purchasing a canoe from a chief whose village lay a short distance from the Ugambi upon the bank of a tributary.

Thereafter the little party of fugitives fled up the broad Ugambi, and so rapid had their flight become that they no longer received word of their pursuers. At the end of canoe navigation upon the river, they abandoned their canoe and took to the jungle. Here progress became at once arduous, slow, and dangerous.

The second day after leaving the Ugambi the baby fell ill with fever. Anderssen knew what the outcome must be, but he had not the heart to tell Jane Clayton the truth, for he had seen that the young woman had come to love the child almost as passionately as though it had been her own flesh and blood.

As the baby's condition precluded farther advance, Anderssen withdrew a little from the main trail he had been following and built a camp in a natural clearing on the bank of a little river.

Here Jane devoted her every moment to caring for the tiny sufferer, and as though her sorrow and anxiety were not all that she could bear, a further blow came with the sudden announcement of one of the Mosula porters who had been foraging in the jungle adjacent that Rokoff and his party were camped quite close to them, and were evidently upon their trail to this little nook which all had thought so excellent a hiding-place.

This information could mean but one thing, and that they must break camp and fly onward regardless of the baby's condition. Jane Clayton knew the traits of the Russian well enough to be positive that he would separate her from the child the moment that he recaptured them, and she knew that separation would mean the immediate death of the baby.

As they stumbled forward through the tangled vegetation along an old and almost overgrown game trail the Mosula porters deserted them one by one.

The men had been staunch enough in their devotion and loyalty as long as they were in no danger of being overtaken by the Russian and his party. They had heard, however, so much of the atrocious disposition of Rokoff that they had grown to hold him in mortal terror, and now that they knew he was close upon them their timid hearts would fortify them no longer, and as quickly as possible they deserted the three whites.

Yet on and on went Anderssen and the girl. The Swede went ahead, to hew a way through the brush where the path was entirely overgrown, so that on this march it was necessary that the young woman carry the child.

All day they marched. Late in the afternoon they realized that they had failed. Close behind them they heard the noise of a large *safari* advancing along the trail which they had cleared for their pursuers.

When it became quite evident that they must be overtaken in a short time Anderssen hid Jane behind a large tree, covering her and the child with brush.

"There is a village about a mile farther on," he said to her. "The Mosula told me its location before they deserted us. Ay try to lead the Russian off your trail, then you go on to the village. Ay tank the chief ban friendly to white men—the Mosula tal me he ban. Anyhow, that was all we can do.

"After while you get chief to tak you down by the Mosula village at the sea again, an' after a while a ship is sure to put into the mouth of the Ugambi. Then you be all right. Gude-by an' gude luck to you, lady!"

"But where are you going, Sven?" asked Jane. "Why can't you hide here and go back to the sea with me?"

"Ay gotta tal the Russian you ban dead, so that he don't luke for you no more," and Anderssen grinned.

"Why can't you join me then after you have told him that?" insisted the girl.

Anderssen shook his head.

"Ay don't tank Ay join anybody any more after Ay tal the Russian you ban dead," he said.

"You don't mean that you think he will kill you?" asked Jane, and yet in her heart she knew that that was exactly what the great scoundrel would do in revenge for his having been thwarted by the Swede. Anderssen did not reply, other than to warn her to silence and point toward the path along which they had just come.

"I don't care," whispered Jane Clayton. "I shall not let you die to save me if I can prevent it in any way. Give me your revolver. I can use that, and together we may be able to hold them off until we can find some means of escape."

"It won't work, lady," replied Anderssen. "They would only get us both, and then Ay couldn't do you no good at all. Think of the kid, lady, and what it would be for you both to fall into Rokoff's hands again. For his sake you must do what Ay say. Here, take my rifle and ammunition; you may need them."

He shoved the gun and bandoleer into the shelter beside Jane. Then he was gone.

She watched him as he returned along the path to meet the oncoming *safari* of the Russian. Soon a turn in the trail hid him from view.

Her first impulse was to follow. With the rifle she might be of assistance to him, and, further, she could not bear the terrible thought of being left alone at the mercy of the fearful jungle without a single friend to aid her.

She started to crawl from her shelter with the intention of running after Anderssen as fast as she could. As she drew the baby close to her she glanced down into its little face.

How red it was! How unnatural the little thing looked. She raised the cheek to hers. It was fiery hot with fever!

With a little gasp of terror Jane Clayton rose to her feet in the jungle path. The rifle and bandoleer lay forgotten in the shelter beside her. Anderssen was forgotten, and Rokoff, and her great peril.

All that rioted through her fear-mad brain was the fearful fact that this little, helpless child was stricken with the terrible jungle-fever, and that she was helpless to do aught to allay its sufferings—sufferings that were sure to come during ensuing intervals of partial consciousness.

Her one thought was to find someone who could help her—some woman who had had children of her own—and with the thought came recollection of the friendly village of which Anderssen had spoken. If she could but reach it—in time!

There was no time to be lost. Like a startled antelope she turned and fled up the trail in the direction Anderssen had indicated.

From far behind came the sudden shouting of men, the sound of shots, and then silence. She knew that Anderssen had met the Russian.

A half-hour later she stumbled, exhausted, into a little thatched village. Instantly she was surrounded by men, women, and children. Eager, curious, excited natives plied her with a hundred questions, no one of which she could understand or answer.

All that she could do was to point tearfully at the baby, now wailing piteously in her arms, and repeat over and over, "Fever—fever—fever."

The blacks did not understand her words, but they saw the cause of her trouble, and soon a young woman had pulled her into a hut and with several others was doing her poor best to quiet the child and allay its agony.

The witch doctor came and built a little fire before the infant, upon which he boiled some strange concoction in a small earthen pot, making weird passes above it and mumbling strange, monotonous chants. Presently he dipped a zebra's tail into the brew, and with further mutterings and incantations sprinkled a few drops of the liquid over the baby's face.

After he had gone the women sat about and moaned and wailed until Jane thought that she should go mad; but, knowing that they were doing it all out of the kindness of their hearts, she endured the frightful waking nightmare of those awful hours in dumb and patient suffering.

It must have been well toward midnight that she became conscious of a sudden commotion in the village. She heard the voices of the natives raised in controversy, but she could not understand the words.

Presently she heard footsteps approaching the hut in which she squatted before a bright fire with the baby on her lap. The little thing lay very still now, its lids, half-raised, showed the pupils horribly upturned.

Jane Clayton looked into the little face with fear-haunted eyes. It was not her baby—not her flesh and blood—but how close, how dear the tiny, helpless thing had become to her. Her heart, bereft of its own, had gone out to this poor, little, nameless waif, and lavished upon it all the love that had been denied her during the long, bitter weeks of her captivity aboard the *Kincaid.*

She saw that the end was near, and though she was terrified at contemplation of her loss, still she hoped that it would come quickly now and end the sufferings of the little victim.

The footsteps she had heard without the hut now halted before the door. There was a whispered colloquy, and a moment later M'ganwazam, chief of the tribe, entered. She had seen but little of him, as the women had taken her in hand almost as soon as she had entered the village.

M'ganwazam, she now saw, was an evil-appearing savage with every mark of brutal degeneracy writ large upon his bestial countenance. To Jane Clayton he looked more gorilla than human. He tried to converse with her, but without success, and finally he called to someone without.

In answer to his summons another Negro entered—a man of very different appearance from M'ganwazam—so different, in fact, that Jane Clayton immediately decided that he was of another tribe. This man acted as interpreter, and almost from the first question that M'ganwazam put to her, Jane felt an intuitive conviction that the savage was attempting to draw information from her for some ulterior motive.

She thought it strange that the fellow should so suddenly have become interested in her plans, and especially in her intended destination when her journey had been interrupted at his village.

Seeing no reason for withholding the information, she told him the truth; but when he asked if she expected to meet her husband at the end of the trip, she shook her head negatively.

Then he told her the purpose of his visit, talking through the interpreter.

"I have just learned," he said, "from some men who live by the side of the great water, that your husband followed you up the Ugambi for several marches, when he was at last set upon by natives and killed. Therefore I have told you this that you might not waste your time in a long journey if you expected to meet your husband at the end of it; but instead could turn and retrace your steps to the coast."

Jane thanked M'ganwazam for his kindness, though her heart was numb with suffering at this new blow. She who had suffered so much was at last beyond reach of the keenest of misery's pangs, for her senses were numbed and calloused.

With bowed head she sat staring with unseeing eyes upon the face of the baby in her lap. M'ganwazam had left the hut. Sometime later she heard a noise at the entrance—another had entered. One of the women sitting opposite her threw a faggot upon the dying embers of the fire between them.

With a sudden flare it burst into renewed flame, lighting up the hut's interior as though by magic.

The flame disclosed to Jane Clayton's horrified gaze that the baby was quite dead. How long it had been so she could not guess.

A choking lump rose to her throat, her head drooped in silent misery upon the little bundle that she had caught suddenly to her breast.

For a moment the silence of the hut was unbroken. Then the native woman broke into a hideous wail.

A man coughed close before Jane Clayton and spoke her name.

With a start she raised her eyes to look into the sardonic countenance of Nikolas Rokoff.

13

Escape

For a moment Rokoff stood sneering down upon Jane Clayton, then his eyes fell to the little bundle in her lap. Jane had drawn one corner of the blanket over the child's face, so that to one who did not know the truth it seemed but to be sleeping.

"You have gone to a great deal of unnecessary trouble," said Rokoff, "to bring the child to this village. If you had attended to your own affairs I should have brought it here myself.

"You would have been spared the dangers and fatigue of the journey. But I suppose I must thank you for relieving me of the inconvenience of having to care for a young infant on the march.

"This is the village to which the child was destined from the first. M'ganwazam will rear him carefully, making a good cannibal of him, and if you ever chance to return to civilization it will doubtless afford you much food for thought as you compare the luxuries and comforts of your life with the details of the life your son is living in the village of the Waganwazam.

"Again I thank you for bringing him here for me, and now I must ask you to surrender him to me, that I may turn him over to his foster parents." As he concluded Rokoff held out his hands for the child, a nasty grin of vindictiveness upon his lips.

To his surprise Jane Clayton rose and, without a word of protest, laid the little bundle in his arms.

"Here is the child," she said. "Thank God he is beyond your power to harm."

Grasping the import of her words, Rokoff snatched the blanket from the child's face to seek confirmation of his fears. Jane Clayton watched his expression closely.

She had been puzzled for days for an answer to the question of Rokoff's knowledge of the child's identity. If she had been in doubt before the last shred of that doubt was wiped away as she witnessed the terrible anger of the Russian as he looked upon the dead face of the baby and realized that at the last moment his dearest wish for vengeance had been thwarted by a higher power.

Almost throwing the body of the child back into Jane Clayton's arms, Rokoff stamped up and down the hut, pounding the air with his clenched fists and cursing terribly. At last he halted in front of the young woman, bringing his face down close to hers.

"You are laughing at me," he shrieked. "You think that you have beaten me—eh? I'll show you, as I have shown the miserable ape you call 'husband,' what it means to interfere with the plans of Nikolas Rokoff.

"You have robbed me of the child. I cannot make him the son of a cannibal chief, but"—and he paused as though to let the full meaning of his threat sink deep—"I can make the mother the wife of a cannibal, and that I shall do—after I have finished with her myself."

If he had thought to wring from Jane Clayton any sign of terror he failed miserably. She was beyond that. Her brain and nerves were numb to suffering and shock.

To his surprise a faint, almost happy smile touched her lips. She was thinking with thankful heart that this poor little corpse was not that of her own wee Jack, and that—best of all—Rokoff evidently did not know the truth.

She would have liked to have flaunted the fact in his face, but she dared not. If he continued to believe that the child had been hers, so much safer would be the real Jack wherever he might be. She had, of course, no knowledge of the whereabouts of her little son—she did not know, even, that he still lived, and yet there was the chance that he might.

It was more than possible that without Rokoff's knowledge this child had been substituted for hers by one of the Russian's confederates, and that even now her son might be safe with friends in London, where there were many, both able and willing, to have paid any ransom which the traitorous conspirator might have asked for the safe release of Lord Greystoke's son.

She had thought it all out a hundred times since she had discovered that the baby which Anderssen had placed in her arms that night upon the *Kincaid* was not her own, and it had been a constant and growing source of happiness to her to dream the whole fantasy through in its every detail.

No, the Russian must never know that this was not her baby. She realized that her position was hopeless—with Anderssen and her husband dead there was no one in all the world with a desire to succour her who knew where she might be found.

Rokoff's threat, she realized, was no idle one. That he would do, or attempt to do, all that he had promised, she was perfectly sure; but at the worst it meant but a little earlier release from the hideous anguish that she had been enduring. She must find some way to take her own life before the Russian could harm her further.

Just now she wanted time—time to think and prepare herself for the end. She felt that she could not take the last, awful step until she had exhausted every possibility of escape. She did not care to live unless she might find her way back to her own child, but slight as such a hope appeared she would not admit its impossibility until the last moment had come, and she faced the fearful reality of choosing between the final alternatives—Nikolas Rokoff on one hand and self-destruction upon the other.

"Go away!" she said to the Russian. "Go away and leave me in peace with my dead. Have you not brought sufficient misery and anguish upon me without attempting to harm me further? What wrong have I ever done you that you should persist in persecuting me?"

"You are suffering for the sins of the monkey you chose when you might have had the love of a gentleman—of Nikolas Rokoff," he replied. "But where is the use in discussing the matter? We shall bury the child here, and you will return with me at once to my own

camp. Tomorrow I shall bring you back and turn you over to your
new husband—the lovely M'ganwazam. Come!"

He reached out for the child. Jane, who was on her feet now,
turned away from him.

"I shall bury the body," she said. "Send some men to dig a
grave outside the village."

Rokoff was anxious to have the thing over and get back to his
camp with his victim. He thought he saw in her apathy a resignation to her fate. Stepping outside the hut, he motioned her to
follow him, and a moment later, with his men, he escorted Jane
beyond the village, where beneath a great tree the blacks scooped
a shallow grave.

Wrapping the tiny body in a blanket, Jane laid it tenderly in the
black hole, and, turning her head that she might not see the
mouldy earth falling upon the pitiful little bundle, she breathed a
prayer beside the grave of the nameless waif that had won its way
to the innermost recesses of her heart.

Then, dry-eyed but suffering, she rose and followed the Russian through the Stygian blackness of the jungle, along the
winding, leafy corridor that led from the village of M'ganwazam,
the black cannibal, to the camp of Nikolas Rokoff, the white fiend.

Beside them, in the impenetrable thickets that fringed the
path, rising to arch above it and shut out the moon, the girl could
hear the stealthy, muffled footfalls of great beasts, and ever round
about them rose the deafening roars of hunting lions, until the
earth trembled to the mighty sound.

The porters lighted torches now and waved them upon either
hand to frighten off the beasts of prey. Rokoff urged them to
greater speed, and from the quavering note in his voice Jane
Clayton knew that he was weak from terror.

The sounds of the jungle night recalled most vividly the days
and nights that she had spent in a similar jungle with her forest
god—with the fearless and unconquerable Tarzan of the Apes.
Then there had been no thoughts of terror, though the jungle
noises were new to her, and the roar of a lion had seemed the most
awe-inspiring sound upon the great earth.

How different would it be now if she knew that he was somewhere there in the wilderness, seeking her! Then, indeed, would
there be that for which to live, and every reason to believe that succour was close at hand—but he was dead! It was incredible that it
should be so.

There seemed no place in death for that great body and those
mighty thews. Had Rokoff been the one to tell her of her lord's

passing she would have known that he lied. There could be no reason, she thought, why M'ganwazam should have deceived her. She did not know that the Russian had talked with the savage a few minutes before the chief had come to her with his tale.

At last they reached the rude *boma* that Rokoff's porters had thrown up round the Russian's camp. Here they found all in turmoil. She did not know what it was all about, but she saw that Rokoff was very angry, and from bits of conversation which she could translate she gleaned that there had been further desertions while he had been absent, and that the deserters had taken the bulk of his food and ammunition.

When he had done venting his rage upon those who remained he returned to where Jane stood under guard of a couple of his white sailors. He grasped her roughly by the arm and started to drag her toward his tent. The girl struggled and fought to free herself, while the two sailors stood by, laughing at the rare treat.

Rokoff did not hesitate to use rough methods when he found that he was to have difficulty in carrying out his designs. Repeatedly he struck Jane Clayton in the face, until at last, half-conscious, she was dragged within his tent.

Rokoff's boy had lighted the Russian's lamp, and now at a word from his master he made himself scarce. Jane had sunk to the floor in the middle of the enclosure. Slowly her numbed senses were returning to her and she was commencing to think very fast indeed. Quickly her eyes ran round the interior of the tent, taking in every detail of its equipment and contents.

Now the Russian was lifting her to her feet and attempting to drag her to the camp cot that stood at one side of the tent. At his belt hung a heavy revolver. Jane Clayton's eyes riveted themselves upon it. Her palm itched to grasp the huge butt. She feigned again to swoon, but through her half-closed lids she waited her opportunity.

It came just as Rokoff was lifting her upon the cot. A noise at the tent door behind him brought his head quickly about and away from the girl. The butt of the gun was not an inch from her hand. With a single, lightning-like move she snatched the weapon from its holster, and at the same instant Rokoff turned back toward her, realizing his peril.

She did not dare fire for fear the shot would bring his people about him, and with Rokoff dead she would fall into hands no better than his and to a fate probably even worse than he alone could have imagined. The memory of the two brutes who stood and laughed as Rokoff struck her was still vivid.

As the rage and fear-filled countenance of the Slav turned toward her Jane Clayton raised the heavy revolver high above the pasty face and with all her strength dealt the man a terrific blow between the eyes.

Without a sound he sank, limp and unconscious, to the ground. A moment later the girl stood beside him—for a moment at least free from the menace of his lust.

Outside the tent she again heard the noise that had distracted Rokoff's attention. What it was she did not know, but, fearing the return of the servant and the discovery of her deed, she stepped quickly to the camp table upon which burned the oil lamp and extinguished the smudgy, evil-smelling flame.

In the total darkness of the interior she paused for a moment to collect her wits and plan for the next step in her venture for freedom.

About her was a camp of enemies. Beyond these foes a black wilderness of savage jungle peopled by hideous beasts of prey and still more hideous human beasts.

There was little or no chance that she could survive even a few days of the constant dangers that would confront her there; but the knowledge that she had already passed through so many perils unscathed, and that somewhere out in the faraway world a little child was doubtless at that very moment crying for her, filled her with determination to make the effort to accomplish the seemingly impossible and cross that awful land of horror in search of the sea and the remote chance of succour she might find there.

Rokoff's tent stood almost exactly in the centre of the *boma*. Surrounding it were the tents and shelters of his white companions and the natives of his *safari*. To pass through these and find egress through the *boma* seemed a task too fraught with insurmountable obstacles to warrant even the slightest consideration, and yet there was no other way.

To remain in the tent until she should be discovered would be to set at naught all that she had risked to gain her freedom, and so with stealthy step and every sense alert she approached the back of the tent to set out upon the first stage of her adventure.

Groping along the rear of the canvas wall, she found that there was no opening there. Quickly she returned to the side of the unconscious Russian. In his belt her groping fingers came upon the hilt of a long hunting-knife, and with this she cut a hole in the back wall of the tent.

Silently she stepped without. To her immense relief she saw that the camp was apparently asleep. In the dim and flickering light of the dying fires she saw but a single sentry, and he was dozing upon his haunches at the opposite side of the enclosure.

Keeping the tent between him and herself, she crossed between the small shelters of the native porters to the *boma* wall beyond.

Outside, in the darkness of the tangled jungle, she could hear the roaring of lions, the laughing of hyenas, and the countless, nameless noises of the midnight jungle.

For a moment she hesitated, trembling. The thought of the prowling beasts out there in the darkness was appalling. Then, with a sudden brave toss of her head, she attacked the thorny *boma* wall with her delicate hands. Torn and bleeding though they were, she worked on breathlessly until she had made an opening through which she could worm her body, and at last she stood outside the enclosure.

Behind her lay a fate worse than death, at the hands of human beings.

Before her lay an almost certain fate—but it was only death—sudden, merciful, and honourable death.

Without a tremor and without regret she darted away from the camp, and a moment later the mysterious jungle had closed about her.

14

Alone in the Jungle

TAMBUDZA, LEADING TARZAN of the Apes toward the camp of the Russian, moved very slowly along the winding jungle path, for she was old and her legs stiff with rheumatism.

So it was that the runners dispatched by M'ganwazam to warn Rokoff that the white giant was in his village and that he would be slain that night reached the Russian's camp before Tarzan and his ancient guide had covered half the distance.

The guides found the white man's camp in a turmoil. Rokoff had that morning been discovered stunned and bleeding within his tent. When he had recovered his senses and realized that Jane Clayton had escaped, his rage was boundless.

Rushing about the camp with his rifle, he had sought to shoot down the native sentries who had allowed the young woman to elude their vigilance, but several of the other whites, realizing that they were already in a precarious position owing to the numerous desertions that Rokoff's cruelty had brought about, seized and disarmed him.

Then came the messengers from M'ganwazam, but scarce had they told their story and Rokoff was preparing to depart with them for their village when other runners, panting from the exertions of their swift flight through the jungle, rushed breathless into the firelight, crying that the great white giant had escaped from M'ganwazam and was already on his way to wreak vengeance against his enemies.

Instantly confusion reigned within the encircling *boma*. The blacks belonging to Rokoff's *safari* were terror-stricken at the thought of the proximity of the white giant who hunted through the jungle with a fierce pack of apes and panthers at his heels.

Before the whites realized what had happened the superstitious fears of the natives had sent them scurrying into the bush—their own carriers as well as the messengers from M'ganwazam—but even in their haste they had not neglected to take with them every article of value upon which they could lay their hands.

Thus Rokoff and the seven white sailors found themselves deserted and robbed in the midst of a wilderness.

The Russian, following his usual custom, berated his companions, laying all the blame upon their shoulders for the events which had led up to the almost hopeless condition in which they now found themselves; but the sailors were in no mood to brook his insults and his cursing.

In the midst of this tirade one of them drew a revolver and fired point-blank at the Russian. The fellow's aim was poor, but his act so terrified Rokoff that he turned and fled for his tent.

As he ran his eyes chanced to pass beyond the *boma* to the edge of the forest, and there he caught a glimpse of that which sent his craven heart cold with a fear that almost expunged his terror of the seven men at his back, who by this time were all firing in hate and revenge at his retreating figure.

What he saw was the giant figure of an almost naked white man emerging from the bush.

Darting into his tent, the Russian did not halt in his flight, but kept right on through the rear wall, taking advantage of the long slit that Jane Clayton had made the night before.

The terror-stricken Muscovite scurried like a hunted rabbit through the hole that still gaped in the *boma*'s wall at the point where his own prey had escaped, and as Tarzan approached the camp upon the opposite side Rokoff disappeared into the jungle in the wake of Jane Clayton.

As the ape-man entered the *boma* with old Tambudza at his elbow the seven sailors, recognizing him, turned and fled in the opposite direction. Tarzan saw that Rokoff was not among them, and so he let them go their way—his business was with the Russian, whom he expected to find in his tent. As to the sailors, he was sure that the jungle would exact from them expiation for their villainies, nor, doubtless, was he wrong, for his were the last white man's eyes to rest upon any of them.

Finding Rokoff's tent empty, Tarzan was about to set out in search of the Russian when Tambudza suggested to him that the departure of the white man could only have resulted from word reaching him from M'ganwazam that Tarzan was in his village.

"He has doubtless hastened there," argued the old woman. "If you would find him let us return at once."

Tarzan himself thought that this would probably prove to be the fact, so he did not waste time in an endeavour to locate the Russian's trail, but, instead, set out briskly for the village of M'ganwazam, leaving Tambudza to plod slowly in his wake.

His one hope was that Jane was still safe and with Rokoff. If this was the case, it would be but a matter of an hour or more before he should be able to wrest her from the Russian.

He knew now that M'ganwazam was treacherous and that he might have to fight to regain possession of his wife. He wished that Mugambi, Sheeta, Akut, and the balance of the pack were with him, for he realized that single-handed it would be no child's play to bring Jane safely from the clutches of two such scoundrels as Rokoff and the wily M'ganwazam.

To his surprise he found no sign of either Rokoff or Jane in the village, and as he could not trust the word of the chief, he wasted no time in futile inquiry. So sudden and unexpected had been his return, and so quickly had he vanished into the jungle after learning that those he sought were not among the Waganwazam, that old M'ganwazam had no time to prevent his going.

Swinging through the trees, he hastened back to the deserted camp he had so recently left, for here, he knew, was the logical place to take up the trail of Rokoff and Jane.

Arrived at the *boma*, he circled carefully about the outside of the enclosure until, opposite a break in the thorny wall, he came to indications that something had recently passed into the jungle. His acute sense of smell told him that both of those he sought had fled from the camp in this direction, and a moment later he had taken up the trail and was following the faint spoor.

Far ahead of him a terror-stricken young woman was slinking along a narrow game-trail, fearful that the next moment would bring her face to face with some savage beast or equally savage man. As she ran on, hoping against hope that she had hit upon the direction that would lead her eventually to the great river, she came suddenly upon a familiar spot.

At one side of the trail, beneath a giant tree, lay a little heap of loosely piled brush—to her dying day that little spot of jungle would be indelibly impressed upon her memory. It was where Anderssen had hidden her—where he had given up his life in the vain effort to save her from Rokoff.

At sight of it she recalled the rifle and ammunition that the man had thrust upon her at the last moment. Until now she had forgotten them entirely. Still clutched in her hand was the revolver she had snatched from Rokoff's belt, but that could contain at most not over six cartridges—not enough to furnish her with food and protection both on the long journey to the sea.

With bated breath she groped beneath the little mound, scarce daring to hope that the treasure remained where she had left it; but, to her infinite relief and joy, her hand came at once upon the barrel of the heavy weapon and then upon the bandoleer of cartridges.

As she threw the latter about her shoulder and felt the weight of the big game-gun in her hand a sudden sense of security suffused her. It was with new hope and a feeling almost of assured success that she again set forward upon her journey.

That night she slept in the crotch of a tree, as Tarzan had so often told her that he was accustomed to doing, and early the next morning was upon her way again. Late in the afternoon, as she was about to cross a little clearing, she was startled at the sight of a huge ape coming from the jungle upon the opposite side.

The wind was blowing directly across the clearing between them, and Jane lost no time in putting herself downwind from the huge creature. Then she hid in a clump of heavy bush and watched, holding the rifle ready for instant use.

Slowly the monster advanced across the clearing, sniffing at the ground from time to time, as though following spoor by scent. Scarcely had the great anthropoid taken a dozen steps into the clearing before another of his kind followed from the jungle, and then another and another, until five of the ferocious beasts were in plain sight of the terrified girl crouching in her hiding place with the heavy rifle ready for instant use.

To her consternation she saw that the apes were pausing in the center of the clearing. They came together in a little knot, where they stood looking backward, as though in expectation of the coming of others of their tribe.

Jane wished that they would go on, for she knew that at any moment some little, eddying gust of wind might carry her scent down to their nostrils, and then what would the protection of her rifle amount to in the face of those gigantic muscles and mighty fangs?

Her eyes moved back and forth between the apes and the edge of the jungle toward which they were gazing until at last she perceived the object of their halt and the thing that they awaited. They were being stalked.

Of this she was positive, as she saw the lithe, sinewy form of a panther glide noiselessly from the jungle at the point at which the apes had emerged but a moment before.

Quickly the beast trotted across the clearing toward the anthropoids. Jane wondered at their apparent apathy, and a moment later her wonder turned to amazement as she saw the great cat come quite close to the apes, who appeared entirely unconcerned by its presence, and, squatting down in their midst, fell assiduously to the business of preening, which occupies most of the waking hours of the cat family.

If the young woman was surprised by the sight of these natural enemies fraternizing, it was with emotions little short of fear for her own sanity that she presently saw a tall, muscular warrior enter the clearing and join the group of savage beasts assembled there.

At first sight of the man she had been positive that he would be torn to pieces, and she had half risen from her shelter, raising her rifle to her shoulder to do what she could to avert the man's terrible fate.

Now she saw that he seemed actually conversing with the beasts—issuing orders to them.

Presently the entire company filed on across the clearing and disappeared in the jungle upon the opposite side.

With a gasp of mingled incredulity and relief Jane Clayton staggered to her feet and fled on away from the terrible horde that had just passed her, while a half-mile behind her another individual, following the same trail as she, lay frozen with terror behind an ant-hill as the hideous band passed quite close to him.

This one was Rokoff; but he had recognized the members of the awful aggregation as allies of Tarzan of the Apes. No sooner, therefore, had the beasts passed him than he rose and raced through the jungle as fast as he could go, in order that he might put as much distance as possible between himself and these frightful beasts.

So it happened that as Jane Clayton came to the bank of the river, down which she hoped to float to the ocean and eventual rescue, Nikolas Rokoff was but a short distance in her rear.

Upon the bank the girl saw a great dugout drawn half-way from the water and tied securely to a nearby tree.

This, she felt, would solve the question of transportation to the sea could she but launch the huge, unwieldy craft. Unfastening the rope that had moored it to the tree, Jane pushed frantically upon the bow of the heavy canoe, but for all the results that were apparent she might as well have been attempting to shove the earth out of its orbit.

She was about winded when it occurred to her to try working the dugout into the stream by loading the stern with ballast and then rocking the bow back and forth along the bank until the craft eventually worked itself into the river.

There were no stones or rocks available, but along the shore she found quantities of driftwood deposited by the river at a slightly higher stage. These she gathered and piled far in the stern of the boat, until at last, to her immense relief, she saw the bow rise gently from the mud of the bank and the stern drift slowly with the current until it again lodged a few feet farther down-stream.

Jane found that by running back and forth between the bow and stern she could alternately raise and lower each end of the boat as she shifted her weight from one end to the other, with the result that each time she leaped to the stern the canoe moved a few inches farther into the river.

As the success of her plan approached more closely to fruition she became so wrapped in her efforts that she failed to note the figure of a man standing beneath a huge tree at the edge of the jungle from which he had just emerged.

He watched her and her labors with a cruel and malicious grin upon his swarthy countenance.

The boat at last became so nearly free of the retarding mud and of the bank that Jane felt positive that she could pole it off into deeper water with one of the paddles which lay in the bottom of the rude craft. With this end in view she seized upon one of these implements and had just plunged it into the river bottom close to the shore when her eyes happened to rise to the edge of the jungle.

As her gaze fell upon the figure of the man a little cry of terror rose to her lips. It was Rokoff.

He was running toward her now and shouting to her to wait or he would shoot—though he was entirely unarmed it was difficult to discover just how he intended making good his threat.

Jane Clayton knew nothing of the various misfortunes that had befallen the Russian since she had escaped from his tent, so she believed that his followers must be close at hand.

However, she had no intention of falling again into the man's clutches. She would rather die at once than that that should happen her. Another minute and the boat would be free.

Once in the current of the river she would be beyond Rokoff's power to stop her, for there was no other boat upon the shore, and no man, and certainly not the cowardly Rokoff, would dare to attempt to swim the crocodile-infested water in an effort to overtake her.

Rokoff, on his part, was bent more upon escape than aught else. He would gladly have forgone any designs he might have had upon Jane Clayton would she but permit him to share this means of escape that she had discovered. He would promise anything if she would let him come aboard the dugout, but he did not think that it was necessary to do so.

He saw that he could easily reach the bow of the boat before it cleared the shore, and then it would not be necessary to make promises of any sort. Not that Rokoff would have felt the slightest compunction in ignoring any promises he might have made the girl, but he disliked the idea of having to sue for favor with one who had so recently assaulted and escaped him.

Already he was gloating over the days and nights of revenge that would be his while the heavy dugout drifted its slow way to the ocean.

Jane Clayton, working furiously to shove the boat beyond his reach, suddenly realized that she was to be successful, for with a little lurch the dugout swung quickly into the current, just as the Russian reached out to place his hand upon its bow.

His fingers did not miss their goal by a half-dozen inches. The girl almost collapsed with the reaction from the terrific mental, physical, and nervous strain under which she had been labouring for the past few minutes. But, thank Heaven, at last she was safe!

Even as she breathed a silent prayer of thanksgiving, she saw a sudden expression of triumph lighten the features of the cursing Russian, and at the same instant he dropped suddenly to the ground, grasping firmly upon something which wriggled through the mud toward the water.

Jane Clayton crouched, wide-eyed and horror-stricken, in the bottom of the boat as she realized that at the last instant success had been turned to failure, and that she was indeed again in the power of the malignant Rokoff.

For the thing that the man had seen and grasped was the end of the trailing rope with which the dugout had been moored to the tree.

15

Down the Ugambi

HALFWAY BETWEEN THE Ugambi and the village of the Waganwazam, Tarzan came upon the pack moving slowly along his old spoor. Mugambi could scarce believe that the trail of the Russian and the mate of his savage master had passed so close to that of the pack.

It seemed incredible that two human beings should have come so close to them without having been detected by some of the marvelously keen and alert beasts; but Tarzan pointed out the spoor of the two he trailed, and at certain points the black could see that the man and the woman must have been in hiding as the pack passed them, watching every move of the ferocious creatures.

It had been apparent to Tarzan from the first that Jane and Rokoff were not traveling together. The spoor showed distinctly that the young woman had been a considerable distance ahead of the Russian at first, though the farther the ape-man continued along the trail the more obvious it became that the man was rapidly overhauling his quarry.

At first there had been the spoor of wild beasts over the footprints of Jane Clayton, while upon the top of all Rokoff's spoor showed that he had passed over the trail after the animals had left their records upon the ground. But later there were fewer and fewer animal imprints occurring between those of Jane's and the Russian's feet, until as he approached the river the ape-man became aware that Rokoff could not have been more than a few hundred yards behind the girl.

He felt they must be close ahead of him now, and, with a little thrill of expectation, he leaped rapidly forward ahead of the pack. Swinging swiftly through the trees, he came out upon the river-bank at the very point at which Rokoff had overhauled Jane as she endeavoured to launch the cumbersome dugout.

In the mud along the bank the ape-man saw the footprints of the two he sought, but there was neither boat nor people there when he arrived, nor, at first glance, any sign of their whereabouts.

It was plain that they had shoved off a native canoe and embarked upon the bosom of the stream, and as the ape-man's eye ran swiftly down the course of the river beneath the shadows of the overarching trees he saw in the distance, just as it rounded a bend that shut it off from his view, a drifting dugout in the stern of which was the figure of a man.

Just as the pack came in sight of the river they saw their agile leader racing down the river's bank, leaping from hummock to hummock of the swampy ground that spread between them and a little promontory which rose just where the river curved inward from their sight.

To follow him it was necessary for the heavy, cumbersome apes to make a wide detour, and Sheeta, too, who hated water. Mugambi followed after them as rapidly as he could in the wake of the great white master.

A half-hour of rapid travelling across the swampy neck of land and over the rising promontory brought Tarzan, by a short cut, to the inward bend of the winding river, and there before him upon the bosom of the stream he saw the dugout, and in its stern Nikolas Rokoff.

Jane was not with the Russian.

At sight of his enemy the broad scar upon the ape-man's brow burned scarlet, and there rose to his lips the hideous, bestial challenge of the bull-ape.

Rokoff shuddered as the weird and terrible alarm fell upon his ears. Cowering in the bottom of the boat, his teeth chattering in terror, he watched the man he feared above all other creatures upon the face of the earth as he ran quickly to the edge of the water.

Even though the Russian knew that he was safe from his enemy, the very sight of him threw him into a frenzy of trembling cowardice, which became frantic hysteria as he saw the white giant dive fearlessly into the forbidding waters of the tropical river.

With steady, powerful strokes the ape-man forged out into the stream toward the drifting dugout. Now Rokoff seized one of the paddles lying in the bottom of the craft, and, with terrorwide eyes still glued upon the living death that pursued him, struck out madly in an effort to augment the speed of the unwieldy canoe.

And from the opposite bank a sinister ripple, unseen by either man, moving steadily toward the half-naked swimmer.

Tarzan had reached the stern of the craft at last. One hand upstretched grasped the gunwale. Rokoff sat frozen with fear, unable to move a hand or foot, his eyes riveted upon the face of his nemesis.

Then a sudden commotion in the water behind the swimmer caught his attention. He saw the ripple, and he knew what caused it.

At the same instant Tarzan felt mighty jaws close upon his right leg. He tried to struggle free and raise himself over the side of the boat. His efforts would have succeeded had not this unexpected interruption galvanized the malign brain of the Russian into instant action with its sudden promise of deliverance and revenge.

Like a venomous snake the man leaped toward the stern of the boat, and with a single swift blow struck Tarzan across the head with the heavy paddle. The ape-man's fingers slipped from their hold upon the gunwale.

There was a short struggle at the surface, and then a swirl of waters, a little eddy, and a burst of bubbles soon smoothed out by the flowing current marked for the instant the spot where Tarzan of the Apes, Lord of the Jungle, disappeared from the sight of men beneath the gloomy waters of the dark and forbidding Ugambi.

Weak from terror, Rokoff sank shuddering into the bottom of the dugout. For a moment he could not realize the good fortune that had befallen him—all that he could see was the figure of a silent, struggling white man disappearing beneath the surface of the river to unthinkable death in the slimy mud of the bottom.

Slowly all that it meant to him filtered into the mind of the Russian, and then a cruel smile of relief and triumph touched his lips;

but it was short-lived, for just as he was congratulating himself that he was now comparatively safe to proceed upon his way to the coast unmolested, a mighty pandemonium rose from the river-bank close by.

As his eyes sought the authors of the frightful sound he saw standing upon the shore, glaring at him with hate-filled eyes, a devil-faced panther surrounded by the hideous apes of Akut, and in the forefront of them a giant black warrior who shook his fist at him, threatening him with terrible death.

The nightmare of that flight down the Ugambi with the hideous horde racing after him by day and by night, now abreast of him, now lost in the mazes of the jungle far behind for hours and once for a whole day, only to appear again upon his trail grim, relentless, and terrible, reduced the Russian from a strong and robust man to an emaciated, white-haired, fear-gibbering thing forever the bay and the ocean broke upon his hopeless vision.

Past populous villages he had fled. Time and again warriors had put out in their canoes to intercept him, but each time the hideous horde had swept into view to send the terrified natives shrieking back to the shore to lose themselves in the jungle.

Nowhere in his flight had he seen aught of Jane Clayton. Not once had his eyes rested upon her since that moment at the river's brim his hand had closed upon the rope attached to the bow of her dugout and he had believed her safely in his power again, only to be thwarted an instant later as the girl snatched up a heavy express rifle from the bottom of the craft and leveled it full at his breast.

Quickly he had dropped the rope then and seen her float away beyond his reach, but a moment later he had been racing up-stream toward a little tributary in the mouth of which was hidden the canoe in which he and his party had come thus far upon their journey in pursuit of the girl and Anderssen.

What had become of her?

There seemed little doubt in the Russian's mind, however, but that she had been captured by warriors from one of the several villages she would have been compelled to pass on her way down to the sea. Well, he was at least rid of most of his human enemies.

But at that he would gladly have had them all back in the land of the living could he thus have been freed from the menace of the frightful creatures who pursued him with awful relentlessness, screaming and growling at him every time they came within sight of him. The one that filled him with the greatest terror was the pan-ther—the flaming-eyed, devil-faced panther whose grinning jaws gaped wide at him by day, and whose fiery orbs gleamed wickedly out across the water from the Cimmerian blackness of the jungle nights.

The sight of the mouth of the Ugambi filled Rokoff with renewed hope, for there, upon the yellow waters of the bay, floated the *Kincaid* at anchor. He had sent the little steamer away to coal while he had gone up the river, leaving Paulvitch in charge of her, and he could have cried aloud in his relief as he saw that she had returned in time to save him.

Frantically he alternately paddled furiously toward her and rose to his feet waving his paddle and crying aloud in an attempt to attract the attention of those on board. But loud as he screamed his cries awakened no answering challenge from the deck of the silent craft.

Upon the shore behind him a hurried backward glance revealed the presence of the snarling pack. Even now, he thought, these manlike devils might yet find a way to reach him even upon the deck of the steamer unless there were those there to repel them with firearms.

What could have happened to those he had left upon the *Kincaid*? Where was Paulvitch? Could it be that the vessel was deserted, and that, after all, he was doomed to be overtaken by the terrible fate that he had been flying from through all these hideous days and nights? He shivered as might one upon whose brow death has already laid his clammy finger.

Yet he did not cease to paddle frantically toward the steamer, and at last, after what seemed an eternity, the bow of the dugout bumped against the timbers of the *Kincaid*. Over the ship's side hung a monkey-ladder, but as the Russian grasped it to ascend to the deck he heard a warning challenge from above, and, looking up, gazed into the cold, relentless muzzle of a rifle.

After Jane Clayton, with rifle leveled at the breast of Rokoff, had succeeded in holding him off until the dugout in which she had taken refuge had drifted out upon the bosom of the Ugambi beyond the man's reach, she had lost no time in paddling to the swiftest sweep of the channel, nor did she for long days and weary nights cease to hold her craft to the most rapidly moving part of the river, except when during the hottest hours of the day she had been wont to drift as the current would take her, lying prone in the bottom of the canoe, her face sheltered from the sun with a great palm leaf.

Thus only did she gain rest upon the voyage; at other times she continually sought to augment the movement of the craft by wielding the heavy paddle.

Rokoff, on the other hand, had used little or no intelligence in his flight along the Ugambi, so that more often than not his craft had drifted in the slow-going eddies, for he habitually hugged the bank farthest from that along which the hideous horde pursued and menaced him.

Thus it was that, though he had put out upon the river but a short time subsequent to the girl, yet she had reached the bay fully two hours ahead of him. When she had first seen the anchored ship upon the quiet water, Jane Clayton's heart had beat fast with hope and thanksgiving, but as she drew closer to the craft and saw that it was the *Kincaid*, her pleasure gave place to the gravest misgivings.

It was too late, however, to turn back, for the current that carried her toward the ship was much too strong for her muscles. She could not have forced the heavy dugout upstream against it, and all that was left her was to attempt either to make the shore without being seen by those upon the deck of the *Kincaid*, or to throw herself upon their mercy—otherwise she must be swept out to sea.

She knew that the shore held little hope of life for her, as she had no knowledge of the location of the friendly Mosula village to which Anderssen had taken her through the darkness of the night of their escape from the *Kincaid*.

With Rokoff away from the steamer it might be possible that by offering those in charge a large reward they could be induced to carry her to the nearest civilized port. It was worth risking—if she could make the steamer at all.

The current was bearing her swiftly down the river, and she found that only by dint of the utmost exertion could she direct the awkward craft toward the vicinity of the *Kincaid*. Having reached the decision to board the steamer, she now looked to it for aid, but to her surprise the decks appeared to be empty and she saw no sign of life aboard the ship.

The dugout was drawing closer and closer to the bow of the vessel, and yet no hail came over the side from any lookout aboard. In a moment more, Jane realized, she would be swept beyond the steamer, and then, unless they lowered a boat to rescue her, she would be carried far out to sea by the current and the swift ebb tide that was running.

The young woman called loudly for assistance, but there was no reply other than the shrill scream of some savage beast upon the jungle-shrouded shore. Frantically Jane wielded the paddle in an effort to carry her craft close alongside the steamer.

For a moment it seemed that she should miss her goal by but a few feet, but at the last moment the canoe swung close beneath the steamer's bow and Jane barely managed to grasp the anchor chain.

Heroically she clung to the heavy iron links, almost dragged from the canoe by the strain of the current upon her craft. Beyond her she saw a monkey-ladder dangling over the steamer's side. To release her hold upon the chain and chance clambering to the ladder as her canoe was swept beneath it seemed beyond the pale of possibility, yet to remain clinging to the anchor chain appeared equally as futile.

Finally her glance chanced to fall upon the rope in the bow of the dugout, and, making one end of this fast to the chain, she succeeded in drifting the canoe slowly down until it lay directly beneath the ladder. A moment later, her rifle slung about her shoulders, she had clambered safely to the deserted deck.

Her first task was to explore the ship, and this she did, her rifle ready for instant use should she meet with any human menace aboard the *Kincaid*. She was not long in discovering the cause of the apparently deserted condition of the steamer, for in the forecastle she found the sailors, who had evidently been left to guard the ship, deep in drunken slumber.

With a shudder of disgust she clambered above, and to the best of her ability closed and made fast the hatch above the heads of the sleeping guard. Next she sought the galley and food, and, having appeased her hunger, she took her place on deck, determined that none should board the *Kincaid* without first having agreed to her demands.

For an hour or so nothing appeared upon the surface of the river to cause her alarm, but then, about a bend upstream, she saw a canoe appear in which sat a single figure. It had not proceeded far in her direction before she recognized the occupant as Rokoff, and when the fellow attempted to board he found a rifle staring him in the face.

When the Russian discovered who it was that repelled his advance he became furious, cursing and threatening in a most horrible manner; but, finding that these tactics failed to frighten or move the girl, he at last fell to pleading and promising.

Jane had but a single reply for his every proposition, and that was that nothing would ever persuade her to permit Rokoff upon the same vessel with her. That she would put her threats into action and shoot him should he persist in his endeavour to board the ship he was convinced.

So, as there was no other alternative, the great coward dropped back into his dugout and, at imminent risk of being swept to sea, finally succeeded in making the shore far down the bay and upon the opposite side from that on which the horde of beasts stood snarling and roaring.

Jane Clayton knew that the fellow could not alone and unaided bring his heavy craft back upstream to the *Kincaid*, and so she had no further fear of an attack by him. The hideous crew upon the shore she thought she recognized as the same that had passed her in the jungle far up the Ugambi several days before, for it seemed quite beyond reason that there should be more than one such a strangely assorted pack; but what had brought them downstream to the mouth of the river she could not imagine.

Toward the day's close the girl was suddenly alarmed by the shouting of the Russian from the opposite bank of the stream, and a moment later, following the direction of his gaze, she was terrified to see a ship's boat approaching from upstream, in which, she felt assured, there could be only members of the *Kincaid*'s missing crew—only heartless ruffians and enemies.

16

In the Darkness of the Night

WHEN TARZAN OF the Apes realized that he was in the grip of the great jaws of a crocodile he did not, as an ordinary man might have done, give up all hope and resign himself to his fate.

Instead, he filled his lungs with air before the huge reptile dragged him beneath the surface, and then, with all the might of his great muscles, fought bitterly for freedom. But out of his native element the ape-man was too greatly handicapped to do more than excite the monster to greater speed as it dragged its prey swiftly through the water.

Tarzan's lungs were bursting for a breath of pure fresh air. He knew that he could survive but a moment more, and in the last paroxysm of his suffering he did what he could to avenge his own death.

His body trailed out beside the slimy carcass of his captor, and into the tough armour the ape-man attempted to plunge his stone knife as he was borne to the creature's horrid den.

His efforts but served to accelerate the speed of the crocodile, and just as the ape-man realized that he had reached the limit of his endurance he felt his body dragged to a muddy bed and his nostrils rise above the water's surface. All about him was the blackness of the pit—the silence of the grave.

For a moment Tarzan of the Apes lay gasping for breath upon the slimy, evil-smelling bed to which the animal had borne him. Close at his side he could feel the cold, hard plates of the creature's coat rising and falling as though with spasmodic efforts to breathe.

For several minutes the two lay thus, and then a sudden convulsion of the giant carcass at the man's side, a tremor, and a stiffening brought Tarzan to his knees beside the crocodile. To his utter amazement he found that the beast was dead. The slim knife had found a vulnerable spot in the scaly armour.

Staggering to his feet, the ape-man groped about the reeking, oozy den. He found that he was imprisoned in a subterranean chamber amply large enough to have accommodated a dozen or more of the huge animals such as the one that had dragged him thither.

He realized that he was in the creature's hidden nest far under the bank of the stream, and that doubtless the only means of ingress or egress lay through the submerged opening through which the crocodile had brought him.

His first thought, of course, was of escape, but that he could make his way to the surface of the river beyond and then to the shore seemed highly improbable. There might be turns and windings in the neck of the passage, or, most to be feared, he might meet another of the slimy inhabitants of the retreat upon his journey outward.

Even should he reach the river in safety, there was still the danger of his being again attacked before he could effect a safe landing. Still there was no alternative, and, filling his lungs with the close and reeking air of the chamber, Tarzan of the Apes dived into the dark and watery hole which he could not see but had felt out and found with his feet and legs.

The leg which had been held within the jaws of the crocodile was badly lacerated, but the bone had not been broken, nor were the muscles or tendons sufficiently injured to render it useless. It gave him excruciating pain, that was all.

But Tarzan of the Apes was accustomed to pain, and gave it no further thought when he found that the use of his legs was not greatly impaired by the sharp teeth of the monster.

Rapidly he crawled and swam through the passage which inclined downward and finally upward to open at last into the river bottom but a few feet from the shore line. As the ape-man reached the surface he saw the heads of two great crocodiles but a short distance from him. They were making rapidly in his direction, and with a superhuman effort the man struck out for the overhanging branches of a nearby tree.

Nor was he a moment too soon, for scarcely had he drawn himself to the safety of the limb than two gaping mouths snapped venomously below him. For a few minutes Tarzan rested in the tree that had proved the means of his salvation. His eyes scanned the river as far downstream as the tortuous channel would permit, but there was no sign of the Russian or his dugout.

When he had rested and bound up his wounded leg he started on in pursuit of the drifting canoe. He found himself upon the opposite side of the river to that at which he had entered the stream, but as his quarry was upon the bosom of the water it made little difference to the ape-man upon which side he took up the pursuit.

To his intense chagrin he soon found that his leg was more badly injured than he had thought, and that its condition seriously impeded his progress. It was only with the greatest difficulty that he could proceed faster than a walk upon the ground, and in the trees he discovered that it not only impeded his progress, but rendered traveling distinctly dangerous.

From the old negress, Tambudza, Tarzan had gathered a suggestion that now filled his mind with doubts and misgivings. When the old woman had told him of the child's death she had also added that the white woman, though grief-stricken, had confided to her that the baby was not hers.

Tarzan could see no reason for believing that Jane could have found it advisable to deny her identity or that of the child; the only explanation that he could put upon the matter was that, after all, the white woman who had accompanied his son and the Swede into the jungle fastness of the interior had not been Jane at all.

The more he gave thought to the problem, the more firmly convinced he became that his son was dead and his wife still safe in

London, and in ignorance of the terrible fate that had overtaken her first-born.

After all, then, his interpretation of Rokoff's sinister taunt had been erroneous, and he had been bearing the burden of a double apprehension needlessly—at least so thought the ape-man. From this belief he garnered some slight surcease from the numbing grief that the death of his little son had thrust upon him.

And such a death! Even the savage beast that was the real Tarzan, inured to the sufferings and horrors of the grim jungle, shuddered as he contemplated the hideous fate that had overtaken the innocent child.

As he made his way painfully towards the coast, he let his mind dwell so constantly upon the frightful crimes which the Russian had perpetrated against his loved ones that the great scar upon his forehead stood out almost continuously in the vivid scarlet that marked the man's most relentless and bestial moods of rage. At times he startled even himself and sent the lesser creatures of the wild jungle scampering to their hiding places as involuntary roars and growls rumbled from his throat.

Could he but lay his hand upon the Russian!

Twice upon the way to the coast bellicose natives ran threateningly from their villages to bar his further progress, but when the awful cry of the bull-ape thundered upon their affrighted ears, and the great white giant charged bellowing upon them, they had turned and fled into the bush, nor ventured thence until he had safely passed.

Though his progress seemed tantalizingly slow to the ape-man whose idea of speed had been gained by such standards as the lesser apes attain, he made, as a matter of fact, almost as rapid progress as the drifting canoe that bore Rokoff on ahead of him, so that he came to the bay and within sight of the ocean just after darkness had fallen upon the same day that Jane Clayton and the Russian ended their flights from the interior.

The darkness lowered so heavily upon the black river and the encircling jungle that Tarzan, even with eyes accustomed to much use after dark, could make out nothing a few yards from him. His idea was to search the shore that night for signs of the Russian and the woman who he was certain must have preceded Rokoff down the Ugambi. That the *Kincaid* or other ship lay at anchor but a hundred yards from him he did not dream, for no light showed on board the steamer.

Even as he commenced his search his attention was suddenly attracted by a noise that he had not at first perceived—the stealthy dip of paddles in the water some distance from the shore, and about opposite the point at which he stood. Motionless as a statue he stood listening to the faint sound.

Presently it ceased, to be followed by a shuffling noise that the ape-man's trained ears could interpret as resulting from but a single cause—the scraping of leather-shod feet upon the rounds of a ship's monkey-ladder, And yet, as far as he could see, there was no ship there—nor might there be one within a thousand miles.

As he stood thus, peering out into the darkness of the cloud-enshrouded night, there came to him from across the water, like a slap in the face, so sudden and unexpected was it, the sharp staccato of an exchange of shots and then the scream of a woman.

Wounded though he was, and with the memory of his recent horrible experience still strong upon him, Tarzan of the Apes did not hesitate as the notes of that frightened cry rose shrill and piercing upon the still night air. With a bound he cleared the intervening bush—there was a splash as the water closed about him—and then, with powerful strokes, he swam out into the impenetrable night with no guide save the memory of an illusive cry, and for company the hideous denizens of an equatorial river.

The boat that had attracted Jane's attention as she stood guard upon the deck of the *Kincaid* had been perceived by Rokoff upon one bank and Mugambi and the horde upon the other. The cries of the Russian had brought the dugout first to him, and then, after a conference, it had been turned toward the *Kincaid*, but before ever it covered half the distance between the shore and the steamer a rifle had spoken from the latter's deck and one of the sailors in the bow of the canoe had crumpled and fallen into the water.

After that they went more slowly, and presently, when Jane's rifle had found another member of the party, the canoe withdrew to the shore, where it lay as long as daylight lasted.

The savage, snarling pack upon the opposite shore had been directed in their pursuit by the black warrior, Mugambi, chief of the Wagambi. Only he knew which might be foe and which friend of their lost master.

Could they have reached either the canoe or the *Kincaid* they would have made short work of any whom they found there, but the gulf of black water intervening shut them off from farther advance as effectually as though it had been the broad ocean that separated them from their prey.

Mugambi knew something of the occurrences which had led up to the landing of Tarzan upon Jungle Island and the pursuit of the whites up the Ugambi. He knew that his savage master sought his wife and child who had been stolen by the wicked white man whom they had followed far into the interior and now back to the sea.

He believed also that this same man had killed the great white giant whom he had come to respect and love as he had never loved the greatest chiefs of his own people. And so in the wild breast of Mugambi burned an iron resolve to win to the side of the wicked one and wreak vengeance upon him for the murder of the ape-man.

But when he saw the canoe come down the river and take in Rokoff, when he saw it make for the *Kincaid*, he realized that only by possessing himself of a canoe could he hope to transport the beasts of the pack within striking distance of the enemy.

So it happened that even before Jane Clayton fired the first shot into Rokoff's canoe the beasts of Tarzan had disappeared into the jungle.

After the Russian and his party, which consisted of Paulvitch and the several men he had left upon the *Kincaid* to attend to the matter of coaling, had retreated before her fire, Jane realized that it would be but a temporary respite from their attentions which she had gained, and with the conviction came a determination to make a bold and final stroke for freedom from the menacing threat of Rokoff's evil purpose.

With this idea in view she opened negotiations with the two sailors she had imprisoned in the forecastle, and having forced their consent to her plans, upon pain of death should they attempt disloyalty, she released them just as darkness closed about the ship.

With ready revolver to compel obedience, she let them up one by one, searching them carefully for concealed weapons as they stood with hands elevated above their heads. Once satisfied that they were unarmed, she set them to work cutting the cable which held the *Kincaid* to her anchorage, for her bold plan was nothing less than to set the steamer adrift and float with her out into the open sea, there to trust to the mercy of the elements, which she was confident would be no more merciless than Nikolas Rokoff should he again capture her.

There was, too, the chance that the *Kincaid* might be sighted by some passing ship, and as she was well stocked with provisions and water—the men had assured her of this fact—and as the season of storm was well over, she had every reason to hope for the eventual success of her plan.

The night was deeply overcast, heavy clouds riding low above the jungle and the water—only to the west, where the broad ocean spread beyond the river's mouth, was there a suggestion of lessening gloom.

It was a perfect night for the purposes of the work in hand.

Her enemies could not see the activity aboard the ship nor mark her course as the swift current bore her outward into the ocean. Before daylight broke the ebb-tide would have carried the *Kincaid* well into the Benguela current which flows northward along the coast of Africa, and, as a south wind was prevailing, Jane hoped to be out of sight of the mouth of the Ugambi before Rokoff could become aware of the departure of the steamer.

Standing over the labouring seamen, the young woman breathed a sigh of relief as the last strand of the cable parted and she knew that the vessel was on its way out of the maw of the savage Ugambi.

With her two prisoners still beneath the coercing influence of her rifle, she ordered them upon deck with the intention of again imprisoning them in the forecastle; but at length she permitted herself to be influenced by their promises of loyalty and the arguments which they put forth that they could be of service to her, and permitted them to remain above.

For a few minutes the *Kincaid* drifted rapidly with the current, and then, with a grinding jar, she stopped in midstream. The ship had run upon a low-lying bar that splits the channel about a quarter of a mile from the sea.

For a moment she hung there, and then, swinging round until her bow pointed toward the shore, she broke adrift once more.

At the same instant, just as Jane Clayton was congratulating herself that the ship was once more free, there fell upon her ears from a point up the river about where the *Kincaid* had been anchored the rattle of musketry and a woman's scream—shrill, piercing, fear-laden.

The sailors heard the shots with certain conviction that they announced the coming of their employer, and as they had no relish for the plan that would consign them to the deck of a drifting derelict, they whispered together a hurried plan to overcome the young woman and hail Rokoff and their companions to their rescue.

It seemed that fate would play into their hands, for with the reports of the guns Jane Clayton's attention had been distracted from her unwilling assistants, and instead of keeping one eye upon them as she had intended doing, she ran to the bow of the *Kincaid* to peer through the darkness toward the source of the disturbance upon the river's bosom.

Seeing that she was off her guard, the two sailors crept stealthily upon her from behind.

The scraping upon the deck of the shoes of one of them startled the girl to a sudden appreciation of her danger, but the warning had come too late.

As she turned, both men leaped upon her and bore her to the deck, and as she went down beneath them she saw, outlined against the lesser gloom of the ocean, the figure of another man clamber over the side of the *Kincaid*.

After all her pains her heroic struggle for freedom had failed. With a stifled sob she gave up the unequal battle.

17

On the Deck of the "Kincaid"

WHEN MUGAMBI HAD turned back into the jungle with the pack he had a definite purpose in view. It was to obtain a dugout wherewith to transport the beasts of Tarzan to the side of the *Kincaid*. Nor was he long in coming upon the object which he sought.

Just at dusk he found a canoe moored to the bank of a small tributary of the Ugambi at a point where he had felt certain that he should find one.

Without loss of time he piled his hideous fellows into the craft and shoved out into the stream. So quickly had they taken possession of the canoe that the warrior had not noticed that it was already occupied. The huddled figure sleeping in the bottom had entirely escaped his observation in the darkness of the night that had now fallen.

But no sooner were they afloat than a savage growling from one of the apes directly ahead of him in the dugout attracted his attention to a shivering and cowering figure that trembled between him and the great anthropoid. To Mugambi's astonishment he saw that it was a native woman. With difficulty he kept the ape from her throat, and after a time succeeded in quelling her fears.

It seemed that she had been fleeing from marriage with an old man she loathed and had taken refuge for the night in the canoe she had found upon the river's edge.

Mugambi did not wish her presence, but there she was, and rather than lose time by returning her to the shore the black permitted her to remain on board the canoe.

As quickly as his awkward companions could paddle the dugout down-stream toward the Ugambi and the *Kincaid* they moved through the darkness. It was with difficulty that Mugambi could make out the shadowy form of the steamer, but as he had it between himself and the ocean it was much more apparent than to one upon either shore of the river.

As he approached it he was amazed to note that it seemed to be receding from him, and finally he was convinced that the vessel was moving down-stream. Just as he was about to urge his creatures to renewed efforts to overtake the steamer the outline of another canoe burst suddenly into view not three yards from the bow of his own craft.

At the same instant the occupants of the strange canoe discovered the proximity of Mugambi's horde, but they did not at first recognize the nature of the fearful crew. A man in the bow of the oncoming boat challenged them just as the two dugouts were about to touch.

For answer came the menacing growl of a panther, and the fellow found himself gazing into the flaming eyes of Sheeta, who had raised himself with his forepaws upon the bow of the boat, ready to leap in upon the occupants of the other craft.

Instantly Rokoff realized the peril that confronted him and his fellows. He gave a quick command to fire upon the occupants of the other canoe, and it was this volley and the scream of the terrified native woman in the canoe with Mugambi that both Tarzan and Jane had heard.

Before the slower and less skilled paddlers in Mugambi's canoe could press their advantage and effect a boarding of the enemy the latter had turned swiftly downstream and were paddling for their lives in the direction of the *Kincaid*, which was now visible to them.

The vessel after striking upon the bar had swung loose again into a slow-moving eddy, which returns upstream close to the southern shore of the Ugambi only to circle out once more and join the downward flow a hundred yards or so farther up. Thus the *Kincaid* was returning Jane Clayton directly into the hands of her enemies.

It so happened that as Tarzan sprang into the river the vessel was not visible to him, and as he swam out into the night he had no idea that a ship drifted so close at hand. He was guided by the sounds which he could hear coming from the two canoes.

As he swam he had vivid recollections of the last occasion upon which he had swum in the waters of the Ugambi, and with them a sudden shudder shook the frame of the giant.

But, though he twice felt something brush his legs from the slimy depths below him, nothing seized him, and of a sudden he quite forgot about crocodiles in the astonishment of seeing a dark mass loom suddenly before him where he had still expected to find the open river.

So close was it that a few strokes brought him up to the thing, when to his amazement his outstretched hand came in contact with a ship's side.

As the agile ape-man clambered over the vessel's rail there came to his sensitive ears the sound of a struggle at the opposite side of the deck.

Noiselessly he sped across the intervening space.

The moon had risen now, and, though the sky was still banked with clouds, a lesser darkness enveloped the scene than that which had blotted out all sight earlier in the night. His keen eyes, therefore, saw the figures of two men grappling with a woman.

That it was the woman who had accompanied Anderssen toward the interior he did not know, though he suspected as much, as he was now quite certain that this was the deck of the *Kincaid* upon which chance had led him.

But he wasted little time in idle speculation. There was a woman in danger of harm from two ruffians, which was enough excuse for the ape-man to project his giant thews into the conflict without further investigation.

The first that either of the sailors knew that there was a new force at work upon the ship was the falling of a mighty hand upon a shoulder of each. As if they had been in the grip of a fly-wheel, they were jerked suddenly from their prey.

"What means this?" asked a low voice in their ears.

They were given no time to reply, however, for at the sound of that voice the young woman had sprung to her feet and with a little cry of joy leaped toward their assailant.

"Tarzan!" she cried.

The ape-man hurled the two sailors across the deck, where they rolled, stunned and terrified, into the scuppers upon the opposite side, and with an exclamation of incredulity gathered the girl into his arms.

Brief, however, were the moments for their greeting.

Scarcely had they recognized one another than the clouds above them parted to show the figures of a half-dozen men clambering over the side of the *Kincaid* to the steamer's deck.

Foremost among them was the Russian. As the brilliant rays of the equatorial moon lighted the deck, and he realized that the man before him was Lord Greystoke, he screamed hysterical commands to his followers to fire upon the two.

Tarzan pushed Jane behind the cabin near which they had been standing, and with a quick bound started for Rokoff. The men behind the Russian, at least two of them, raised their rifles and fired at the charging ape-man; but those behind them were otherwise engaged—for up the monkey-ladder in their rear was thronging a hideous horde.

First came five snarling apes, huge, manlike beasts, with bared fangs and slavering jaws; and after them a giant black warrior, his long spear gleaming in the moonlight.

Behind him again scrambled another creature, and of all the horrid horde it was this they most feared—Sheeta, the panther, with gleaming jaws agape and fiery eyes blazing at them in the mightiness of his hate and of his blood lust.

The shots that had been fired at Tarzan missed him, and he would have been upon Rokoff in another instant had not the great coward dodged backward between his two henchmen, and, screaming in hysterical terror, bolted forward toward the forecastle.

For the moment Tarzan's attention was distracted by the two men before him, so that he could not at the time pursue the Russian. About him the apes and Mugambi were battling with the balance of the Russian's party.

Beneath the terrible ferocity of the beasts the men were soon scampering in all directions—those who still lived to scamper, for the great fangs of the apes of Akut and the tearing talons of Sheeta already had found more than a single victim.

Four, however, escaped and disappeared into the forecastle, where they hoped to barricade themselves against further assault. Here they found Rokoff, and, enraged at his desertion of them in their moment of peril, no less than at the uniformly brutal treatment it had been his wont to accord them, they gloated upon the opportunity now offered them to revenge themselves in part upon their hated employer.

Despite his prayers and grovelling pleas, therefore, they hurled him bodily out upon the deck, delivering him to the mercy of the fearful things from which they had themselves just escaped.

Tarzan saw the man emerge from the forecastle—saw and recognized his enemy; but another saw him even as soon.

It was Sheeta, and with grinning jaws the mighty beast slunk silently toward the terror-stricken man.

When Rokoff saw what it was that stalked him his shrieks for help filled the air, as with trembling knees he stood, as one paralyzed, before the hideous death that was creeping upon him.

Tarzan took a step toward the Russian, his brain burning with a raging fire of vengeance. At last he had the murderer of his son at his mercy. His was the right to avenge.

Once Jane had stayed his hand that time that he sought to take the law into his own power and mete to Rokoff the death that he had so long merited; but this time none should stay him.

His fingers clenched and unclenched spasmodically as he approached the trembling Russ, beastlike and ominous as a brute of prey.

Presently he saw that Sheeta was about to forestall him, robbing him of the fruits of his great hate.

He called sharply to the panther, and the words, as if they had broken a hideous spell that had held the Russian, galvanized him into sudden action. With a scream he turned and fled toward the bridge.

After him pounced Sheeta the panther, unmindful of his master's warning voice.

Tarzan was about to leap after the two when he felt a light touch upon his arm. Turning, he found Jane at his elbow.

"Do not leave me," she whispered. "I am afraid."

Tarzan glanced behind her.

All about were the hideous apes of Akut. Some, even, were approaching the young woman with bared fangs and menacing guttural warnings.

The ape-man warned them back. He had forgotten for the moment that these were but beasts, unable to differentiate his friends and his foes. Their savage natures were roused by their recent battle with the sailors, and now all flesh outside the pack was meat to them.

Tarzan turned again toward the Russian, chagrined that he should have to forgo the pleasure of personal revenge— unless the man should escape Sheeta. But as he looked he saw that there could be no hope of that. The fellow had retreated to the end of the bridge, where he now stood trembling and wide-eyed, facing the beast that moved slowly toward him.

The panther crawled with belly to the planking, uttering uncanny mouthings. Rokoff stood as though petrified, his eyes protruding from their sockets, his mouth agape, and the cold sweat of terror clammy upon his brow.

Below him, upon the deck, he had seen the great anthropoids, and so had not dared to seek escape in that direction. In fact, even now one of the brutes was leaping to seize the bridge-rail and draw himself up to the Russian's side.

Before him was the panther, silent and crouched.

Rokoff could not move. His knees trembled. His voice broke in inarticulate shrieks. With a last piercing wail he sank to his knees—and then Sheeta sprang.

Full upon the man's breast the tawny body hurtled, tumbling the Russian to his back.

As the great fangs tore at the throat and chest, Jane Clayton turned away in horror; but not so Tarzan of the Apes. A cold smile of satisfaction touched his lips. The scar upon his forehead that had burned scarlet faded to the normal hue of his tanned skin and disappeared.

Rokoff fought furiously but futilely against the growling, rending fate that had overtaken him. For all his countless crimes he was punished in the brief moment of the hideous death that claimed him at the last.

After his struggles ceased Tarzan approached, at Jane's suggestion, to wrest the body from the panther and give what remained of it decent human burial; but the great cat rose snarling above its kill, threatening even the master it loved in its savage way, so that rather than kill his friend of the jungle, Tarzan was forced to relinquish his intentions.

All that night Sheeta, the panther, crouched upon the grisly thing that had been Nikolas Rokoff. The bridge of the *Kincaid* was slippery with blood. Beneath the brilliant tropic moon the great beast feasted until, when the sun rose the following morning, there remained of Tarzan's great enemy only gnawed and broken bones.

Of the Russian's party, all were accounted for except Paulvitch. Four were prisoners in the *Kincaid*'s forecastle. The rest were dead.

With these men Tarzan got up steam upon the vessel, and with the knowledge of the mate, who happened to be one of those surviving, he planned to set out in quest of Jungle Island; but as the morning dawned there came with it a heavy gale from the west which raised a sea into which the mate of the *Kincaid* dared not venture. All that day the ship lay within the shelter of the mouth of the river; for, though night witnessed a lessening of the wind, it was thought safer to wait for daylight before attempting the navigation of the winding channel to the sea.

Upon the deck of the steamer the pack wandered without let or hindrance by day, for they had soon learned through Tarzan and Mugambi that they must harm no one upon the *Kincaid*; but at night they were confined below.

Tarzan's joy had been unbounded when he learned from his wife that the little child who had died in the village of M'ganwazam was not their son. Who the baby could have been, or what had become of their own, they could not imagine, and as both Rokoff and Paulvitch were gone, there was no way of discovering.

There was, however, a certain sense of relief in the knowledge that they might yet hope. Until positive proof of the baby's death reached them there was always that to buoy them up.

It seemed quite evident that their little Jack had not been brought aboard the *Kincaid*. Anderssen would have known of it had such been the case, but he had assured Jane time and time again that the little one he had brought to her cabin the night he aided her to escape was the only one that had been aboard the *Kincaid* since she lay at Dover.

18

Paulvitch Plots Revenge

As JANE AND Tarzan stood upon the vessel's deck recounting to one another the details of the various adventures through which each had passed since they had parted in their London home, there glared at them from beneath scowling brows a hidden watcher upon the shore.

Through the man's brain passed plan after plan whereby he might thwart the escape of the Englishman and his wife, for so long as the vital spark remained within the vindictive brain of Alexander Paulvitch none who had aroused the enmity of the Russian might be entirely safe.

Plan after plan he formed only to discard each either as impracticable, or unworthy the vengeance his wrongs demanded. So warped by faulty reasoning was the criminal mind of Rokoff's lieutenant that he could not grasp the real truth of that which lay between himself and the ape-man and see that always the fault had been, not with the English lord, but with himself and his confederate.

And at the rejection of each new scheme Paulvitch arrived always at the same conclusion—that he could accomplish naught while half the breadth of the Ugambi separated him from the object of his hatred.

But how was he to span the crocodile-infested waters? There was no canoe nearer than the Mosula village, and Paulvitch was none too sure that the *Kincaid* would still be at anchor in the river when he returned should he take the time to traverse the jungle to the distant village and return with a canoe. Yet there was no other way, and so, convinced that thus alone might he hope to reach his prey, Paulvitch, with a parting scowl at the two figures upon the *Kincaid*'s deck, turned away from the river.

Hastening through the dense jungle, his mind centered upon his one fetich—revenge—the Russian forgot even his terror of the savage world through which he moved.

Baffled and beaten at every turn of Fortune's wheel, reacted upon time after time by his own malign plotting, the principal victim of his own criminality, Paulvitch was yet so blind as to imagine that his greatest happiness lay in a continuation of the plottings and schemings which had ever brought him and Rokoff to disaster, and the latter finally to a hideous death.

As the Russian stumbled on through the jungle toward the Mosula village there presently crystallized within his brain a plan which seemed more feasible than any that he had as yet considered.

He would come by night to the side of the *Kincaid*, and once aboard, would search out the members of the ship's original crew who had survived the terrors of this frightful expedition, and enlist them in an attempt to wrest the vessel from Tarzan and his beasts.

In the cabin were arms and ammunition, and hidden in a secret receptacle in the cabin table was one of those infernal machines, the construction of which had occupied much of Paulvitch's spare time when he had stood high in the confidence of the Nihilists of his native land.

That was before he had sold them out for immunity and gold to the police of Petrograd. Paulvitch winced as he recalled the denunciation of him that had fallen from the lips of one of his former comrades ere the poor devil expiated his political sins at the end of a hempen rope.

But the infernal machine was the thing to think of now. He could do much with that if he could but get his hands upon it. Within the little hardwood case hidden in the cabin table rested sufficient potential destructiveness to wipe out in the fraction of a second every enemy aboard the *Kincaid*.

Paulvitch licked his lips in anticipatory joy, and urged his tired legs to greater speed that he might not be too late to the ship's anchorage to carry out his designs.

All depended, of course, upon when the *Kincaid* departed. The Russian realized that nothing could be accomplished beneath the light of day. Darkness must shroud his approach to the ship's side, for should he be sighted by Tarzan or Lady Greystoke he would have no chance to board the vessel.

The gale that was blowing was, he believed, the cause of the delay in getting the *Kincaid* under way, and if it continued to blow until night then the chances were all in his favour, for he knew that there was little likelihood of the ape-man attempting to navigate the tortuous channel of the Ugambi while darkness lay upon the surface of the water, hiding the many bars and the numerous small islands which are scattered over the expanse of the river's mouth.

It was well after noon when Paulvitch came to the Mosula village upon the bank of the tributary of the Ugambi. Here he was received with suspicion and unfriendliness by the native chief, who, like all those who came in contact with Rokoff or Paulvitch, had suffered in some manner from the greed, the cruelty, or the lust of the two Muscovites.

When Paulvitch demanded the use of a canoe the chief grumbled a surly refusal and ordered the white man from the village. Surrounded by angry, muttering warriors who seemed to be but waiting some slight pretext to transfix him with their menacing spears the Russian could do naught else than withdraw.

A dozen fighting men led him to the edge of the clearing, leaving him with a warning never to show himself again in the vicinity of their village.

Stifling his anger, Paulvitch slunk into the jungle; but once beyond the sight of the warriors he paused and listened intently.

He could hear the voices of his escort as the men returned to the village, and when he was sure that they were not following him he wormed his way through the bushes to the edge of the river, still determined some way to obtain a canoe.

Life itself depended upon his reaching the *Kincaid* and enlisting the survivors of the ship's crew in his service, for to be abandoned here amidst the dangers of the African jungle where he had won the enmity of the natives was, he well knew, practically equivalent to a sentence of death.

A desire for revenge acted as an almost equally powerful incentive to spur him into the face of danger to accomplish his design, so that it was a desperate man that lay hidden in the foliage beside the little river searching with eager eyes for some sign of a small canoe which might be easily handled by a single paddle.

Nor had the Russian long to wait before one of the awkward little skiffs which the Mosula fashion came in sight upon the bosom of the river. A youth was paddling lazily out into midstream from a point beside the village. When he reached the channel he allowed the sluggish current to carry him slowly along while he lolled indolently in the bottom of his crude canoe.

All ignorant of the unseen enemy upon the river's bank the lad floated slowly down the stream while Paulvitch followed along the jungle path a few yards behind him.

A mile below the village the black boy dipped his paddle into the water and forced his skiff toward the bank. Paulvitch, elated by the chance which had drawn the youth to the same side of the river as that along which he followed rather than to the opposite side where he would have been beyond the stalker's reach, hid in the brush close beside the point at which it was evident the skiff would touch the bank of the slow-moving stream, which seemed jealous of each fleeting instant which drew it nearer to the broad and muddy Ugambi where it must for ever lose its identity in the larger stream that would presently cast its waters into the great ocean.

Equally indolent were the motions of the Mosula youth as he drew his skiff beneath an overhanging limb of a great tree that leaned down to implant a farewell kiss upon the bosom of the departing water, caressing with green fronds the soft breast of its languorous love.

And, snake-like, amidst the concealing foliage lay the malevolent Russ. Cruel, shifty eyes gloated upon the outlines of the coveted canoe, and measured the stature of its owner, while the crafty brain weighed the chances of the white man should physical encounter with the black become necessary.

Only direst necessity could drive Alexander Paulvitch to personal conflict; but it was indeed dire necessity which goaded him on to action now.

There was time, just time enough, to reach the *Kincaid* by nightfall. Would the black fool never quit his skiff? Paulvitch squirmed and fidgeted. The lad yawned and stretched. With exasperating deliberateness he examined the arrows in his quiver, tested his bow, and looked to the edge upon the hunting-knife in his loin-cloth.

Again he stretched and yawned, glanced up at the riverbank, shrugged his shoulders, and lay down in the bottom of his canoe for a little nap before he plunged into the jungle after the prey he had come forth to hunt.

Paulvitch half rose, and with tensed muscles stood glaring down upon his unsuspecting victim. The boy's lids drooped and closed. Presently his breast rose and fell to the deep breaths of slumber. The time had come!

The Russian crept stealthily nearer. A branch rustled beneath his weight and the lad stirred in his sleep. Paulvitch drew his revolver and leveled it upon the black. For a moment he remained in rigid quiet, and then again the youth relapsed into undisturbed slumber.

The white man crept closer. He could not chance a shot until there was no risk of missing. Presently he leaned close above the Mosula. The cold steel of the revolver in his hand insinuated itself nearer and nearer to the breast of the unconscious lad. Now it stopped but a few inches above the strongly beating heart.

But the pressure of a finger lay between the harmless boy and eternity. The soft bloom of youth still lay upon the brown cheek, a smile half parted the beardless lips. Did any qualm of conscience point its disquieting finger of reproach at the murderer?

To all such was Alexander Paulvitch immune. A sneer curled his bearded lip as his forefinger closed upon the trigger of his revolver. There was a loud report. A little hole appeared above the heart of the sleeping boy, a little hole about which lay a blackened rim of powder-burned flesh.

The youthful body half rose to a sitting posture. The smiling lips tensed to the nervous shock of a momentary agony which the conscious mind never apprehended, and then the dead sank limply back into that deepest of slumbers from which there is no awakening.

The killer dropped quickly into the skiff beside the killed. Ruthless hands seized the dead boy heartlessly and raised him to the low gunwale. A little shove, a splash, some widening ripples broken by the sudden surge of a dark, hidden body from the slimy depths, and the coveted canoe was in the sole possession of the white man—more savage than the youth whose life he had taken.

Casting off the tie rope and seizing the paddle, Paulvitch bent feverishly to the task of driving the skiff downward toward the Ugambi at top speed.

Night had fallen when the prow of the bloodstained craft shot out into the current of the larger stream. Constantly the Russian strained his eyes into the increasing darkness ahead in vain endeavour to pierce the black shadows which lay between him and the anchorage of the *Kincaid*.

Was the ship still riding there upon the waters of the Ugambi, or had the ape-man at last persuaded himself of the safety of venturing forth into the abating storm? As Paulvitch forged ahead with the current he asked himself these questions, and many more beside, not the least disquieting of which were those which related to his future should it chance that the *Kincaid* had already steamed away, leaving him to the merciless horrors of the savage wilderness.

In the darkness it seemed to the paddler that he was fairly flying over the water, and he had become convinced that the ship had left her moorings and that he had already passed the spot at which she had lain earlier in the day, when there appeared before him beyond a projecting point which he had but just rounded the flickering light from a ship's lantern.

Alexander Paulvitch could scarce restrain an exclamation of triumph. The *Kincaid* had not departed! Life and vengeance were not to elude him after all.

He stopped paddling the moment that he descried the gleaming beacon of hope ahead of him. Silently he drifted down the muddy waters of the Ugambi, occasionally dipping his paddle's blade gently into the current that he might guide his primitive craft to the vessel's side.

As he approached more closely the dark bulk of a ship loomed before him out of the blackness of the night. No sound came from the vessel's deck. Paulvitch drifted, unseen, close to the *Kincaid*'s side. Only the momentary scraping of his canoe's nose against the ship's planking broke the silence of the night.

Trembling with nervous excitement, the Russian remained motionless for several minutes; but there was no sound from the great bulk above him to indicate that his coming had been noted.

Stealthily he worked his craft forward until the stays of the bowsprit were directly above him. He could just reach them. To make his canoe fast there was the work of but a minute or two, and then the man raised himself quietly aloft.

A moment later he dropped softly to the deck. Thoughts of the hideous pack which tenanted the ship induced cold tremors along the spine of the cowardly prowler; but life itself depended upon the success of his venture, and so he was enabled to steel himself to the frightful chances which lay before him.

No sound or sign of watch appeared upon the ship's deck. Paulvitch crept stealthily toward the forecastle. All was silence. The hatch was raised, and as the man peered downward he saw one of the *Kincaid*'s crew reading by the light of the smoky lantern depending from the ceiling of the crew's quarters.

Paulvitch knew the man well, a surly cut-throat upon whom he figured strongly in the carrying out of the plan which he had conceived. Gently the Russ lowered himself through the aperture to the rounds of the ladder which led into the forecastle.

He kept his eyes turned upon the reading man, ready to warn him to silence the moment that the fellow discovered him; but so deeply immersed was the sailor in the magazine that the Russian came, unobserved, to the forecastle floor.

There he turned and whispered the reader's name. The man raised his eyes from the magazine—eyes that went wide for a moment as they fell upon the familiar countenance of Rokoff's lieutenant, only to narrow instantly in a scowl of disapproval.

"The devil!" he ejaculated. "Where did you come from? We all thought you were done for and gone where you ought to have gone a long time ago. His lordship will be mighty pleased to see you."

Paulvitch crossed to the sailor's side. A friendly smile lay on the Russian's lips, and his right hand was extended in greeting, as though the other might have been a dear and long lost friend. The sailor ignored the proffered hand, nor did he return the other's smile.

"I've come to help you," explained Paulvitch. "I'm going to help you get rid of the Englishman and his beasts—then there will be no danger from the law when we get back to civilization. We can sneak in on them while they sleep—that is Greystoke, his wife, and that black scoundrel, Mugambi. Afterward it will be a simple matter to clean up the beasts. Where are they?"

"They're below," replied the sailor, "but just let me tell you something, Paulvitch. You haven't got no more show to turn us men against the Englishman than nothing. We had all we wanted of you and that other beast. He's dead, an' if I don't miss my guess a whole lot you'll be dead too before long. You two treated us like dogs, and if you think we got any love for you you better forget it."

"You mean to say that you're going to turn against me?" demanded Paulvitch.

The other nodded, and then after a momentary pause, during which an idea seemed to have occurred to him, he spoke again.

"Unless," he said, "you can make it worth my while to let you go before the Englishman finds you here."

"You wouldn't turn me away in the jungle, would you?" asked Paulvitch. "Why, I'd die there in a week."

"You'd have a chance there," replied the sailor. "Here, you wouldn't have no chance. Why, if I woke up my maties here they'd probably cut your heart out of you before the Englishman got a chance at you at all. It's mighty lucky for you that I'm the one to be awake now and not none of the others."

"You're crazy," cried Paulvitch. "Don't you know that the Englishman will have you all hanged when he gets you back where the law can get hold of you?"

"No, he won't do nothing of the kind," replied the sailor. "He's told us as much, for he says that there wasn't nobody to blame but you and Rokoff—the rest of us was just tools. See?"

For half an hour the Russian pleaded or threatened as the mood seized him. Sometimes he was upon the verge of tears, and again he was promising his listener either fabulous rewards or condign punishment; but the other was obdurate.

He made it plain to the Russian that there were but two plans open to him—either he must consent to being turned over immediately to Lord Greystoke, or he must pay to the sailor, as a price for permission to quit the *Kincaid* unmolested, every cent of money and article of value upon his person and in his cabin.

"And you'll have to make up your mind mighty quick," growled the man, "for I want to turn in. Come now, choose—his lordship or the jungle?"

"You'll be sorry for this," grumbled the Russian.

"Shut up," admonished the sailor. "If you get funny I may change my mind, and keep you here after all."

Now Paulvitch had no intention of permitting himself to fall into the hands of Tarzan of the Apes if he could possibly avoid it, and while the terrors of the jungle appalled him they were, to his mind, infinitely preferable to the certain death which he knew he merited and for which he might look at the hands of the ape-man.

"Is anyone sleeping in my cabin?" he asked.

The sailor shook his head. "No," he said, "Lord and Lady

Greystoke have the captain's cabin. The mate is in his own, and there ain't no one in yours."

"I'll go and get my valuables for you," said Paulvitch.

"I'll go with you to see that you don't try any funny business," said the sailor, and he followed the Russian up the ladder to the deck.

At the cabin entrance the sailor halted to watch, permitting Paulvitch to go alone to his cabin. Here he gathered together his few belongings that were to buy him the uncertain safety of escape, and as he stood for a moment beside the little table on which he had piled them he searched his brain for some feasible plan either to ensure his safety or to bring revenge upon his enemies.

And presently as he thought there recurred to his memory the little black box which lay hidden in a secret receptacle beneath a false top upon the table where his hand rested.

The Russian's face lighted to a sinister gleam of malevolent satisfaction as he stooped and felt beneath the table top. A moment later he withdrew from its hiding place the thing he sought. He had lighted the lantern swinging from the beams overhead that he might see to collect his belongings, and now he held the black box well in the rays of the lamplight, while he fingered at the clasp that fastened its lid.

The lifted cover revealed two compartments within the box. In one was a mechanism which resembled the works of a small clock. There also was a little battery of two dry cells. A wire ran from the clockwork to one of the poles of the battery, and from the other pole through the partition into the other compartment, a second wire returning directly to the clockwork.

Whatever lay within the second compartment was not visible, for a cover lay over it and appeared to be sealed in place by asphaltum. In the bottom of the box, beside the clockwork, lay a key, and this Paulvitch now withdrew and fitted to the winding stem.

Gently he turned the key, muffling the noise of the winding operation by throwing a couple of articles of clothing over the box. All the time he listened intently for any sound which might indicate that the sailor or another were approaching his cabin; but none came to interrupt his work.

When the winding was completed the Russian set a pointer upon a small dial at the side of the clockwork, then he replaced the cover upon the black box, and returned the entire machine to its hiding place in the table.

A sinister smile curled the man's bearded lips as he gathered up his valuables, blew out the lamp, and stepped from his cabin to the side of the waiting sailor.

"Here are my things," said the Russian, "now let me go."

"I'll first take a look in your pockets," replied the sailor. "You might have overlooked some trifling thing that won't be of no use to you in the jungle, but that'll come in mighty handy to a poor sailorman in London. Ah! just as I feared," he ejaculated an instant later as he withdrew a roll of banknotes from Paulvitch's inside coat pocket.

The Russian scowled, muttering an imprecation; but nothing could be gained by argument, and so he did his best to reconcile himself to his loss in the knowledge that the sailor would never reach London to enjoy the fruits of his thievery.

It was with difficulty that Paulvitch restrained a consuming desire to taunt the man with a suggestion of the fate that would presently overtake him and the other members of the *Kincaid*'s company; but fearing to arouse the fellow's suspicions, he crossed the deck and lowered himself in silence into his canoe.

A minute or two later he was paddling toward the shore to be swallowed up in the darkness of the jungle night, and the terrors of a hideous existence from which, could he have had even a slight foreknowledge of what awaited him in the long years to come, he would have fled to the certain death of the open sea rather than endure it.

The sailor, having made sure that Paulvitch had departed, returned to the forecastle, where he hid away his booty and turned into his bunk, while in the cabin that had belonged to the Russian there ticked on and on through the silences of the night the little mechanism in the small black box which held for the unconscious sleepers upon the ill-starred *Kincaid* the coming vengeance of the thwarted Russian.

19

The Last of the "Kincaid"

SHORTLY AFTER THE break of day Tarzan was on deck noting the condition of the weather. The wind had abated. The sky was cloudless. Every condition seemed ideal for the commencement of the return voyage to Jungle Island, where the beasts were to be left. And then—home!

The ape-man aroused the mate and gave instructions that the *Kincaid* sail at the earliest possible moment. The remaining members of the crew, safe in Lord Greystoke's assurance that they would not be prosecuted for their share in the villainies of the two Russians, hastened with cheerful alacrity to their several duties.

The beasts, liberated from the confinement of the hold, wandered about the deck, not a little to the discomfiture of the crew in whose minds there remained a still vivid picture of the savagery of the beasts in conflict with those who had gone to their deaths beneath the fangs and talons which even now seemed itching for the soft flesh of further prey.

Beneath the watchful eyes of Tarzan and Mugambi, however, Sheeta and the apes of Akut curbed their desires, so that the men worked about the deck amongst them in far greater security than they imagined.

At last the *Kincaid* slipped down the Ugambi and ran out upon the shimmering waters of the Atlantic. Tarzan and Jane Clayton watched the verdure-clad shoreline receding in the ship's wake, and for once the ape-man left his native soil without one single pang of regret.

No ship that sailed the seven seas could have borne him away from Africa to resume his search for his lost boy with half the speed that the Englishman would have desired, and the slow-moving *Kincaid* seemed scarce to move at all to the impatient mind of the bereaved father.

Yet the vessel made progress even when she seemed to be standing still, and presently the low hills of Jungle Island became distinctly visible upon the western horizon ahead.

In the cabin of Alexander Paulvitch the thing within the black box ticked, ticked, ticked, with apparently unending monotony; but yet, second by second, a little arm which protruded from the periphery of one of its wheels came nearer and nearer to another little arm which projected from the hand which Paulvitch had set at a certain point upon the dial beside the clockwork. When those two arms touched one another the ticking of the mechanism would cease—forever.

Jane and Tarzan stood upon the bridge looking out toward Jungle Island. The men were forward, also watching the land grow upward out of the ocean. The beasts had sought the shade of the galley, where they were curled up in sleep. All was quiet and peace upon the ship, and upon the waters.

Suddenly, without warning, the cabin roof shot up into the air, a cloud of dense smoke puffed far above the *Kincaid*, there was a terrific explosion which shook the vessel from stem to stern.

Instantly pandemonium broke loose upon the deck. The apes of Akut, terrified by the sound, ran hither and thither, snarling and growling. Sheeta leaped here and there, screaming out his startled terror in hideous cries that sent the ice of fear straight to the hearts of the *Kincaid*'s crew.

Mugambi, too, was trembling. Only Tarzan of the Apes and his wife retained their composure. Scarce had the debris settled than the ape-man was among the beasts, quieting their fears, talking to them in low, pacific tones, stroking their shaggy bodies, and assuring them, as only he could, that the immediate danger was over.

An examination of the wreckage showed that their greatest danger, now, lay in fire, for the flames were licking hungrily at the splintered wood of the wrecked cabin, and had already found a foothold upon the lower deck through a great jagged hole which the explosion had opened.

By a miracle no member of the ship's company had been injured by the blast, the origin of which remained for ever a total mystery to all but one—the sailor who knew that Paulvitch had been aboard the *Kincaid* and in his cabin the previous night. He guessed the truth; but discretion sealed his lips. It would, doubtless, fare none too well for the man who had permitted the arch-enemy of them all aboard the ship in the watches of the night, where later he might set an infernal machine to blow them all to kingdom come. No, the man decided that he would keep this knowledge to himself.

As the flames gained headway it became apparent to Tarzan that whatever had caused the explosion had scattered some highly inflammable substance upon the surrounding woodwork, for the water which they poured in from the pump seemed rather to spread than to extinguish the blaze.

Fifteen minutes after the explosion great, black clouds of smoke were rising from the hold of the doomed vessel. The flames had reached the engine-room, and the ship no longer moved toward the shore. Her fate was as certain as though the waters already had closed above her charred and smoking remains.

"It is useless to remain aboard her longer," remarked the ape-man to the mate. "There is no telling but there may be other explosions, and as we cannot hope to save her, the safest thing which we can do is to take to the boats without further loss of time and make land."

Nor was there any other alternative. Only the sailors could bring away any belongings, for the fire, which had not yet reached the forecastle, had consumed all in the vicinity of the cabin which the explosion had not destroyed.

Two boats were lowered, and as there was no sea the landing was made with infinite ease. Eager and anxious, the beasts of Tarzan sniffed the familiar air of their native island as the small boats drew in toward the beach, and scarce had their keels grated upon the sand than Sheeta and the apes of Akut were over the bows and racing swiftly toward the jungle.

A half-sad smile curved the lips of the ape-man as he watched them go.

"Good-bye, my friends," he murmured. "You have been good and faithful allies, and I shall miss you."

"They will return, will they not, dear?" asked Jane Clayton, at his side.

"They may and they may not," replied the ape-man. "They have been ill at ease since they were forced to accept so many human beings into their confidence. Mugambi and I alone affected them less, for he and I are, at best, but half human. You, however, and the members of the crew are far too civilized for my beasts— it is you whom they are fleeing. Doubtless they feel that they cannot trust themselves in the close vicinity of so much perfectly good food without the danger that they may help themselves to a mouthful some time by mistake."

Jane laughed. "I think they are just trying to escape you," she retorted. "You are always making them stop something which they see no reason why they should not do. Like little children they are doubtless delighted at this opportunity to flee from the zone of parental discipline. If they come back, though, I hope they won't come by night."

"Or come hungry, eh?" laughed Tarzan.

For two hours after landing the little party stood watching the burning ship which they had abandoned. Then there came faintly to them from across the water the sound of a second explosion. The *Kincaid* settled rapidly almost immediately thereafter, and sank within a few minutes.

The cause of the second explosion was less a mystery than that of the first, the mate attributing it to the bursting of the boilers when the flames had finally reached them; but what had caused the first explosion was a subject of considerable speculation among the stranded company.

20

Jungle Island Again

THE FIRST CONSIDERATION of the party was to locate fresh water and make camp, for all knew that their term of existence upon Jungle Island might be drawn out to months, or even years.

Tarzan knew the nearest water, and to this he immediately led the party. Here the men fell to work to construct shelters and rude furniture while Tarzan went into the jungle after meat, leaving the faithful Mugambi and the Mosula woman to guard Jane, whose safety he would never trust to any member of the *Kincaid*'s cut-throat crew.

Lady Greystoke suffered far greater anguish than any other of the castaways, for the blow to her hopes and her already cruelly lacerated mother-heart lay not in her own privations but in the knowledge that she might now never be able to learn the fate of her first-born or do aught to discover his whereabouts, or ameliorate his condition—a condition which imagination naturally pictured in the most frightful forms.

For two weeks the party divided the time amongst the various duties which had been allotted to each. A daylight watch was maintained from sunrise to sunset upon a bluff near the camp—a jutting shoulder of rock which overlooked the sea. Here, ready for instant lighting, was gathered a huge pile of dry branches, while from a lofty pole which they had set in the ground there floated an improvised distress signal fashioned from a red undershirt which belonged to the mate of the *Kincaid*.

But never a speck upon the horizon that might be sail or smoke rewarded the tired eyes that in their endless, hopeless vigil strained daily out across the vast expanse of ocean.

It was Tarzan who suggested, finally, that they attempt to construct a vessel that would bear them back to the mainland. He alone could show them how to fashion rude tools, and when the idea had taken root in the minds of the men they were eager to commence their labours.

But as time went on and the Herculean nature of their task became more and more apparent they fell to grumbling, and to quarrelling among themselves, so that to the other dangers were now added dissension and suspicion.

More than before did Tarzan now fear to leave Jane among the half brutes of the *Kincaid*'s crew; but hunting he must do, for none other could so surely go forth and return with meat as he. Sometimes Mugambi spelled him at the hunting; but the black's spear and arrows were never so sure of results as the rope and knife of the ape-man.

Finally the men shirked their work, going off into the jungle by twos to explore and to hunt. All this time the camp had had no sight of Sheeta, or Akut and the other great apes, though Tarzan had sometimes met them in the jungle as he hunted.

And as matters tended from bad to worse in the camp of the castaways upon the east coast of Jungle Island, another camp came into being upon the north coast.

Here, in a little cove, lay a small schooner, the *Cowrie*, whose decks had but a few days since run red with the blood of her officers and the loyal members of her crew, for the *Cowrie* had fallen upon bad days when it had shipped such men as Gust and Momulla the Maori and that archfiend Kai Shang of Fachan.

There were others, too, ten of them all told, the scum of the South Sea ports; but Gust and Momulla and Kai Shang were the brains and cunning of the company. It was they who had instigated the mutiny that they might seize and divide the catch of pearls which constituted the wealth of the *Cowrie*'s cargo.

It was Kai Shang who had murdered the captain as he lay asleep in his berth, and it had been Momulla the Maori who had led the attack upon the officer of the watch.

Gust, after his own peculiar habit, had found means to delegate to the others the actual taking of life. Not that Gust entertained any scruples on the subject, other than those which induced in him a rare regard for his own personal safety. There is always a certain element of risk to the assassin, for victims of deadly assault are seldom prone to personal safety. There is always a certain element of risk to go so far as to dispute the issue with the murderer. It was this chance of dispute which Gust preferred to forgo.

But now that the work was done the Swede aspired to the position of highest command among the mutineers. He had even gone so far as to appropriate and wear certain articles belonging to the murdered captain of the *Cowrie*—articles of apparel which bore upon them the badges and insignia of authority.

Kai Shang was peeved. He had no love for authority, and certainly not the slightest intention of submitting to the domination of an ordinary Swede sailor.

The seeds of discontent were, therefore, already planted in the camp of the mutineers of the *Cowrie* at the north edge of Jungle Island. But Kai Shang realized that he must act with circumspection, for Gust alone of the motley horde possessed sufficient knowledge of navigation to get them out of the South Atlantic and around the cape into more congenial waters where they might find a market for their ill-gotten wealth, and no questions asked.

The day before they sighted Jungle Island and discovered the little landlocked harbor upon the bosom of which the *Cowrie* now rode quietly at anchor, the watch had discovered the smoke and funnels of a warship upon the southern horizon.

The chance of being spoken and investigated by a man-of-war appealed not at all to any of them, so they put into hiding for a few days until the danger should have passed.

And now Gust did not wish to venture out to sea again. There was no telling, he insisted, but that the ship they had seen was actually searching for them. Kai Shang pointed out that such could not be the case since it was impossible for any human being other than themselves to have knowledge of what had transpired aboard the *Cowrie*.

But Gust was not to be persuaded. In his wicked heart he nursed a scheme whereby he might increase his share of the booty by something like one hundred per cent. He alone could sail the *Cowrie*, therefore the others could not leave Jungle Island without him; but what was there to prevent Gust, with just sufficient men to man the schooner, slipping away from Kai Shang, Momulla the Maori, and some half of the crew when opportunity presented?

It was for this opportunity that Gust waited. Some day there would come a moment when Kai Shang, Momulla, and three or four of the others would be absent from camp, exploring or hunting. The Swede racked his brain for some plan whereby he might successfully lure from the sight of the anchored ship those whom he had determined to abandon.

To this end he organized hunting party after hunting party, but always the devil of perversity seemed to enter the soul of Kai Shang, so that that wily celestial would never hunt except in the company of Gust himself.

One day Kai Shang spoke secretly with Momulla the Maori, pouring into the brown ear of his companion the suspicions which he harbored concerning the Swede. Momulla was for going immediately and running a long knife through the heart of the traitor.

It is true that Kai Shang had no other evidence than the natural cunning of his own knavish soul—but he imagined in the intentions of Gust what he himself would have been glad to accomplish had the means lain at hand.

But he dared not let Momulla slay the Swede, upon whom they depended to guide them to their destination. They decided, however, that it would do no harm to attempt to frighten Gust into acceding to their demands, and with this purpose in mind the Maori sought out the self-constituted commander of the party.

When he broached the subject of immediate departure Gust again raised his former objection—that the warship might very probably be patrolling the sea directly in their southern path, waiting for them to make the attempt to reach other waters.

Momulla scoffed at the fears of his fellow, pointing out that as no one aboard any warship knew of their mutiny there could be no reason why they should be suspected.

"Ah!" exclaimed Gust, "there is where you are wrong. There is where you are lucky that you have an educated man like me to tell you what to do. You are an ignorant savage, Momulla, and so you know nothing of wireless."

The Maori leaped to his feet and laid his hand upon the hilt of his knife.

"I am no savage," he shouted.

"I was only joking," the Swede hastened to explain. "We are old friends, Momulla; we cannot afford to quarrel, at least not while old Kai Shang is plotting to steal all the pearls from us. If he could find a man to navigate the *Cowrie* he would leave us in a minute. All his talk about getting away from here is just because he has some scheme in his head to get rid of us."

"But the wireless," asked Momulla. "What has the wireless to do with our remaining here?"

"Oh yes," replied Gust, scratching his head. He was wondering if the Maori were really so ignorant as to believe the preposterous lie he was about to unload upon him. "Oh yes! You see every warship is equipped with what they call a wireless apparatus. It lets them talk to other ships hundreds of miles away, and it lets them listen to all that is said on these other ships. Now, you see, when you fellows were shooting up the *Cowrie* you did a whole lot of loud talking, and there isn't any doubt but that that warship was a-lyin' off south of us listenin' to it all. Of course they might not have learned the name of the ship, but they heard enough to know that the crew of some ship was mutinying and killin' her officers. So you see they'll be waiting to search every ship they sight for a long time to come, and they may not be far away now."

When he had ceased speaking the Swede strove to assume an air of composure that his listener might not have his suspicions aroused as to the truth of the statements that had just been made.

Momulla sat for some time in silence, eyeing Gust. At last he rose.

"You are a great liar," he said. "If you don't get us on our way by tomorrow you'll never have another chance to lie, for I heard two of the men saying that they'd like to run a knife into you and that if you kept them in this hole any longer they'd do it."

"Go and ask Kai Shang if there is not a wireless," replied Gust. "He will tell you that there is such a thing and that vessels can talk to one another across hundreds of miles of water. Then say to the two men who wish to kill me that if they do so they will never live to spend their share of the swag, for only I can get you safely to any port."

So Momulla went to Kai Shang and asked him if there was such an apparatus as a wireless by means of which ships could talk with each other at great distances, and Kai Shang told him that there was.

Momulla was puzzled; but still he wished to leave the island, and was willing to take his chances on the open sea rather than to remain longer in the monotony of the camp.

"If we only had someone else who could navigate a ship!" wailed Kai Shang.

That afternoon Momulla went hunting with two other Maoris. They hunted toward the south, and had not gone far from camp when they were surprised by the sound of voices ahead of them in the jungle.

They knew that none of their own men had preceded them, and as all were convinced that the island was uninhabited, they were inclined to flee in terror on the hypothesis that the place was haunted—possibly by the ghosts of the murdered officers and men of the *Cowrie*.

But Momulla was even more curious than he was superstitious, and so he quelled his natural desire to flee from the supernatural. Motioning his companions to follow his example, he dropped to his hands and knees, crawling forward stealthily and with quakings of heart through the jungle in the direction from which came the voices of the unseen speakers.

Presently, at the edge of a little clearing, he halted, and there he breathed a deep sigh of relief, for plainly before him he saw two flesh-and-blood men sitting upon a fallen log and talking earnestly together.

One was Schneider, mate of the *Kincaid*, and the other was a seaman named Schmidt.

"I think we can do it, Schmidt," Schneider was saying. "A good canoe wouldn't be hard to build, and three of us could paddle it to the mainland in a day if the wind was right and the sea reasonably calm. There ain't no use waiting for the men to build a big enough boat to take the whole party, for they're sore now and sick of working like slaves all day long. It ain't none of our business anyway to save the Englishman. Let him look out for himself, says I." He paused for a moment, and then eyeing the other to note the effect of his next words, he continued, "But we might take the woman. It would be a shame to leave a nice-lookin' piece like she is in such a Gott-forsaken hole as this here island."

Schmidt looked up and grinned.

"So that's how she's blowin', is it?" he asked. "Why didn't you say so in the first place? Wot's in it for me if I help you?"

"She ought to pay us well to get her back to civilization,"

explained Schneider, "an' I tell you what I'll do, I'll just whack up with the two men that helps me. I'll take half an' they can divide the other half—you an' whoever the other bloke is. I'm sick of this place, an' the sooner I get out of it the better I'll like it. What do you say?"

"Suits me," replied Schmidt. "I wouldn't know how to reach the mainland myself, an' know that none o' the other fellows would, so's you're the only one what knows anything of naviga- tion, you're the fellow I'll tie to."

Momulla the Maori pricked up his ears. He had a smattering of every tongue that is spoken upon the seas, and more than a few times had he sailed on English ships, so that he understood fairly well all that had passed between Schneider and Schmidt since he had stumbled upon them.

He rose to his feet and stepped into the clearing. Schneider and his companion started as nervously as though a ghost had risen before them. Schneider reached for his revolver. Momulla raised his right hand, palm forward, as a sign of his pacific intentions.

"I am a friend," he said. "I heard you; but do not fear that I will reveal what you have said. I can help you, and you can help me." He was addressing Schneider. "You can navigate a ship, but you have no ship. We have a ship, but no one to navigate it. If you will come with us and ask no questions we will let you take the ship where you will after you have landed us at a certain port, the name of which we will give you later. You can take the woman of whom you speak, and we will ask no questions either. Is it a bargain?"

Schneider desired more information, and got as much as Momulla thought best to give him. Then the Maori suggested that they speak with Kai Shang. The two members of the *Kincaid*'s company followed Momulla and his fellows to a point in the jungle close by the camp of the mutineers. Here Momulla hid them while he went in search of Kai Shang, first admonishing his Maori companions to stand guard over the two sailors lest they change their minds and attempt to escape. Schneider and Schmidt were virtually prisoners, though they did not know it.

Presently Momulla returned with Kai Shang, to whom he had briefly narrated the details of the stroke of good fortune that had come to them. The Chinaman spoke at length with Schneider, until, notwithstanding his natural suspicion of the sincerity of all men, he became quite convinced that Schneider was quite as much of a rogue as himself and that the fellow was anxious to leave the island.

These two premises accepted there could be little doubt that Schneider would prove trustworthy in so far as accepting the command of the *Cowrie* was concerned; after that Kai Shang knew that he could find means to coerce the man into submission to his further wishes.

When Schneider and Schmidt left them and set out in the direction of their own camp, it was with feelings of far greater relief than they had experienced in many a day. Now at last they saw a feasible plan for leaving the island upon a seaworthy craft. There would be no more hard labour at shipbuilding, and no risking their lives upon a crudely built makeshift that would be quite as likely to go to the bottom as it would to reach the mainland.

Also, they were to have assistance in capturing the woman, or rather women, for when Momulla had learned that there was a black woman in the other camp he had insisted that she be brought along as well as the white woman.

As Kai Shang and Momulla entered their camp, it was with a realization that they no longer needed Gust. They marched straight to the tent in which they might expect to find him at that hour of the day, for though it would have been more comfortable for the entire party to remain aboard the ship, they had mutually decided that it would be safer for all concerned were they to pitch their camp ashore.

Each knew that in the heart of the others was sufficient treachery to make it unsafe for any member of the party to go ashore leaving the others in possession of the *Cowrie*, so not more than two or three men at a time were ever permitted aboard the vessel unless all the balance of the company was there too.

As the two crossed toward Gust's tent the Maori felt the edge of his long knife with one grimy, calloused thumb. The Swede would have felt far from comfortable could he have seen this significant action, or read what was passing amid the convolutions of the brown man's cruel brain.

Now it happened that Gust was at that moment in the tent occupied by the cook, and this tent stood but a few feet from his own. So that he heard the approach of Kai Shang and Momulla, though he did not, of course, dream that it had any special significance for him.

Chance had it, though, that he glanced out of the doorway of the cook's tent at the very moment that Kai Shang and Momulla approached the entrance to his, and he thought that he noted a stealthiness in their movements that comported poorly with amicable or friendly intentions, and then, just as they two slunk within the interior, Gust caught a glimpse of the long knife which Momulla the Maori was then carrying behind his back.

The Swede's eyes opened wide, and a funny little sensation

assailed the roots of his hairs. Also he turned almost white beneath his tan. Quite precipitately he left the cook's tent. He was not one who required a detailed exposition of intentions that were quite all too obvious.

As surely as though he had heard them plotting, he knew that Kai Shang and Momulla had come to take his life. The knowledge that he alone could navigate the *Cowrie* had, up to now, been sufficient assurance of his safety; but quite evidently something had occurred of which he had no knowledge that would make it quite worth the while of his coconspirators to eliminate him.

Without a pause Gust darted across the beach and into the jungle. He was afraid of the jungle; uncanny noises that were indeed frightful came forth from its recesses—the tangled mazes of the mysterious country back of the beach.

But if Gust was afraid of the jungle he was far more afraid of Kai Shang and Momulla. The dangers of the jungle were more or less problematical, while the danger that menaced him at the hands of his companions was a perfectly well-known quantity, which might be expressed in terms of a few inches of cold steel, or the coil of a light rope. He had seen Kai Shang garrotte a man at Pai-sha in a dark alleyway back of Loo Kotai's place. He feared the rope, therefore, more than he did the knife of the Maori; but he feared them both too much to remain within reach of either. Therefore he chose the pitiless jungle.

21

The Law of the Jungle

IN TARZAN'S CAMP, by dint of threats and promised rewards, the ape-man had finally succeeded in getting the hull of a large skiff almost completed. Much of the work he and Mugambi had done with their own hands in addition to furnishing the camp with meat.

Schneider, the mate, had been doing considerable grumbling, and had at last openly deserted the work and gone off into the jungle with Schmidt to hunt. He said that he wanted a rest, and Tarzan, rather than add to the unpleasantness which already made camp life almost unendurable, had permitted the two men to depart without a remonstrance.

Upon the following day, however, Schneider affected a feeling of remorse for his action, and set to work with a will upon the skiff. Schmidt also worked good-naturedly, and Lord Greystoke congratulated himself that at last the men had awakened to the necessity for the labor which was being asked of them and to their obligations to the balance of the party.

It was with a feeling of greater relief than he had experienced for many a day that he set out that noon to hunt deep in the jungle for a herd of small deer which Schneider reported that he and Schmidt had seen there the day before.

The direction in which Schneider had reported seeing the deer was toward the south-west, and to that point the ape-man swung easily through the tangled verdure of the forest.

And as he went there approached from the north a half-dozen ill-featured men who went stealthily through the jungle as go men bent upon the commission of a wicked act.

They thought that they traveled unseen; but behind them, almost from the moment they quitted their own camp, a tall man crept upon their trail. In the man's eyes were hate and fear, and a great curiosity. Why went Kai Shang and Momulla and the others thus stealthily toward the south? What did they expect to find there? Gust shook his low-browed head in perplexity. But he would know. He would follow them and learn their plans, and then if he could thwart them he would—that went without question.

At first he had thought that they searched for him; but finally his better judgment assured him that such could not be the case, since they had accomplished all they really desired by chasing him out of camp. Never would Kai Shang or Momulla go to such pains to slay him or another unless it would put money into their pockets, and as Gust had no money it was evident that they were searching for someone else.

Presently the party he trailed came to a halt. Its members concealed themselves in the foliage bordering the game trail along which they had come. Gust, that he might the better observe, clambered into the branches of a tree to the rear of them, being careful that the leafy fronds hid him from the view of his erstwhile mates.

He had not long to wait before he saw a strange white man approach carefully along the trail from the south.

At sight of the newcomer Momulla and Kai Shang arose from their places of concealment and greeted him. Gust could not overhear what passed between them. Then the man returned in the direction from which he had come.

He was Schneider. Nearing his camp he circled to the opposite side of it, and presently came running in breathlessly. Excitedly he hastened to Mugambi.

"Quick!" he cried. "Those apes of yours have caught Schmidt and will kill him if we do not hasten to his aid. You alone can call them off. Take Jones and Sullivan—you may need help—and get to him as quick as you can. Follow the game trail south for about a mile. I will remain here. I am too spent with running to go back with you," and the mate of the *Kincaid* threw himself upon the ground, panting as though he was almost done for.

Mugambi hesitated. He had been left to guard the two women. He did not know what to do, and then Jane Clayton, who had heard Schneider's story, added her pleas to those of the mate.

"Do not delay," she urged. "We shall be all right here. Mr. Schneider will remain with us. Go, Mugambi. The poor fellow must be saved."

Schmidt, who lay hidden in a bush at the edge of the camp, grinned. Mugambi, heeding the commands of his mistress, though still doubtful of the wisdom of his action, started off toward the south, with Jones and Sullivan at his heels.

No sooner had he disappeared than Schmidt rose and darted north into the jungle, and a few minutes later the face of Kai Shang of Fachan appeared at the edge of the clearing. Schneider saw the Chinaman, and motioned to him that the coast was clear.

Jane Clayton and the Mosula woman were sitting at the opening of the former's tent, their backs toward the approaching ruffians. The first intimation that either had of the presence of strangers in camp was the sudden appearance of a half-dozen ragged villains about them.

"Come!" said Kai Shang, motioning that the two arise and follow him.

Jane Clayton sprang to her feet and looked about for Schneider, only to see him standing behind the newcomers, a grin upon his face. At his side stood Schmidt. Instantly she saw that she had been made the victim of a plot.

"What is the meaning of this?" she asked, addressing the mate.

"It means that we have found a ship and that we can now escape from Jungle Island," replied the man.

"Why did you send Mugambi and the others into the jungle?" she inquired.

"They are not coming with us—only you and I, and the Mosula woman."

"Come!" repeated Kai Shang, and seized Jane Clayton's wrist.

One of the Maoris grasped the black woman by the arm, and when she would have screamed struck her across the mouth.

Mugambi raced through the jungle toward the south. Jones and Sullivan trailed far behind. For a mile he continued upon his way to the relief of Schmidt, but no signs saw he of the missing man or of any of the apes of Akut.

At last he halted and called aloud the summons which he and Tarzan had used to hail the great anthropoids. There was no response. Jones and Sullivan came up with the black warrior as the latter stood voicing his weird call. For another half-mile the black searched, calling occasionally.

Finally the truth flashed upon him, and then, like a frightened deer, he wheeled and dashed back toward camp. Arriving there, it was but a moment before full confirmation of his fears was impressed upon him. Lady Greystoke and the Mosula woman were gone. So, likewise, was Schneider.

When Jones and Sullivan joined Mugambi he would have killed them in his anger, thinking them parties to the plot; but they finally succeeded in partially convincing him that they had known nothing of it.

As they stood speculating upon the probable whereabouts of the women and their abductor, and the purpose which Schneider had in mind in taking them from camp, Tarzan of the Apes swung from the branches of a tree and crossed the clearing toward them.

His keen eyes detected at once that something was radically wrong, and when he had heard Mugambi's story his jaws clicked angrily together as he knitted his brows in thought.

What could the mate hope to accomplish by taking Jane Clayton from a camp upon a small island from which there was no escape from the vengeance of Tarzan? The ape-man could not believe the fellow such a fool, and then a slight realization of the truth dawned upon him.

Schneider would not have committed such an act unless he had been reasonably sure that there was a way by which he could quit Jungle Island with his prisoners. But why had he taken the black woman as well? There must have been others, one of whom wanted the dusky female.

"Come," said Tarzan, "there is but one thing to do now, and that is to follow their trail."

As he finished speaking a tall, ungainly figure emerged from the jungle north of the camp. He came straight toward the four men. He was an entire stranger to all of them, not one of whom had dreamed that another human being than those of their own camp dwelt upon the unfriendly shores of Jungle Island.

It was Gust. He came directly to the point.

"Your women were stolen," he said. "If you want ever to see them again, come quickly and follow me. If we do not hurry the *Cowrie* will be standing out to sea by the time we reach her anchorage."

"Who are you?" asked Tarzan. "What do you know of the theft of my wife and the black woman?"

"I heard Kai Shang and Momulla the Maori plot with two men of your camp. They had chased me from our camp, and would have killed me. Now I will get even with them. Come!"

Gust led the four men of the *Kincaid*'s camp at a rapid trot through the jungle toward the north. Would they come to the sea in time? But a few more minutes would answer the question.

And when at last the little party did break through the last of the screening foliage, and the harbour and the ocean lay before them, they realized that fate had been most cruelly unkind, for the *Cowrie* was already under sail and moving slowly out of the mouth of the harbour into the open sea.

What were they to do? Tarzan's broad chest rose and fell to the force of his pent emotions. The last blow seemed to have fallen, and if ever in all his life Tarzan of the Apes had had occasion to abandon hope it was now that he saw the ship bearing his wife to some frightful fate moving gracefully over the rippling water, so very near and yet so hideously far away.

In silence he stood watching the vessel. He saw it turn toward the east and finally disappear around a headland on its way he knew not whither. Then he dropped upon his haunches and buried his face in his hands.

It was after dark that the five men returned to the camp on the east shore. The night was hot and sultry. No slightest breeze ruffled the foliage of the trees or rippled the mirror-like surface of the ocean. Only a gentle swell rolled softly in upon the beach.

Never had Tarzan seen the great Atlantic so ominously at peace. He was standing at the edge of the beach gazing out to sea in the direction of the mainland, his mind filled with sorrow and hopelessness, when from the jungle close behind the camp came the uncanny wail of a panther.

There was a familiar note in the weird cry, and almost mechanically Tarzan turned his head and answered. A moment later the tawny figure of Sheeta slunk out into the half-light of the beach. There was no moon, but the sky was brilliant with stars. Silently the savage brute came to the side of the man. It had been long since Tarzan had seen his old fighting companion, but the soft purr was sufficient to assure him that the animal still recalled the bonds which had united them in the past.

The ape-man let his fingers fall upon the beast's coat, and as Sheeta pressed close against his leg he caressed and fondled the wicked head while his eyes continued to search the blackness of the waters.

Presently he started. What was that? He strained his eyes into the night. Then he turned and called aloud to the men smoking upon their blankets in the camp. They came running to his side; but Gust hesitated when he saw the nature of Tarzan's companion.

"Look!" cried Tarzan. "A light! A ship's light! It must be the *Cowrie*. They are becalmed." And then with an exclamation of renewed hope, "We can reach them! The skiff will carry us easily."

Gust demurred. "They are well armed," he warned. "We could not take the ship—just five of us."

"There are six now," replied Tarzan, pointing to Sheeta, "and we can have more still in a half-hour. Sheeta is the equivalent of twenty men, and the few others I can bring will add full a hundred to our fighting strength. You do not know them."

The ape-man turned and raised his head toward the jungle, while there pealed from his lips, time after time, the fearsome cry of the bull-ape who would summon his fellows.

Presently from the jungle came an answering cry, and then another and another. Gust shuddered. Among what sort of creatures had fate thrown him? Were not Kai Shang and Momulla to be preferred to this great white giant who stroked a panther and called to the beasts of the jungle?

In a few minutes the apes of Akut came crashing through the underbrush and out upon the beach, while in the meantime the five men had been struggling with the unwieldy bulk of the skiff's hull.

By dint of Herculean efforts they had managed to get it to the water's edge. The oars from the two small boats of the *Kincaid*, which had been washed away by an offshore wind the very night that the party had landed, had been in use to support the canvas of the sailcloth tents. These were hastily requisitioned, and by the time Akut and his followers came down to the water all was ready for embarkation.

Once again the hideous crew entered the service of their master, and without question took up their places in the skiff. The four men, for Gust could not be prevailed upon to accompany the party, fell to the oars, using them paddle-wise, while some of the apes followed their example, and presently the ungainly skiff was moving quietly out to sea in the direction of the light which rose and fell gently with the swell.

A sleepy sailor kept a poor vigil upon the *Cowrie*'s deck, while in the cabin below Schneider paced up and down arguing with Jane Clayton. The woman had found a revolver in a table drawer in the room in which she had been locked, and now she kept the mate of the *Kincaid* at bay with the weapon.

The Mosula woman kneeled behind her, while Schneider paced up and down before the door, threatening and pleading and promising, but all to no avail. Presently from the deck above came a shout of warning and a shot. For an instant Jane Clayton relaxed her vigilance, and turned her eyes toward the cabin skylight. Simultaneously Schneider was upon her.

The first intimation the watch had that there was another craft within a thousand miles of the *Cowrie* came when he saw the head and shoulders of a man poked over the ship's side. Instantly the fellow sprang to his feet with a cry and levelled his revolver at the intruder. It was his cry and the subsequent report of the revolver which threw Jane Clayton off her guard.

Upon deck the quiet of fancied security soon gave place to the wildest pandemonium. The crew of the *Cowrie* rushed above armed with revolvers, cutlasses, and the long knives that many of them habitually wore; but the alarm had come too late. Already the beasts of Tarzan were upon the ship's deck, with Tarzan and the two men of the *Kincaid*'s crew.

In the face of the frightful beasts the courage of the mutineers wavered and broke. Those with revolvers fired a few scattering shots and then raced for some place of supposed safety. Into the shrouds went some; but the apes of Akut were more at home there than they.

Screaming with terror the Maoris were dragged from their lofty perches. The beasts, uncontrolled by Tarzan who had gone in search of Jane, loosed the full fury of their savage natures upon the unhappy wretches who fell into their clutches.

Sheeta, in the meanwhile, had felt his great fangs sink into but a single jugular. For a moment he mauled the corpse, and then he spied Kai Shang darting down the companionway toward his cabin.

With a shrill scream Sheeta was after him—a scream which awoke an almost equally uncanny cry in the throat of the terror-stricken Chinaman.

But Kai Shang reached his cabin a fraction of a second ahead of the panther, and leaping within slammed the door—just too late. Sheeta's great body hurtled against it before the catch engaged, and a moment later Kai Shang was gibbering and shrieking in the back of an upper berth.

Lightly Sheeta sprang after his victim, and presently the wicked days of Kai Shang of Fachan were ended, and Sheeta was gorging himself upon tough and stringy flesh.

A moment scarcely had elapsed after Schneider leaped upon Jane Clayton and wrenched the revolver from her hand, when the door of the cabin opened and a tall and half-naked white man stood framed within the portal.

Silently he leaped across the cabin. Schneider felt sinewy fingers at his throat. He turned his head to see who had attacked him, and his eyes went wide when he saw the face of the ape-man close above his own.

Grimly the fingers tightened upon the mate's throat. He tried to scream, to plead, but no sound came forth. His eyes protruded as he struggled for freedom, for breath, for life.

Jane Clayton seized her husband's hands and tried to drag them from the throat of the dying man; but Tarzan only shook his head.

"Not again," he said quietly. "Before have I permitted scoundrels to live, only to suffer and to have you suffer for my mercy. This time we shall make sure of one scoundrel—sure that he will never again harm us or another," and with a sudden wrench he twisted the neck of the perfidious mate until there was a sharp crack, and the man's body lay limp and motionless in the ape-man's grasp. With a gesture of disgust Tarzan tossed the corpse aside. Then he returned to the deck, followed by Jane and the Mosula woman.

The battle there was over. Schmidt and Momulla and two others alone remained alive of all the company of the *Cowrie*, for they had found sanctuary in the forecastle. The others had died, horribly, and as they deserved, beneath the fangs and talons of the beasts of Tarzan, and in the morning the sun rose on a grisly sight upon the deck of the unhappy *Cowrie*; but this time the blood which stained her white planking was the blood of the guilty and not of the innocent.

Tarzan brought forth the men who had hidden in the forecastle, and without promises of immunity from punishment forced them to help work the vessel—the only alternative was immediate death.

A stiff breeze had risen with the sun, and with canvas spread the *Cowrie* set in toward Jungle Island, where a few hours later, Tarzan picked up Gust and bid farewell to Sheeta and the apes of Akut, for here he set the beasts ashore to pursue the wild and natural life they loved so well; nor did they lose a moment's time in disappearing into the cool depths of their beloved jungle.

That they knew that Tarzan was to leave them may be doubted—except possibly in the case of the more intelligent Akut, who alone of all the others remained upon the beach as the small boat drew away toward the schooner, carrying his savage lord and master from him.

And as long as their eyes could span the distance, Jane and Tarzan, standing upon the deck, saw the lonely figure of the shaggy anthropoid motionless upon the surf-beaten sands of Jungle Island.

It was three days later that the *Cowrie* fell in with H.M. sloop-of-war *Shorewater*, through whose wireless Lord Greystoke soon got in communication with London. Thus he learned that which filled his and his wife's heart with joy and thanksgiving—little Jack was safe at Lord Greystoke's town house.

It was not until they reached London that they learned the details of the remarkable chain of circumstances that had preserved the infant unharmed.

It developed that Rokoff, fearing to take the child aboard the *Kincaid* by day, had hidden it in a low den where nameless infants were harbored, intending to carry it to the steamer after dark.

His confederate and chief lieutenant, Paulvitch, true to the long years of teaching of his wily master, had at last succumbed to the treachery and greed that had always marked his superior, and, lured by the thoughts of the immense ransom that he might win by returning the child unharmed, had divulged the secret of its parentage to the woman who maintained the foundling asylum. Through her he had arranged for the substitution of another infant, knowing full well that never until it was too late would Rokoff suspect the trick that had been played upon him.

The woman had promised to keep the child until Paulvitch returned to England; but she, in turn, had been tempted to betray her trust by the lure of gold, and so had opened negotiations with Lord Greystoke's solicitors for the return of the child.

Esmeralda, the old Negro nurse whose absence on a vacation in America at the time of the abduction of little Jack had been attributed by her as the cause of the calamity, had returned and positively identified the infant.

The ransom had been paid, and within ten days of the date of his kidnapping the future Lord Greystoke, none the worse for his experience, had been returned to his father's home.

And so that last and greatest of Nikolas Rokoff's many rascalities had not only miserably miscarried through the treachery he had taught his only friend, but it had resulted in the archvillain's death, and given to Lord and Lady Greystoke a peace of mind that neither could ever have felt so long as the vital spark remained in the body of the Russian and his malign mind was free to formulate new atrocities against them.

Rokoff was dead, and while the fate of Paulvitch was unknown, they had every reason to believe that he had succumbed to the dangers of the jungle where last they had seen him—the malicious tool of his master.

And thus, in so far as they might know, they were to be freed forever from the menace of these two men—the only enemies which Tarzan of the Apes ever had had occasion to fear, because they struck at him cowardly blows, through those he loved.

It was a happy family party that were reunited in Greystoke House the day that Lord Greystoke and his lady landed upon English soil from the deck of the *Shorewater*.

Accompanying them were Mugambi and the Mosula woman whom he had found in the bottom of the canoe that night upon the bank of the little tributary of the Ugambi.

The woman had preferred to cling to her new lord and master rather than return to the marriage she had tried to escape.

Tarzan had proposed to them that they might find a home upon his vast African estates in the land of the Waziri, where they were to be sent as soon as opportunity presented itself.

Possibly we shall see them all there amid the savage romance of the grim jungle and the great plains where Tarzan of the Apes loves best to be.

Who knows?

THE SON
OF TARZAN

TO
HULBERT BURROUGHS

1

THE LONG BOAT of the *Marjorie W.* was floating down the broad Ugambi with ebb tide and current. Her crew were lazily enjoying this respite from the arduous labor of rowing up stream. Three miles below them lay the *Marjorie W.* herself, quite ready to sail so soon as they should have clambered aboard and swung the long boat to its davits. Presently the attention of every man was drawn from his dreaming or his gossiping to the northern bank of the river. There, screaming at them in a cracked falsetto and with skinny arms outstretched, stood a strange apparition of a man.

"Wot the 'ell?" ejaculated one of the crew.

"A white man!" muttered the mate, and then: "Man the oars, boys, and we'll just pull over an' see what he wants."

When they came close to the shore they saw an emaciated creature with scant white locks tangled and matted. The thin, bent body was naked but for a loincloth. Tears were rolling down the sunken pock-marked cheeks. The man jabbered at them in a strange tongue.

"Rooshun," hazarded the mate. "Savvy English?" he called to the man.

He did, and in that tongue, brokenly and haltingly, as though it had been many years since he had used it, he begged them to take him with them away from this awful country. Once on board the *Marjorie W.* the stranger told his rescuers a pitiful tale of privation, hardships, and torture, extending over a period of ten years. How he happened to have come to Africa he did not tell them, leaving them to assume he had forgotten the incidents of his life prior to the frightful ordeals that had wrecked him mentally and physically. He did not even tell them his true name, and so they knew him only as Michael Sabrov, nor was there any resemblance

159

between this sorry wreck and the virile, though unprincipled, Alexander Paulvitch of old.

It had been ten years since the Russian had escaped the fate of his friend, the archfiend Rokoff, and not once, but many times during those ten years had Paulvitch cursed the fate that had given to Nikolas Rokoff death and immunity from suffering while it had meted to him the hideous terrors of an existence infinitely worse than the death that persistently refused to claim him.

Paulvitch had taken to the jungle when he had seen the beasts of Tarzan and their savage lord swarm the deck of the *Kincaid*, and in his terror lest Tarzan pursue and capture him he had stumbled on deep into the jungle, only to fall at last into the hands of one of the savage cannibal tribes that had felt the weight of Rokoff's evil temper and cruel brutality. Some strange whim of the chief of this tribe saved Paulvitch from death only to plunge him into a life of misery and torture. For ten years he had been the butt of the village, beaten and stoned by the women and children, cut and slashed and disfigured by the warriors; a victim of often recurring fevers of the most malignant variety. Yet he did not die. Smallpox laid its hideous clutches upon him, leaving him unspeakably branded with its repulsive marks. Between it and the attentions of the tribe the countenance of Paulvitch was so altered that his own mother could not have recognized in the pitiful mask he called his face a single familiar feature. A few scraggly, yellow-white locks had supplanted the thick, dark hair that had covered his head. His limbs were bent and twisted, he walked with a shuffling, unsteady gait, his body doubled forward. His teeth were gone—knocked out by his savage masters. Even his mentality was but a sorry mockery of what it once had been.

They took him aboard the *Marjorie W.*, and there they fed and nursed him. He gained a little in strength; but his appearance never altered for the better—a human derelict, battered and wrecked, they had found him; a human derelict, battered and wrecked, he would remain until death claimed him. Though still in his thirties, Paulvitch could easily have passed for eighty. Inscrutable Nature had demanded of the accomplice a greater penalty than his principal had paid.

In the mind of Paulvitch there lingered no thoughts of revenge—only a dull hatred of the man whom he and Rokoff had tried to break, and failed. There was hatred, too, of the memory of Rokoff, for Rokoff had led him into the horrors he had undergone. There was hatred of the police of a score of cities from which he had had to flee. There was hatred of law, hatred of order, hatred of everything. Every moment of the man's waking life was filled with morbid thought of hatred—he had become mentally as he was physically in outward appearance, the personification of the blighting emotion of Hate. He had little or nothing to do with the men who had rescued him. He was too weak to work and too morose for company, and so they quickly left him alone to his own devices.

The *Marjorie W.* had been chartered by a syndicate of wealthy manufacturers, equipped with a laboratory and a staff of scientists, and sent out to search for some natural product which the manufacturers who footed the bills had been importing from South America at an enormous cost. What the product was none on board the *Marjorie W.* knew except the scientists, nor is it of any moment to us, other than that it led the ship to a certain island off the coast of Africa after Paulvitch had been taken aboard.

The ship lay at anchor off the coast for several weeks. The monotony of life aboard her became trying for the crew. They went often ashore, and finally Paulvitch asked to accompany them—he too was tiring of the blighting sameness of existence upon the ship.

The island was heavily timbered. Dense jungle ran down almost to the beach. The scientists were far inland, prosecuting their search for the valuable commodity that native rumor upon the mainland had led them to believe might be found here in marketable quantity. The ship's company fished, hunted, and explored. Paulvitch shuffled up and down the beach, or lay in the shade of the great trees that skirted it. One day, as the men were gathered at a little distance inspecting the body of a panther that had fallen to the gun of one of them who had been hunting inland, Paulvitch lay sleeping beneath his tree. He was awakened by the touch of a hand upon his shoulder. With a start he sat up to see a huge, anthropoid ape squatting at his side, inspecting him intently. The Russian was thoroughly frightened. He glanced toward the sailors—they were a couple of hundred yards away. Again the ape plucked at his shoulder, jabbering plaintively. Paulvitch saw no menace in the inquiring gaze, or in the attitude of the beast. He got slowly to his feet. The ape rose at his side.

Half doubled, the man shuffled cautiously away toward the sailors. The ape moved with him, taking one of his arms. They had come almost to the little knot of men before they were seen, and by this time Paulvitch had become assured that the beast meant no harm. The animal evidently was accustomed to the association of human beings. It occurred to the Russian that the ape represented a certain considerable money value, and before they reached the sailors he had decided he should be the one to profit by it.

When the men looked up and saw the oddly paired couple shuffling toward them they were filled with amazement, and started on a run toward the two. The ape showed no sign of fear. Instead he grasped each sailor by the shoulder and peered long and earnestly into his face. Having inspected them all he returned to Paulvitch's side, disappointment written strongly upon his countenance and in his carriage.

The men were delighted with him. They gathered about, asking Paulvitch many questions, and examining his companion. The Russian told them that the ape was his—nothing further would he offer—but kept harping continually upon the same theme, "The ape is mine. The ape is mine." Tiring of Paulvitch, one of the men essayed a pleasantry. Circling about behind the ape he prodded the anthropoid in the back with a pin. Like a flash the beast wheeled upon its tormentor, and, in the brief instant of turning, the placid, friendly animal was metamorphosed to a frenzied demon of rage. The broad grin that had sat upon the sailor's face as he perpetrated his little joke froze to an expression of terror. He attempted to dodge the long arms that reached for him; but, failing, drew a long knife that hung at his belt. With a single wrench the ape tore the weapon from the man's grasp and flung it to one side, then his yellow fangs were buried in the sailor's shoulder.

With sticks and knives the man's companions fell upon the beast, while Paulvitch danced around the cursing snarling pack mumbling and screaming pleas and threats. He saw his visions of wealth rapidly dissipating before the weapons of the sailors.

The ape, however, proved no easy victim to the superior numbers that seemed fated to overwhelm him. Rising from the sailor who had precipitated the battle he shook his giant shoulders, freeing himself from two of the men that were clinging to his back, and with mighty blows of his open palms felled one after another of his attackers, leaping hither and thither with the agility of a small monkey.

The fight had been witnessed by the captain and mate who were just landing from the *Marjorie W.*, and Paulvitch saw these two now running forward with drawn revolvers while the two sailors who had brought them ashore trailed at their heels. The ape stood looking about him at the havoc he had wrought, but whether he was awaiting a renewal of the attack or was deliberating which of his foes he should exterminate first Paulvitch could not guess. What he could guess, however, was that the moment the two officers came within firing distance of the beast they would put an end to him in short order unless something were done and done quickly to prevent it. The ape had made no move to attack the Russian but even so the man was none too sure of what might happen were he to interfere with the savage beast, now thoroughly aroused to bestial rage, and with the smell of new spilled blood fresh in its nostrils. For an instant he hesitated, and then again there rose before him the dreams of affluence which this great anthropoid would doubtless turn to realities once Paulvitch had landed him safely in some great metropolis like London.

The captain was shouting to him now to stand aside that he might have a shot at the animal; but instead Paulvitch shuffled to the ape's side, and though the man's hair quivered at its roots he mastered his fear and laid hold of the ape's arm.

"Come!" he commanded, and tugged to pull the beast from among the sailors, many of whom were now sitting up in wide-eyed fright or crawling away from their conqueror upon hands and knees.

Slowly the ape permitted itself to be led to one side, nor did it show the slightest indication of a desire to harm the Russian. The captain came to a halt a few paces from the odd pair.

"Get aside, Sabrov!" he commanded. "I'll put that brute where he won't chew up any more able seamen."

"It wasn't his fault, captain," pleaded Paulvitch. "Please don't shoot him. The men started it—they attacked him first. You see, he's perfectly gentle—and he's mine—he's mine—he's mine! I won't let you kill him," he concluded, as his half-wrecked mentality pictured anew the pleasure that money would buy in London—money that he could not hope to possess without some such windfall as the ape represented.

The captain lowered his weapon. "The men started it, did they?" he repeated. "How about that?" and he turned toward the sailors who had by this time picked themselves from the ground, none of them much the worse for his experience except the fellow who had been the cause of it, and who would doubtless nurse a sore shoulder for a week or so.

"Simpson done it," said one of the men. "He stuck a pin into the monk from behind, and the monk got him—which served him bloomin' well right—an' he got the rest of us, too, for which I can't blame him, since we all jumped him to once."

The captain looked at Simpson, who sheepishly admitted the truth of the allegation, then he stepped over to the ape as though to discover for himself the sort of temper the beast possessed, but it was noticeable that he kept his revolver cocked and leveled as he did so. However, he spoke soothingly to the animal who squatted at the Russian's side looking first at one and then another of the sailors. As the captain approached him the ape half rose and waddled forward to meet him. Upon his countenance was the same strange, searching expression that had marked his scrutiny of each of the sailors he had first encountered. He came quite close to the officer and laid a paw upon one of the man's shoulders, studying his face intently for a long moment, then came the expression of disappointment accompanied by what was almost a human sigh, as he turned away to peer in the same curious fashion into the faces of the mate and the two sailors who had arrived with the officers. In each instance he sighed and passed on, returning at length to Paulvitch's side, where he squatted down once more; thereafter evincing little or no interest in any of the other men, and apparently forgetful of his recent battle with them.

When the party returned aboard the *Marjorie W.*, Paulvitch was accompanied by the ape, who seemed anxious to follow him. The captain interposed no obstacles to the arrangement, and so the great anthropoid was tacitly admitted to membership in the ship's company. Once aboard he examined each new face minutely, evincing the same disappointment in each instance that had marked his scrutiny of the others. The officers and scientists aboard often discussed the beast, but they were unable to account satisfactorily for the strange ceremony with which he greeted each new face. Had he been discovered upon the mainland, or any other place than the almost unknown island that had been his home, they would have concluded that he had formerly been a pet of man; but that theory was not tenable in the face of the isolation of his uninhabited island. He seemed continually to be searching for someone, and during the first days of the return voyage from the island he was often discovered nosing about in various parts of the ship; but after he had seen and examined each face of the ship's company, and explored every corner of the vessel he lapsed into utter indifference of all about him. Even the Russian elicited only casual interest when he brought him food. At other times the ape appeared merely to tolerate him. He never showed affection for him, or for anyone else upon the *Marjorie W.*, nor did he at any time evince any indication of the savage temper that had marked his resentment of the attack of the sailors upon him at the time that he had come among them.

Most of his time was spent in the eye of the ship scanning the horizon ahead, as though he were endowed with sufficient reason to know that the vessel was bound for some port where there would be other human beings to undergo his searching scrutiny. All in all,

Ajax, as he had been dubbed, was considered the most remarkable and intelligent ape that any one aboard the *Marjorie W.* ever had seen. Nor was his intelligence the only remarkable attribute he owned. His stature and physique were, for an ape, awe inspiring. That he was old was quite evident, but if his age had impaired his physical or mental powers in the slightest it was not apparent.

And so at length the *Marjorie W.* came to England, and there the officers and the scientists, filled with compassion for the pitiful wreck of a man they had rescued from the jungles, furnished Paulvitch with funds and bid him and his Ajax Godspeed.

Upon the dock and all through the journey to London the Russian had his hands full with Ajax. Each new face of the thousands that came within the anthropoid's ken must be carefully scrutinized, much to the horror of many of his victims; but at last, failing, apparently, to discover whom he sought, the great ape relapsed into morbid indifference, only occasionally evincing interest in a passing face.

In London, Paulvitch went directly with his prize to a certain famous animal trainer. This man was much impressed with Ajax with the result that he agreed to train him for a lion's share of the profits of exhibiting him, and in the meantime to provide for the keep of both the ape and his owner.

And so came Ajax to London, and there was forged another link in the chain of strange circumstances that were to affect the lives of many people.

2

Mr. HAROLD MOORE was a bilious-countenanced, studious young man. He took himself very seriously, and life, and his work, which latter was the tutoring of the young son of a British nobleman. He felt that his charge was not making the progress that his parents had a right to expect, and he was now conscientiously explaining this fact to the boy's mother.

"It's not that he isn't bright," he was saying, "if that were true I should have hopes of succeeding, for then I might bring to bear all my energies in overcoming his obtuseness; but the trouble is that he is exceptionally intelligent, and learns so quickly that I can find no fault in the matter of the preparation of his lessons. What concerns me, however, is that fact that he evidently takes no interest whatever in the subjects we are studying. He merely accomplishes each lesson as a task to be rid of as quickly as possible and I am sure that no lesson ever again enters his mind until the hours of study and recitation once more arrive. His sole interests seem to be feats of physical prowess and the reading of everything that he can get hold of relative to savage beasts and the lives and customs of uncivilized peoples; but particularly do stories of animals appeal to him. He will sit for hours together poring over the work of some African explorer, and upon two occasions I have found him setting up in bed at night reading Carl Hagenbeck's book on men and beasts."

The boy's mother tapped her foot nervously upon the hearth rug.

"You discourage this, of course?" she ventured.

Mr. Moore shuffled embarrassedly.

"I—ah—essayed to take the book from him," he replied, a slight flush mounting his sallow cheek, "but—ah—your son is quite muscular for one so young."

"He wouldn't let you take it?" asked the mother.

"He would not," confessed the tutor. "He was perfectly good-natured about it; but he insisted upon pretending that he was a gorilla and that I was a chimpanzee attempting to steal food from him. He leaped upon me with the most savage growls I ever heard, lifted me completely above his head, hurled me upon his bed, and after going through a pantomime indicative of choking me to death he stood upon my prostrate form and gave voice to a most fearsome shriek, which he explained was the victory cry of a bull ape. Then he carried me to the door, shoved me out into the hall, and locked me from his room."

For several minutes neither spoke again. It was the boy's mother who finally broke the silence.

"It is very necessary, Mr. Moore," she said, "that you do everything in your power to discourage this tendency in Jack, he—" but she got no further. A loud "Whoop!" from the direction of the window brought them both to their feet. The room was upon the second floor of the house, and opposite the window to which their attention had been attracted was a large tree, a branch of which spread to within a few feet of the sill. Upon this branch now they both discovered the subject of their recent conversation, a tall, well-built boy, balancing with ease upon the bending limb and uttering loud shouts of glee as he noted the terrified expressions upon the faces of his audience.

The mother and tutor both rushed toward the window but before they had crossed half the room the boy had leaped nimbly to the sill and entered the apartment with them.

" 'The wild man from Borneo has just come to town,' " he sang, dancing a species of war dance about his terrified mother and scandalized tutor, and ending by throwing his arms about the former's neck and kissing her upon either cheek.

"Oh, Mother," he cried, "there's a wonderful, educated ape being shown at one of the music halls. Willie Grimsby saw it last night. He says it can do everything but talk. It rides a bicycle, eats with knife and fork, counts up to ten, and ever so many other wonderful things, and can I go and see it too? Oh, please, Mother— please let me."

Patting the boy's cheek affectionately, the mother shook her head negatively. "No, Jack," she said, "you know I do not approve of such exhibitions."

"I don't see why not, Mother," replied the boy. "All the other fellows go and they go to the Zoo, too, and you'll never let me do even that. Anybody'd think I was a girl or—or a mollycoddle. Oh, Father," he exclaimed, as the door opened to admit a tall gray-eyed man. "Oh, Father, can't I go?"

"Go where, my son?" asked the newcomer.

"He wants to go to a music hall to see a trained ape," said the mother, looking warningly at her husband.

"Who, Ajax?" questioned the man.

The boy nodded.

"Well, I don't know that I blame you, my son," said the father, "I wouldn't mind seeing him myself. They say he is very wonderful, and that for an anthropoid he is unusually large. Let's all go, Jane—what do you say?" And he turned toward his wife, but that lady only shook her head in a most positive manner, and turning to Mr. Moore asked him if it was not time that he and Jack were in the study for the morning recitations. When the two had left she turned toward her husband.

"John," she said, "something must be done to discourage Jack's

tendency toward anything that may excite the cravings for the
savage life which I fear he has inherited from you. You know from
your own experience how strong is the call of the wild at times.
You know that often it has necessitated a stern struggle on your
part to resist the almost insane desire which occasionally over-
whelms you to plunge once again into the jungle life that claimed
you for so many years, and at the same time you know, better than
any other, how frightful a fate it would be for Jack, were the trail
to the savage jungle made either alluring or easy to him."

"I doubt if there is any danger of his inheriting a taste for jungle
life from me," replied the man, "for I cannot conceive that such a
thing may be transmitted from father to son. And sometimes, Jane,
I think that in your solicitude for his future you go a bit too far in
your restrictive measures. His love for animals—his desire, for
example, to see this trained ape—is only natural in a healthy,
normal boy of his age. Just because he wants to see Ajax is no
indication that he would wish to marry an ape, and even should he,
far be it from you Jane to have the right to cry 'shame!' " and John
Clayton, Lord Greystoke, put an arm about his wife, laughing
good-naturedly down into her upturned face before he bent his
head and kissed her. Then, more seriously, he continued: "You
have never told Jack anything concerning my early life, nor have
you permitted me to, and in this I think that you have made a mistake. Had I been able to tell him of the experiences of Tarzan of
the Apes I could doubtless have taken much of the glamour and
romance from jungle life that naturally surrounds it in the minds of
those who have had no experience of it. He might then have prof-
ited by my experience, but now, should the jungle lust ever claim
him, he will have nothing to guide him but his own impulses, and
I know how powerful these may be in the wrong direction at
times."

But Lady Greystoke only shook her head as she had a hundred
other times when the subject had claimed her attention in the past.

"No, John," she insisted, "I shall never give my consent to the
implanting in Jack's mind of any suggestion of the savage life
which we both wish to preserve him from."

It was evening before the subject was again referred to and then
it was raised by Jack himself. He had been sitting, curled in a large
chair, reading, when he suddenly looked up and addressed his
father.

"Why," he asked, coming directly to the point, "can't I go and
see Ajax?"

"Your mother does not approve," replied his father.

"Do you?"

"That is not the question," evaded Lord Greystoke. "It is enough that your mother objects."

"I am going to see him," announced the boy, after a few moments of thoughtful silence. "I am not different from Willie Grimsby, or any other of the fellows who have been to see him. It did not harm them and it will not harm me. I could go without telling you; but I would not do that. So I tell you now, beforehand, that I am going to see Ajax."

There was nothing disrespectful or defiant in the boy's tone or manner. His was merely a dispassionate statement of facts. His father could scarce repress either a smile or a show of the admiration he felt for the manly course his son had pursued.

"I admire your candor, Jack," he said. "Permit me to be candid, as well. If you go to see Ajax without permission, I shall punish you. I have never inflicted corporal punishment upon you, but I warn you that should you disobey your mother's wishes in this instance, I shall."

"Yes, sir," replied the boy; and then: "I shall tell you, sir, when I have been to see Ajax."

Mr. Moore's room was next to that of his youthful charge, and it was the tutor's custom to have a look into the boy's each evening as the former was about to retire. This evening he was particularly careful not to neglect his duty, for he had just come from a conference with the boy's father and mother in which it had been impressed upon him that he must exercise the greatest care to prevent Jack visiting the music hall where Ajax was being shown. So, when he opened the boy's door at about half after nine, he was greatly excited, though not entirely surprised to find the future Lord Greystoke fully dressed for the street and about to crawl from his open bed room window.

Mr. Moore made a rapid sprint across the apartment; but the waste of energy was unnecessary, for when the boy heard him within the chamber and realized that he had been discovered he turned back as though to relinquish his planned adventure.

"Where were you going?" panted the excited Mr. Moore.

"I am going to see Ajax," replied the boy, quietly.

"I am astonished," cried Mr. Moore; but a moment later he was infinitely more astonished, for the boy, approaching close to him, suddenly seized him about the waist, lifted him from his feet and threw him face downward upon the bed, shoving his face deep into a soft pillow.

"Be quiet," admonished the victor, "or I'll choke you."

Mr. Moore struggled; but his efforts were in vain. Whatever else Tarzan of the Apes may or may not have handed down to his son he had at least bequeathed him almost as marvelous a physique as he himself had possessed at the same age. The tutor was as putty in the boy's hands. Kneeling upon him, Jack tore strips from a sheet and bound the man's hands behind his back. Then he rolled him over and stuffed a gag of the same material between his teeth, securing it with a strip wound about the back of his victim's head. All the while he talked in a low, conversational tone.

"I am Waja, chief of the Waji," he explained, "and you are Mohammed Dubn, the Arab sheik, who would murder my people and steal my ivory," and he dexterously trussed Mr. Moore's hobbled ankles up behind to meet his hobbled wrists. "Ah—ha! Villain! I have you in me power at last. I go; but I shall return!" And the son of Tarzan skipped across the room, slipped through the open window, and slid to liberty by way of the down spout from an eaves trough.

Mr. Moore wriggled and struggled about the bed. He was sure that he should suffocate unless aid came quickly. In his frenzy of terror he managed to roll off the bed. The pain and shock of the fall jolted him back to something like sane consideration of his plight. Where before he had been unable to think intelligently because of the hysterical fear that had claimed him he now lay quietly searching for some means of escape from his dilemma. It finally occurred to him that the room in which Lord and Lady Greystoke had been sitting when he left them was directly beneath that in which he lay upon the floor. He knew that some time had elapsed since he had come upstairs and that they might be gone by this time, for it seemed to him that he had struggled about the bed, in his efforts to free himself, for an eternity. But the best that he could do was to attempt to attract attention from below, and so, after many failures, he managed to work himself into a position in which he could tap the toe of his boot against the floor. This he proceeded to do at short intervals, until, after what seemed a very long time, he was rewarded by hearing footsteps ascending the stairs, and presently a knock upon the door. Mr. Moore tapped vigorously with his toe—he could not reply in any other way. The knock was repeated after a moment's silence. Again Mr. Moore tapped. Would they never open the door! Laboriously he rolled in the direction of succor. If he could get his back against the door he could then tap upon its base, when surely he must be heard. The knocking was repeated a little louder, and finally a voice called: "Mr. Jack!"

It was one of the house men—Mr. Moore recognized the fellow's voice. He came near to bursting a blood vessel in an endeavor to scream "come in" through the stifling gag. After a moment the man knocked again, quite loudly and again called the boy's name. Receiving no reply he turned the knob, and at the same instant a sudden recollection filled the tutor anew with numbing terror—he had, himself, locked the door behind him when he had entered the room.

He heard the servant try the door several times and then depart. Upon which Mr. Moore swooned.

In the meantime Jack was enjoying to the full the stolen pleasures of the music hall. He had reached the temple of mirth just as Alex's act was commencing, and having purchased a box seat was now leaning breathlessly over the rail watching every move of the great ape, his eyes wide in wonder. The trainer was not slow to note the boy's handsome, eager face, and as one of Ajax's biggest hits consisted in an entry to one or more boxes during his performance, ostensibly in search of a long-lost relative, as the trainer explained, the man realized the effectiveness of sending him into the box with the handsome boy, who, doubtless, would be terror stricken by proximity to the shaggy, powerful beast.

When the time came, therefore, for the ape to return from the wings in reply to an encore the trainer directed its attention to the boy who chanced to be the sole occupant of the box in which he sat. With a spring the huge anthropoid leaped from the stage to the boy's side; but if the trainer had looked for a laughable scene of fright he was mistaken. A broad smile lighted the boy's features as he laid his hand upon the shaggy arm of his visitor. The ape, grasping the boy by either shoulder, peered long and earnestly into his face, while the latter stroked his head and talked to him in a low voice.

Never had Ajax devoted so long a time to an examination of another as he did in this instance. He seemed troubled and not a little excited, jabbering and mumbling to the boy, and now caressing him, as the trainer had never seen him caress a human being before. Presently he clambered over into the box with him and snuggled down close to the boy's side. The audience was delighted; but they were still more delighted when the trainer, the period of his act having elapsed, attempted to persuade Ajax to leave the box. The ape would not budge. The manager, becoming excited at the delay, urged the trainer to greater haste, but when the latter entered the box to drag away the reluctant Ajax he was met by bared fangs and menacing growls.

The audience was delirious with joy. They cheered the ape. They cheered the boy, and they hooted and jeered at the trainer and the manager, which luckless individual had inadvertently shown himself and attempted to assist the trainer.

Finally, reduced to desperation and realizing that this show of mutiny upon the part of his valuable possession might render the animal worthless for exhibition purposes in the future if not immediately subdued, the trainer had hastened to his dressing room and procured a heavy whip. With this he now returned to the box; but when he had threatened Ajax with it but once he found himself facing two infuriated enemies instead of one, for the boy had leaped to his feet, and seizing a chair was standing ready at the ape's side to defend his new found friend. There was no longer a smile upon his handsome face. In his gray eyes was an expression which gave the trainer pause, and beside him stood the giant anthropoid growling and ready.

What might have happened, but for a timely interruption, may only be surmised; but that the trainer would have received a severe mauling, if nothing more, was clearly indicated by the attitudes of the two who faced him.

It was a pale-faced man who rushed into the Greystoke library to announce that he had found Jack's door locked and had been able to obtain no response to his repeated knocking and calling other than a strange tapping and the sound of what might have been a body moving about upon the floor.

Four steps at a time John Clayton took the stairs that led to the floor above. His wife and the servant hurried after him. Once he called his son's name in a loud voice; but receiving no reply he launched his great weight, backed by all the undiminished power of his giant muscles, against the heavy door. With a snapping of iron butts and a splintering of wood the obstacle burst inward.

At its foot lay the body of the unconscious Mr. Moore, across whom it fell with a resounding thud. Through the opening leaped Tarzan, and a moment later the room was flooded with light from a dozen electric bulbs.

It was several minutes before the tutor was discovered, so completely had the door covered him; but finally he was dragged forth, his gag and bonds cut away, and a liberal application of cold water had hastened returning consciousness.

"Where is Jack?" was John Clayton's first question, and then, "Who did this?" as the memory of Rokoff and the fear of a second abduction seized him.

Slowly Mr. Moore staggered to his feet. His gaze wandered about the room. Gradually he collected his scattered wits. The details of his recent harrowing experience returned to him.

"I tender my resignation, sir, to take effect at once," were his first words. "You do not need a tutor for your son—what he needs is a wild animal trainer."

"But where is he?" cried Lady Greystoke.

"He has gone to see Ajax."

It was with difficulty that Tarzan restrained a smile, and after satisfying himself that the tutor was more scared than injured, he ordered his closed car around and departed in the direction of a certain well-known music hall.

3

As THE TRAINER, with raised lash, hesitated an instant at the entrance to the box where the boy and the ape confronted him, a tall broad-shouldered man pushed past him and entered. As his eyes fell upon the newcomer a slight flush mounted the boy's cheeks.

"Father!" he exclaimed.

The ape gave one look at the English lord, and then leaped toward him, calling out in excited jabbering. The man, his eyes going wide in astonishment, stopped as though turned to stone.

"Akut!" he cried.

The boy looked, bewildered, from the ape to his father, and from his father to the ape. The trainer's jaw dropped as he listened to what followed, for from the lips of the Englishman flowed the gutterals of an ape that were answered in kind by the huge anthropoid that now clung to him.

And from the wings a hideously bent and disfigured old man watched the tableau in the box, his pock-marked features working spasmodically in varying expressions that might have marked every sensation in the gamut from pleasure to terror.

"Long have I looked for you, Tarzan," said Akut. "Now that I have found you I shall come to your jungle and live there always."

The man stroked the beast's head. Through his mind there was running rapidly a train of recollection that carried him far into the depths of the primeval African forest where this huge, man-like beast had fought shoulder to shoulder with him years before. He saw the black Mugambi wielding his deadly knob-stick, and beside them, with bared fangs and bristling whiskers, Sheeta the terrible; and pressing close behind savage and the savage panther, the hideous apes of Akut. The man sighed. Strong within him surged the jungle lust that he had thought dead. Ah! if he could go back even for a brief month of it, to feel again the brush of leafy branches against his naked hide; to smell the musty rot of dead vegetation—frankincense and myrrh to the jungle born; to sense the noiseless coming of the great carnivora upon his trail; to hunt and to be hunted; to kill! The picture was alluring. And then came another picture—a sweet-faced woman, still young and beautiful; friends; a home; a son. He shrugged his giant shoulders.

"It cannot be, Akut," he said, "but if you would return, I shall see that it is done. You could not be happy here—I may not be happy there."

The trainer stepped forward. The ape bared his fangs, growling.

"Go with him, Akut," said Tarzan of the Apes. "I will come and see you tomorrow."

The beast moved sullenly to the trainer's side. The latter, at John Clayton's request, told where they might be found. Tarzan turned toward his son.

"Come!" he said, and the two left the theater. Neither spoke for several minutes after they had entered the limousine. It was the boy who broke the silence.

"The ape knew you," he said, "and you spoke together in the ape's tongue. How did the ape know you, and how did you learn his language?"

And then, briefly and for the first time, Tarzan of the Apes told his son of his early life—of the birth in the jungle, of the death of his parents, and of how Kala, the great she-ape, had suckled and raised him from infancy almost to manhood. He told him, too, of the dangers and the horrors of the jungle; of the great beasts that stalked one by day and by night; of the periods of drought, and of the cataclysmic rains; of hunger; of cold; of intense heat; of nakedness and fear and suffering. He told him of all those things that seem most horrible to the creature of civilization in the hope that the knowledge of them might expunge from the lad's mind any inherent desire for the jungle. Yet they were the very things that made the memory of the jungle what it was to Tarzan—that made up the composite jungle life he loved. And in the telling he forgot one thing—the principal thing—that the boy at his side, listening with eager ears, was the son of Tarzan of the Apes.

After the boy had been tucked away in bed—and without the threatened punishment—John Clayton told his wife of the events of the evening, and that he had at last acquainted the boy with the facts of his jungle life. The mother, who had long foreseen that her son must some time know of those frightful years during which his father had roamed the jungle, a naked, savage beast of prey, only shook her head, hoping against hope that the lure she knew was still strong in the father's breast had not been transmitted to his son.

Tarzan visited Akut the following day, but though Jack begged to be allowed to accompany him he was refused. This time Tarzan saw the pock-marked old owner of the ape, whom he did not recognize as the wily Paulvitch of former days. Tarzan, influenced by Akut's pleadings, broached the question of the ape's purchase; but Paulvitch would not name any price, saying that he would consider the matter.

When Tarzan returned home Jack was all excitement to hear the details of his visit, and finally suggested that his father buy the ape and bring it home. Lady Greystoke was horrified at the suggestion. The boy was insistent. Tarzan explained that he had wished to purchase Akut and return him to his jungle home, and to this the mother assented. Jack asked to be allowed to visit the ape, but again he was met with flat refusal. He had the address, however, which the trainer had given his father, and two days later he found the opportunity to elude his new tutor—who had replaced the terrified Mr. Moore—and after a considerable search through a section of London which he had never before visited, he found the smelly little quarters of the pock-marked old man. The old fellow himself replied to his knocking, and when he stated that he had come to see Ajax, opened the door and admitted him to the little room which he and the great ape occupied. In former years Paulvitch had been a fastidious scoundrel; but ten years of hideous life among the cannibals of Africa had eradicated the last vestige of niceness from his habits. His apparel was wrinkled and soiled. His hands were unwashed, his few straggling locks uncombed. His room was a jumble of filthy disorder. As the boy entered he saw the great ape squatting upon the bed, the coverlets of which were a tangled wad of filthy blankets and ill-smelling quilts. At sight of the youth the ape leaped to the floor and shuffled forward. The man, not recognizing his visitor and fearing that the ape meant mischief, stepped between them, ordering the ape back to the bed.

"He will not hurt me," cried the boy. "We are friends, and before, he was my father's friend. They knew one another in the jungle. My father is Lord Greystoke. He does not know that I have come here. My mother forbid my coming; but I wished to see Ajax, and I will pay you if you will let me come here often and see him."

At the mention of the boy's identity Paulvitch's eyes narrowed. Since he had first seen Tarzan again from the wings of the theater there had been forming in his deadened brain the beginnings of a desire for revenge. It is a characteristic of the weak and criminal to attribute to others the misfortunes that are the result of their own wickedness, and so now it was that Paulvitch was slowly recalling the events of his past life and as he did so laying at the door of the man whom he and Rokoff had so assiduously attempted to ruin and murder all the misfortunes that had befallen him in the failure of their various schemes against their intended victim.

He saw at first no way in which he could, with safety to himself, wreak vengeance upon Tarzan through the medium of Tarzan's son; but that great possibilities for revenge lay in the boy was apparent to him, and so he determined to cultivate the lad in the hope that fate would play into his hands in some way in the future. He told the boy all that he knew of his father's past life in the jungle and when he found that the boy had been kept in ignorance of all these things for so many years, and that he had been forbidden visiting the zoological gardens; that he had had to bind and gag his tutor to find an opportunity to come to the music hall and see Ajax, he guessed immediately the nature of the great fear that lay in the hearts of the boy's parents—that he might crave the jungle as his father had craved it.

And so Paulvitch encouraged the boy to come and see him often, and always he played upon the lad's craving for tales of the savage world with which Paulvitch was all too familiar. He left him alone with Akut much, and it was not long until he was surprised to learn that the boy could make the great beast understand him—that he had actually learned many of the words of the primitive language of the anthropoids.

During this period Tarzan came several times to visit Paulvitch. He seemed anxious to purchase Ajax, and at last he told the man frankly that he was prompted not only by a desire upon his part to return the beast to the liberty of his native jungle; but also because his wife feared that in some way her son might learn the whereabouts of the ape and through his attachment for the beast become imbued with the roving instinct which, as Tarzan explained to Paulvitch, had so influenced his own life.

The Russian could scarce repress a smile as he listened to Lord Greystoke's words, since scarce a half hour had passed since the future Lord Greystoke had been sitting upon the disordered bed jabbering away to Ajax with all the fluency of a born ape.

It was during this interview that a plan occurred to Paulvitch, and as a result of it he agreed to accept a certain fabulous sum for the ape, and upon receipt of the money to deliver the beast to a vessel that was sailing south from Dover for Africa two days later. He had a double purpose in accepting Clayton's offer. Primarily, the money consideration influenced him strongly, as the ape was no longer a source of revenue to him, having consistently refused to perform upon the stage after having discovered Tarzan. It was as though the beast had suffered himself to be brought from his jungle home and exhibited before thousands of curious spectators for the sole purpose of searching out his long lost friend and master, and, having found him, considered further mingling with the common herd of humans unnecessary. However that may be, the fact remained that no amount of persuasion could influence him even to show himself upon the music hall stage, and upon the single occasion that the trainer attempted force the results were such that the unfortunate man considered himself lucky to have escaped with his life. All that saved him was the accidental presence of Jack Clayton, who had been permitted to visit the animal in the dressing room reserved for him at the music hall, and had immediately interfered when he saw that the savage beast meant serious mischief.

And after the money consideration, strong in the heart of the Russian was the desire for revenge, which had been growing with constant brooding over the failures and miseries of his life, which he attributed to Tarzan; the latest, and by no means the least, of which was Ajax's refusal to longer earn money for him. The ape's refusal he traced directly to Tarzan, finally convincing himself that the ape-man had instructed the great anthropoid to refuse to go upon the stage.

Paulvitch's naturally malign disposition was aggravated by the weakening and warping of his mental and physical faculties through torture and privation. From cold, calculating, highly intelligent perversity it had deteriorated into the indiscriminating, dangerous menace of the mentally defective. His plan, however, was sufficiently cunning to at least cast a doubt upon the assertion that his mentality was wandering. It assured him first of the competence which Lord Greystoke had promised to pay him for the deportation of the ape, and then of revenge upon his benefactor through the son he idolized. That part of his scheme was crude and brutal—it lacked the refinement of torture that had marked the master strokes of the Paulvitch of old, when he had worked with that virtuoso of villainy, Nikolas Rokoff—but it at least assured Paulvitch of immunity from responsibility, placing that upon the ape, who would thus also be punished for his refusal longer to support the Russian.

Everything played with fiendish unanimity into Paulvitch's hands. As chance would have it, Tarzan's son overheard his father relating to the boy's mother the steps he was taking to return Akut safely to his jungle home, and having overheard he begged them to bring the ape home that he might have him for a play-fellow. Tarzan would not have been averse to this plan; but Lady Greystoke was horrified at the very thought of it. Jack pleaded with his mother; but all unavailingly. She was obdurate, and at last the lad appeared to acquiesce in his mother's decision that the ape must be returned to Africa and the boy to school, from which he had been absent on vacation.

He did not attempt to visit Paulvitch's room again that day, but instead busied himself in other ways. He had always been well supplied with money, so that when necessity demanded he had no difficulty in collecting several hundred pounds. Some of this money he invested in various strange purchases which he managed to smuggle into the house, undetected, when he returned late in the afternoon.

The next morning, after giving his father time to precede him and conclude his business with Paulvitch, the lad hastened to the Russian's room. Knowing nothing of the man's true character the boy dared not take him fully into his confidence for fear that the old fellow would not only refuse to aid him, but would report the whole affair to his father. Instead, he simply asked permission to take Ajax to Dover. He explained that it would relieve the old man of a tiresome journey, as well as placing a number of pounds in his pocket, for the lad purposed paying the Russian well.

"You see," he went on, "there will be no danger of detection since I am supposed to be leaving on an afternoon train for school. Instead I will come here after they have left me on board the train. Then I can take Ajax to Dover, you see, and arrive at school only a day late. No one will be the wiser, no harm will be done, and I shall have had an extra day with Ajax before I lose him forever."

The plan fitted perfectly with that which Paulvitch had in mind. Had he known what further the boy contemplated he would doubtless have entirely abandoned his own scheme of revenge and aided the boy whole heartedly in the consummation of the lad's, which would have been better for Paulvitch, could he have but read the future but a few short hours ahead.

That afternoon Lord and Lady Greystoke bid their son goodbye and saw him safely settled in a first-class compartment of the railway carriage that would set him down at school in a few hours. No sooner had they left him, however, than he gathered his bags together, descended from the compartment and sought a cab stand outside the station. Here he engaged a cabby to take him to the Russian's address. It was dusk when he arrived. He found Paulvitch awaiting him. The man was pacing the floor nervously. The ape was tied with a stout cord to the bed. It was the first time that Jack had ever seen Ajax thus secured. He looked questioningly at Paulvitch. The man, mumbling, explained that he believed the animal had guessed that he was to be sent away and he feared he would attempt to escape.

Paulvitch carried another piece of cord in his hand. There was a noose in one end of it which he was continually playing with. He walked back and forth, up and down the room. His pock-marked features were working horribly as he talked silent to himself. The boy had never seen him thus—it made him uneasy. At last Paulvitch stopped on the opposite side of the room, far from the ape.

"Come here," he said to the lad. "I will show you how to secure the ape should he show signs of rebellion during the trip."

The lad laughed. "It will not be necessary," he replied. "Ajax will do whatever I tell him to do."

The old man stamped his foot angrily. "Come here, as I tell you," he repeated. "If you do not do as I say you shall not accompany the ape to Dover—I will take no chances upon his escaping."

Still smiling, the lad crossed the room and stood before the Russian.

"Turn around, with your back toward me," directed the latter, "that I may show you how to bind him quickly."

The boy did as he was bid, placing his hands behind him when Paulvitch told him to do so. Instantly the old man slipped the running noose over one of the lad's wrists, took a couple of half hitches about his other wrist, and knotted the cord.

The moment that the boy was secured the attitude of the man changed. With an angry oath he wheeled his prisoner about, tripped him and hurled him violently to the floor, leaping upon his breast as he fell. From the bed the ape growled and struggled with his bonds. The boy did not cry out—a trait inherited from his savage sire whom long years in the jungle following the death of his foster mother, Kala the great ape, had taught that there was none to come to the succor of the fallen.

Paulvitch's fingers sought the lad's throat. He grinned down horribly into the face of his victim.

"Your father ruined me," he mumbled. "This will pay him. He will think that the ape did it. I will tell him that the ape did it. That I left him alone for a few minutes, and that you sneaked in and the ape killed you. I will throw your body upon the bed after I have choked the life from you, and when I bring your father he will see the ape squatting over it," and the twisted fiend cackled in gloating laughter. His fingers closed upon the boy's throat.

Behind them the growling of the maddened beast reverberated against the walls of the little room. The boy paled, but no other sign of fear or panic showed upon his countenance. He was the son of Tarzan. The fingers tightened their grip upon his throat. It was with difficulty that he breathed, gaspingly. The ape lunged against the stout cord that held him. Turning, he wrapped the cord about his hands, as a man might have done, and surged heavily backward. The great muscles stood out beneath his shaggy hide. There was a rending as of splintered wood—the cord held, but a portion of the footboard of the bed came away.

At the sound Paulvitch looked up. His hideous face went white with terror—the ape was free.

With a single bound the creature was upon him. The man shrieked. The brute wrenched him from the body of the boy. Great fingers sunk into the man's flesh. Yellow fangs gaped close to his throat—he struggled, futilely—and when they closed, the soul of Paulvitch passed into the keeping of the demons who had long been awaiting it.

The boy struggled to his feet, assisted by Akut. For two hours under the instructions of the former the ape worked upon the knots that secured his friend's wrists. Finally they gave up their secret, and the boy was free. Then he opened one of his bags and drew forth some garments. His plans had been well made. He did not consult the beast, which did all that he directed. Together they slunk from the house, but no casual observer might have noted that one of them was an ape.

4

THE KILLING OF the friendless old Russian, Michael Sabrov, by his great trained ape, was a matter for newspaper comment for a few days. Lord Greystoke read of it, and while taking special precautions not to permit his name to become connected with the affair, kept himself well posted as to the police search for the anthropoid.

As was true of the general public, his chief interest in the matter centered about the mysterious disappearance of the slayer. Or at least this was true until he learned, several days subsequent to the tragedy, that his son Jack had not reported at the public school en route for which they had seen him safely ensconced in a railway carriage. Even then the father did not connect the disappearance of his son with the mystery surrounding the whereabouts of the ape. Nor was it until a month later that careful investigation revealed the fact that the boy had left the train before it pulled out of the station at London, and the cab driver had been found who had driven him to the address of the old Russian, that Tarzan of the Apes realized that Akut had in some way been connected with the disappearance of the boy.

Beyond the moment that the cab driver had deposited his fare beside the curb in front of the house in which the Russian had been quartered there was no clue. No one had seen either the boy or the ape from that instant—at least no one who still lived. The proprietor of the house identified the picture of the lad as that of one who had been a frequent visitor in the room of the old man. Aside from this he knew nothing. And there, at the door of a grimy, old building in the slums of London, the searchers came to a blank wall—baffled.

The day following the death of Paulvitch a youth, accompanying his invalid grandmother, boarded a steamer at Dover. The old lady was heavily veiled, and so weakened by age and sickness that she had to be wheeled aboard the vessel in an invalid chair.

The boy would permit none but himself to wheel her, and with his own hands assisted her from the chair to the interior of their stateroom—and that was the last that was seen of the old lady by the ship's company until the pair disembarked. The boy even insisted upon doing the work of their cabin steward, since, as he explained, his grandmother was suffering from a nervous disposition that made the presence of strangers extremely distasteful to her.

Outside the cabin—and none there was aboard who knew what he did in the cabin—the lad was just as any other healthy, normal English boy might have been. He mingled with his fellow passengers, became a prime favorite with the officers, and struck up numerous friendships among the common sailors. He was generous and unaffected, yet carried an air of dignity and strength of character that inspired his many new friends with admiration as well as affection for him.

Among the passengers there was an American named Condon, a noted blackleg and crook who was "wanted" in a half dozen of the larger cities of the United States. He had paid little attention to the boy until on one occasion he had seen him accidentally display a roll of banknotes. From then on Condon cultivated the youthful Briton. He learned, easily, that the boy was traveling alone with his invalid grandmother, and that their destination was a small port on the west coast of Africa, a little below the equator; that their name was Billings, and that they had no friends in the little settlement for which they were bound. Upon the point of their purpose in visiting the place Condon found the boy reticent, and so he did not push the matter—he had learned all that he cared to know as it was.

Several times Condon attempted to draw the lad into a card game; but his victim was not interested, and the black looks of several of the other men passengers decided the American to find other means of transferring the boy's bank roll to his own pocket.

At last came the day that the steamer dropped anchor in the lee of a wooded promontory where a score or more of sheet-iron shacks making an unsightly blot upon the fair face of nature proclaimed the fact that civilization had set its heel. Straggling upon the outskirts were the thatched huts of natives, picturesque in their primeval savagery, harmonizing with the background of tropical jungle and accentuating the squalid hideousness of the white man's pioneer architecture.

The boy, leaning over the rail, was looking far beyond the man-made town deep into the God-made jungle. A little shiver of anticipation tingled his spine, and then, quite without volition, he found himself gazing into the loving eyes of his mother and the strong face of the father which mirrored, beneath its masculine strength, a love no less than the mother's eyes proclaimed. He felt himself weakening in his resolve. Nearby one of the ship's officers was shouting orders to a flotilla of native boats that was approaching to lighter the consignment of the steamer's cargo destined for this tiny post.

"When does the next steamer for England touch here?" the boy asked.

"The *Emanuel* ought to be along most any time now," replied the officer. "I figgered we'd find her here," and he went on with his bellowing remarks to the dusky horde drawing close to the steamer's side.

The task of lowering the boy's grandmother over the side to a waiting canoe was rather difficult. The lad insisted on being always at her side, and when at last she was safely ensconced in the bottom of the craft that was to bear them shoreward her grandson dropped catlike after her. So interested was he in seeing her comfortably disposed that he failed to notice the little package that had worked from his pocket as he assisted in lowering the sling that contained the old woman over the steamer's side, nor did he notice it even as it slipped out entirely and dropped into the sea.

Scarcely had the boat containing the boy and the old woman started for the shore than Condon hailed a canoe upon the other side of the ship, and after bargaining with its owner finally lowered his baggage and himself aboard. Once ashore he kept out of sight of the two-story atrocity that bore the legend "Hotel" to lure unsuspecting wayfarers to its multitudinous discomforts. It was quite dark before he ventured to enter and arrange for accommodations.

In a back room upon the second floor the lad was explaining, not without considerable difficulty, to his grandmother that he had decided to return to England upon the next steamer. He was endeavoring to make it plain to the old lady that she might remain in Africa if she wished but that for his part his conscience demanded that he return to his father and mother, who doubtless were even now suffering untold sorrow because of his absence; from which it may be assumed that his parents had not been acquainted with the plans that he and the old lady had made for their adventure into African wilds.

Having come to a decision the lad felt a sense of relief from the worry that had haunted him for many sleepless nights. When he closed his eyes in sleep it was to dream of a happy reunion with those at home. And as he dreamed, Fate, cruel and inexorable, crept stealthily upon him through the dark corridor of the squalid building in which he slept—Fate in the form of the American crook, Condon.

Cautiously the man approached the door of the lad's room. There he crouched listening until assured by the regular breathing of those within that both slept. Quietly he inserted a slim, skeleton key in the lock of the door. With deft fingers, long accustomed to the silent manipulation of the bars and bolts that guarded other men's property, Condon turned the key and the knob simultaneously. Gentle pressure upon the door swung it slowly inward upon its hinges. The man entered the room, closing the door behind him. The moon was temporarily overcast by heavy clouds. The interior of the apartment was shrouded in gloom. Condon groped his way toward the bed. In the far corner of the room something moved—moved with a silent stealthiness which transcended even the trained silence of the burglar. Condon heard nothing. His attention was riveted upon the bed in which he thought to find a young boy and his helpless, invalid grandmother.

The American sought only the bank roll. If he could possess himself of this without detection, well and good; but were he to meet resistance he was prepared for that too. The lad's clothes lay across a chair beside the bed. The American's fingers felt swiftly through them—the pockets contained no roll of crisp, new notes. Doubtless they were beneath the pillows of the bed. He stepped closer toward the sleeper; his hand was already half way beneath the pillow when the thick cloud that had obscured the moon rolled aside and the room was flooded with light. At the same instant the boy opened his eyes and looked straight into those of Condon. The man was suddenly conscious that the boy was alone in the bed. Then he clutched for his victim's throat. As the lad rose to meet him Condon heard a low growl at his back, then he felt his wrists seized by the boy, and realized that beneath those tapering, white fingers played muscles of steel.

He felt other hands at his throat, rough hairy hands that reached over his shoulders from behind. He cast a terrified glance backward, and the hairs of his head stiffened at the sight his eyes revealed, for grasping him from the rear was a huge, man-like ape. The bared fighting fangs of the anthropoid were close to his throat. The lad pinioned his wrists. Neither uttered a sound. Where was the grandmother? Condon's eyes swept the room in a single all-inclusive glance. His eyes bulged in horror at the realization of the truth which that glance revealed. In the power of what creatures of hideous mystery had he placed himself! Frantically he fought to beat off the lad that he might turn upon the fearsome thing at his back. Freeing one hand he struck a savage blow at the lad's face. His act seemed to unloose a thousand devils in the hairy creature clinging to his throat. Condon heard a low and savage snarl. It was the last thing that the American ever heard in this life. Then he was dragged backward upon the floor, a heavy body fell upon him, powerful teeth fastened themselves in his jugular, his head whirled in the sudden blackness which rims eternity—a moment later the ape rose from his prostrate form; but Condon did not know—he was quite dead.

The lad, horrified, sprang from the bed to lean over the body of the man. He knew that Akut had killed in his defense, as he had killed Michael Sabrov; but here, in savage Africa, far from home and friends what would they do to him and his faithful ape? The lad knew that the penalty of murder was death. He even knew that an accomplice might suffer the death penalty with the principal. Who was there here who would plead for them? All would be against them. It was little more than a half-civilized community, and the chances were that they would drag Akut and him forth in the morning and hang them both to the nearest tree—he had read of such things being done in America, and Africa was worse even and wilder than the great West of his mother's native land. Yes, they would both be hanged in the morning!

Was there no escape? He thought in silence for a few moments, and then, with an exclamation of relief, he struck his palms together and turned toward his clothing upon the chair. Money would do anything! Money would save him and Akut! He felt for the bank roll in the pocket in which he had been accustomed to carry it. It was not there! Slowly at first and at last frantically he searched through the remaining pockets of his clothing. Then he dropped upon his hands and knees and examined the floor. Lighting the lamp he moved the bed to one side and, inch by inch, felt over the entire floor. Beside the body of Condon he hesitated, but at last he nerved himself to touch it. Rolling it over he sought beneath it for the money. Nor was it there. He guessed that Condon had entered their room to rob; but he did not believe that the man had had time to possess himself of the money; however, as it was nowhere else, it must be upon the body of the dead man. Again and again he went over the room, only to return each time to the corpse; but no where could he find the money.

He was half-frantic with despair. What were they to do? In the morning they would be discovered and killed. For all his inherited size and strength he was, after all, only a little boy—a frightened, homesick little boy—reasoning faultily from the meager experience of childhood. He could think of but a single glaring fact—they had killed a fellow man, and they were among savage strangers, thirsting for the blood of the first victim whom fate cast into their clutches. This much he had gleaned from penny-dreadfuls.

And they must have money!

Again he approached the corpse. This time resolutely. The ape squatted in a corner watching his young companion. The youth commenced to remove the American's clothing piece by piece, and, piece by piece, he examined each garment minutely. Even to the shoes he searched with painstaking care, and when the last article had been removed and scrutinized he dropped back upon the bed with dilated eyes that saw nothing in the present—only a grim tableau of the future in which two forms swung silently from the limb of a great tree.

How long he sat thus he did not know; but finally he was aroused by a noise coming from the floor below. Springing quickly to his feet he blew out the lamp, and crossing the floor silently locked the door. Then he turned toward the ape, his mind made up.

Last evening he had been determined to start for home at the first opportunity, to beg the forgiveness of his parents for this mad adventure. Now he knew that he might never return to them. The blood of a fellow man was upon his hands—in his morbid reflections he had long since ceased to attribute the death of Condon to the ape. The hysteria of panic had fastened the guilt upon himself. With money he might have bought justice; but penniless!—ah, what hope could there be for strangers without money here?

But what had become of the money? He tried to recall when last he had seen it. He could not, nor, could he, would he have been able to account for its disappearance, for he had been entirely unconscious of the falling of the little package from his pocket into the sea as he clambered over the ship's side into the waiting canoe that bore him to shore.

Now he turned toward Akut. "Come!" he said, in the language of the great apes. Forgetful of the fact that he wore only a thin pajama suit he led the way to the open window. Thrusting his head out he listened attentively. A single tree grew a few feet from the window. Nimbly the lad sprang to its bole, clinging cat-like for an instant before he clambered quietly to the ground below. Close behind him came the great ape. Two hundred yards away a spur of the jungle ran close to the straggling town. Toward this the lad led the way. None saw them, and a moment later the jungle swallowed them, and John Clayton, future Lord Greystoke, passed from the eyes and the knowledge of men.

It was late the following morning that a native houseman knocked upon the door of the room that had been assigned to Mrs. Billings and her grandson. Receiving no response he inserted his pass key in the lock, only to discover that another key was already there, but from the inside. He reported the fact to Herr Skopf, the proprietor, who at once made his way to the second floor where he, too, pounded vigorously upon the door. Receiving no reply he bent to the key hole in an attempt to look through into the room beyond. In so doing, being portly, he lost his balance, which necessitated putting a palm to the floor to maintain his equilibrium. As he did so he felt something soft and thick and wet beneath his fingers. He raised his open palm before his eyes in the dim light of the corridor and peered at it. Then he gave a little shudder, for even in the semi-darkness he saw a dark red stain upon his hand. Leaping to his feet he hurled his shoulder against the door. Herr Skopf is a heavy man—or at least he was then—I have not seen him for several years. The frail door collapsed beneath his weight, and Herr Skopf stumbled precipitately into the room beyond.

Before him lay the greatest mystery of his life. Upon the floor at his feet was the dead body of a strange man. The neck was broken and the jugular severed as by the fangs of a wild beast. The body was entirely naked, the clothing being strewn about the corpse. The old lady and her grandson were gone. The window was open. They must have disappeared through the window for the door had been locked from the inside.

But how could the boy have carried his invalid grandmother

from a second story window to the ground? It was preposterous. Again Herr Skopf searched the small room. He noticed that the bed was pulled well away from the wall—why? He looked beneath it again for the third or fourth time. The two were gone, and yet his judgment told him that the old lady could not have gone without porters to carry her down as they had carried her up the previous day.

Further search deepened the mystery. All the clothing of the two was still in the room—if they had gone then they must have gone naked or in their night clothes. Herr Skopf shook his head; then he scratched it. He was baffled. He had never heard of Sherlock Holmes or he would have lost no time in invoking the aid of that celebrated sleuth, for here was a real mystery: An old woman—an invalid who had to be carried from the ship to her room in the hotel—and a handsome lad, her grandson, had entered a room on the second floor of his hostelry the day before. They had had their evening meal served in their room— that was the last that had been seen of them. At nine the following morning the corpse of a strange man had been the sole occupant of that room. No boat had left the harbor in the meantime—there was not a railroad within hundreds of miles—there was no other white settlement that the two could reach under several day of arduous marching accompanied by a well-equipped *safari*. They had simply vanished into thin air, for the native he had sent to inspect the ground beneath the open window had just returned to report that there was no sign of a footstep there, and what sort of creatures were they who could have dropped that distance to the soft turf without leaving spoor? Herr Skopf shuddered. Yes, it was a great mystery—there was something uncanny about the whole thing—he hated to think about it, and he dreaded the coming of night.

It was a great mystery to Herr Skopf—and, doubtless, still is.

5

CAPTAIN ARMAND JACOT of the Foreign Legion sat upon an outspread saddle blanket at the foot of a stunted palm tree. His broad shoulders and his close-cropped head rested in luxurious ease against the rough bole of the palm. His long legs were stretched straight before him overlapping the meager blanket, his spurs buried in the sandy soil of the little desert oasis. The captain was taking his ease after a long day of weary riding across the shifting sands of the desert.

Lazily he puffed upon his cigarette and watched his orderly who was preparing his evening meal. Captain Armand Jacot was well satisfied with himself and the world. A little to his right rose the noisy activity of his troop of sun-tanned veterans, released for the time from the irksome trammels of discipline, relaxing tired muscles, laughing, joking, and smoking as they, too, prepared to eat after a twelve hour fast. Among them, silent and taciturn, squatted five white-robed Arabs, securely bound and under heavy guard.

It was the sight of these that filled Captain Armand Jacot with the pleasurable satisfaction of a duty well-performed. For a long, hot, gaunt month he and his little troop had scoured the places of the desert waste in search of a band of marauders to the sin-stained account of which were charged innumerable thefts of camels, horses, and goats, as well as murders enough to have sent the whole unsavory gang to the guillotine several times over.

A week before, he had come upon them. In the ensuing battle he had lost two of his own men, but the punishment inflicted upon the marauders had been severe almost to extinction. A half dozen, perhaps, had escaped; but the balance, with the exception of the five prisoners, had expiated their crimes before the nickel jacketed bullets of the legionaries. And, best of all, the ring leader, Achmet ben Houdin, was among the prisoners.

From the prisoners Captain Jacot permitted his mind to traverse the remaining miles of sand to the little garrison post where, upon the morrow, he should find awaiting him with eager welcome his wife and little daughter. His eyes softened to the memory of them, as they always did. Even now he could see the beauty of the mother reflected in the childish lines of little Jeanne's face, and both those faces would be smiling up into his as he swung from his tired mount late the following afternoon. Already he could feel a soft cheek pressed close to each of his—velvet against leather.

His reverie was broken in upon by the voice of a sentry summoning a noncommissioned officer. Captain Jacot raised his eyes. The sun had not yet set, but the shadows of the few trees huddled about the water hole and of his men and their horses stretched far away into the east across the now golden sand. The sentry was pointing in this direction, and the corporal, through narrowed lids, was searching the distance. Captain Jacot rose to his feet. He was not a man content to see through the eyes of others. He must see for himself. Usually he saw things long before others were aware that there was anything to see—a trait that had won for him the sobriquet of Hawk. Now he saw, just beyond the long shadows, a dozen specks rising and falling among the sands. They disappeared and reappeared, but always they grew larger. Jacot recognized them immediately. They were horsemen— horsemen of the desert. Already a sergeant was running toward him. The entire camp was straining its eyes into the distance. Jacot gave a few terse orders to the sergeant who saluted, turned upon his heel and returned to the men. Here he gathered a dozen who saddled their horses, mounted and rode out to meet the strangers. The remaining men disposed themselves in readiness for instant action. It was not entirely beyond the range of possibilities that the horsemen riding thus swiftly toward the camp might be friends of the prisoners bent upon the release of their kinsmen by a sudden attack. Jacot doubted this, however, since the strangers were evidently making no attempt to conceal their presence. They were galloping rapidly toward the camp in plain view of all. There might be treachery lurking beneath their fair appearance; but none who knew The Hawk would be so gullible as to hope to trap him thus.

The sergeant with his detail met the Arabs two hundred yards from the camp. Jacot could see him in conversation with a tall, white-robed figure—evidently the leader of the band. Presently the sergeant and this Arab rode side by side toward camp. Jacot awaited them. The two reined in and dismounted before him.

"Sheik Amor ben Khatour," announced the sergeant by way of introduction.

Captain Jacot eyed the newcomer. He was acquainted with nearly every principal Arab within a radius of several hundred miles. This man he never had seen. He was a tall, weather-beaten, sour looking man of sixty or more. His eyes were narrow and evil. Captain Jacot did not relish his appearance.

"Well?" he asked, tentatively.

The Arab came directly to the point.

"Achmet ben Houdin is my sister's son," he said. "If you will give him into my keeping I will see that he sins no more against the laws of the French."

Jacot shook his head. "That cannot be," he replied. "I must take him back with me. He will be properly and fairly tried by a civil court. If he is innocent he will be released."

"And if he is not innocent?" asked the Arab.

"He is charged with many murders. For any one of these, if he is proved guilty, he will have to die."

The Arab's left hand was hidden beneath his burnous. Now he withdrew it disclosing a large goatskin purse, bulging and heavy with coins. He opened the mouth of the purse and let a handful of the contents trickle into the palm of his right hand—all were pieces of good French gold. From the size of the purse and its bulging proportions Captain Jacot concluded that it must contain a small fortune. Sheik Amor ben Khatour dropped the spilled gold pieces one by one back into the purse. Jacot was eyeing him narrowly. They were alone. The sergeant, having introduced the visitor, had withdrawn to some little distance—his back was toward them. Now the sheik, having returned all the gold pieces, held the bulging purse outward upon his open palm toward Captain Jacot.

"Achmet ben Houdin, my sister's son, *might* escape tonight," he said. "Eh?"

Captain Armand Jacot flushed to the roots of his close-cropped hair. Then he went very white and took a half-step toward the Arab. His fists were clenched. Suddenly he thought better of whatever impulse was moving him.

"Sergeant!" he called. The noncommissioned officer hurried toward him, saluting as his heels clicked together before his superior.

"Take this black dog back to his people," he ordered. "See that they leave at once. Shoot the first man who comes within range of camp tonight."

Sheik Amor ben Khatour drew himself up to his full height. His evil eyes narrowed. He raised the bag of gold level with the eyes of the French officer.

"You will pay more than this for the life of Achmet ben Houdin, my sister's son," he said. "And as much again for the name that you have called me and a hundredfold in sorrow in the bargain."

"Get out of here!" growled Captain Armand Jacot, "before I kick you out."

All of this happened some three years before the opening of this tale. The trail of Achmet ben Houdin and his accomplices is a matter of record—you may verify it if you care to. He met the death he deserved, and he met it with the stoicism of the Arab.

A month later little Jeanne Jacot, the seven-year-old daughter of Captain Armand Jacot, mysteriously disappeared. Neither the wealth of her father and mother, or all the powerful resources of the great republic were able to wrest the secret of her whereabouts from the inscrutable desert that had swallowed her and her abductor.

A reward of such enormous proportions was offered that many adventurers were attracted to the hunt. This was no case for the modern detective of civilization, yet several of these threw themselves into the search—the bones of some are already bleaching beneath the African sun upon the silent sands of the Sahara.

Two Swedes, Carl Jenssen and Sven Malbihn, after three years of following false leads at last gave up the search far to the south of the Sahara to turn their attention to the more profitable business of ivory poaching. In a great district they were already known for their relentless cruelty and their greed for ivory. The natives feared and hated them. The European governments in whose possessions they worked had long sought them; but, working their way slowly out of the north they had learned many things in the no-man's-land south of the Sahara which gave them immunity from capture through easy avenues of escape that were unknown to those who pursued them. Their raids were sudden and swift. They seized ivory and retreated into the trackless wastes of the north before the guardians of the territory they raped could be made aware of their presence. Relentlessly they slaughtered elephants themselves as well as stealing ivory from the natives. Their following consisted of a hundred or more renegade Arabs and Negro slaves—a fierce, relentless band of cut-throats. Remember them—Carl Jenssen and Sven Malbihn, yellow-bearded, Swedish giants—for you will meet them later.

In the heart of the jungle, hidden away upon the banks of a small unexplored tributary of a large river that empties into the Atlantic not so far from the equator, lay a small, heavily palisaded village. Twenty palm-thatched, beehive huts sheltered its black population, while a half-dozen goatskin tents in the center of the clearing housed the score of Arabs who found shelter here while, by trading and raiding, they collected the cargoes which their ships of the desert bore northward twice each year to the market of Timbuktu.

Playing before one of the Arab tents was a little girl of ten—a black-haired, black-eyed little girl who, with her nut-brown skin and graceful carriage looked every inch a daughter of the desert. Her little fingers were busily engaged in fashioning a skirt of grasses for a much-disheveled doll which a kindly disposed slave had made for her a year or two before. The head of the doll was rudely chipped from ivory, while the body was a rat skin stuffed with grass. The arms and legs were bits of wood, perforated at one end and sewn to the rat skin torso. The doll was quite hideous and altogether disreputable and soiled, but Meriem thought it the most beautiful and adorable thing in the whole world, which is not so strange in view of the fact that it was the only object within that world upon which she might bestow her confidence and her love.

Everyone else with whom Meriem came in contact was, almost without exception, either indifferent to her or cruel. There was, for example, the old black hag who looked after her, Mabunu—toothless, filthy and ill tempered. She lost no opportunity to cuff the little girl, or even inflict minor tortures upon her, such as pinching, or, as she had twice done, searing the tender flesh with hot coals. And there was The Sheik, her father. She feared him more than she did Mabunu. He often scolded her for nothing, quite habitually terminating his tirades by cruelly beating her, until her little body was black and blue.

But when she was alone she was happy, playing with Geeka, or decking her hair with wild flowers, or making ropes of grasses. She was always busy and always singing—when they left her alone. No amount of cruelty appeared sufficient to crush the innate happiness and sweetness from her full little heart. Only when The Sheik was near was she quiet and subdued. Him she feared with a fear that was at times almost hysterical terror. She feared the gloomy jungle too—the cruel jungle that surrounded the little village with chattering monkeys and screaming birds by day and the roaring and coughing and moaning of the carnivora by night. Yes, she feared the jungle; but so much more did she fear The Sheik that many times it was in her childish head to run away, out into the terrible jungle forever rather than longer to face the ever present terror of her father.

As she sat there this day before The Sheik's goatskin tent, fashioning a skirt of grasses for Geeka, The Sheik appeared suddenly approaching. Instantly the look of happiness faded from the child's face. She shrunk aside in an attempt to scramble from the path of the leathern-faced old Arab; but she was not quick enough. With a brutal kick the man sent her sprawling upon her face, where she lay quite still, tearless but trembling. Then, with an oath at her, the man passed into the tent. The old, black hag shook with appreciative laughter, disclosing an occasional and lonesome yellow fang.

When she was sure The Sheik had gone, the little girl crawled to the shady side of the tent, where she lay quite still, hugging Geeka close to her breast, her little form racked at long intervals with choking sobs. She dared not cry aloud, since that would have brought The Sheik upon her again. The anguish in her little heart was not alone the anguish of physical pain; but that infinitely more pathetic anguish—of love denied a childish heart that yearns for love.

Little Meriem could scarce recall any other existence than that of the stern cruelty of The Sheik and Mabunu. Dimly, in the back of her childish memory there lurked a blurred recollection of a gentle mother; but Meriem was not sure but that even this was but a dream picture induced by her own desire for the caresses she never received, but which she lavished upon the much loved Geeka. Never was such a spoiled child as Geeka. Its little mother, far from fashioning her own conduct after the example set her by her father and nurse, went to the extreme of indulgence. Geeka was kissed a thousand times a day. There was play in which Geeka was naughty; but the little mother never punished. Instead, she caressed and fondled; her attitude influenced solely by her own pathetic desire for love.

Now, as she pressed Geeka close to her, her sobs lessened gradually, until she was able to control her voice, and pour out her misery into the ivory ear of her only confidante.

"Geeka loves Meriem," she whispered. "Why does The Sheik, my father, not love me, too? Am I so naughty? I try to be good; but I never know why he strikes me, so I cannot tell what I have done which displeases him. Just now he kicked me and hurt me so, Geeka; but I was only sitting before the tent making a skirt for you. That must be wicked, or he would not have kicked me for it. But why is it wicked, Geeka? Oh dear! I do not know, I do not know. I wish, Geeka, that I were dead. Yesterday the hunters brought in the body of *el adrea. El adrea* was quite dead. No more will he slink silently upon his unsuspecting prey. No more will his great head and his maned shoulders strike terror to the hearts of the grass eaters at the drinking ford by night. No more will his thundering roar shake the ground. *El adrea* is dead. They beat his body terribly when it was brought into the village; but *el adrea* did not mind. He did not feel the blows, for he was dead. When I am dead, Geeka, neither shall I feel the blows of Mabunu, or the kicks of The Sheik, my father. Then shall I be happy. Oh, Geeka, how I wish that I were dead!"

If Geeka contemplated a remonstrance it was cut short by sounds of altercation beyond the village gates. Meriem listened. With the curiosity of childhood she would have liked to have run down there and learn what it was that caused the men to talk so loudly. Others of the village were already trooping in the direction of the noise. But Meriem did not dare. The Sheik would be there, doubtless, and if he saw her it would be but another opportunity to abuse her, so Meriem lay still and listened.

Presently she heard the crowd moving up the street toward The Sheik's tent. Cautiously she stuck her little head around the edge of the tent. She could not resist the temptation, for the sameness of the village life was monotonous, and she craved diversion. What she saw was two strangers—white men. They were alone, but as they approached she learned from the talk of the natives that surrounded them that they possessed a considerable following that was camped outside the village. They were coming to palaver with The Sheik.

The old Arab met them at the entrance to his tent. His eyes narrowed wickedly when they had appraised the newcomers. They stopped before him, exchanging greetings. They had come to trade for ivory they said. The Sheik grunted. He had no ivory. Meriem gasped. She knew that in a nearby hut the great tusks were piled almost to the roof. She poked her little head further forward to get a better view of the strangers. How white their skins! How yellow their great beards!

Suddenly one of them turned his eyes in her direction. She tried to dodge back out of sight, for she feared all men; but he saw her.

Meriem noticed the look of almost shocked surprise that crossed his face. The Sheik saw it too, and guessed the cause of it.

"I have no ivory," he repeated. "I do not wish to trade. Go away. Go now."

He stepped from his tent and almost pushed the strangers about in the direction of the gates. They demurred, and then The Sheik threatened. It would have been suicide to have disobeyed, so the two men turned and left the village, making their way immediately to their own camp.

The Sheik returned to his tent; but he did not enter it. Instead he walked to the side where little Meriem lay close to the goatskin wall, very frightened. The Sheik stooped and clutched her by the arm. Viciously he jerked her to her feet, dragged her to the entrance of the tent, and shoved her viciously within. Following her he again seized her, beating her ruthlessly.

"Stay within!" he growled. "Never let the strangers see thy face. Next time you show yourself to strangers I shall kill you!"

With a final vicious cuff he knocked the child into a far corner of the tent, where she lay stifling her moans, while The Sheik paced to and fro muttering to himself. At the entrance sat Mabunu, muttering and chuckling.

In the camp of the strangers one was speaking rapidly to the other.

"There is no doubt of it, Malbihn," he was saying. "Not the slightest; but why the old scoundrel hasn't claimed the reward long since is what puzzles me."

"There are some things dearer to an Arab, Jenssen, than money," returned the first speaker—"revenge is one of them."

"Anyhow it will not harm to try the power of gold," replied Jenssen.

Malbihn shrugged.

"Not on The Sheik," he said. "We might try it on one of his people; but The Sheik will not part with his revenge for gold. To offer it to him would only confirm his suspicions that we must have awakened when we were talking to him before his tent. If we got away with our lives, then, we should be fortunate."

"Well, try bribery, then," assented Jenssen.

But bribery failed—grewsomely. The tool they selected after a stay of several days in their camp outside the village was a tall, old headman of The Sheik's native contingent. He fell to the lure of the shining metal, for he had lived upon the coast and knew the power of gold. He promised to bring them what they craved, late that night.

Immediately after dark the two white men commenced to make arrangements to break camp. By midnight all was prepared. The porters lay beside their loads, ready to swing them aloft at a moment's notice. The armed *askaris* loitered between the balance of the *safari* and the Arab village, ready to form a rear guard for the retreat that was to begin the moment that the head man brought that which the white masters awaited.

Presently there came the sound of footsteps along the path from the village. Instantly the *askaris* and the whites were on the alert. More than a single man was approaching. Jenssen stepped forward and challenged the newcomers in a low whisper.

"Who comes?" he queried.

"Mbeeda," came the reply.

Mbeeda was the name of the traitorous head man. Jenssen was satisfied, though he wondered why Mbeeda had brought others with him. Presently he understood. The thing they fetched lay upon a litter borne by two men. Jenssen cursed beneath his breath. Could the fool be bringing them a corpse? They had paid for a living prize!

The bearers came to a halt before the white men.

"This has your gold purchased," said one of the two. They set the litter down, turned and vanished into the darkness toward the village. Malbihn looked at Jenssen, a crooked smile twisting his lips. The thing upon the litter was covered with a piece of cloth.

"Well?" queried the latter. "Raise the covering and see what you have bought. Much money shall we realize on a corpse—especially after the six months beneath the burning sun that will be consumed in carrying it to its destination!"

"The fool should have known that we desired her alive," grumbled Malbihn, grasping a corner of the cloth and jerking the cover from the thing that lay upon the litter.

At sight of what lay beneath both men stepped back—involuntary oaths upon their lips—for there before them lay the dead body of Mbeeda, the faithless head man.

Five minutes later the *safari* of Jenssen and Malbihn was forcing its way rapidly toward the west, nervous *askaris* guarding the rear from the attack they momentarily expected.

6

H IS FIRST NIGHT in the jungle was one which the son of Tarzan held longest in his memory. No savage carnivora menaced him. There was never a sign of hideous barbarian. Or, if there were, the boy's troubled mind took no cognizance of them. His conscience was harassed by the thought of his mother's suffering. Self-blame plunged him into the depths of misery. The killing of the American caused him little or no remorse. The fellow had earned his fate. Jack's regret on this score was due mainly to the effect which the death of Condon had had upon his own plans. Now he could not return directly to his parents as he had planned. Fear of the primitive, borderland law, of which he had read highly colored, imaginary tales, had thrust him into the jungle a fugitive. He dared not return to the coast at this point—not that he was so greatly influenced through personal fear as from a desire to shield his father and mother from further sorrow and from the shame of having their honored name dragged through the sordid degradation of a murder trial.

With returning day the boy's spirits rose. With the rising sun rose new hope within his breast. He would return to civilization by another way. None would guess that he had been connected with the killing of the stranger in the little out-of-the-way trading post upon a remote shore.

Crouched close to the great ape in the crotch of a tree the boy had shivered through an almost sleepless night. His light pajamas had been but little protection from the chill dampness of the jungle, and only that side of him which was pressed against the warm body of his shaggy companion approximated to comfort. And so he welcomed the rising sun with its promise of warmth as well as light—the blessed sun, dispeller of physical and mental ills.

He shook Akut into wakefulness.

"Come," he said. "I am cold and hungry. We will search for food, out there in the sunlight," and he pointed to an open plain, dotted with stunted trees and strewn with jagged rock.

The boy slid to the ground as he spoke, but the ape first looked carefully about, sniffing the morning air. Then, satisfied that no danger lurked near, he descended slowly to the ground beside the boy.

"Numa, and Sabor his mate, feast upon those who descend first and look afterward, while those who look first and descend afterward live to feast themselves." Thus the old ape imparted to the son of Tarzan the boy's first lesson in jungle lore. Side by side they set off across the rough plain, for the boy wished first to be warm. The ape showed him the best places to dig for rodents and worms; but the lad only gagged at the thought of devouring the repulsive things. Some eggs they found, and these he sucked raw, as also he ate roots and tubers which Akut unearthed. Beyond the plain and across a low bluff they came upon water—brackish, ill-smelling stuff in a shallow water hole, the sides and bottom of which were trampled by the feet of many beasts. A herd of zebra galloped away as they approached.

The lad was too thirsty by now to cavil at anything even remotely resembling water, so he drank his fill while Akut stood with raised head, alert for any danger. Before the ape drank he cautioned the boy to be watchful; but as he drank he raised his head from time to time to cast a quick glance toward a clump of bushes a hundred yards away upon the opposite side of the water hole. When he had done he rose and spoke to the boy, in the language that was their common heritage—the tongue of the great apes.

"There is no danger near?" he asked.

"None," replied the boy. "I saw nothing move while you drank."

"Your eyes will help you but little in the jungle," said the ape.

"Here, if you would live, you must depend upon your ears and your nose but most upon your nose. When we came down to drink I knew that no danger lurked near upon this side of the water hole, for else the zebras would have discovered it and fled before we came; but upon the other side toward which the wind blows danger might lie concealed. We could not smell it for its scent is being blown in the other direction, and so I bent my ears and eyes down wind where my nose cannot travel."

"And you found—nothing?" asked the lad, with a laugh.

"I found Numa crouching in that clump of bushes where the tall grasses grow," and Akut pointed.

"A lion?" exclaimed the boy. "How do you know? I can see nothing."

"Numa is there, though," replied the great ape. "First I heard him sigh. To you the sigh of Numa may sound no different from the other noises which the wind makes among the grasses and the trees; but later you must learn to know the sigh of Numa. Then I watched and at last I saw the tall grasses moving at one point to a force other than the force of the wind. See, they are spread there upon either side of Numa's great body, and as he breathes—you see? You see the little motion at either side that is not caused by the wind—the motion that none of the other grasses have?"

The boy strained his eyes—better eyes than the ordinary boy inherits—and at last he gave a little exclamation of discovery.

"Yes," he said, "I see. He lies there," and he pointed. "His head is toward us. Is he watching us?"

"Numa is watching us," replied Akut, "but we are in little danger, unless we approach too close, for he is lying upon his kill. His belly is almost full, or we should hear him crunching the bones. He is watching us in silence merely from curiosity. Presently he will resume his feeding or he will rise and come down to the water for a drink. As he neither fears or desires us he will not try to hide his presence from us; but now is an excellent time to learn to know Numa, for you must learn to know him well if you would live long in the jungle. Where the great apes are many Numa leaves us alone. Our fangs are long and strong, and we can fight; but when we are alone and he is hungry we are no match for him. Come, we will circle him and catch his scent. The sooner you learn to know it the better; but keep close to the trees, as we go around him, for Numa often does that which he is least expected to do. And keep your ears and your eyes and your nose open. Remember always that there may be an enemy behind every bush, in every tree and amongst every clump of jungle grass. While you are avoiding Numa do not run into the jaws of Sabor, his mate. Follow me," and Akut set off in a wide circle about the water hole and the crouching lion.

The boy followed close upon his heels, his every sense upon the alert, his nerves keyed to the highest pitch of excitement. This was life! For the instant he forgot his resolutions of a few minutes past to hasten to the coast at some other point than that at which he had landed and make his way immediately back to London. He thought now only of the savage joy of living, and of pitting one's wits and prowess against the wiles and might of the savage jungle brood which haunted the broad plains and the gloomy forest aisles of the great, untamed continent. He knew no fear. His father had had none to transmit to him; but honor and conscience he did have and these were to trouble him many times as they battled with his inherent love of freedom for possession of his soul.

They had passed but a short distance to the rear of Numa when the boy caught the unpleasant odor of the carnivore. His face lighted with a smile. Something told him that he would have known that scent among a myriad of others even if Akut had not told him that a lion lay near. There was a strange familiarity—a weird familiarity in it that made the short hairs rise at the nape of his neck, and brought his upper lip into an involuntary snarl that bared his fighting fangs. There was a sense of stretching of the skin about his ears, for all the world as though those members were flattening back against his skull in preparation for deadly combat. His skin tingled. He was aglow with a pleasurable sensation that he never before had known. He was, upon the instant, another creature—wary, alert, ready. Thus did the scent of Numa, the lion, transform the boy into a beast.

He had never seen a lion—his mother had gone to great pains to prevent it. But he had devoured countless pictures of them, and now he was ravenous to feast his eyes upon the king of beasts in the flesh. As he trailed Akut he kept an eye cocked over one shoulder, rearward, in the hope that Numa might rise from his kill and reveal himself. Thus it happened that he dropped some little way behind Akut, and the next he knew he was recalled suddenly to a contemplation of other matters than the hidden Numa by a shrill scream of warning from the ape. Turning his eyes quickly in the direction of his companion, the boy saw her, standing in the path directly before him, which sent tremors of excitement racing along every nerve of his body. With body half-merging from a clump of bushes in which she must have lain hidden, stood a sleek and beautiful lioness. Her yellow-green eyes were round and staring, boring straight into the eyes of the boy. Not ten paces separated them. Twenty paces behind the lioness stood the great ape, bellowing instructions to the boy and hurling taunts at the lioness in an evident effort to attract her attention from the lad while he gained the shelter of a nearby tree.

But Sabor was not to be diverted. She had her eyes upon the lad.

He stood between her and her mate, between her and the kill. It was suspicious. Probably he had ulterior designs upon her lord and master or upon the fruits of their hunting. A lioness is short tempered. Akut's bellowing annoyed her. She uttered a little rumbling growl, taking a step toward the boy.

"The tree!" screamed Akut.

The boy turned and fled, and at the same instant the lioness charged. The tree was but a few paces away. A limb hung ten feet from the ground, and as the boy leaped for it the lioness leaped for him. Like a monkey he pulled himself up and to one side. A great forepaw caught him a glancing blow at the hips—just grazing him. One curved talon hooked itself into the waist band of his pajama trousers, ripping them from him as the lioness sped by. Half-naked the lad drew himself to safety as the beast turned and leaped for him once more.

Akut, from a nearby tree, jabbered and scolded, calling the lioness all manner of foul names. The boy, patterning his conduct after that of his preceptor, unstoppered the vials of his invective upon the head of the enemy, until in realization of the futility of words as weapons he bethought himself of something heavier to hurl. There was nothing but dead twigs and branches at hand, but these he flung at the upturned, snarling face of Sabor just as his father had before him twenty years ago, when as a boy he too had taunted and tantalized the great cats of the jungle.

The lioness fretted about the bole of the tree for a short time; but finally, either realizing the uselessness of her vigil, or prompted by the pangs of hunger, she stalked majestically away and disappeared in the brush that hid her lord, who had not once shown himself during the altercation.

Freed from their retreats Akut and the boy came to the ground, to take up their interrupted journey once more. The old ape scolded the lad for his carelessness.

"Had you not been so intent upon the lion behind you you might have discovered the lioness much sooner than you did," he said.

"But you passed right by her without seeing her," retorted the boy.

Akut was chagrined.

"It is thus," he said, "that jungle folk die. We go cautiously for a lifetime, and then, just for an instant, we forget, and—" he ground his teeth in mimicry of the crunching of great jaws in flesh. "It is a lesson," he resumed. "You have learned that you may not for too long keep your eyes and your ears and your nose all bent in the same direction."

That night the son of Tarzan was colder than he ever had been in all his life. The pajama trousers had not been heavy; but they had been much heavier than nothing. And the next day he roasted in the hot sun, for again their way led much across wide and tree-less plains.

It was still in the boy's mind to travel to the south, and circle back to the coast in search of another outpost of civilization. He had said nothing of this plan to Akut, for he knew that the old ape would look with displeasure upon any suggestion that savored of separation.

For a month the two wandered on, the boy learning rapidly the laws of the jungle; his muscles adapting themselves to the new mode of life that had been thrust upon them. The thews of the sire had been transmitted to the son—it needed only the hardening of use to develop them. The lad found that it came quite naturally to him to swing through the trees. Even at great heights he never felt the slightest dizziness, and when he had caught the knack of the swing and the release, he could hurl himself through space from branch to branch with even greater agility than the heavier Akut.

And with exposure came a toughening and hardening of his smooth, white skin, browning now beneath the sun and wind. He had removed his pajama jacket one day to bathe in a little stream that was too small to harbor crocodiles, and while he and Akut had been disporting themselves in the cool waters a monkey had dropped down from the overhanging trees, snatched up the boy's single remaining article of civilized garmenture, and scampered away with it.

For a time Jack was angry; but when he had been without the jacket for a short while he began to realize that being half-clothed is infinitely more uncomfortable than being entirely naked. Soon he did not miss his clothing in the least, and from that he came to revel in the freedom of his unhampered state. Occasionally a smile would cross his face as he tried to imagine the surprise of his schoolmates could they but see him now. They would envy him. Yes, how they would envy him. He felt sorry for them at such times, and again as he thought of them amid luxuries and comforts of their English homes, happy with their fathers and mothers, a most uncomfortable lump would arise into the boy's throat, and he would see a vision of his mother's face through a blur of mist that came unbidden to his eyes. Then it was that he urged Akut onward, for now they were headed westward toward the coast.

The old ape thought that they were searching for a tribe of his own kind, nor did the boy disabuse his mind of this belief. It would do to tell Akut of his real plans when they had come within sight of civilization.

One day as they were moving slowly along beside a river they came unexpectedly upon a native village. Some children were playing beside the water. The boy's heart leaped within his breast at sight of them—for over a month he had seen no human being. What if these were naked savages? What if their skins were black? Were they not creatures fashioned in the mold of their Maker, as was he? They were his brothers and sisters! He started toward them. With a low warning Akut laid a hand upon his arm to hold him back. The boy shook himself free, and with a shout of greeting ran forward toward the ebon players.

The sound of his voice brought every head erect. Wide eyes viewed him for an instant, and then, with screams of terror, the children turned and fled toward the village. At their heels ran their mothers, and from the village gate, in response to the alarm, came a score of warriors, hastily snatched spears and shields ready in their hands.

At sight of the consternation he had wrought the boy halted. The glad smile faded from his face as with wild shouts and menacing gestures the warriors ran toward him. Akut was calling to him from behind to turn and flee, telling him that the blacks would kill him. For a moment he stood watching them coming, then he raised his hand with the palm toward them in signal for them to halt, calling out at the same time that he came as a friend—that he had only wanted to play with their children. Of course they did not understand a word that he addressed to them, and their answer was what any naked creature who had run suddenly out of the jungle upon their women and children might have expected—a shower of spears. The missiles struck all about the boy, but none touched him. Again his spine tingled and the short hairs lifted at the nape of his neck and along the top of his scalp. His eyes narrowed. Sudden hatred flared in them to wither the expression of glad friendliness that had lighted them but an instant before. With a low snarl, quite similar to that of a baffled beast, he turned and ran into the jungle. There was Akut awaiting him in a tree. The ape urged him to hasten in flight, for the wise old anthropoid knew that they two, naked and unarmed, were no match for the sinewy black warriors who would doubtless make some sort of search for them through the jungle.

But a new power moved the son of Tarzan. He had come with

a boy's glad and open heart to offer his friendship to these people who were human beings like himself. He had been met with suspicion and spears. They had not even listened to him. Rage and hatred consumed him. When Akut urged speed he held back. He wanted to fight, yet his reason made it all too plain that it would be but a foolish sacrifice of his life to meet these armed men with his naked hands and his teeth—already the boy thought of his teeth, of his fighting fangs, when possibility of combat loomed close.

Moving slowly through the trees he kept his eyes over his shoulder, though he no longer neglected the possibilities of other dangers which might lurk on either hand or ahead—his experience with the lioness did not need a repetition to insure the permanency of the lesson it had taught. Behind he could hear the savages advancing with shouts and cries. He lagged further behind until the pursuers were in sight. They did not see him, for they were not looking among the branches of the trees for human quarry. The lad kept just ahead of them. For a mile perhaps they continued the search, and then they turned back toward the village. Here was the boy's opportunity, that for which he had been waiting, while the hot blood of revenge coursed through his veins until he saw his pursuers through a scarlet haze.

When they turned back he turned and followed them. Akut was no longer in sight. Thinking that the boy followed he had gone on further ahead. He had no wish to tempt fate within range of those deadly spears. Slinking silently from tree to tree the boy dogged the footsteps of the returning warriors. At last one dropped behind his fellows as they followed a narrow path toward the village. A grim smile lit the lad's face. Swiftly he hurried forward until he moved almost above the unconscious black—stalking him as Sheeta, the panther, stalked his prey, as the boy had seen Sheeta do on many occasions.

Suddenly and silently he leaped forward and downward upon the broad shoulders of his prey. In the instant of contact his fingers sought and found the man's throat. The weight of the boy's body hurled the black heavily to the ground, the knees in his back knocking the breath from him as he struck. Then a set of strong, white teeth fastened themselves in his neck, and muscular fingers closed tighter upon his windpipe. For a time the warrior struggled frantically, throwing himself about in an effort to dislodge his antagonist; but all the while he was weakening and all the while the grim and silent thing he could not see clung tenaciously to him, and dragged him slowly into the bush to one side of the trail.

Hidden there at last, safe from the prying eyes of searchers, should they miss their fellow and return for him, the lad choked the life from the body of his victim. At last he knew by the sudden struggle, followed by limp relaxation, that the warrior was dead. Then a strange desire seized him. His whole being quivered and thrilled. Involuntarily he leaped to his feet and placed one foot upon the body of his kill. His chest expanded. He raised his face toward the heavens and opened his mouth to voice a strange, weird cry that seemed screaming within him for outward expression, but no sound passed his lips—he just stood there for a full minute, his face turned toward the sky, his breast heaving to the pent emotion, like an animate statue of vengeance.

The silence which marked the first great kill of the son of Tarzan was to typify all his future kills, just as the hideous victory cry of the bull ape had marked the kills of his mighty sire.

7

AKUT, DISCOVERING THAT the boy was not close behind him, turned back to search for him. He had gone but a short distance in return when he was brought to a sudden and startled halt by sight of a strange figure moving through the trees toward him. It was the boy, yet could it be? In his hand was a long spear, down his back hung an oblong shield such as the black warriors who had attacked them had worn, and upon ankle and arm were bands of iron and brass, while a loincloth was twisted about the youth's middle. A knife was thrust through its folds.

When the boy saw the ape he hastened forward to exhibit his trophies. Proudly he called attention to each of his newly won possessions. Boastfully he recounted the details of his exploit.

"With my bare hands and my teeth I killed him," he said. "I would have made friends with them but they chose to be my ene-

And now that I have a spear I shall show Numa, too, what it means to have me for a foe. Only the white men and the great apes, Akut, are our friends. Them we shall seek, all others must we avoid or kill. This have I learned of the jungle."

They made a detour about the hostile village, and resumed their journey toward the coast. The boy took much pride in his new weapons and ornaments. He practiced continually with the spear, throwing it at some object ahead hour by hour as they traveled their loitering way, until he gained a proficiency such as only youthful muscles may attain too speedily. All the while his training went on under the guidance of Akut. No longer was there a single jungle spoor but was an open book to the keen eyes of the lad, and those other indefinite spoor that elude the senses of civilized man and are only partially appreciable to his savage cousin came to be familiar friends of the eager boy. He could differentiate the innumerable species of the herbivora by scent, and he could tell, too, whether an animal was approaching or departing merely by the waxing or waning strength of its effluvium. Nor did he need the evidence of his eyes to tell him whether there were two lions or four up wind—a hundred yards away or half a mile.

Much of this had Akut taught him, but far more was instinctive knowledge—a species of strange intuition inherited from his father. He had come to love the jungle life. The constant battle of wits and senses against the many deadly foes that lurked by day and by night along the pathway of the wary and the unwary appealed to the spirit of adventure which breathes strong in the heart of every red-blooded son of primordial Adam. Yet, though he loved it, he had not let his selfish desires outweigh the sense of duty that had brought him to a realization of the moral wrong which lay beneath the adventurous escapade that had brought him to Africa. His love of father and mother was strong within him, too strong to permit unalloyed happiness which was undoubtedly causing them days of sorrow. And so he held tight to his determination to find a port upon the coast where he might communicate with them and receive funds for his return to London. There he felt sure that he could now persuade his parents to let him spend at least a portion of his time upon those African estates which from little careless remarks dropped at home he knew his father possessed. That would be something, better at least than a lifetime of the cramped and cloying restrictions of civilization.

And so he was rather contented than otherwise as he made his way in the direction of the coast, for while he enjoyed the liberty and the savage pleasures of the wild his conscience was at the same time clear, for he knew that he was doing all that lay in his power to return to his parents. He rather looked forward, too, to meeting white men again—creatures of his own kind—for there had been many occasions upon which he had longed for other companionship than that of the old ape. The affair with the blacks still rankled in his heart. He had approached them in such innocent good fellowship and with such childlike assurance of a hospitable welcome that the reception which had been accorded him had proved a shock to his boyish ideals. He no longer looked upon the black man as his brother; but rather as only another of the innumerable foes of the bloodthirsty jungle—a beast of prey which walked upon two feet instead of four.

But if the blacks were his enemies there were those in the world who were not. There were those who always would welcome him with open arms; who would accept him as a friend and brother, and with whom he might find sanctuary from every enemy. Yes, there were always white men. Somewhere along the coast or even in the depths of the jungle itself there were white men. To them he would be a welcome visitor. They would befriend him. And there were also the great apes—the friends of his father and of Akut. How glad they would be to receive the son of Tarzan of the Apes! He hoped that he could come upon them before he found a trading post upon the coast. He wanted to be able to tell his father that he had known his old friends of the jungle, that he had hunted with them, that he had joined with them in their savage life, and their fierce, primeval ceremonies—the strange ceremonies of which Akut had tried to tell him. It cheered him immensely to dwell upon these happy meetings. Often he rehearsed the long speech which he would make to the apes, in which he would tell them of the life of their former king since he had left them.

At other times he would play at meeting with white men. Then he would enjoy their consternation at sight of a naked white boy trapped in the war togs of a black warrior and roaming the jungle with only a great ape as his companion.

And so the days passed, and with the traveling and the hunting and the climbing the boy's muscles developed and his agility increased until even phlegmatic Akut marvelled at the prowess of his pupil. And the boy, realizing his great strength and reveling in it, became careless. He strode through the jungle, his proud head erect, defying danger. Where Akut took to the trees at the first scent of Numa, the lad laughed in the face of the king of beasts and walked boldly past him. Good fortune was with him for a long time. The lions he met were well-fed, perhaps, or the very boldness of the strange creature which invaded their domain so filled them with surprise that thoughts of attack were banished from their minds as they stood, round-eyed, watching his approach and his departure. Whatever the cause, however, the fact remains that on many occasions the boy passed within a few paces of some great lion without arousing more than a warning growl.

But no two lions are necessarily alike in character or temper. They differ as greatly as do individuals of the human family. Because ten lions act similarly under similar conditions one cannot say that the eleventh lion will do likewise—the chances are that he will not. The lion is a creature of high nervous development. He thinks, therefore he reasons. Having a nervous system and brains he is the possessor of temperament, which is affected variously by extraneous causes. One day the boy met the eleventh lion. The former was walking across a small plain upon which grew little clumps of bushes. Akut was a few yards to the left of the lad who was the first to discover the presence of Numa.

"Run, Akut," called the boy, laughing. "Numa lies hid in the bushes to my right. Take to the trees. Akut! I, the son of Tarzan, will protect you," and the boy, laughing, kept straight along his way which led close beside the brush in which Numa lay concealed.

The ape shouted to him to come away, but the lad only flourished his spear and executed an improvised war dance to show his contempt for the king of beasts. Closer and closer to the dread destroyer he came, until, with a sudden, angry growl, the lion rose from his bed not ten paces from the youth. A huge fellow he was, this lord of the jungle and the desert. A shaggy mane clothed his shoulders. Cruel fangs armed his great jaws. His yellow-green eyes blazed with hatred and challenge.

The boy, with his pitifully inadequate spear ready in his hand, realized quickly that this lion was different from the others he had met; but he had gone too far now to retreat. The nearest tree lay several yards to his left—the lion could be upon him before he had covered half the distance, and that the beast intended to charge none could doubt who looked upon him now. Beyond the lion was a thorn tree—only a few feet beyond him. It was the nearest sanctuary but Numa stood between it and his prey.

The feel of the long spear shaft in his hand and the sight of the tree beyond the lion gave the lad an idea—a preposterous idea—a ridiculous, forlorn hope of an idea; but there was no time now to weigh chances—there was but a single chance, and that was the thorn tree. If the lion charged it would be too late—the lad must charge first, and to the astonishment of Akut and none the less of Numa, the boy leaped swiftly toward the beast. Just for a second was the lion motionless with surprise and in that second Jack Clayton put to the crucial test an accomplishment which he had practiced at school.

Straight for the savage brute he ran, his spear held butt foremost across his body. Akut shrieked in terror and amazement. The lion stood with wide, round eyes awaiting the attack, ready to rear upon his hind feet and receive this rash creature with blows that could crush the skull of a buffalo.

Just in front of the lion the boy placed the butt of his spear upon the ground, gave a mighty spring, and, before the bewildered beast could guess the trick that had been played upon him, sailed over the lion's head into the rending embrace of the thorn tree—safe but lacerated.

Akut had never before seen a pole-vault. Now he leaped up and down within the safety of his own tree, screaming taunts and boasts at the discomfited Numa, while the boy, torn and bleeding, sought some position in his thorny retreat in which he might find the least agony. He had saved his life; but at considerable cost in suffering. It seemed to him that the lion would never leave, and it was a full hour before the angry brute gave up his vigil and strode majestically away across the plain. When he was at a safe distance the boy extricated himself from the thorn tree; but not without inflicting new wounds upon his already tortured flesh.

It was many days before the outward evidence of the lesson he had learned had left him; while the impression upon his mind was one that was to remain with him for life. Never again did he uselessly tempt fate.

He took long chances often in his after life; but only when the taking of chances might further the attainment of some cherished end—and, always thereafter, he practiced pole-vaulting.

For several days the boy and the ape lay up while the former recovered from the painful wounds inflicted by the sharp thorns. The great anthropoid licked the wounds of his human friend, nor, aside from this, did they receive other treatment, but they soon healed, for healthy flesh quickly replaces itself.

When the lad felt fit again the two continued their journey toward the coast, and once more the boy's mind was filled with pleasurable anticipation.

And at last the much dreamed of moment came. They were passing through a tangled forest when the boy's sharp eyes discovered from the lower branches through which he was traveling an old but well-marked spoor—a spoor that set his heart to leaping—the spoor of man, of white men, for among the prints of naked feet were the well defined outlines of European made boots. The trail, which marked the passage of a good-sized company, pointed north at right angles to the course the boy and the ape were taking toward the coast.

Doubtless these white men knew the nearest coast settlement. They might even be headed for it now. At any rate it would be worth while overtaking them if even only for the pleasure of meeting again creatures of his own kind. The lad was all excitement; palpitant with eagerness to be off in pursuit. Akut demurred. He wanted nothing of men. To him the lad was a fellow ape, for he was the son of the king of apes. He tried to dissuade the boy, telling him that soon they should come upon a tribe of their own folk where some day when he was older the boy should be king as his father had before him. But Jack was obdurate. He insisted that he wanted to see white men again. He wanted to send a message to his parents. Akut listened and as he listened the intuition of the beast suggested the truth to him—the boy was planning to return to his own kind.

The thought filled the old ape with sorrow. He loved the boy as he had loved the father, with the loyalty and faithfulness of a hound for its master. In his ape brain and his ape heart he had nursed the hope that he and the lad would never be separated. He saw all his fondly cherished plans fading away, and yet he remained loyal to the lad and to his wishes. Though disconsolate he gave in to the boy's determination to pursue the *safari* of the white men, accompanying him upon what he believed would be their last journey together.

The spoor was but a couple of days old when the two discovered it, which meant that the slow-moving caravan was but a few hours distant from them whose trained and agile muscles could carry their bodies swiftly through the branches above the tangled undergrowth which had impeded the progress of the laden carriers of the white men.

The boy was in the lead, excitement and anticipation carrying him ahead of his companion to whom the attainment of their goal meant only sorrow. And it was the boy who first saw the rear guard of the caravan and the white men he had been so anxious to overtake.

Stumbling along the tangled trail of those ahead a dozen heavily laden blacks who, from fatigue or sickness, had dropped behind were being prodded by the black soldiers of the rear guard, kicked when they fell, and then roughly jerked to their feet and hustled onward. On either side walked a giant white man, heavy blonde beards almost obliterating their countenances. The boy's lips formed a glad cry of salutation as his eyes first discovered the whites—a cry that was never uttered, for almost immediately he witnessed that which turned his happiness to anger as he saw that both the white men were wielding heavy whips brutally upon the naked backs of the poor devils staggering along beneath loads that would have overtaxed the strength and endurance of strong men at the beginning of a new day.

Every now and then the rear guard and the white men cast apprehensive glances rearward as though momentarily expecting the materialization of some long expected danger from that quarter. The boy had paused after his first sight of the caravan, and now was following slowly in the wake of the sordid, brutal spectacle. Presently Akut came up with him. To the beast there was less of horror in the sight than to the lad, yet even the great ape growled beneath his breath at useless torture being inflicted upon the helpless slaves. He looked at the boy. Now that he had caught up with the creatures of his own kind, why was it that he did not rush forward and greet them? He put the question to his companion.

"They are fiends," muttered the boy. "I would not travel with such as they, for if I did I should set upon them and kill them the first time they beat their people as they are beating them now; but," he added, after a moment's thought, "I can ask them the whereabouts of the nearest port, and then, Akut, we can leave them."

The ape made no reply, and the boy swung to the ground and started at a brisk walk toward the *safari*. He was a hundred yards away, perhaps, when one of the whites caught sight of him. The man gave a shout of alarm, instantly levelling his rifle upon the boy and firing. The bullet struck just in front of its mark, scattering turf and fallen leaves against the lad's legs. A second later the other white and the black soldiers of the rear guard were firing hysterically at the boy.

Jack leaped behind a tree, unhit. Days of panic ridden flight through the jungle had filled Carl Jenssen and Sven Malbihn with jangling nerves and their native boys with unreasoning terror. Every new note from behind sounded to their frightened ears the coming of The Sheik and his bloodthirsty entourage. They were in a blue funk, and the sight of the naked white warrior stepping silently out of the jungle through which they had just passed had been sufficient shock to let loose in action all the pent nerve energy of Malbihn, who had been the first to see the strange apparition. And Malbihn's shout and shot had set the others going.

When their nervous energy had spent itself and they came to take stock of what they had been fighting it developed that Malbihn alone had seen anything clearly. Several of the blacks averred that they too had obtained a good view of the creature but their descriptions of it varied so greatly that Jenssen, who had seen nothing himself, was inclined to be a trifle skeptical. One of the blacks insisted that the thing had been eleven feet tall, with a man's body and the head of an elephant. Another had seen *three* immense Arabs with huge, black beards; but when, after conquering their nervousness, the rear guard advanced upon the enemy's position to investigate they found nothing, for Akut and the boy had retreated out of range of the unfriendly guns.

Jack was disheartened and sad. He had not entirely recovered from the depressing effect of the unfriendly reception he had received at the hands of the blacks, and now he had found an even more hostile one accorded him by men of his own color.

"The lesser beasts flee from me in terror," he murmured, half to himself, "the greater beasts are ready to tear me to pieces at sight. Black men would kill me with their spears or arrows. And now white men, men of my own kind, have fired upon me and driven me away. Are all the creatures of the world my enemies? Has the son of Tarzan no friend other than Akut?"

The old ape drew closer to the boy.

"There are the great apes," he said. "They only will be the friends of Akut's friend. Only the great apes will welcome the son of Tarzan. You have seen that men want nothing of you. Let us go now and continue our search for the great apes—our people."

The language of the great apes is a combination of monosyllabic gutturals, amplified by gestures and signs. It may not be literally translated into human speech; but as near as may be this is what Akut said to the boy.

The two proceeded in silence for some time after Akut had spoken. The boy was immersed in deep thought—bitter thoughts in which hatred and revenge predominated. Finally he spoke: "Very well, Akut," he said, "we will find our friends, the great apes."

The anthropoid was overjoyed; but he gave no outward demonstration of his pleasure. A low grunt was his only response, and a moment later he had limped nimbly upon a small and unwary rodent that had been surprised at a fatal distance from its burrow.

Tearing the unhappy creature in two Akut handed the lion's share
to the lad.

8

A YEAR HAD passed since the two Swedes had been driven in
terror from the savage country where The Sheik held sway. Little
Meriem still played with Geeka, lavishing all her childish love
upon the now almost hopeless ruin of what had never, even in its
palmiest days, possessed even a slight degree of loveliness. But to
Meriem, Geeka was all that was sweet and adorable. She carried
to the deaf ears of the battered ivory head all her sorrows, all her
hopes and all her ambitions, for even in the face of hopelessness,
in the clutches of the dread authority from which there was no
escape, little Meriem yet cherished hopes and ambitions. It is true
that her ambitions were rather nebulous in form, consisting chiefly
of a desire to escape with Geeka to some remote and unknown
spot where there were no Sheiks, no Mabunus—where *el adrea*
could find no entrance, and where she might play all day surrounded only by flowers and birds and the harmless little monkeys
playing in the tree tops.

The Sheik had been away for a long time, conducting a caravan
of ivory, skins, and rubber far into the north. The interim had been
one of great peace for Meriem. It is true that Mabunu had still been
with her, to pinch or beat her as the mood seized the villainous old
hag; but Mabunu was only one. When The Sheik was there also
there were two of them, and The Sheik was stronger and more
brutal even than Mabunu. Little Meriem often wondered why the
grim old man hated her so. It is true that he was cruel and unjust to
all with whom he came in contact, but to Meriem he reserved his
greatest cruelties, his most studied injustices.

Today Meriem was squatting at the foot of a large tree which grew inside the palisade close to the edge of the village. She was fashioning a tent of leaves for Geeka. Before the tent were some pieces of wood and small leaves and a few stones. These were the household utensils. Geeka was cooking dinner. As the little girl played she prattled continuously to her companion, propped in a sitting position with a couple of twigs. She was totally absorbed in the domestic duties of Geeka—so much so that she did not note the gentle swaying of the branches of the tree above her as they bent to the body of the creature that had entered them stealthily from the jungle.

In happy ignorance the little girl played on, while from above two steady eyes looked down upon her—unblinking, unwavering. There was none other than the little girl in this part of the village, which had been almost deserted since The Sheik had left long months before upon his journey toward the north.

And out in the jungle, an hour's march from the village, The Sheik was leading his returning caravan homeward.

A year had passed since the white men had fired upon the lad and driven him back into the jungle to take up his search for the only remaining creatures to whom he might look for companionship—the great apes. For months the two had wandered eastward, deeper and deeper into the jungle. The year had done much for the boy—turning his already mighty muscles to thews of steel, developing his woodcraft to a point where it verged upon the uncanny, perfecting his arboreal instincts, and training him in the use of both natural and artificial weapons.

He had become at last a creature of marvelous physical powers and mental cunning. He was still but a boy, yet so great was his strength that the powerful anthropoid with which he often engaged in mimic battle was no match for him. Akut had taught him to fight as the bull ape fights, nor ever was there a teacher better fitted to instruct in the savage warfare of primordial man, or a pupil better equipped to profit by the lessons of a master.

As the two searched for a band of the almost extinct species of ape to which Akut belonged they lived upon the best the jungle afforded. Antelope and zebra fell to the boy's spear, or were dragged down by the two powerful beasts of prey who leaped upon them from some overhanging limb or from the ambush of the undergrowth beside the trail to the water hole or the ford.

The pelt of a leopard covered the nakedness of the youth; but the wearing of it had not been dictated by any prompting of modesty. With the rifle shots of the white men showering about him he had reverted to the savagery of the beast that is inherent in each of us, but that flamed more strongly in this boy whose father had been raised a beast of prey. He wore his leopard skin at first in response to a desire to parade a trophy of his prowess, for he had slain the leopard with his knife in a hand-to-hand combat. He saw that the skin was beautiful, which appealed to his barbaric sense of ornamentation, and when it stiffened and later commenced to decompose because of his having no knowledge of how to cure or tan it was with sorrow and regret that he discarded it. Later, when he chanced upon a lone, black warrior wearing the counterpart of it, soft and clinging and beautiful from proper curing, it required but an instant to leap from above upon the shoulders of the unsuspecting black, sink a keen blade into his heart and possess the rightly preserved hide.

There were no after-qualms of conscience. In the jungle might is right, nor does it take long to inculcate this axiom in the mind of a jungle dweller, regardless of what his past training may have been. That the black would have killed him had he had the chance the boy knew full well. Neither he nor the black were any more sacred than the lion, or the buffalo, the zebra or the deer, or any other of the countless creatures who roamed, or slunk, or flew, or wriggled through the dark mazes of the forest. Each had but a single life, which was sought by many. The greater number of enemies slain the better chance to prolong that life. So the boy smiled and donned the finery of the vanquished, and went his way with Akut, searching, always searching for the elusive anthropoids who were to welcome them with open arms. And at last they found them. Deep in the jungle, buried far from sight of man, they came upon such another little natural arena as had witnessed the wild ceremony of the Dum-Dum in which the boy's father had taken part long years before.

First, at a great distance, they heard the beating of the drum of the great apes. They were sleeping in the safety of a huge tree when the booming sound smote upon their ears. Both awoke at once. Akut was the first to interpret the strange cadence.

"The great apes!" he growled. "They dance the Dum-Dum. Come, Korak, son of Tarzan, let us go to our people."

Months before Akut had given the boy a name of his own choosing, since he could not master the mangiven name of Jack. Korak is as near as it may be interpreted into human speech. In the language of the apes it means Killer. Now the Killer rose upon the branch of the great tree where he had been sleeping with his back braced against the stem. He stretched his lithe young muscles, the moonlight filtering through the foliage from above dappling his brown skin with little patches of light.

The ape, too, stood up, half squatting after the manner of his kind. Low growls rumbled from the bottom of his deep chest—growls of excited anticipation. The boy growled in harmony with the ape. Then the anthropoid slid softly to the ground. Close by, in the direction of the booming drum, lay a clearing which they must cross. The moon flooded it with silvery light. Half-erect, the great ape shuffled into the full glare of the moon. At his side, swinging gracefully along in marked contrast to the awkwardness of his companion, strode the boy, the dark, shaggy coat of the one brushing against the smooth, clear hide of the other. The lad was humming now, a music hall air that had found its way to the forms of the great English public school that was to see him no more. He was happy and expectant. The moment he had looked forward to for so long was about to be realized. He was coming into his own. He was coming home. As the months had dragged or flown along, retarded or spurred on as privation or adventure predominated, thoughts of his own home, while oft recurring, had become less vivid. The old life had grown to seem more like a dream than a reality, and the balking of his determination to reach the coast and return to London had finally thrown the hope of realization so remotely into the future that it too now seemed little more than a pleasant but hopeless dream.

Now all thoughts of London and civilization were crowded so far into the background of his brain that they might as well have been non-existent. Except for form and mental development he was as much an ape as the great, fierce creature at his side.

In the exuberance of his joy he slapped his companion roughly on the side of the head. Half in anger, half in play the anthropoid turned upon him, his fangs bared and glistening. Long, hairy arms reached out to seize him, and, as they had done a thousand times before, the two clinched in mimic battle, rolling upon the sward, striking, growling and biting, though never closing their teeth in more than a rough pinch. It was wondrous practice for them both. The boy brought into play wrestling tricks that he had learned at school, and many of these Akut learned to use and to foil. And from the ape the boy learned the methods that had been handed down to Akut from some common ancestor of them both, who had roamed the teeming earth when ferns were trees and crocodiles were birds.

But there was one art the boy possessed which Akut could not

master, though he did achieve fair proficiency in it for an ape—
boxing. To have his bull-like charges stopped and crumpled with
a suddenly planted fist upon the end of his snout, or a painful jolt
in the short ribs, always surprised Akut. It angered him too, and at
such times his mighty jaws came nearer to closing in the soft flesh
of his friend than at any other, for he was still an ape, with an ape's
short temper and brutal instincts; but the difficulty was in catching
his tormentor while his rage lasted, for when he lost his head and
rushed madly into close quarters with the boy he discovered that
the stinging hail of blows released upon him always found their
mark and effectually stopped him—effectually and painfully.
Then he would withdraw growling viciously, backing away with
grinning jaws distended, to sulk for an hour or so.

Tonight they did not box. Just for a moment or two they
wrestled playfully, until the scent of Sheeta, the panther, brought
them to their feet, alert and wary. The great cat was passing
through the jungle in front of them. For a moment it paused, listening. The boy and the ape growled menacingly in chorus and the
carnivore moved on.

Then the two took up their journey toward the sound of the
Dum-Dum. Louder and louder came the beating of the drum.
Now, at last, they could hear the growling of the dancing apes, and
strong to their nostrils came the scent of their kind. The lad
trembled with excitement. The hair down Akut's spine stiffened—
the symptoms of happiness and anger are often similar.

Silently they crept through the jungle as they neared the
meeting place of the apes. Now they were in the trees, worming
their way forward, alert for sentinels. Presently through a break in
the foliage the scene burst upon the eager eyes of the boy. To Akut
it was a familiar one; but to Korak it was all new. His nerves tingled at the savage sight. The great bulls were dancing in the moonlight, leaping in an irregular circle about the flat-topped earthen
drum about which three old females sat beating its resounding top
with sticks worn smooth by long years of use.

Akut, knowing the temper and customs of his kind, was too
wise to make their presence known until the frenzy of the dance
had passed. After the drum was quiet and the bellies of the tribe
well-filled he would hail them. Then would come a parley, after
which he and Korak would be accepted into membership by the
community. There might be those who would object; but such
could be overcome by brute force, of which he and the lad had
an ample surplus. For weeks, possibly months, their presence
might cause ever decreasing suspicion among others of the tribe;

but eventually they would become as born brothers to these strange apes.

He hoped that they had been among those who had known Tarzan, for that would help in the introduction of the lad and in the consummation of Akut's dearest wish, that Korak should become king of the apes. It was with difficulty, however, that Akut kept the boy from rushing into the midst of the dancing anthropoids—an act that would have meant the instant extermination of them both, since the hysterical frenzy into which the great apes work themselves during the performance of their strange rites is of such a nature that even the most ferocious of the carnivora give them a wide berth at such times.

As the moon declined slowly toward the lofty, foliaged horizon of the amphitheater the booming of the drum decreased and lessened were the exertions of the dancers, until, at last, the final note was struck and the huge beasts turned to fall upon the feast they had dragged hither for the orgy.

From what he had seen and heard Akut was able to explain to Korak that the rites proclaimed the choosing of a new king, and he pointed out to the boy the massive figure of the shaggy monarch, come into his kingship, no doubt, as many human rulers have come into theirs—by the murder of his predecessor.

When the apes had filled their bellies and many of them had sought the bases of the trees to curl up in sleep Akut plucked Korak by the arm.

"Come," he whispered. "Come slowly. Follow me. Do as Akut does."

Then he advanced slowly through the trees until he stood upon a bough overhanging one side of the amphitheater. Here he stood in silence for a moment. Then he uttered a low growl. Instantly a score of apes leaped to their feet. Their savage little eyes sped quickly around the periphery of the clearing. The king ape was the first to see the two figures upon the branch. He gave voice to an ominous growl. Then he took a few lumbering steps in the direction of the intruders. His hair was bristling. His legs were stiff, imparting a halting, jerky motion to his gait. Behind him pressed a number of bulls.

He stopped just a little before he came beneath the two—just far enough to be beyond their spring. Wary king! Here he stood rocking himself to and fro upon his short legs, baring his fangs in hideous grinnings, rumbling out an ever increasing volume of growls, which were slowly but steadily increasing to the proportions of roars. Akut knew that he was an attack upon them. The old ape did not wish to fight. He had come with the boy to cast his lot with the tribe.

"I am Akut," he said. "This is Korak. Korak is the son of Tarzan who was king of the apes. I, too, was king of the apes who dwelt in the midst of the great waters. We have come to hunt with you, to fight with you. We are great hunters. We are mighty fighters. Let us come in peace."

The king ceased his rocking. He eyed the pair from beneath his beetling brows. His bloodshot eyes were savage and crafty. His kingship was very new and he was jealous of it. He feared the encroachments of two strange apes. The sleek, brown, hairless body of the lad spelled "man," and man he feared and hated.

"Go away!" he growled. "Go away, or I will kill you."

The eager lad, standing behind the great Akut, had been pulsing with anticipation and happiness. He wanted to leap down among these hairy monsters and show them that he was their friend, that he was one of them. He had expected that they would receive him with open arms, and now the words of the king ape filled him with indignation and sorrow. The blacks had set upon him and driven him away. Then he had turned to the white men—to those of his own kind—only to hear the ping of bullets where he had expected words of cordial welcome. The great apes had remained his final hope. To them he looked for the companionship man had denied him. Suddenly rage overwhelmed him.

The king ape was almost directly beneath him. The others were formed in a half circle several yards behind the king. They were watching events interestedly. Before Akut could guess his intention, or prevent, the boy leaped to the ground directly in the path of the king, who had now succeeded in stimulating himself to a frenzy of fury.

"I am Korak!" shouted the boy. "I am the Killer. I came to live among you as a friend. You want to drive me away. Very well, then, I shall go; but before I go I shall show you that the son of Tarzan is your master, as his father was before him—that he is not afraid of your king or you."

For an instant the king ape had stood motionless with surprise. He had expected no such rash action upon the part of either of the intruders. Akut was equally surprised. Now he shouted excitedly for Korak to come back, for he knew that in the sacred arena the other bulls might be expected to come to the assistance of their king against an outsider, though there was small likelihood that the king would need assistance. Once those mighty jaws closed upon the boy's soft neck the end would come quickly. To leap to his rescue would mean death for Akut, too; but the brave old ape never hesitated. Bristling and growling, he dropped to the sward just as the king ape charged.

The beast's hands clutched for their hold as the animal sprang upon the lad. The fierce jaws were wide distended to bury the yellow fangs deeply in the brown hide. Korak, too, leaped forward to meet the attack; but leaped crouching, beneath the outstretched arms. At the instant of contact the lad pivoted on one foot, and with all the weight of his body and the strength of his trained muscles drove a clenched fist into the bull's stomach. With a gasping shriek the king ape collapsed, clutching futilely for the agile, naked creature nimbly sidestepping from his grasp.

Howls of rage and dismay broke from the bull apes behind the fallen king, as with murder in their savage little hearts they rushed forward upon Korak and Akut; but the old ape was too wise to court any such unequal encounter. To have counseled the boy to retreat now would have been futile, and Akut knew it. To delay even a second in argument would have sealed the death warrants of them both. There was but a single hope and Akut seized it. Grasping the lad around the waist he lifted him bodily from the ground, and turning ran swiftly toward another tree which swung low branches above the arena. Close upon their heels swarmed the hideous mob; but Akut, old though he was and burdened by the weight of the struggling Korak, was still fleeter than his pursuers.

With a bound he grasped a low limb, and with the agility of a little monkey swung himself and the boy to temporary safety. Nor did he hesitate even here; but raced on through the jungle night, bearing his burden to safety. For a time the bulls pursued; but presently, as the swifter outdistanced the slower and found themselves separated from their fellows they abandoned the chase, standing roaring and screaming until the jungle reverberated to their hideous noises. Then they turned and retraced their way to the amphitheater.

When Akut felt assured that they were no longer pursued he stopped and released Korak. The boy was furious.

"Why did you drag me away?" he cried. "I would have taught them! I would have taught them all! Now they will think that I am afraid of them."

"What they think cannot harm you," said Akut. "You are alive. If I had not brought you away you would be dead now and so would I. Do you not know that even Numa slinks from the path of the great apes when there are many of them and they are mad?"

9

I<small>T WAS AN</small> unhappy Korak who wandered aimlessly through the jungle the day following his inhospitable reception by the great apes. His heart was heavy from disappointment. Unsatisfied vengeance smoldered in his breast. He looked with hatred upon the denizens of his jungle world, bearing his fighting fangs and growling at those that came within radius of his senses. The mark of his father's early life was strong upon him and enhanced by months of association with beasts, from whom the imitative faculty of youth had absorbed a countless number of little mannerisms of the predatory creatures of the wild.

He bared his fangs now as naturally and upon as slight provocation as Sheeta, the panther, bared his. He growled as ferociously as Akut himself. When he came suddenly upon another beast his quick crouch bore a strange resemblance to the arching of a cat's back. Korak, the killer, was looking for trouble. In his heart of hearts he hoped to meet the king ape who had driven him from the amphitheater. To this end he insisted upon remaining in the vicinity; but the exigencies of the perpetual search for food led them several miles further away during day.

They were moving slowly down wind, and warily because the advantage was with whatever beast might chance to be hunting ahead of them, where their scent-spoor was being borne by the light breeze. Suddenly the two halted simultaneously. Two heads were cocked upon one side. Like creatures hewn from solid rock they stood immovable, listening. Not a muscle quivered. For several seconds they remained thus, then Korak advanced cautiously a few yards and leaped nimbly into a tree. Akut followed close upon his heels. Neither had made a noise that would have been appreciable to human ears at a dozen paces.

Stopping often to listen they crept forward through the trees. That both were greatly puzzled was apparent from the questioning looks they cast at one another from time to time. Finally the lad caught a glimpse of a palisade a hundred yards ahead, and beyond it the tops of some goatskin tents and a number of thatched huts. His lip upcurled in a savage snarl. Blacks! How he hated them. He signed to Akut to remain where he was while he advanced to reconnoiter.

Woe betide the unfortunate villager whom The Killer came upon now. Slinking through the lower branches of the trees, leaping lightly from one jungle giant to its neighbor where the distance was not too great, or swinging from one hand hold to another Korak came silently toward the village. He heard a voice beyond the palisade and toward that he made his way. A great tree overhung the enclosure at the very point from which the voice came. Into this Korak crept. His spear was ready in his hand. His ears told him of the proximity of a human being. All that his eyes required was a single glance to show him his target. Then, lightning like, the missile would fly to its goal. With raised spear he crept among the branches of the tree glaring narrowly downward in search of the owner of the voice which rose to him from below.

At last he saw a human back. The spear hand flew to the limit of the throwing position to gather the force that would send the iron shod missile completely through the body of the unconscious victim. And then The Killer paused. He leaned forward a little to get a better view of the target. Was it to insure more perfect aim, or had there been that in the graceful lines and the childish curves of the little body below him that had held in check the spirit of murder running riot in his veins?

He lowered his spear cautiously that it might make no noise by scraping against foliage or branches. Quietly he crouched in a comfortable position along a great limb and there he lay with wide eyes looking down in wonder upon the creature he had crept upon to kill—looking down upon a little girl, a little nut brown maiden. The snarl had gone from his lip. His only expression was one of interested attention—he was trying to discover what the girl was doing. Suddenly a broad grin overspread his face, for a turn of the girl's body had revealed Geeka of the ivory head and the rat skin torso—Geeka of the splinter limbs and the disreputable appearance. The little girl raised the marred face to hers and rocking herself backward and forward crooned a plaintive Arab lullaby to the doll. A softer light entered the eyes of The Killer. For a long hour that passed very quickly to him Korak lay with gaze riveted upon the playing child. Not once had he had a view of the girl's full face. For the most part he saw only a mass of wavy, black hair, one brown little shoulder exposed upon the side where her single robe was caught beneath her arm, and a shapely knee protruding from beneath her garment as she sat cross legged upon the ground. A tilt of the head as she emphasized some maternal admonition to the passive Geeka revealed occasionally a rounded cheek or a piquant little chin. Now she was shaking a slim finger at Geeka, reprovingly, and again she crushed to her heart this only object upon which she might lavish the untold wealth of her childish affections.

Korak, momentarily forgetful of his bloody mission, permitted the fingers of his spear hand to relax a little their grasp upon the shaft of his formidable weapon. It slipped, almost falling; but the occurrence recalled The Killer to himself. It reminded him of his purpose in slinking stealthily upon the owner of the voice that had attracted his vengeful attention. He glanced at the spear, with its well-worn grip and cruel, barbed head. Then he let his eyes wander again to the dainty form below him. In imagination he saw the heavy weapon shooting downward. He saw it pierce the tender flesh, driving its way deep into the yielding body. He saw the ridiculous doll drop from its owner's arms to lie sprawled and pathetic beside the quivering body of the little girl. The Killer shuddered, scowling at the inanimate iron and wood of the spear as though they constituted a sentient being endowed with a malignant mind.

Korak wondered what the girl would do were he to drop suddenly from the tree to her side. Most likely she would scream and run away. Then would come the men of the village with spears and guns and set upon him. They would either kill him or drive him away. A lump rose in the boy's throat. He craved the companionship of his own kind, though he scarce realized how greatly. He would have liked to slip down beside the little girl and talk with her, though he knew from the words he had overheard that she spoke a language with which he was unfamiliar. They could have talked by signs a little. That would have been better than nothing. Too, he would have been glad to see her face. What he had glimpsed assured him that she was pretty; but her strongest appeal to him lay in the affectionate nature revealed by her gentle mothering of the grotesque doll.

At last he hit upon a plan. He would attract her attention, and reassure her by a smiling greeting from a greater distance. Silently he wormed his way back into the tree. It was his intention to hail her from beyond the palisade, giving her the feeling of security which he imagined the stout barricade would afford.

He had scarcely left his position in the tree when his attention was attracted by a considerable noise upon the opposite side of the village. By moving a little he could see the gate at the far end of the main street. A number of men, women and children were running toward it. It swung open, revealing the head of a caravan upon the opposite side. In trooped the motley organization—black slaves and dark hued Arabs of the northern deserts; cursing camel drivers urging on their vicious charges; overburdened donkeys, waving sadly pendulous ears while they endured with stoic patience the brutalities of their masters; goats, sheep and horses. Into the village they all trooped behind a tall, sour, old man, who rode without greetings to those who shrunk from his path directly to a large goatskin tent in the center of the village. Here he spoke to a wrinkled hag.

Korak, from his vantage spot, could see it all. He saw the old man asking questions of the black woman, and then he saw the latter point toward a secluded corner of the village which was hidden from the main street by the tents of the Arabs and the huts of the natives in the direction of the tree beneath which the little girl played. This was doubtless her father, thought Korak. He had been away and his first thought upon returning was of his little daughter. How glad she would be to see him! How she would run and throw herself into his arms, to be crushed to his breast and covered with his kisses. Korak sighed. He thought of his own father and mother far away in London.

He returned to his place in the tree above the girl. If he couldn't have happiness of this sort himself he wanted to enjoy the happiness of others. Possibly if he made himself known to the old man he might be permitted to come to the village occasionally as a friend. It would be worth trying. He would wait until the old Arab had greeted his daughter, then he would make his presence known with signs of peace.

The Arab was striding softly toward the girl. In a moment he would be beside her, and then how surprised and delighted she would be! Korak's eyes sparkled in anticipation—and now the old man stood behind the little girl. His stern old face was still unrelaxed. The child was yet unconscious of his presence. She prattled on to the unresponsive Geeka. Then the old man coughed. With a start the child glanced quickly up over her shoulder. Korak could see her full face now. It was very beautiful in its sweet and innocent childishness—all soft and lovely curves. He could see her great, dark eyes. He looked for the happy love light that would follow recognition; but it did not come. Instead, terror, stark, paralyzing terror, was mirrored in her eyes, in the expression of her mouth, in the tense, cowering attitude of her body. A grim smile curved the thin, cruel lip of the Arab. The child essayed to crawl away; but before she could get out of his reach the old man kicked her brutally, sending her sprawling upon the grass. Then he followed her up to seize and strike her as was his custom.

Above them, in the tree, a beast crouched where a moment before had been a boy—a beast with dilating nostrils and bared fangs—a beast that trembled with rage.

The Sheik was stooping to reach for the girl when The Killer dropped to the ground at his side. His spear was still in his left hand but he had forgotten it. Instead his right fist was clenched and as The Sheik took a backward step, astonished by the sudden materialization of this strange apparition apparently out of clear air, the heavy fist landed full upon his mouth backed by the weight of the young giant and the terrific power of his more than human muscles.

Bleeding and senseless The Sheik sank to earth. Korak turned toward the child. She had regained her feet and stood wide eyed and frightened, looking first into his face and then, horror struck, at the recumbent figure of The Sheik. In an involuntary gesture of protection The Killer threw an arm about the girl's shoulders and stood waiting for the Arab to regain consciousness. For a moment they remained thus, when the girl spoke.

"When he regains his senses he will kill me," she said, in Arabic.

Korak could not understand her. He shook his head, speaking to her first in English and then in the language of the great apes; but neither of these was intelligible to her. She leaned forward and touched the hilt of the long knife that the Arab wore. Then she raised her clasped hand above her head and drove an imaginary blade into her breast above her heart. Korak understood. The old man would kill her. The girl came to his side again and stood there trembling. She did not fear him. Why should she? He had saved her from a terrible beating at the hands of The Sheik. Never, in her memory, had another so befriended her. She looked up into his face. It was a boyish, handsome face, nut-brown like her own. She admired the spotted leopard skin that circled his lithe body from one shoulder to his knees. The metal anklets and armlets adorning him aroused her envy. Always had she coveted something of the kind; but never had The Sheik permitted her more than the single cotton garment that barely sufficed to cover her nakedness. No furs or silks or jewelry had there ever been for little Meriem.

And Korak looked at the girl. He had always held girls in a species of contempt. Boys who associated with them were, in his estimation, mollycoddles. He wondered what he should do. Could he leave her here to be abused, possibly murdered, by the villainous old Arab? No! But, on the other hand, could he take her into the jungle with him? What could he accomplish burdened by a weak and frightened girl? She would scream at her own shadow when the moon came out upon the jungle night and the great beasts roamed, moaning and roaring, through the darkness.

He stood for several minutes buried in thought. The girl watched his face, wondering what was passing in his mind. She, too, was thinking of the future. She feared to remain and suffer the vengeance of The Sheik. There was no one in all the world to whom she might turn, other than this half-naked stranger who had dropped miraculously from the clouds to save her from one of The Sheik's accustomed beatings. Would her new friend leave her now? Wistfully she gazed at his intent face. She moved a little closer to him, laying a slim, brown hand upon his arm. The contact awakened the lad from his absorption. He looked down at her, and then his arm went about her shoulder once more, for he saw tears upon her lashes.

"Come," he said. "The jungle is kinder than man. You shall live in the jungle and Korak and Akut will protect you."

She did not understand his words, but the pressure of his arm drawing her away from the prostrate Arab and the tents was quite intelligible. One little arm crept about his waist and together they walked toward the palisade. Beneath the great tree that had harbored Korak while he watched the girl at play he lifted her in his arms and throwing her lightly across his shoulder leaped nimbly into the lower branches. Her arms were about his neck and from one little hand Geeka dangled down his straight young back.

And so Meriem entered the jungle with Korak, trusting, in her childish innocence, the stranger who had befriended her, and perhaps influenced in her belief in him by that strange intuitive power possessed by woman. She had no conception of what the future might hold. She did not know, nor could she have guessed the manner of life led by her protector. Possibly she pictured a distant village similar to that of The Sheik in which lived other white men like the stranger. That she was to be taken into the savage, primeval life of a jungle beast could not have occurred to her. Had it, her little heart would have palpitated with fear. Often had she wished to run away from the cruelties of The Sheik and Mabunu; but the dangers of the jungle always had deterred her.

The two had gone but a short distance from the village when the girl spied the huge proportions of the great Akut. With a half-stifled scream she clung more closely to Korak, and pointed fearfully toward the ape.

Akut, thinking that The Killer was returning with a prisoner, came growling toward them—a little girl aroused no more sympathy in the beast's heart than would a full-grown bull ape. She was a stranger and therefore to be killed. He bared his yellow fangs as he approached, and to his surprise The Killer bared his likewise, but he bared them at Akut, and snarled menacingly.

"Ah," thought Akut, "The Killer has taken a mate," and so, obedient to the tribal laws of his kind, he left them alone, becoming suddenly absorbed in a fuzzy caterpillar of peculiarly succulent appearance. The larva disposed of, he glanced from the corner of an eye at Korak. The youth had deposited his burden upon a large limb, where she clung desperately to keep from falling.

"She will accompany us," said Korak to Akut, jerking a thumb in the direction of the girl. "Do not harm her. We will protect her."

Akut shrugged. To be burdened by the young of man was in no way to his liking. He could see from her evident fright at her position on the branch, and from the terrified glances she cast in his direction that she was hopelessly unfit. By all the ethics of Akut's training and inheritance the unfit should be eliminated; but if The Killer wished this there was nothing to be done about it but to tolerate her. Akut certainly didn't want her—of that he was quite positive. Her skin was too smooth and hairless. Quite snake-like, in fact, and her face was most unattractive. Not at all like that of a certain lovely she he had particularly noticed among the apes in the amphitheater the previous night. Ah, there was true feminine beauty for one!—a great, generous mouth; lovely, yellow fangs, and the cutest, softest side whiskers! Akut sighed. Then he rose, expanded his great chest and strutted back and forth along a substantial branch, for even a puny thing like this she of Korak's might admire his fine coat and his graceful carriage.

But poor little Meriem only shrank closer to Korak and almost wished that she were back in the village of The Sheik where the terrors of existence were of human origin, and so more or less familiar. The hideous ape frightened her. He was so large and so ferocious in appearance. His actions she could only interpret as a menace, for how could she guess that he was parading to excite admiration? Nor could she know of the bond of fellowship which existed between this great brute and the godlike youth who had rescued her from the Sheik.

Meriem spent an evening and a night of unmitigated terror. Korak and Akut led her along dizzy ways as they searched for food. Once they hid her in the branches of a tree while they stalked a nearby buck. Even her natural terror of being left alone in the awful jungle was submerged in a greater horror as she saw the man and the beast spring simultaneously upon their prey and drag it down, as she saw the handsome face of her preserver contorted in a bestial snarl; as she saw his strong, white teeth buried in the soft flesh of the kill.

When he came back to her blood smeared his face and hands and breast and she shrank from him as he offered her a huge hunk of hot, raw meat. He was evidently much disturbed by her refusal to eat, and when, a moment later, he scampered away into the forest to return with fruit for her she was once more forced to alter her estimation of him. This time she did not shrink, but acknowledged his gift with a smile that, had she known it, was more than ample payment to the affection starved boy.

The sleeping problem vexed Korak. He knew that the girl could not balance herself in safety in a tree crotch while she slept, nor would it be safe to permit her to sleep upon the ground open to the attacks of prowling beasts of prey. There was but a single solution that presented itself—he must hold her in his arms all night. And that he did, with Akut braced upon one side of her and he upon the other, so that she was warmed by the bodies of them both.

She did not sleep much until the night was half spent; but at last Nature overcame her terrors of the black abyss beneath and the hairy body of the wild beast at her side, and she fell into a deep slumber which outlasted the darkness. When she opened her eyes the sun was well up. At first she could not believe in the reality of her position. Her head had rolled from Korak's shoulder so that her eyes were directed upon the hairy back of the ape. At sight of it she shrank away. Then she realized that someone was holding her, and turning her head she saw the smiling eyes of the youth regarding her. When he smiled she could not fear him, and now she shrank closer against him in natural revulsion toward the rough coat of the brute upon her other side.

Korak spoke to her in the language of the apes; but she shook her head, and spoke to him in the language of the Arab, which was as unintelligible to him as was ape speech to her. Akut sat up and looked at them. He could understand what Korak said but the girl made only foolish noises that were entirely unintelligible and ridiculous. Akut could not understand what Korak saw in her to attract him. He looked at her long and steadily, appraising her carefully, then he scratched his head, rose and shook himself.

His movement gave the girl a little start—she had forgotten Akut for the moment. Again she shrank from him. The beast saw that she feared him, and being a brute enjoyed the evidence of the terror his brutishness inspired. Crouching, he extended his huge hand stealthily toward her, as though to seize her. She shrank still further away. Akut's eyes were busy drinking in the humor of the situation—he did not see the narrowing eyes of the boy upon him, nor the shortening neck as the broad shoulders rose in a characteristic attitude of preparation for attack. As the ape's fingers were about to close upon the girl's arm the youth rose suddenly with a short, vicious growl. A clenched fist flew before Meriem's eyes to land full upon the snout of the astonished Akut. With an explosive bellow the anthropoid reeled backward and tumbled from the tree.

Korak stood glaring down upon him when a sudden swish in the bushes close by attracted his attention. The girl too was looking down; but she saw nothing but the angry ape scrambling to his feet. Then, like a bolt from a cross bow, a mass of spotted, yellow fur shot into view straight for Akut's back. It was Sheeta, the leopard.

10

As the leopard leaped for the great ape Meriem gasped in surprise and horror—not for the impending fate of the anthropoid, but at the act of the youth who but an instant before had angrily struck his strange companion; for scarce had the carnivore burst into view than with drawn knife the youth had leaped far out above him, so that as Sheeta was almost in the act of sinking fangs and talons in Akut's broad back The Killer landed full upon the leopard's shoulders.

The cat halted in mid air, missed the ape by but a hair's breadth, and with horrid snarlings rolled over upon its back, clutching and clawing in an effort to reach and dislodge the antagonist biting at its neck and knifing it in the side.

Akut, startled by the sudden rush from his rear, and following hoary instinct, was in the tree beside the girl with an agility little short of marvelous in so heavy a beast. But the moment that he turned to see what was going on below him brought him as quickly to the ground again. Personal differences were quickly forgotten in the danger which menaced his human companion, nor was he a whit less eager to jeopardize his own safety in the service of his friend than Korak had been to succor him.

The result was that Sheeta presently found two ferocious creatures tearing him to ribbons. Shrieking, snarling and growling, the three rolled hither and thither among the underbrush, while with staring eyes the sole spectator of the battle royal crouched trembling in the tree above them hugging Geeka frantically to her breast.

It was the boy's knife which eventually decided the battle, and as the fierce feline shuddered convulsively and rolled over upon its side the youth and the ape rose and faced one another across the prostrate carcass. Korak jerked his head in the direction of the little girl in the tree.

"Leave her alone," he said, "she is mine."

Akut grunted, blinked his bloodshot eyes, and turned toward the body of Sheeta. Standing erect upon it he threw out his great chest, raised his face toward the heavens and gave voice to so horrid a scream that once again the little girl shuddered and shrank. It was the victory cry of the bull ape that has made a kill. The boy only looked on for a moment in silence; then he leaped into the tree again to the girl's side. Akut presently rejoined them. For a few minutes he busied himself licking his wounds, then he wandered off to hunt his breakfast.

For many months the strange life of the three went on unmarked by any unusual occurrences. At least without any occurrences that seemed unusual to the youth or the ape; but to the little girl it was a constant nightmare of horrors for days and weeks, until she too became accustomed to gazing into the eyeless sockets of death and to the feel of the icy wind of his shroudlike mantle. Slowly she learned the rudiments of the only common medium of thought exchange which her companions possessed— the language of the great apes. More quickly she perfected herself in jungle craft, so that the time soon came when she was an important factor in the chase, watching while the others slept, or helping them to trace the spoor of whatever prey they might be stalking. Akut accepted her on a footing which bordered upon equality when it was necessary for them to come into close contact; but for the most part he avoided her. The youth always was kind to her, and if there were many occasions upon which he felt the burden of her presence he hid it from her. Finding that the night damp and chill caused her discomfort and even suffering, Korak constructed a tight little shelter high among the swaying branches of a giant tree. Here little Meriem slept in comparative warmth and safety, while The Killer and the ape perched upon nearby branches, the former always before the entrance to the lofty domicile, where he best could guard its inmate from the dangers of arboreal enemies. They were too high to feel much fear of Sheeta; but there was always Histah, the snake, to strike terror to one's soul, and the great baboons who lived nearby, and who, while never attacking always bared their fangs and barked at any of the trio when they passed near them.

After the construction of the shelter the activities of the three became localized. They ranged less widely, for there was always the necessity of returning to their own tree at nightfall. A river flowed near by. Game and fruit were plentiful, as were fish also. Existence had settled down to the daily humdrum of the wild—the search for food and the sleeping upon full bellies. They looked no further ahead than today. If the youth thought of his past and of those who longed for him in the distant metropolis it was in a detached and impersonal sort of way as though that other life belonged to another creature than himself. He had given up hope of returning to civilization, for since his various rebuffs at the hands of those to whom he had looked for friendship he had wandered so far inland as to realize that he was completely lost in the mazes of the jungle.

Then, too, since the coming of Meriem he had found in her that one thing which he had most missed before in his savage, jungle life—human companionship. In his friendship for her there was appreciable no trace of sex influence of which he was cognizant. They were friends—companions—that was all. Both might have been boys, except for the half tender and always masterful manifestation of the protective instinct which was apparent in Korak's attitude.

The little girl idolized him as she might have idolized an indulgent brother had she had one. Love was a thing unknown to either; but as the youth neared manhood it was inevitable that it should come to him as it did to every other savage, jungle male.

As Meriem became proficient in their common language the pleasures of their companionship grew correspondingly, for now they could converse and aided by the mental powers of their human heritage they amplified the restricted vocabulary of the apes until talking was transformed from a task into an enjoyable pastime. When Korak hunted, Meriem usually accompanied him, for she had learned the fine art of silence, when silence was desirable. She could pass through the branches of the great trees now with all the agility and stealth of The Killer himself. Great heights no longer appalled her. She swung from limb to limb, or she raced through the mighty branches, surefooted, lithe, and fearless. Korak was very proud of her, and even old Akut grunted in approval where before he had growled in contempt.

A distant village of blacks had furnished her with a mantle of fur and feathers, with copper ornaments, and weapons, for Korak would not permit her to go unarmed, or unversed in the use of the weapons he stole for her. A leather thong over one shoulder supported the ever present Geeka who was still the recipient of her most sacred confidences. A light spear and a long knife were her weapons of offense or defense. Her body, rounding into the fulness of an early maturity, followed the lines of a Greek goddess; but there the similarity ceased, for her face was beautiful.

As she grew more accustomed to the jungle and the ways of its wild denizens fear left her. As time wore on she even hunted alone when Korak and Akut were prowling at a great distance, as they were sometimes forced to do when game was scarce in their immediate vicinity. Upon these occasions she usually confined her endeavors to the smaller animals though sometimes she brought down a deer, and once even Horta, the boar—a great tusker that even Sheeta might have thought twice before attacking.

In their stamping grounds in the jungle the three were familiar figures. The little monkeys knew them well, often coming close to chatter and frolic about them. When Akut was by, the small folk kept their distance, but with Korak they were less shy and when both the males were gone they would come close to Meriem, tugging at her ornaments or playing with Geeka, who was a never ending source of amusement to them. The girl played with them and fed them, and when she was alone they helped her to pass the long hours until Korak's return.

Nor were they worthless as friends. In the hunt they helped her locate her quarry. Often they would come racing through the trees to her side to announce the near presence of antelope or giraffe, or with excited warnings of the proximity of Sheeta or Numa. Luscious, sun-kissed fruits which hung far out upon the frail bough of the jungle's waving crest were brought to her by these tiny, nimble allies. Sometimes they played tricks upon her; but she was always kind and gentle with them and in their wild, half-human way they were kind to her and affectionate. Their language being similar to that of the great apes Meriem could converse with them though the poverty of their vocabulary rendered these exchanges anything but feasts of reason. For familiar objects they had names, as well as for those conditions which induced pain or pleasure, joy, sorrow, or rage. These root words were so similar to those in use among the great anthropoids as to suggest that the language of the Manus was the mother tongue. Dreams, aspirations, hopes, the past, the sordid exchange. Dreams, aspirations, hopes, the past, the future held no place in the conversation of Manu, the monkey. All was of the present—particularly of filling his belly and catching lice.

Poor food was this to nourish the mental appetite of a girl just upon the brink of womanhood. And so, finding Manu only amusing as an occasional playfellow or pet, Meriem poured out her sweetest soul thoughts into the deaf ears of Geeka's ivory head. To Geeka she spoke in Arabic, knowing that Geeka, being but a doll, could not understand the language of Korak and Akut, and that the language of Korak and Akut being that of male apes contained nothing of interest to an Arab doll.

Geeka had undergone a transformation since her little mother had left the village of The Sheik. Her garmenture now reflected in miniature that of Meriem. A tiny bit of leopard skin covered her ratskin torso from shoulder to splinter knee. A band of braided grasses about her brow held in place a few gaudy feathers from the parakeet, while other bits of grass were fashioned into imitations of arm and leg ornaments of metal. Geeka was a perfect little savage; but at heart she was unchanged, being the same omnivorous listener as of yore. An excellent trait in Geeka was that she never interrupted in order to talk about herself. Today was no exception. She had been listening attentively to Meriem for an hour, propped against the bole of a tree while her lithe, young mistress stretched catlike and luxurious along a swaying branch before her.

"Little Geeka," said Meriem, "our Korak has been gone for a long time today. We miss him, little Geeka, do we not? It is dull and lonesome in the great jungle when our Korak is away. What will he bring us this time, eh? Another shining band of metal for Meriem's ankle? Or a soft, doeskin loin cloth from the body of a black she? He tells me that it is harder to get the possessions of the shes, for he will not kill them as he does the males, and they fight savagely when he leaps upon them to wrest their ornaments from them. Then come the males with spears and arrows and Korak takes to the trees. Sometimes he takes the she with him and high among the branches divests her of the things he wishes to bring home to Meriem. He says that the blacks fear him now, and at the first sight of him the women and children run shrieking to their huts; but he follows them within, and it is not often that he returns without arrows for himself and a present for Meriem. Korak is mighty among the jungle people—our Korak, Geeka—no, *my* Korak!"

Meriem's conversation was interrupted by the sudden plunge of an excited little monkey that landed upon her shoulders in a flying leap from a neighboring tree.

"Climb!" he cried. "Climb! The Mangani are coming."

Meriem glanced lazily over her shoulder at the excited disturber of her peace.

"Climb, yourself, little Manu," she said. "The only Mangani in our jungle are Korak and Akut. It is they you have seen returning from the hunt. Some day you will see your own shadow, little Manu, and then you will be frightened to death."

But the monkey only screamed his warning more lustily before he raced upward toward the safety of the high terrace where Mangani, the great ape, could not follow. Presently Meriem heard the sound of approaching bodies swinging through the trees. She listened attentively. There were two and they were great apes—Korak and Akut. To her Korak was an ape—a Mangani, for as such the three always described themselves. Man was an enemy, so they did not think of themselves as belonging any longer to the same genus. Tarmangani, or great white ape, which described the white man in their language, did not fit them all. Gomangani—great black ape, or Negro—described none of them so they called themselves plain Mangani.

Meriem decided that she would feign slumber and play a joke on Korak. So she lay very still with eyes tightly closed. She heard the two approaching closer and closer. They were in the adjoining tree now and must have discovered her, for they had halted. Why were they so quiet? Why did not Korak call out his customary greeting? The quietness was ominous. It was followed presently by a very stealthy sound—one of them was creeping upon her. Was Korak planning a joke upon his own account? Well, she would fool him. Cautiously she opened her eyes the tiniest bit, and as she did so her heart stood still. Creeping silently toward her was a huge bull ape that she never before had seen. Behind him was another like him.

With the agility of a squirrel Meriem was upon her feet and at the same instant the great bull lunged for her. Leaping from limb to limb the girl fled through the jungle while close behind her came the two great apes. Above them raced a bevy of screaming, chattering monkeys, hurling taunts and insults at the Mangani, and encouragement and advice to the girl.

From tree to tree swung Meriem working ever upward toward the smaller branches which would not bear the weight of her pursuers. Faster and faster came the bull apes after her. The clutching fingers of the foremost were almost upon her again and again, but she eluded them by sudden bursts of speed or reckless chances as she threw herself across dizzy spaces.

Slowly she was gaining her way to the greater heights where safety lay, when, after a particularly daring leap, the swaying branch she grasped bent low beneath her weight, nor whipped upward again as it should have done. Even before the rending sound which followed Meriem knew that she had misjudged the strength of the limb. It gave slowly at first. Then there was a ripping as it parted from the trunk. Releasing her hold Meriem dropped among the foliage beneath, clutching for a new support. She found it a dozen feet below the broken limb. She had fallen thus many times before, so that she had no particular terror of a fall—it was the delay which appalled her most, and rightly, for scarce had she scrambled to a place of safety than the body of the huge ape dropped at her side and a great, hairy arm went about her waist.

Almost at once the other ape reached his companion's side. He made a lunge at Meriem; but her captor swung her to one side, bared his fighting fangs and growled ominously. Meriem struggled to escape. She struck at the hairy breast and bearded cheek. She fastened her strong, white teeth in one shaggy forearm. The ape cuffed her viciously across the face, then he had to turn his attention to his fellow who quite evidently desired the prize for his own.

The captor could not fight to advantage upon the swaying bough, burdened as he was by a squirming, struggling captive, so he dropped quickly to the ground beneath. The other followed him, and here they fought, occasionally abandoning their duel to pursue and recapture the girl who took every advantage of her captors' preoccupation in battle to break away in attempted escape; but always they overtook her, and first one and then the other possessed her as they struggled to tear one another to pieces for the prize.

Often the girl came in for many blows that were intended for a hairy foe, and once she was felled, lying unconscious while the apes, relieved of the distraction of detaining her by force, tore into one another in fierce and terrible combat.

Above them screamed the little monkeys, racing hither and thither in a frenzy of hysterical excitement. Back and forth over the battle field flew countless birds of gorgeous plumage, squawking their hoarse cries of rage and defiance. In the distance a lion roared.

The larger bull was slowly tearing his antagonist to pieces. They rolled upon the ground biting and striking. Again, erect upon their hind legs they pulled and tugged like human wrestlers; but always the giant fangs found their bloody part to play until both combatants and the ground about them were red with gore.

Meriem, through it all, lay still and unconscious upon the ground. At last one found a permanent hold upon the jugular of the other and thus they went down for the last time. For several minutes they lay with scarce a struggle. It was the larger bull who arose alone from the last embrace. He shook himself. A deep growl rumbled from his hairy throat. He waddled back and forth between the body of the girl and that of his vanquished foe. Then he stood upon the latter and gave tongue to his hideous challenge. The little monkeys broke, screaming, in all directions as the terrifying noise broke upon their ears. The gorgeous birds took wing and fled. Once again the lion roared, this time at a greater distance.

The great ape waddled once more to the girl's side. He turned her over upon her back, and stooping commenced to sniff and listen about her face and breast. She lived. The monkeys were returning. They came in swarms, and from above hurled down insults upon the victor.

The ape showed his displeasure by baring his teeth and growling up at them. Then he stooped and lifting the girl to his shoulder waddled off through the jungle. In his wake followed the angry mob.

11

KORAK, RETURNING FROM the hunt, heard the jabbering of the excited monkeys. He knew that something was seriously amiss. Histah, the snake, had doubtless coiled his slimy folds about some careless Manu. The youth hastened ahead. The monkeys were Meriem's friends. He would help them if he could. He traveled rapidly along the middle terrace. In the tree by Meriem's shelter he deposited his trophies of the hunt and called aloud to her. There was no answer. He dropped quickly to a lower level. She might be hiding from him.

Upon a great branch where Meriem often swung at indolent ease he saw Geeka propped against the tree's great bole. What could it mean? Meriem had never left Geeka thus alone before. Korak picked up the doll and tucked it in his belt. He called again, more loudly; but no Meriem answered his summons. In the distance the jabbering of the excited Manus was growing less distinct.

Could their excitement be in any way connected with Meriem's disappearance? The bare thought was enough. Without waiting for Akut who was coming slowly along some distance in his rear, Korak swung rapidly in the direction of the chattering mob. But a few minutes sufficed to overtake the rearmost. At sight of him they fell to screaming and pointing downward ahead of them, and a moment later Korak came within sight of the cause of their rage.

The youth's heart stood still in terror as he saw the limp body of the girl across the hairy shoulders of a great ape. That she was dead he did not doubt, and in that instant there arose within him a something which he did not try to interpret nor could have had he tried; but all at once the whole world seemed centered in that tender, graceful body, that frail little body, hanging so pitifully limp and helpless across the bulging shoulders of the brute.

He knew then that little Meriem was his world—his sun, his moon, his stars—with her going had gone all light and warmth and happiness. A groan escaped his lips, and after that a series of hideous roars, more bestial than the beasts', as he dropped plummet-like in mad descent toward the perpetrator of this hideous crime.

The bull ape turned at the first note of this new and menacing voice, and as he turned a new flame was added to the rage and hatred of The Killer, for he saw that the creature before him was none other than the king ape which had driven him away from the great anthropoids to whom he had looked for friendship and asylum.

Dropping the body of the girl to the ground the bull turned to battle anew for possession of his expensive prize; but this time he looked for an easy conquest. He too recognized Korak. Had he not chased him away from the amphitheater without even having to lay a fang or paw upon him? With lowered head and bulging shoulders he rushed headlong for the smooth-skinned creature who was daring to question his right to his prey.

They met head on like two charging bulls, to go down together tearing and striking. Korak forgot his knife. Rage and bloodlust such as his could be satisfied only by the feel of hot flesh between rending fangs, by the gush of new life blood against his bare skin, for, though he did not realize it, Korak, The Killer, was fighting for something more compelling than hate or revenge—he was a great male fighting another male for a she of his own kind.

So impetuous was the attack of the man-ape that he found his hold before the anthropoid could prevent him—a savage hold, with strong jaws closed upon a pulsing jugular, and there he clung, with closed eyes, while his fingers sought another hold upon the shaggy throat.

It was then that Meriem opened her eyes. At the sight before her they went wide.

"Korak!" she cried. "Korak! My Korak! I knew that you would come. Kill him, Korak! Kill him!" And with flashing eyes and heaving bosom the girl, coming to her feet, ran to Korak's side to encourage him. Nearby lay The Killer's spear, where he had flung it as he charged the ape. The girl saw it and snatched it up. No faintness overcame her in the face of this battle primeval at her feet. For her there was no hysterical reaction from the nerve strain of her own personal encounter with the bull. She was excited; but cool and entirely unafraid. Her Korak was battling with another Mangani that would have stolen her; but she did not seek the safety of an overhanging bough there to watch the battle from afar, as would a she Mangani. Instead she placed the point of Korak's spear against the bull ape's side and plunged the sharp point deep into the savage heart. Korak had not needed her aid, for the great bull had been already as good as dead, with the blood gushing from his torn jugular; but Korak rose smiling with a word of approbation for his helper.

How tall and fine she was! Had she changed suddenly within the few hours of his absence, or had his battle with the ape affected his vision? He might have been looking at Meriem through new eyes for the many startling and wonderful surprises his gaze revealed. How long it had been since he had found her in her father's village, a little Arab girl, he did not know, for time is of no import in the jungle and so he had kept no track of the passing days. But he realized, as he looked upon her now, that she was no longer such a little girl as he had first seen playing with Geeka beneath the great tree just within the palisade. The change must have been very gradual to have eluded his notice until now. And what was it that had caused him to realize it so suddenly? His gaze wandered from the girl to the body of the dead bull. For the first time there flashed to his understanding the explanation of the reason for the girl's attempted abduction. Korak's eyes went wide and then they closed to narrow slits of rage as he stood glaring down upon the abysmal brute at his feet. When next his glance rose to Meriem's face a slow flush suffused his own. Now, indeed, was he looking upon her through new eyes—the eyes of a man looking upon a maid.

Akut had come up just as Meriem had speared Korak's antagonist. The exultation of the old ape was keen. He strutted, stifflegged and truculent about the body of the fallen enemy. He growled and upcurved his long, flexible lip. His hair bristled. He was paying no attention to Meriem and Korak. Back in the uttermost recesses of his little brain something was stirring—something which the sight and smell of the great bull had aroused. The outward manifestation of the germinating idea was one of bestial rage; but the inner sensations were pleasurable in the extreme. The scent of the great bull and the sight of his huge and hairy figure had wakened in the heart of Akut a longing for the companionship of his own kind. So Korak was not alone undergoing a change.

And Meriem? She was a woman. It is woman's divine right to love. Always she had loved Korak. He was her big brother.

Meriem alone underwent no change. She was still happy in the companionship of her Korak. She still loved him—as a sister loves an indulgent brother—and she was very, very proud of him. In all the jungle there was no other creature so strong, so handsome, or so brave.

Korak came close to her. There was a new light in his eyes as she looked up into them; but she did not understand it. She did not realize how close they were to maturity, nor aught of all the difference in their lives the look in Korak's eyes might mean.

"Meriem," he whispered and his voice was husky as he laid a brown hand upon her bare shoulder. "Meriem!" Suddenly he crushed her to him. She looked up into his face, laughing, and then he bent and kissed her full upon the mouth. Even then she did not understand. She did not recall ever having been kissed before. It was very nice. Meriem liked it. She thought it was Korak's way of showing how glad he was that the great ape had not succeeded in running away with her. She was glad too, so she put her arms about The Killer's neck and kissed him again and again. Then, discovering the doll in his belt she transferred it to her own possession, kissing it as she had kissed Korak.

Korak wanted to say something. He wanted to tell her how he loved her; but the emotion of his love choked him and the vocabulary of the Mangani was limited.

There came a sudden interruption. It was from Akut—a sudden, low growl, no louder than those he had been giving vent to the while he pranced about the dead bull, nor half so loud in fact; but of a timbre that bore straight to the perceptive faculties of the jungle beast ingrained in Korak. It was a warning. Korak looked quickly up from the glorious vision of the sweet face so close to his. Now his other faculties awoke. His ears, his nostrils were on the alert. Something was coming!

The Killer moved to Akut's side. Meriem was just behind them. The three stood like carved statues gazing into the leafy tangle of the jungle. The noise that had attracted their attention increased, and presently a great ape broke through the underbrush a few paces from where they stood. The beast halted at sight of them. He gave a warning grunt back over his shoulder, and a moment later coming cautiously another bull appeared. He was followed by others—both bulls and females with young, until two score hairy monsters stood glaring at the three. It was the tribe of the dead king ape. Akut was the first to speak. He pointed to the body of the dead bull.

"Korak, mighty fighter, has killed your king," he grunted.

"There is none greater in all the jungle than Korak, son of Tarzan. Now Korak is king. What bull is greater than Korak?" It was a challenge to any bull who might care to question Korak's right to the kingship. The apes jabbered and chattered and growled among themselves for a time. At last a young bull came slowly forward rocking upon his short legs, bristling, growling, terrible.

The beast was enormous, and in the full prime of his strength. He belonged to that almost extinct species for which white men have long sought upon the information of the natives of the more inaccessible jungles. Even the natives seldom see these great, hairy, primordial men.

Korak advanced to meet the monster. He, too, was growling. In his mind a plan was revolving. To close with this powerful, untired brute after having just passed through a terrific battle with another of his kind would have been to tempt defeat. He must find an easier way to victory. Crouching, he prepared to meet the charge which he knew would soon come, nor did he have long to wait. His antagonist paused only for sufficient time to permit him to recount for the edification of the audience and the confounding of Korak a brief résumé of his former victories, of his prowess, and of what he was about to do to this puny Tarmangani. Then he charged.

With clutching fingers and wide opened jaws he came down upon the waiting Korak with the speed of an express train. Korak did not move until the great arms swung to embrace him, then he dropped low beneath them, swung a terrific right to the side of the beast's jaw as he sidestepped his rushing body, and swinging quickly about stood ready over the fallen ape where he sprawled upon the ground.

It was a surprised anthropoid that attempted to scramble to its feet. Froth flecked its hideous lips. Red were the little eyes. Blood curdling roars tumbled from the deep chest. But it did not reach its feet. The Killer stood waiting above it, and the moment that the hairy chin came upon the proper level another blow that would have felled an ox sent the ape over backward.

Again and again the beast struggled to arise, but each time the mighty Tarmangani stood waiting with ready fist and pile driver blow to bowl him over. Weaker and weaker became the efforts of the bull. Blood smeared his face and breast. A red stream trickled from nose and mouth. The crowd that had cheered him on at first with savage yells, now jeered him—their approbation was for the Tarmangani.

"Kagoda?" inquired Korak, as he sent the bull down once more.

Again the stubborn bull essayed to scramble to his feet. Again The Killer struck him a terrific blow. Again he put the question, *kagoda*—have you had enough?

For a moment the bull lay motionless. Then from between battered lips came the single word: *"Kagoda!"*

"Then rise and go back among your people," said Korak. "I do not wish to be king among people who once drove me from them. Keep your own ways, and we will keep ours. When we meet we may be friends, but we shall not live together."

An old bull came slowly toward The Killer.

"You have killed our king," he said. "You have defeated him who would have been king. You could have killed him had you wished. What shall we do for a king?"

Korak turned toward Akut.

"There is your king," he said. But Akut did not want to be separated from Korak, although he was anxious enough to remain with his own kind. He wanted Korak to remain, too. He said as much.

The youth was thinking of Meriem—of what would be best and safest for her. If Akut went away with the apes there would be but one to watch over and protect her. On the other hand were they to join the tribe he would never feel safe to leave Meriem behind when he went out to hunt, for the passions of the ape-folk are not ever well controlled. Even a female might develop an insane hatred for the slender white girl and kill her during Korak's absence.

"We will live near you," he said, at last. "When you change your hunting ground we will change ours, Meriem and I, and so remain near you; but we shall not dwell among you."

Akut raised objections to this plan. He did not wish to be separated from Korak. At first he refused to leave his human friend for the companionship of his own kind; but when he saw the last of the tribe wandering off into the jungle again and his glance rested upon the lithe figure of the dead king's young mate as she cast admiring glances at her lord's successor the call of blood would not be denied. With a farewell glance toward his beloved Korak he turned and followed the she ape into the labyrinthine mazes of the wood.

After Korak had left the village of the blacks following his last thieving expedition, the screams of his victim and those of the other women and children had brought the warriors in from the forest and the river. Great was the excitement and hot was the rage of the men when they learned that the white devil had again entered their homes, frightened their women and stolen arrows and ornaments and food.

Even their superstitious fear of this weird creature who hunted with a huge bull ape was overcome in their desire to wreak vengeance upon him and rid themselves for good and all of the menace of his presence in the jungle.

And so it was that a score of the fleetest and most doughty warriors of the tribe set out in pursuit of Korak and Akut but a few minutes after they had left the scene of The Killer's many depredations.

The youth and the ape had traveled slowly and with no precautions against a successful pursuit. Nor was their attitude of careless indifference to the blacks at all remarkable. So many similar raids had gone unpunished that the two had come to look upon the Negroes with contempt. The return journey led them straight up wind. The result being that the scent of their pursuers was borne away from them, so they proceeded upon their way in total ignorance of the fact that tireless trackers but little less expert in the mysteries of woodcraft than themselves were dogging their trail with savage insistence.

The little party of warriors was led by Kovudoo, the chief; a middle-aged savage of exceptional cunning and bravery. It was he who first came within sight of the quarry which they had followed for hours by the mysterious methods of their almost uncanny powers of observation, intuition, and even scent.

Kovudoo and his men came upon Korak, Akut and Meriem after the killing of the king ape, the noise of the combat having led them at last straight to their quarry. The sight of the slender white girl had amazed the savage chief and held him gazing at the trio for a moment before ordering his warriors to rush out upon their prey. In that moment it was that the great apes came and again the blacks remained awestruck witnesses to the palaver, and the battle between Korak and the young bull.

But now the apes had gone, and the white youth and the white maid stood alone in the jungle. One of Kovudoo's men leaned close to the ear of his chief. "Look!" he whispered, and pointed to something that dangled at the girl's side. "When my brother and I were slaves in the village of The Sheik my brother made that thing for The Sheik's little daughter—she played with it always and called it after my brother, whose name is Geeka. Just before we escaped some one came and struck down The Sheik, stealing his daughter away. If this is she The Sheik will pay you well for her return."

Korak's arm had again gone around the shoulders of Meriem. Love raced hot through his young veins. Civilization was but a half-remembered state—London as remote as ancient Rome. In all the world there were but they two—Korak, The Killer, and Meriem, his mate. Again he drew her close to him and covered her willing lips with his hot kisses. And then from behind him broke a hideous bedlam of savage war cries and a score of shrieking blacks were upon them.

Korak turned to give battle. Meriem with her own light spear stood by his side. An avalanche of barbed missiles flew about them. One pierced Korak's shoulder, another his leg, and he went down.

Meriem was unscathed for the blacks had intentionally spared her. Now they rushed forward to finish Korak and make good the girl's capture; but as they came there came also from another point in the jungle the great Akut and at his heels the huge bulls of his new kingdom.

Snarling and roaring they rushed upon the black warriors when they saw the mischief they had already wrought. Kovudoo, realizing the danger of coming to close quarters with these mighty ape-men, seized Meriem and called upon his warriors to retreat. For a time the apes followed them, and several of the blacks were badly mauled and one killed before they succeeded in escaping. Nor would they have gotten off thus easily had Akut not been more concerned with the condition of the wounded Korak than with the fate of the girl upon whom he had always looked as more or less of an interloper and an unquestioned burden.

Korak lay bleeding and unconscious when Akut reached his side. The great ape tore the heavy spears from his flesh, licked the wounds and then carried his friend to the lofty shelter that Korak had constructed for Meriem. Further than this the brute could do nothing. Nature must accomplish the rest unaided or Korak must die.

He did not die, however. For days he lay helpless with fever, while Akut and the apes hunted close by that they might protect him from such birds and beasts as might reach his lofty retreat. Occasionally Akut brought him juicy fruits which helped to slake his thirst and allay his fever, and little by little his powerful constitution overcame the effects of the spear thrusts. The wounds healed and his strength returned. All during his rational moments as he had lain upon the soft furs which lined Meriem's nest he had suffered more acutely from fears for Meriem than from the pain of his own wounds. For her he must live. For her he must regain his strength that he might set out in search of her. What had the blacks done to her? Did she still live, or had they sacrificed her to their lust for torture and human flesh? Korak almost trembled with terror as the most hideous possibilities of the girl's fate suggested themselves to him out of his knowledge of the customs of Kovudoo's tribe.

The days dragged their weary lengths along, but at last he had sufficiently regained his strength to crawl from the shelter and make his way unaided to the ground. Now he lived more upon raw meat, for which he was entirely dependent on Akut's skill and generosity. With the meat diet his strength returned more rapidly, and at last he felt that he was fit to undertake the journey to the village of the blacks.

12

Two TALL, BEARDED white men moved cautiously through the jungle from their camp beside a wide river. They were Carl Jenssen and Sven Malbihn, but little altered in appearance since the day, years before, that they and their *safari* had been so badly frightened by Korak and Akut as the former sought haven with them.

Every year had they come into the jungle to trade with the natives, or to rob them; to hunt and trap; or to guide other white men in the land they knew so well. Always since their experience with The Sheik had they operated at a safe distance from his territory.

Now they were closer to his village than they had been for years, yet safe enough from discovery owing to the uninhabited nature of the intervening jungle and the fear and enmity of Kovudoo's people for The Sheik, who, in time past, had raided and all but exterminated the tribe.

This year they had come to trap live specimens for a European zoological garden, and today they were approaching a trap which they had set in the hope of capturing a specimen of the large baboons that frequented the neighborhood. As they approached the trap they became aware from the noises emanating from its vicinity that their efforts had been crowned with success. The barking and screaming of hundreds of baboons could mean naught else than that one or more of their number had fallen a victim to the allurements of the bait.

The extreme caution of the two men was prompted by former experiences with the intelligent and doglike creatures with which they had to deal. More than one trapper has lost his life in battle with enraged baboons who will hesitate to attack nothing upon one occasion, while upon another a single gun shot will disperse hundreds of them.

Heretofore the Swedes had always watched nearby their trap, for as a rule only the stronger bulls are thus caught, since in their greediness they prevent the weaker from approaching the coveted bait, and when once with the ordinary rude trap woven on the spot of interlaced branches they are able, with the aid of their friends upon the outside, to demolish their prison and escape. But in this instance the trappers had utilized a special steel cage which could withstand all the strength and cunning of a baboon. It was only necessary, therefore, to drive away the herd which they knew were surrounding the prison and wait for their boys who were even now following them to the trap.

As they came within sight of the spot they found conditions precisely as they had expected. A large male was battering frantically against the steel wires of the cage that held him captive. Upon the outside several hundred other baboons were tearing and tugging in his aid, and all were roaring and jabbering and barking at the top of their lungs.

But what neither the Swedes nor the baboons saw was the half-naked figure of a youth hidden in the foliage of a nearby tree. He had come upon the scene at almost the same instant as Jenssen and Malbihn, and was watching the activities of the baboons with every mark of interest.

Korak's relations with the baboons had never been over friendly. A species of armed toleration had marked their occasional meetings. The baboons and Akut had walked stiff legged and growling past one another, while Korak had maintained a bared fang neutrality. So now he was not greatly disturbed by the predicament of their king. Curiosity prompted him to tarry a moment, and in that moment his quick eyes caught the unfamiliar coloration of the clothing of the two Swedes behind a bush not far from him. Now he was all alertness. Who were these interlopers? What was their business in the jungle of the Mangani? Korak slunk noiselessly around them to a point where he might get their scent as well as a better view of them, and scarce had he done so when he recognized them—they were the men who had fired upon him years before. His eyes blazed. He could feel the hairs upon his scalp stiffen at the roots. He watched them with the intentness of a panther about to spring upon its prey.

He saw them rise and, shouting, attempt to frighten away the baboons as they approached the cage. Then one of them raised his rifle and fired into the midst of the surprised and angry herd. For an instant Korak thought that the baboons were about to charge, but two more shots from the rifles of the white men sent them scampering into the trees. Then the two Europeans advanced upon the cage. Korak thought that they were going to kill the king. He cared nothing for the king but he cared less for the two white men. The king had never attempted to kill him—the white men had. The king was a denizen of his own beloved jungle—the white men were aliens. His loyalty therefore was to the baboon against the human. He could speak the language of the baboon—it was identical to that of the great apes. Across the clearing he saw the jabbering horde watching.

Raising his voice he shouted to them. The white men turned at the sound of this new factor behind them. They thought it was another baboon that had circled them; but though they searched the trees with their eyes they saw nothing of the now silent figure hidden by the foliage. Again Korak shouted.

"I am The Killer," he cried. "These men are my enemies and yours. I will help you free your king. Run out upon the strangers when you see me do so, and together we will drive them away and free your king."

And from the baboons came a great chorus: "We will do what you say, Korak."

Dropping from his tree Korak ran toward the two Swedes, and at the same instant three hundred baboons followed his example. At sight of the strange apparition of the half-naked white warrior rushing upon them with uplifted spear Jenssen and Malbihn raised their rifles and fired at Korak; but in the excitement both missed and a moment later the baboons were upon them. Now their only hope of safety lay in escape, and dodging here and there, fighting off the great beasts that leaped upon their backs, they ran into the jungle. Even then they would have died but for the coming of their men whom they met a couple of hundred yards from the cage.

Once the white men had turned in flight Korak gave them no further attention, turning instead to the imprisoned baboon. The fastenings of the door that had eluded the mental powers of the baboons, yielded their secret immediately to the human intelligence of The Killer, and a moment later the king baboon stepped forth to liberty. He wasted no breath in thanks to Korak, nor did the young man expect thanks. He knew that none of the baboons would ever forget his service, though as a matter of fact he did not care if they did. What he had done had been prompted by a desire to be revenged upon the two white men. The baboons could never be of service to him. Now they were racing in the direction of the battle that was being waged between their fellows and the followers of the two Swedes, and as the din of battle subsided in the distance, Korak turned and resumed his journey toward the village of Kovudoo.

On the way he came upon a herd of elephants standing in an open forest glade. Here the trees were too far apart to permit Korak to travel through the branches—a trail he much preferred not only because of its freedom from dense underbrush and the wider field of vision it gave him but from pride in his arboreal ability. It was exhilarating to swing from tree to tree; to test the prowess of his mighty muscles; to reap the pleasurable fruits of his hard won agility. Korak joyed in the thrills of the highflung upper terraces of the great forest, where, unhampered and unhindered, he might laugh down upon the great brutes who must keep forever to the darkness and the gloom of the musty soil.

But here, in this open glade where Tantor flapped his giant ears and swayed his huge bulk from side to side, the ape-man must pass along the surface of the ground—a pygmy amongst giants. A great bull raised his trunk to rattle a low warning as he sensed the coming of an intruder. His weak eyes roved hither and thither but it was his keen scent and acute hearing which first located the ape-man. The herd moved restlessly, prepared for fight, for the old bull had caught the scent of man.

"Peace, Tantor," called The Killer. "It is I, Korak, Tarmangani."

The bull lowered his trunk and the herd resumed their interrupted meditations. Korak passed within a foot of the great bull. A sinuous trunk undulated toward him, touching his brown hide in a half caress. Korak slapped the great shoulder affectionately as he went by. For years he had been upon good terms with Tantor and his people. Of all the jungle folk he loved best the mighty pachyderm—the most peaceful and at the same time the most terrible of them all. The gentle gazelle feared him not, yet Numa, lord of the jungle, gave him a wide berth. Among the younger bulls, the cows and the calves Korak wound his way. Now and then another trunk would run out to touch him, and once a playful calf grasped his legs and upset him.

The afternoon was almost spent when Korak arrived at the village of Kovudoo. There were many natives lolling in shady spots beside the conical huts or beneath the branches of the several trees which had been left standing within the enclosure. Warriors were in evidence upon hand. It was not a good time for a lone enemy to prosecute a search through the village. Korak determined to await the coming of darkness. He was a match for many warriors; but he could not, unaided, overcome an entire tribe—not even for his beloved Meriem. While he waited among the branches and foliage of a nearby tree he searched the village constantly with his keen eyes, and twice he circled it, sniffing the vagrant breezes which puffed erratically from first one point of the compass and then another. Among the various stenches peculiar to a native village the ape-man's sensitive nostrils were finally rewarded by cognizance of the delicate aroma which marked the presence of her he sought. Meriem was there—in one of those huts! But which one he could not know without closer investigation, and so he waited, with the dogged patience of a beast of prey, until night had fallen.

The camp fires of the blacks dotted the gloom with little points of light, casting their feeble rays in tiny circles of luminosity that brought into glistening relief the naked bodies of those who lay or squatted about them. It was then that Korak slid silently from the tree that had hidden him and dropped lightly to the ground within the enclosure.

Keeping well in the shadows of the huts he commenced a systematic search of the village—ears, eyes and nose constantly upon the alert for the first intimation of the near presence of Meriem. His progress must of necessity be slow since not even the keen-eared curs of the savages must guess the presence of a stranger within the gates. How close he came to a detection on several occasions The Killer well knew from the restless whining of several of them.

It was not until he reached the back of a hut at the head of the wide village street that Korak caught again, plainly, the scent of Meriem. With nose close to the thatched wall Korak sniffed eagerly about the structure—tense and palpitant as a hunting hound. Toward the front and the door he made his way when once his nose had assured him that Meriem lay within; but as he rounded the side and came within view of the entrance he saw a burly Negro armed with a long spear squatting at the portal of the girl's prison. The fellow's back was toward him, his figure outlined against the glow of cooking fires further down the street. He was alone. The nearest of his fellows were beside a fire sixty or seventy feet beyond. To enter the hut Korak must either silence the sentry or pass him unnoticed. The danger in the accomplishment of the former alternative lay in the practical certainty of alarming the warriors nearby and bringing them and the balance of the village down upon him. To achieve the latter appeared practically impossible. To you or me it would have been impossible; but Korak, The Killer, was not as you or I.

There was a good twelve inches of space between the broad back of the black and the frame of the doorway. Could Korak pass through behind the savage warrior without detection? The light that fell upon the glistening ebony of the sentry's black skin fell also upon the light brown of Korak's. Should one of the many further down the street chance to look long in this direction they must surely note the tall, light-colored, moving figure; but Korak depended upon their interest in their own gossip to hold their attention fast where it already lay, and upon the firelight near them to prevent them seeing too plainly at a distance into the darkness at the village end where his work lay.

Flattened against the side of the hut, yet not arousing a single warning rustle from its dried thatching, The Killer came closer and closer to the watcher. Now he was at his shoulder. Now he had wormed his sinuous way behind him. He could feel the heat of the naked body against his knees. He could hear the man breathe. He marveled that the dull-witted creature had not long since been alarmed; but the fellow sat there as ignorant of the presence of another as though that other had not existed.

Korak moved scarcely more than an inch at a time, then he would stand motionless for a moment. Thus was he worming his way behind the guard when the latter straightened up, opened his cavernous mouth in a wide yawn, and stretched his arms above his head. Korak stood rigid as stone. Another step and he would be within the hut. The black lowered his arms and relaxed. Behind him was the frame work of the doorway. Often before had it supported his sleepy head, and now he leaned back to enjoy the forbidden pleasure of a cat nap.

But instead of the door frame his head and shoulders came in contact with the warm flesh of a pair of living legs. The exclamation of surprise that almost burst from his lips was throttled in his throat by steel-thewed fingers that closed about his windpipe with the suddenness of thought. The black struggled to arise—to turn upon the creature that had seized him—to wriggle from its hold; but all to no purpose. As he had been held in a mighty vise of iron he could not move. He could not scream. Those awful fingers at his throat but closed more and more tightly. His eyes bulged from their sockets. His face turned an ashy blue. Presently he relaxed once more—this time in the final dissolution from which there is no quickening. Korak propped the dead body against the door frame. There it sat, lifelike in the gloom. Then the ape-man turned and glided into the Stygian darkness of the hut's interior.

"Meriem!" he whispered.

"Korak! My Korak!" came an answering cry, subdued by fear of alarming her captors, and half stifled by a sob of joyful welcome.

The youth knelt and cut the bonds that held the girl's wrists and ankles. A moment later he had lifted her to her feet, and grasping her by the hand led her towards the entrance. Outside the grim sentinel of death kept his grisly vigil. Sniffing at his dead feet whined a mangy native cur. At sight of the two emerging from the hut the beast gave an ugly snarl and an instant later as it caught the scent of the strange white man it raised a series of excited yelps. Instantly the warriors at the nearby fire were attracted. They turned their heads in the direction of the commotion. It was impossible that they should fail to see the white skins of the fugitives.

Korak slunk quickly into the shadows at the hut's side, drawing Meriem with him; but he was too late. The blacks had seen enough to arouse their suspicions and a dozen of them were now running to investigate. The yapping cur was still at Korak's heels leading the searchers unerringly in pursuit. The youth struck viciously at the brute with his long spear; but, long accustomed to dodging blows, the wily creature made a most uncertain target.

Other blacks had been alarmed by the running and shouting of their companions and now the entire population of the village was swarming up the street to assist in the search. Their first discovery was the dead body of the sentry, and a moment later one of the bravest of them had entered the hut and discovered the absence of the prisoner. These startling announcements filled the blacks with a combination of terror and rage; but, seeing no foe in evidence they were enabled to permit their rage to get the better of their terror, and so the leaders, pushed on by those behind them, ran rapidly around the hut in the direction of the yapping of the mangy cur. Here they found a single white warrior making away with their captive, and recognizing him as the author of numerous raids and indignities and believing that they had him cornered and at a disadvantage, they charged savagely upon him.

Korak, seeing that they were discovered, lifted Meriem to his shoulders and ran for the tree which would give them egress from the village. He was handicapped in his flight by the weight of the girl whose legs would but scarce bear her weight, to say nothing of maintaining her in rapid flight, for the tightly drawn bonds that had been about her ankles for so long had stopped circulation and partially paralyzed her extremities.

Had this not been the case the escape of the two would have been a feat of little moment, since Meriem was scarcely a whit less agile than Korak, and fully as much at home in the trees as he. But with the girl on his shoulder Korak could not both run and fight to advantage, and the result was that before he had covered half the distance to the tree a score of native curs attracted by the yelping of their mate and the yells and shouts of their masters had closed in upon the fleeing white man, snapping at his legs and at last succeeding in tripping him. As he went down the hyena-like brutes were upon him, and as he struggled to his feet the blacks closed in.

A couple of them seized the clawing, biting Meriem, and subdued her—a blow upon the head was sufficient. For the ape-man they found more drastic measures would be necessary. Weighted down as he was by dogs and warriors he still managed to struggle to his feet. To right and left he swung crushing blows to the faces of his human antagonists—to the dogs he paid not the slightest attention other than to seize the more persistent and wring their necks with a single quick movement of the wrist.

A knob stick aimed at him by an ebon Hercule he caught and wrested from his antagonist, and then the blacks experienced to the full the possibilities for punishment that lay within those smooth flowing muscles beneath the velvet brown skin of the strange, white giant. He rushed among them with all the force and ferocity of a bull elephant gone mad. Hither and thither he charged striking down the few who had the temerity to stand against him, and it was evident that unless a chance spear thrust brought him down he would rout the entire village and regain his prize. But old Kovudoo was not to be so easily robbed of the ransom which the girl represented, and seeing that their attack which had up to now resulted in a series of individual combats with the white warrior, he called his tribesmen off, and forming them in a compact body about the girl and the two who watched over her bid them do nothing more than repel the assaults of the ape-man.

Again and again Korak rushed against this human barricade bristling with spear points. Again and again he was repulsed, often with severe wounds to caution him to greater wariness. From head to foot he was red with his own blood, and at last, weakening from the loss of it, he came to the bitter realization that alone he could do no more to succor his Meriem.

Presently an idea flashed through his brain. He called aloud to the girl. She had regained consciousness now and replied.

"Korak goes," he shouted, "but he will return and take you from the Gomangani. Good-bye, my Meriem. Korak will come for you again."

"Good-bye!" cried the girl. "Meriem will look for you until you come."

Like a flash, and before they could know his intention or prevent him, Korak wheeled, raced across the village and with a single leap disappeared into the foliage of the great tree that was his highroad to the village of Kovudoo. A shower of spears followed him, but their only harvest was a taunting laugh flung back from out the darkness of the jungle.

13

MERIEM, AGAIN BOUND and under heavy guard in Kovudoo's own hut, saw the night pass and the new day come without bringing the momentarily looked for return of Korak. She had no doubt but that he would come back and less still that he would easily free her from her captivity. To her Korak was little short of omnipotent. He embodied for her all that was finest and strongest and best in her savage world. She gloried in his prowess and worshipped him for the tender thoughtfulness that always had marked his treatment of her. No other within the ken of her memory had ever accorded her the love and gentleness that was his daily offering to her. Most of the gentler attributes of his early childhood had long since been forgotten in the fierce battle for existence which the customs of the mysterious jungle had forced upon him. He was more often savage and bloodthirsty than tender and kindly. His other friends of the wild looked for no gentle tokens of his affection. That he would hunt with them and fight for them was sufficient. If he growled and showed his fighting fangs when they trespassed upon his inalienable rights to the fruits of his kills they felt no anger toward him—only greater respect for the efficient and the fit—for him who could not only kill but protect the flesh of his kill.

But toward Meriem he always had shown more of his human side. He killed primarily for her. It was to the feet of Meriem that he brought the fruits of his labors. It was for Meriem more than for himself that he squatted beside his flesh and growled ominously at whosoever dared sniff too closely to it. When he was cold in the dark days of rain, or thirsty in a prolonged drouth, his discomfort engendered first of all thoughts of Meriem's welfare—after she had been made warm, after her thirst had been slaked, then he turned to the affair of ministering to his own wants.

The softest skins fell gracefully from the graceful shoulders of his Meriem. The sweetest-scented grasses lined her bower where other soft, furry pelts made hers the downiest couch in all the jungle.

What wonder then that Meriem loved her Korak? But she loved him as a little sister might love a big brother who was very good to her. As yet she knew naught of the love of a maid for a man.

So now as she lay waiting for him she dreamed of him and of all that he meant to her. She compared him with The Sheik, her father, and at thought of the stern, grizzled, old Arab she shuddered. Even the savage blacks had been less harsh to her than he. Not understanding their tongue she could not guess what purpose they had in keeping her a prisoner. She knew that man ate man, and she had expected to be eaten; but she had been with them for some time now and no harm had befallen her. She did not know that a runner had been dispatched to the distant village of The Sheik to barter with him for a ransom. She did not know, nor did Kovudoo, that the runner had never reached his destination—that he had fallen in with the *safari* of Jenssen and Malbihn and with the talkativeness of a native to other natives had unfolded his whole mission to the black servants of the two Swedes. These had not been long in retailing the matter to their masters, and the result was that when the runner left their camp to continue his journey he had scarce passed from sight before there came the report of a rifle and he rolled lifeless into the underbrush with a bullet in his back.

A few moments later Malbihn strolled back into the encampment, where he went to some pains to let it be known that he had had a shot at a fine buck and missed. The Swedes knew that their men hated them, and that an overt act against Kovudoo would quickly be carried to the chief at the first opportunity. Nor were they sufficiently strong in either guns or loyal followers to risk antagonizing the wily old chief.

Following this episode came the encounter with the baboons and the strange, white savage who had allied himself with the beasts against the humans. Only by dint of masterful maneuvering and the expenditure of much power had the Swedes been able to repulse the infuriated apes, and even for hours afterward their camp was constantly besieged by hundreds of snarling, screaming devils.

The Swedes, rifles in hand, repelled numerous savage charges which lacked only efficient leadership to have rendered them as effective in results as they were terrifying in appearance. Time and time again the two men thought they saw the smooth-skinned body of the wild ape-man moving among the baboons in the forest, and the belief that he might head a charge upon them proved most disquieting. They would have given much for a clean shot at him, for to him they attributed the loss of their specimen and the ugly attitude of the baboons toward them.

"The fellow must be the same we fired on several years ago," said Malbihn. "That time he was accompanied by a gorilla. Did you get a good look at him, Carl?"

"Yes," replied Jenssen. "He was not five paces from me when I fired at him. He appears to be an intelligent looking European—and not much more than a lad. There is nothing of the imbecile or degenerate in his features or expression, as is usually true in similar cases, where some lunatic escapes into the woods and by living in filth and nakedness wins the title of wild man among the peasants of the neighborhood. No, this fellow is of different stuff—and so infinitely more to be feared. As much as I should like a shot at him I hope he stays away. Should he ever deliberately lead a charge against us I wouldn't give much for our chances if we happened to fail to bag him at the first rush."

But the white giant did not appear again to lead the baboons against them, and finally the angry brutes themselves wandered off into the jungle leaving the frightened *safari* in peace.

The next day the Swedes set out for Kovudoo's village bent on securing possession of the person of the white girl whom Kovudoo's runner had told them lay captive in the chief's village. How they were to accomplish their end they did not know. Force was out of the question, though they would not have hesitated to use it had they possessed it. In former years they had marched rough shod over enormous areas, taking toll by brute force even when kindliness or diplomacy would have accomplished more; but now they were in bad straits—so bad that they had shown their true colors scared twice in a year and then only when they came upon an isolated village, weak in numbers and poor in courage.

Kovudoo was not as these, and though his village was in a way remote from the more populous district to the north his power was such that he maintained an acknowledged suzerainty over the thin thread of villages which connected him with the savage lords to the north. To have antagonized him would have spelled ruin for the Swedes. It would have meant that they might never reach civilization by the northern route. To the west, the village of The Sheik lay directly in their path, barring them effectually. To the east the trail was unknown to them, and to the south there was no trail. So the two Swedes approached the village of Kovudoo with friendly words upon their tongues and deep craft in their hearts.

Their plans were well made. There was no mention of the white prisoner—they chose to pretend that they were not aware that Kovudoo had a white prisoner. They exchanged gifts with the old chief, haggling with his plenipotentiaries over the value of what they were to receive for what they gave, as is customary and proper when one has no ulterior motives. Unwarranted generosity would have aroused suspicion.

During the palaver which followed they retailed the gossip of the villages through which they had passed, receiving in exchange such news as Kovudoo possessed. The palaver was long and tiresome, as these native ceremonies always are to Europeans. Kovudoo made no mention of his prisoner and from his generous offers of guides and presents seemed anxious to assure himself of the speedy departure of his guests. It was Malbihn who, quite casually, near the close of their talk, mentioned the fact that The Sheik was dead. Kovudoo evinced interest and surprise.

"You did not know it?" asked Malbihn. "That is strange. It was during the last moon. He fell from his horse when the beast stepped in a hole. The horse fell upon him. When his men came up The Sheik was quite dead."

Kovudoo scratched his head. He was much disappointed. No Sheik meant no ransom for the white girl. Now she was worthless, unless he utilized her for a feast or—a mate. The latter thought aroused him. He spat at a small beetle crawling through the dust before him. He eyed Malbihn appraisingly. These white men were peculiar. They traveled far from their own villages without women. Yet he knew that they cared for women. But how much did they care for them?—that was the question that disturbed Kovudoo.

"I know where there is a white girl," he said, unexpectedly. "If you wish to buy her she may be had cheap."

Malbihn shrugged. "We have troubles enough, Kovudoo," he said, "without burdening ourselves with an old she-hyena, and as for paying for one—" Malbihn snapped his fingers in derision.

"She is young," said Kovudoo, "and good looking."

The Swedes laughed. "There are no good-looking white women in the jungle, Kovudoo," said Jenssen. "You should be ashamed to try to make fun of old friends."

Kovudoo sprang to his feet. "Come," he said, "I will show you that she is all I say."

Malbihn and Jenssen rose to follow him and as they did so their eyes met, and Malbihn slowly drooped one of his lids in a sly wink. Together they followed Kovudoo toward his hut. In the dim interior they discerned the figure of a woman lying bound upon a sleeping mat.

Malbihn took a single glance and turned away. "She must be a thousand years old, Kovudoo," he said, as he left the hut.

"She is young," cried the savage. "It is dark in here. You cannot see. Wait, I will have her brought out into the sunlight," and he commanded the two warriors who watched the girl to cut the bonds from her ankles and lead her forth for inspection.

Malbihn and Jenssen evinced no eagerness, though both were fairly bursting with it—not to see the girl but to obtain possession of her. They cared not if she had the face of a marmoset, or the figure of pot-bellied Kovudoo himself. All that they wished to know was that she was the girl who had been stolen from The Sheik several years before. They thought that they would recognize her for such if she was indeed the same, but even so the testimony of the runner Kovudoo had sent to The Sheik was such as to assure them that the girl was the one they had once before attempted to abduct.

As Meriem was brought forth from the darkness of the hut's interior the two men turned with every appearance of disinterestedness to glance at her. It was with difficulty that Malbihn suppressed an ejaculation of astonishment. The girl's beauty fairly took his breath from him; but instantly he recovered his poise and turned to Kovudoo.

"Well?" he said to the old chief.

"Is she not both young and good-looking?" asked Kovudoo.

"She is not old," replied Malbihn, "but even so she will be a burden. We did not come from the north after wives—there are more than enough there for us."

Meriem stood looking straight at the white men. She expected nothing from them—they were to her as much enemies as the black men. She hated and feared them all. Malbihn spoke to her in Arabic.

"We are friends," he said. "Would you like to have us take you away from here?"

Slowly and dimly as though from a great distance recollection of the once familiar tongue returned to her.

"I should like to go free," she said, "and go back to Korak."

"You would like to go with us?" persisted Malbihn.

"No," said Meriem.

Malbihn turned to Kovudoo. "She does not wish to go with us," he said.

"You are men," returned the black. "Can you not take her by force?"

"It would only add to our troubles," replied the Swede. "No, Kovudoo, we do not wish her; though, if you wish to be rid of her, we will take her away because of our friendship for you."

Now Kovudoo knew that he had made a sale. They wanted her. So he commenced to bargain, and in the end the person of Meriem passed from the possession of the black chieftain into that of the two Swedes in consideration of six yards of Amerikan, three empty brass cartridge shells and a shiny, new jack knife from New Jersey. And all but Meriem were more than pleased with the bargain.

Kovudoo stipulated but a single condition and that was that the Europeans were to leave his village and take the girl with them as early the next morning as they could get started. After the sale was consummated he did not hesitate to explain his reasons for this demand. He told them of the strenuous attempt of the girl's savage mate to rescue her, and suggested that the sooner they got her out of the country the more likely they were to retain possession of her.

Meriem was again bound and placed under guard, but this time in the tent of the Swedes. Malbihn talked to her, trying to persuade her to accompany them willingly. He told her that they would return her to her own village; but when he discovered that she would rather die than go back to the old sheik, he assured her that they would not take her there, nor, as a matter of fact, had they had an intention of so doing. As he talked with the girl the Swede feasted his eyes upon the beautiful lines of her face and figure. She had grown tall and straight and slender toward maturity since he had seen her in The Sheik's village on that long gone day. For years she had represented to him a certain fabulous reward. In his thoughts she had been but the personification of the pleasures and luxuries that many francs would purchase. Now as she stood before him pulsing with life and loveliness she suggested other seductive and alluring possibilities. He came closer to her and laid his hand upon her. The girl shrank from him. He seized her and she struck him heavily in the mouth as he sought to kiss her. Then Jenssen entered the tent.

"Malbihn!" he almost shouted. "You fool!"

Sven Malbihn released his hold upon the girl and turned toward his companion. His face was red with mortification.

"What the devil are you trying to do?" growled Jenssen. "Would you throw away every chance for the reward? If we maltreat her we not only couldn't collect a sou, but they'd send us to prison for our pains. I thought you had more sense, Malbihn."

"I'm not a wooden man," growled Malbihn.

"You'd better be," rejoined Jenssen, "at least until we have delivered her over in safety and collected what will be coming to us."

"Oh, hell," cried Malbihn. "What's the use? They'll be glad enough to have her back, and by the time we get there with her she'll be only too glad to keep her mouth shut. Why not?"

"Because I say not," growled Jenssen. "I've always let you boss things, Sven; but here's a case where what I say has got to go— because I'm right and you're wrong, and we both know it."

"You're getting damned virtuous all of a sudden," growled Malbihn. "Perhaps you think I have forgotten about the innkeeper's daughter, and little Celella, and that nigger at—"

"Shut up!" snapped Jenssen. "It's not a matter of virtue and you are as well aware of that as I. I don't want to quarrel with you, but so help me God, Sven, you're not going to harm this girl if I have to kill you to prevent it. I've suffered and slaved and been nearly killed forty times in the last nine or ten years trying to accomplish what luck has thrown at our feet at last, and now I'm not going to be robbed of the fruits of success because you happen to be more of a beast than a man. Again I warn you, Sven—" and he tapped the revolver that swung in its holster at his hip.

Malbihn gave his friend an ugly look, shrugged his shoulders, and left the tent. Jenssen turned to Meriem.

"If he bothers you again, call me," he said. "I shall always be near."

The girl had not understood the conversation that had been carried on by her two owners, for it had been in Swedish; but what Jenssen had just said to her in Arabic she understood and from it grasped an excellent idea of what had passed between the two. The expressions upon their faces, their gestures, and Jenssen's final tapping of his revolver before Malbihn had left the tent had all been eloquent of the seriousness of their altercation. Now, toward Jenssen she looked for friendship, and with the innocence of youth she threw herself upon his mercy, begging him to set her free, that she might return to Korak and her jungle life; but she was doomed to another disappointment, for the man only laughed at her roughly and told her that if she tried to escape she would be punished by the very thing that he had just saved her from.

All that night she lay listening for a signal from Korak. All about the jungle life moved through the darkness. To her sensitive ears came sounds that the others in the camp could not hear—sounds that she interpreted as we might interpret the speech of a friend, but not once came a single note that reflected the presence of Korak. But she knew that he would come. Nothing short of death itself could prevent her Korak from returning for her. What delayed him though?

When morning came again and the night had brought no succoring Korak, Meriem's faith and loyalty were still unshaken though misgivings began to assail her as to the safety of her friend. It seemed unbelievable that serious mishap could have overtaken her wonderful Korak who daily passed unscathed through all the terrors of the jungle. Yet morning came, the morning meal was eaten, the camp broken and the disreputable *safari* of the Swedes was on the move northward with still no sign of the rescue the girl momentarily expected.

All that day they marched, and the next and the next, nor did Korak even so much as show himself to the patient little waiter moving, silently and stately, beside her hard captors.

Malbihn remained scowling and angry. He replied to Jenssen's friendly advances in curt monosyllables. To Meriem he did not speak, but on several occasions she discovered him glaring at her from beneath half closed lids—greedily. The look sent a shudder through her. She hugged Geeka closer to her breast and doubly regretted the knife that they had taken from her when she was captured by Kovudoo.

It was on the fourth day that Meriem began definitely to give up hope. Something had happened to Korak. She knew it. He would never come now, and these men would take her far away. Presently they would kill her. She would never see her Korak again.

On this day the Swedes rested, for they had marched rapidly and their men were tired. Malbihn and Jenssen had gone from camp to hunt, taking different directions. They had been gone about an hour when the door of Meriem's tent was lifted and Malbihn entered. The look of a beast was on his face.

14

WITH WIDE EYES fixed upon him, like a trapped creature horrified beneath the mesmeric gaze of a great serpent, the girl watched the approach of the man. Her hands were free, the Swedes having secured her with a length of ancient slave chain fastened at one end to an iron collar padlocked about her neck and at the other to a long stake driven deep into the ground.

Slowly Meriem shrank inch by inch toward the opposite end of the tent. Malbihn followed her. His hands were extended and his fingers half-opened—claw-like—to seize her. His lips were parted, and his breath came quickly, pantingly.

The girl recalled Jenssen's instructions to call him should Malbihn molest her; but Jenssen had gone into the jungle to hunt. Malbihn had chosen his time well. Yet she screamed, loud and shrill, once, twice, a third time, before Malbihn could leap across the tent and throttle her alarming cries with his brute fingers. Then she fought him, as any jungle she might fight, with tooth and nail. The man found her no easy prey. In that slender, young body, beneath the rounded curves and the fine, soft skin, lay the muscles of a young lioness. But Malbihn was no weakling. His character and appearance were brutal, nor did they belie his brawn. He was of giant stature and of giant strength. Slowly he forced the girl back upon the ground, striking her in the face when she hurt him badly either with teeth or nails. Meriem struck back, but she was growing weaker from the choking fingers at her throat.

Out in the jungle Jenssen had brought down two bucks. His hunting had not carried him far afield, nor was he prone to permit it to do so. He was suspicious of Malbihn. The very fact that his companion had refused to accompany him and elected instead to hunt alone in another direction would not, under ordinary circumstances, have seemed fraught with sinister suggestion; but Jenssen knew Malbihn well, and so, having secured meat, he turned immediately back toward camp, while his boys brought in his kill.

He had covered about half the return journey when a scream came faintly to his ears from the direction of camp. He halted to listen. It was repeated twice. Then silence. With a muttered curse Jenssen broke into a rapid run. He wondered if he would be too late. What a fool Malbihn was indeed to thus chance jeopardizing a fortune!

Further away from camp than Jenssen and upon the opposite side another heard Meriem's screams—a stranger who was not even aware of the proximity of white men other than himself—a hunter with a handful of sleek, black warriors. He, too, listened intently for a moment. That the voice was that of a woman in distress he could not doubt, and so he also hastened at a run in the direction of the affrighted voice; but he was much further away than Jenssen so that the latter reached the tent first. What the Swede found there roused no pity within his calloused heart, only anger against his fellow scoundrel. Meriem was still fighting off her attacker. Malbihn still was showering blows upon her. Jenssen, streaming foul curses upon his erstwhile friend, burst into the tent. Malbihn, interrupted, dropped his victim and turned to meet Jenssen's infuriated charge. He whipped a revolver from his hip. Jenssen, anticipating the lightning move of the other's hand, drew almost simultaneously, and both men fired at once. Jenssen was still moving toward Malbihn at the time, but at the flash of the explosion he stopped. His revolver dropped from nerveless fingers. For a moment he staggered drunkenly. Deliberately Malbihn put two more bullets into his friend's body at close range. Even in the midst of the excitement and her terror Meriem found herself wondering at the tenacity of life which the hit man displayed. His eyes were closed, his head dropped forward upon his breast, his hands hung limply before him. Yet still he stood there upon his feet, though he reeled horribly. It was not until the third bullet had found its mark within his body that he lunged forward upon his face. Then Malbihn approached him, and with an oath kicked him viciously. Then he returned once more to Meriem. Again he seized her, and at the same instant the flaps of the tent opened silently and a tall white man stood in the aperture. Neither Meriem or Malbihn saw the newcomer. The latter's back was toward him while his body hid the stranger from Meriem's eyes.

He crossed the tent quickly, stepping over Jenssen's body. The first intimation Malbihn had that he was not to carry out his design without further interruption was a heavy hand upon his shoulder. He wheeled to face an utter stranger—a tall, black-haired, gray-eyed stranger clad in khaki and pith helmet. Malbihn reached for his gun again, but another hand had been quicker than his and he saw the weapon tossed to the ground at the side of the tent—out of reach.

"What is the meaning of this?" the stranger addressed his question to Meriem in a tongue she did not understand. She shook her head and spoke in Arabic. Instantly the man changed his question to that language.

"These men are taking me away from Korak," explained the girl. "This one would have harmed me. The other, whom he had just killed, tried to stop him. They were both very bad men; but this one is the worse. If my Korak were here he would kill him. I suppose you are like them, so you will not kill him."

The stranger smiled. "He deserves killing?" he said. "There is no doubt of that. Once I should have killed him; but not now. I will see, though, that he does not bother you any more."

He was holding Malbihn in a grasp the giant Swede could not break, though he struggled to do so, and he was holding him as easily as Malbihn might have held a little child, yet Malbihn was a huge man, mightily thewed. The Swede began to rage and curse. He struck at his captor, only to be twisted about and held at arm's length. Then he shouted to his boys to come and kill the stranger. In response a dozen strange blacks entered the tent. They, too, were powerful, clean-limbed men, not at all like the mangy crew that followed the Swedes.

"We have had enough foolishness," said the stranger to Malbihn. "You deserve death, but I am not the law. I know now who you are. I have heard of you before. You and your friend here bear a most unsavory reputation. We do not want you in our country. I shall let you go this time; but should you ever return I shall take the law into my own hands. You understand?"

Malbihn blustered and threatened, finishing by applying a most uncomplimentary name to his captor. For this he received a shaking that rattled his teeth. Those who know say that the most painful punishment that can be inflicted upon an adult male, short of injuring him, is a good, old-fashioned shaking. Malbihn received such a shaking.

"Now get out," said the stranger, "and next time you see me remember who I am," and he spoke a name in the Swede's ear— a name that more effectually subdued the scoundrel than many beatings—then he gave him a push that carried him bodily through the tent doorway to sprawl upon the turf beyond.

"Now," he said, turning toward Meriem, "who has the key to this thing about your neck?"

The girl pointed to Jenssen's body. "He carried it always," she said.

The stranger searched the clothing on the corpse until he came upon the key. A moment more Meriem was free.

"Will you let me go back to my Korak?" she asked.

"I will see that you are returned to your people," he replied. "Who are they and where is their village?"

He had been eyeing her strange, barbaric garmenture wonderingly. From her speech she was evidently an Arab girl; but he had never before seen one thus clothed.

"Who are your people? Who is Korak?" he asked again.

"Korak! Why Korak is an ape. I have no other people. Korak and I live in the jungle alone since A'ht went to be king of the apes." She had always thus pronounced Akut's name, for so it had sounded to her when first she came with Korak and the ape. "Korak could have been king, but he would not."

A questioning expression entered the stranger's eyes. He looked at the girl closely.

"So Korak is an ape?" he said. "And what, pray, are you?"

"I am Meriem. I, also, am an ape."

"M-m," was the stranger's only oral comment upon this startling announcement; but what he thought might have been partially interpreted through the pitying light that entered his eyes. He approached the girl and started to lay his hand upon her forehead. She drew back with a savage little growl. A smile touched his lips.

"You need not fear me," he said. "I shall not harm you. I only wish to discover if you have fever—if you are entirely well. If you are we will set forth in search of Korak."

Meriem looked straight into the keen gray eyes. She must have found there an unquestionable assurance of the honorableness of their owner, for she permitted him to lay his palm upon her forehead and feel her pulse. Apparently she had no fever.

"How long have you been an ape?" asked the man.

"Since I was a little girl, many, many years ago, and Korak came and took me from my father who was beating me. Since then I have lived in the trees with Korak and A'ht."

"Where in the jungle lives Korak?" asked the stranger.

Meriem pointed with a sweep of her hand that took in, generously, half the continent of Africa.

"Could you find your way back to him?"

"I do not know," she replied, "but he will find his way to me."

"Then I have a plan," said the stranger. "I live but a few marches from here. I shall take you home where my wife will look after you and care for you until we can find Korak or Korak finds us. If he could find you here he can find you at my village. Is it not so?"

Meriem thought that it was so; but she did not like the idea of not starting immediately back to meet Korak. On the other hand the man had no intention of permitting this poor, insane child to wander further amidst the dangers of the jungle. From whence she had come, or what she had undergone he could not guess, but that her Korak and their life among the apes was but a figment of a disordered mind he could not doubt. He knew the jungle well, and he knew that men have lived alone and naked among the savage beasts for years; but a frail and slender girl! No, it was not possible.

Together they went outside. Malbihn's boys were striking camp in preparation for a hasty departure. The stranger's blacks were conversing with them. Malbihn stood at a distance, angry and glowering. The stranger approached one of his own men.

"Find out where they got this girl," he commanded.

The Negro thus addressed questioned one of Malbihn's followers. Presently he returned to his master.

"They bought her from old Kovudoo," he said. "That is all that this fellow will tell me. He pretends that he knows nothing more, and I guess that he does not. These two white men were very bad men. They did many things that their boys knew not the meanings of. It would be well Bwana, to kill the other."

"I wish that I might; but a new law is come into this part of the jungle. It is not as it was in the old days, Muviri," replied the master.

The stranger remained until Malbihn and his *safari* had disappeared into the jungle toward the north. Meriem, trustful now, stood at his side, Geeka clutched in one slim, brown hand. They talked together, the man wondering at the faltering Arabic of the girl, but attributing it finally to her defective mentality. Could he have known that years had elapsed since she had used it until she was taken by the Swedes he would not have wondered that she had half forgotten it. There was yet another reason why the language of The Sheik had thus readily eluded her; but of that reason she herself could not have guessed the truth any better than could the man.

He tried to persuade her to return with him to his "village" as he called it, or *douar*, in Arabic; but she was insistent upon searching immediately for Korak. As a last resort he determined to take her with him by force rather than sacrifice her life to the insane hallucination which haunted her; but, being a wise man, he determined to humor her first and then attempt to lead her as he would have her go. So when they took up their march it was in the direction of the south, though his own ranch lay almost due east.

By degrees he turned the direction of their way more and more eastward, and greatly was he pleased to note that the girl failed to discover that any change was being made. Little by little she became more trusting. At first she had had but her intuition to guide her belief that this big Tarmangani meant her no harm, but as the days passed and she saw that his kindness and consideration never faltered she came to compare him with Korak, and to be very fond of him; but never did her loyalty to her ape-man flag.

On the fifth day they came suddenly upon a great plain and from the edge of the forest the girl saw in the distance fenced fields and many buildings. At the sight she drew back in astonishment.

"Where are we?" she asked, pointing.

"We could not find Korak," replied the man, "and as our way led near my *douar* I have brought you here to wait and rest with my wife until my men can find your ape, or he finds you. It is better thus, little one. You will be safer with us, and you will be happier."

"I am afraid, Bwana," said the girl. "In thy *douar* they will beat me as did The Sheik, my father. Let me go back into the jungle. There Korak will find me. He would not think to look for me in the douar of a white man."

"No one will beat you, child," replied the man. "I have not done so, have I? Well, here all belong to me. They will treat you well. Here no one is beaten. My wife will be very good to you, and at last Korak will come, for I shall send men to search for him."

The girl shook her head. "They could not bring him, for he would kill them, as all men have tried to kill him. I am afraid. Let me go, Bwana."

"You do not know the way to your own country. You would be lost. The leopards or the lions would get you the first night, and after all you would not find your Korak. It is better that you stay with us. Did I not save you from the bad man? Do you not owe me something for that? Well, then remain with us for a few weeks at least until we can determine what is best for you. You are only a little girl—it would be wicked to permit you to go alone into the jungle."

Meriem laughed. "The jungle," she said, "is my father and my mother. It has been kinder to me than have men. I am not afraid of the jungle. Nor am I afraid of the leopard or the lion. When my time comes I shall die. It may be that a leopard or a lion shall kill me, or it may be a tiny bug no bigger than the end of my littlest finger. When the lion leaps upon me, or the little bug stings me I shall be afraid—oh, then I shall be terribly afraid, I know; but life would be very miserable indeed were I to spend it in terror of the thing that has not yet happened. If it be the lion my terror shall be short of life; but if it be the little bug I may suffer for days before I die. And so I fear the lion least of all. He is great and noisy. I can hear him, or see him, or smell him in time to escape; but any moment I may place a hand or foot on the little bug, and never know that he is there until I feel his deadly sting. No, I do not fear the jungle. I love it. I should rather die than leave it forever; but your *douar* is close beside the jungle. You have been good to me. I will do as you wish, and remain here for a while to wait the coming of my Korak."

"Good!" said the man, and he led the way down toward the flower-covered bungalow behind which lay the barns and out-houses of a well-ordered African farm.

As they came nearer a dozen dogs ran barking toward them— gaunt wolf hounds, a huge great Dane, a nimble-footed collie and a number of yapping, quarrelsome fox terriers. At first their appearance was savage and unfriendly in the extreme; but once they recognized the foremost black warriors, and the white men behind them their attitude underwent a remarkable change. The collie and the fox terriers became frantic with delirious joy, and while the wolf hounds and the great Dane were not a whit less delighted at the return of their master their greetings were of a more dignified nature. Each in turn sniffed at Meriem who displayed not the slightest fear of any of them.

The wolf hounds bristled and growled at the scent of wild beasts that clung to her garment; but when she layed her hand upon their heads and her soft voice murmured caressingly they half-closed their eyes, lifting their upper lips in contented canine smiles. The man was watching them and he too smiled, for it was seldom that these savage brutes took thus kindly to strangers. It was as though in some subtile way the girl had breathed a message of kindred savagery to their savage hearts.

With her slim fingers grasping the collar of a wolf hound upon either side of her Meriem walked on toward the bungalow upon the porch of which a woman dressed in white waved a welcome to her returning lord. There was more fear in the girl's eyes now than there had been in the presence of strange men or savage beasts. She hesitated, turning an appealing glance toward the man.

"This is my wife," he said. "She will be glad to welcome you."

The woman came down the path to meet them. The man kissed her, and turning toward Meriem introduced them, speaking in the Arab tongue the girl understood.

"This is Meriem, my dear," he said, and he told the story of the jungle waif in so far as he knew it.

Meriem saw that the woman was beautiful. She saw that sweetness and goodness were stamped indelibly upon her countenance. She no longer feared her, and when her brief story had been narrated and the woman came and put her arms about her and kissed her and called her "poor little darling" something snapped in Meriem's little heart. She buried her face on the bosom of this new friend in whose voice was the mother tone that Meriem had not heard for so many years that she had forgotten its very existence. She buried her face on the kindly bosom and wept as she had not wept before in all her life—tears of relief and joy that she could not fathom.

And so came Meriem, the savage little Mangani, out of her beloved jungle into the midst of a home of culture and refinement. Already "Bwana" and "My Dear," as she first heard them called and continued to call them, were as father and mother to her. Once her savage fears allayed, she went to the opposite extreme of trustfulness and love. Now she was willing to wait here until they found Korak, or Korak found her. She did not give up that thought—Korak, her Korak always was first.

15

AND OUT IN the jungle, far away, Korak, covered with wounds, stiff with clotted blood, burning with rage and sorrow, swung back upon the trail of the great baboons. He had not found them where he had last seen them, nor in any of their usual haunts; but he sought them along the well-marked spoor they had left behind them, and at last he overtook them. When first he came upon them they were moving slowly but steadily southward in one of those periodic migrations the reasons for which the baboon himself is best able to explain. At sight of the white warrior who came upon them from down wind the herd halted in response to the warning cry of the sentinel that had discovered him. There was much growling and muttering; much stiff-legged circling on the part of the bulls. The mothers, in nervous, high pitched tones, called their young to their sides, and with them moved to safety behind their lords and masters.

Korak called aloud to the king, who, at the familiar voice, advanced slowly, warily, and still stiff-legged. He must have the confirmatory evidence of his nose before venturing to rely too implicitly upon the testimony of his ears and eyes. Korak stood perfectly still. To have advanced then might have precipitated an immediate attack, or, as easily, a panic of flight. Wild beasts are creatures of nerves. It is a relatively simple thing to throw them into a species of hysteria which may induce either a mania for murder, or symptoms of apparent abject cowardice—it is a question, however, if a wild animal ever is actually a coward.

The king baboon approached Korak. He walked around him in an ever decreasing circle—growling, grunting, sniffing. Korak spoke to him.

"I am Korak," he said. "I opened the cage that held you. I saved you from the Termangani. I am Korak, The Killer. I am your friend."

"Huh," grunted the king. "Yes, you are Korak. My ears told me that you were Korak. My eyes told me that you were Korak. Now my nose tells me that you are Korak. My nose is never wrong. I am your friend. Come, we shall hunt together."

"Korak cannot hunt now," replied the ape-man. "The Gomangani have stolen Meriem. They have tied her in their village. They will not let her go. Korak, alone, was unable to set her free. Korak set you free. Now will you bring your people and set Korak's Meriem free?"

"The Gomangani have many sharp sticks which they throw. They pierce the bodies of my people. They kill us. The Gomangani are bad people. They will kill us all if we enter their village."

"The Tarmangani have sticks that make a loud noise and kill at a great distance," replied Korak. "They had these when Korak set you free from their trap. If Korak had run away from them you would now be a prisoner among the Tarmangani."

The baboon scratched his head. In a rough circle about him and the ape-man squatted the bulls of his herd. They blinked their eyes, shouldered one another about for more advantageous positions, scratched in the rotting vegetation upon the chance of unearthing a toothsome worm, or sat listlessly eyeing their king and the strange Mangani, who called himself thus but who more closely resembled the hated Tarmangani. The king looked at some of the older of his subjects, as though inviting suggestion.

"We are too few," grunted one.

"There are the baboons of the hill country," suggested another. "They are as many as the leaves of the forest. They, too, hate the Gomangani. They love to fight. They are very savage. Let us ask them to accompany us. Then can we kill all the Gomangani in the jungle." He rose and growled horribly, bristling his stiff hair.

"That is the way to talk," cried The Killer, "but we do not need the baboons of the hill country. We are enough. It will take a long time to fetch them. Meriem may be dead and eaten before we could free her. Let us set out at once for the village of the Gomangani. If we travel very fast it will not take long to reach it. Then, all at the same time, we can charge into the village, growling and barking. The Gomangani will be very frightened and will run away. While they are gone we can seize Meriem and carry her off. We do not have to kill or be killed—all that Korak wishes is his Meriem."

"We are too few," croaked the old ape again.

"Yes, we are too few," echoed others.

Korak could not persuade them. They would help him, gladly; but they must do it in their own way and that meant enlisting the services of their kinsmen and allies of the hill country. So Korak was forced to give in. All he could do for the present was to urge them to haste, and at his suggestion the king baboon with a dozen of his mightiest bulls agreed to go to the hill country with Korak, leaving the balance of the herd behind.

Once enlisted in the adventure the baboons became quite enthusiastic about it. The delegation set off immediately. They traveled swiftly; but the ape-man found no difficulty in keeping up with them. They made a tremendous racket as they passed through the trees in an endeavor to suggest to enemies in their front that a great herd was approaching, for when the baboons travel in large numbers there is no jungle creature who cares to molest them. When the nature of the country required much travel upon the level, and the distance between trees was great, they moved silently, knowing that the lion and the leopard would not be fooled by noise when they could see plainly for themselves that only a handful of baboons were on the trail.

For two days the party raced through the savage country, passing out of the dense jungle into an open plain, and across this to timbered mountain slopes. Here Korak never before had been. It was a new country to him and the change from the monotony of the circumscribed view in the jungle was pleasing. But he had little desire to enjoy the beauties of nature at this time. Meriem, his Meriem was in danger. Until she was freed and returned to him he had little thought for aught else.

Once in the forest that clothed the mountain slopes the baboons advanced more slowly. Constantly they gave tongue to a plaintive note of calling. Then would follow silence while they listened. At last, faintly from the distance straight ahead came an answer.

The baboons continued to travel in the direction of the voices that floated through the forest to them in the intervals of their own silence. Thus, calling and listening, they came closer to their kinsmen, who, it was evident to Korak, were coming to meet them in great numbers; but when, at last, the baboons of the hill country came in view the ape-man was staggered at the reality that broke upon his vision.

What appeared a solid wall of huge baboons rose from the ground through the branches of the trees to the loftiest terrace to which they dared entrust their weight. Slowly they were approaching, voicing their weird, plaintive call, and behind them, as far as Korak's eyes could pierce the verdure, rose solid walls of their fellows treading close upon their heels. There were thousands of them. The ape-man could not but think of the fate of his little party should some untoward incident arouse even momentarily the rage of fear of a single one of all these thousands.

But nothing such befell. The two kings approached one another, as was their custom, with much sniffing and bristling. They satisfied themselves of each other's identity. Then each scratched the other's back. After a moment they spoke together. Korak's friend explained the nature of their visit, and for the first time Korak showed himself. He had been hiding behind a bush. The excitement among the hill baboons was intense at sight of him. For a moment Korak feared that he should be torn to pieces; but his fear was for Meriem. Should he die there would be none to succor her.

The two kings, however, managed to quiet the multitude, and Korak was permitted to approach. Slowly the hill baboons came closer to him. They sniffed at him from every angle. When he spoke to them in their own tongue they were filled with wonder and delight. They talked to him and listened while he spoke. He told them of Meriem, and of their life in the jungle where they were the friends of all the ape folk from little Manu to Mangani, the great ape.

"The Gomangani, who are keeping Meriem from me, are no friends of yours," he said. "They kill you. The baboons of the low country are too few to go against them. They tell me that you are very many and very brave—that your numbers are as the numbers of the grasses upon the plains or the leaves within the forest, and that even Tantor, the elephant, fears you, so brave you are. They told me that you would be happy to accompany us to the village of the Gomangani and punish these bad people while I, Korak, The Killer, carry away my Meriem."

The king ape puffed out his chest and strutted about very stiff-legged indeed. So also did many of the other great bulls of his nation. They were pleased and flattered by the words of the strange Tarmangani, who called himself Mangani and spoke the language of the hairy progenitors of man.

"Yes," said one, "we of the hill country are mighty fighters. Tantor fears us. Numa fears us. Sheeta fears us. The Gomangani of the hill country are glad to pass us by in peace. I, for one, will come with you to the village of the Gomangani of the low places. I am the king's first he-child. Alone can I kill all the Gomangani of the low country," and he swelled his chest and strutted proudly back and forth, until the itching back of a comrade commanded his industrious attention.

"I am Goob," cried another. "My fighting fangs are long. They are sharp. They are strong. Into the soft flesh of many a Gomangani have they been buried. Alone I slew the sister of Sheeta. Goob will go to the low country with you and kill so many of the Gomangani that there will be none left to count the dead," and then he, too, strutted and pranced before the admiring eyes of the shes and the young.

Korak looked at the king, questioningly.

"Your bulls are very brave," he said, "but braver than any is the king."

Thus addressed, the shaggy bull, still in his prime—else he had been no longer king—growled ferociously. The forest echoed to his lusty challenges. The little baboons clutched fearfully at their mothers' hairy necks. The bulls, electrified, leaped high in air and took up the roaring challenge of their king. The din was terrific.

Korak came close to the king and shouted in his ear, "Come." Then he started off through the forest toward the plain that they must cross on their long journey back to the village of Kovudoo, the Gomangani. The king, still roaring and shrieking, wheeled and followed him. In their wake came the handful of low country baboons and the thousands of the hill clan—savage, wiry, doglike creatures, athirst for blood.

And so they came, upon the second day, to the village of Kovudoo. It was mid-afternoon. The village was sunk in the quiet of the great equatorial sun-heat. The mighty herd traveled quietly now. Beneath the thousands of padded feet the forest gave forth no greater sound than might have been produced by the increased soughing of a stronger breeze through the leafy branches of the trees.

Korak and the two kings were in the lead. Close beside the village they halted until the stragglers had closed up. Now utter silence reigned. Korak, creeping stealthily, entered the tree that overhung the palisade. He glanced behind him. The pack were close upon his heels. The time had come. He had warned them continuously during the long march that no harm must befall the white she who lay a prisoner within the village. All others were their legitimate prey. Then, raising his face toward the sky, he gave voice to a single cry. It was the signal.

In response three thousand hairy bulls leaped screaming and barking into the village of the terrified blacks. Warriors poured from every hut. Mothers gathered their babies in their arms and fled toward the gates as they saw the horrid horde pouring into the village street. Kovudoo marshaled his fighting men about him and, leaping and yelling to arouse their courage, offered a bristling, spear tipped front to the charging horde.

Korak, as he had led the march, led the charge. The blacks were struck with horror and dismay at the sight of this white-skinned youth at the head of a pack of hideous baboons. For an instant they held their ground, hurling their spears once at the advancing multitude; but before they could fit arrows to their bows they wavered, gave, and turned in terrified rout. Into their ranks, upon their backs, sinking strong fangs into the muscles of their necks sprang the baboons and first among them, most ferocious, most bloodthirsty, most terrible was Korak, The Killer.

At the village gates, through which the blacks poured in panic, Korak left them to the tender mercies of his allies and turned himself eagerly toward the hut in which Meriem had been a prisoner. It was empty. One after another the filthy interiors revealed the same disheartening fact—Meriem was in none of them. That she had not been taken by the blacks in their flight from the village Korak knew for he had watched carefully for a glimpse of her among the fugitives.

To the mind of the ape-man, knowing as he did the proclivities of the savages, there was but a single explanation—Meriem had been killed and eaten. With the conviction that Meriem was dead there surged through Korak's brain a wave of blood red rage against those he believed to be her murderer. In the distance he could hear the snarling of the baboons mixed with the screams of their victims, and towards this he made his way. When he came upon them the baboons had commenced to tire of the sport of battle, and the blacks in a little knot were making a new stand, using their knob sticks effectively upon the few bulls who still persisted in attacking them.

Among these broke Korak from the branches of a tree above them—swift, relentless, terrible, he hurled himself upon the savage warriors of Kovudoo. Blind fury possessed him. Too, it protected him by its very ferocity. Like a wounded lioness he was here, there, everywhere, striking terrific blows with hard fists and with the precision and timeliness of the trained fighter. Again and

again he buried his teeth in the flesh of a foeman. He was upon one
and gone again to another before an effective blow could be dealt
him. Yet, though great was the weight of his execution in deter-
mining the result of the combat, it was outweighed by the terror
which he inspired in the simple, superstitious minds of his
foeman. To them this white warrior, who consorted with the great
apes and the fierce baboons, who growled and snarled and
snapped like a beast, was not human. He was a demon of the
forest—a fearsome god of evil whom they had offended, and who
had come out of his lair deep in the jungle to punish them. And
because of this belief there were many who offered but little
defense, feeling as they did the futility of pitting their puny mortal
strength against that of a deity.

Those who could fled, until at last there were no more to pay the
penalty for a deed, which, while not beyond them, they were,
nevertheless, not guilty of. Panting and bloody, Korak paused for
want of further victims. The baboons gathered about him, sated
themselves with blood and battle. They lolled upon the ground,
fagged.

In the distance Kovudoo was gathering his scattered tribesmen,
and taking account of injuries and losses. His people were panic
stricken. Nothing could prevail upon them to remain longer in this
country. They would not even return to the village for their
belongings. Instead they insisted upon continuing their flight until
they had put many miles between themselves and the stamping
ground of the demon who had so bitterly attacked them. And thus
it befell that Korak drove from their homes the only people who
might have aided him in a search for Meriem, and cut off the only
connecting link between him and her from whomsoever might
come in search of him from the *douar* of the kindly Bwana who
had befriended his little jungle sweetheart.

It was a sour and savage Korak who bade farewell to his
baboon allies upon the following morning. They wished him to
accompany them; but the ape-man had no heart for the society of
any. Jungle life had encouraged taciturnity in him. His sorrow had
deepened this to a sullen moroseness that could not brook even the
savage companionship of the ill-natured baboons.

Brooding and despondent he took his solitary way into the
deepest jungle. He moved along the ground when he knew that
Numa was abroad and hungry. He took to the same trees that harbored Sheeta, the panther. He courted death in a hundred ways and
a hundred forms. His mind was ever occupied with reminiscences
of Meriem and the happy years that they had spent together. He

realized now to the full what she had meant to him. The sweet face, the tanned, supple, little body, the bright smile that always had welcomed his return from the hunt haunted him continually.

Inaction soon threatened him with madness. He must be on the go. He must fill his days with labor and excitement that he might forget—that night might find him so exhausted that he should sleep in blessed unconsciousness of his misery until a new day had come.

Had he guessed that by any possibility Meriem might still live he would at least have had hope. His days could have been devoted to searching for her; but he implicitly believed that she was dead.

For a long year he led his solitary, roaming life. Occasionally he fell in with Akut and his tribe, hunting with them for a day or two; or he might travel to the hill country where the baboons had come to accept him as a matter of course; but most of all was he with Tantor, the elephant—the great gray battle ship of the jungle—the super-dreadnaught of his savage world.

The peaceful quiet of the monster bulls, the watchful solicitude of the mother cows, the awkward playfulness of the calves rested, interested, and amused Korak. The life of the huge beasts took his mind, temporarily from his own grief. He came to love them as he loved not even the great apes, and there was one gigantic tusker in particular of which he was very fond—the lord of the herd—a savage beast that was wont to charge a stranger upon the slightest provocation, or upon no provocation whatsoever. And to Korak this mountain of destruction was docile and affectionate as a lap dog.

He came when Korak called. He wound his trunk about the ape-man's body and lifted him to his broad neck in response to a gesture, and there would Korak lie at full length kicking his toes affectionately into the thick hide and brushing the flies from about the tender ears of his colossal chum with a leafy branch torn from a nearby tree by Tantor for the purpose.

And all the while Meriem was scarce a hundred miles away.

16

To MERIEM, IN her new home, the days passed quickly. At first she was all anxiety to be off into the jungle searching for her Korak. Bwana, as she insisted upon calling her benefactor, dissuaded her from making the attempt at once by dispatching a head man with a party of blacks to Kovudoo's village with instructions to learn from the old savage how he came into possession of the white girl and as much of her antecedents as might be culled from the black chieftain. Bwana particularly charged his head men with the duty of questioning Kovudoo relative to the strange character whom the girl called Korak, and of searching for the ape-man if he found the slightest evidence upon which to ground a belief in the existence of such an individual. Bwana was more than fully convinced that Korak was a creature of the girl's disordered imagination. He believed that the terrors and hardships she had undergone during captivity among the blacks and her frightful experience with the two Swedes had unbalanced her mind but as the days passed and he became better acquainted with her and able to observe her under the ordinary conditions of the quiet of his African home he was forced to admit that her strange tale puzzled him not a little, for there was no other evidence whatever that Meriem was not in full possession of her normal faculties.

The white man's wife, whom Meriem had christened "My Dear" from having first heard her thus addressed by Bwana, took not only a deep interest in the little jungle waif because of her forlorn and friendless state, but grew to love her as well for her sunny disposition and natural charm of temperament. And Meriem, similarly impressed by little attributes in the gentle, cultured woman, reciprocated the other's regard and affection.

And so the days flew by while Meriem waited the return of the head man and his party from the country of Kovudoo. They were short days, for into them were crowded many hours of insidious instruction of the unlettered child by the lonely woman. She commenced at once to teach the girl English without forcing it upon her as a task. She varied the instruction with lessons in sewing and deportment, nor once did she let Meriem guess that it was not all play. Nor was this difficult, since the girl was avid to learn. Then there were pretty dresses to be made to take the place of the single leopard skin and in this she found the child as responsive and enthusiastic as any civilized miss of her acquaintance.

A month passed before the head man returned—a month that had transformed the savage, half-naked little Tarmangani into a daintily frocked girl of at least outward civilization. Meriem had progressed rapidly with the intricacies of the English language, for Bwana and My Dear had persistently refused to speak Arabic from the time they had decided that Meriem must learn English, which had been a day or two after her introduction into their home.

The report of the head man plunged Meriem into a period of despondency, for he had found the village of Kovudoo deserted nor, search as he would, could he discover a single native anywhere in the vicinity. For some time he had camped near the village, spending the days in a systematic search of the environs for traces of Meriem's Korak; but in this quest, too, had he failed. He had seen neither apes nor ape-man. Meriem at first insisted upon setting forth herself in search of Korak, but Bwana prevailed upon her to wait. He would go himself, he assured her, as soon as he could find the time, and at last Meriem consented to abide by his wishes; but it was months before she ceased to mourn almost hourly for her Korak.

My Dear grieved with the grieving girl and did her best to comfort and cheer her. She told her that if Korak lived he would find her; but all the time she believed that Korak had never existed beyond the child's dreams. She planned amusements to distract Meriem's attention from her sorrow, and she instituted a well-designed campaign to impress upon the child the desirability of civilized life and customs. Nor was this difficult, as she was soon to learn, for it rapidly became evident that beneath the uncouth savagery of the girl was a bed rock of innate refinement—a nicety of taste and predilection that quite equaled that of her instructor.

My Dear was delighted. She was lonely and childless, and so she lavished upon this little stranger all the mother love that would have gone to her own had she had one. The result was that by the end of the first year none might have guessed that Meriem ever had existed beyond the lap of culture and luxury.

She was sixteen now, though she easily might have passed for nineteen, and she was very good to look upon, with her black hair and her tanned skin and all the freshness and purity of health and innocence. Yet she still nursed her secret sorrow, though she no longer mentioned it to My Dear. Scarce an hour passed that did not bring its recollection of Korak, and its poignant yearning to see him again.

Meriem spoke English fluently now, and read and wrote it as well. One day My Dear spoke jokingly to her in French and to her surprise Meriem replied in the same tongue—slowly, it is true, and haltingly; but none the less in excellent French, such, though, as a little child might use. Thereafter they spoke a little French each day, and My Dear often marveled that the girl learned this language with a facility that was at times almost uncanny. At first Meriem had puckered her narrow, arched, little eye brows as though trying to force recollection of something all but forgotten which the new words suggested, and then, to her own astonishment as well as to that of her teacher she had used other French words than those in the lessons—used them properly and with a pronunciation that the English woman knew was more perfect than her own; but Meriem could neither read nor write what she spoke so well, and as My Dear considered a knowledge of correct English of the first importance, other than conversational French was postponed for a later day.

"You doubtless heard French spoken at times in your father's *douar*," suggested My Dear, as the most reasonable explanation.

Meriem shook her head.

"It may be," she said, "but I do not recall ever having seen a Frenchman in my father's company—he hated them and would have nothing whatever to do with them, and I am quite sure that I never heard any of these words before, yet at the same time I find them all familiar. I cannot understand it."

"Neither can I," agreed My Dear.

It was about this time that a runner brought a letter that, when she learned the contents, filled Meriem with excitement. Visitors were coming! A number of English ladies and gentlemen had accepted My Dear's invitation to spend a month of hunting and exploring with them. Meriem was all expectancy. What would these strangers be like? Would they be as nice to her as had Bwana and My Dear, or would they be like the other white folk she had known—cruel and relentless. My Dear assured her that they all were gentle folk and that she would find them kind, considerate and honorable.

To My Dear's surprise there was none of the shyness of the wild creature in Meriem's anticipation of the visit of strangers.

She looked forward to their coming with curiosity and with a certain pleasurable anticipation when once she was assured that they would not bite her. In fact she appeared no different than would any pretty young miss who had learned of the expected coming of company.

Korak's image was still often in her thoughts, but it aroused now a less well-defined sense of bereavement. A quiet sadness pervaded Meriem when she thought of him; but the poignant grief of her loss when it was young no longer goaded her to desperation. Yet she was still loyal to him. She still hoped that some day he would find her, nor did she doubt for a moment but that he was searching for her if he still lived. It was this last suggestion that caused her the greatest perturbation. Korak might be dead. It scarce seemed possible that one so well-equipped to meet the emergencies of jungle life should have succumbed so young; yet when she had last seen him he had been beset by a horde of armed warriors, and should he have returned to the village again, as she well knew he must have, he may have been killed. Even her Korak could not, single handed, slay an entire tribe.

At last the visitors arrived. There were three men and two women—the wives of the two older men. The youngest member of the party was Hon. Morison Baynes, a young man of considerable wealth who, having exhausted all the possibilities for pleasure offered by the capitals of Europe, had gladly seized upon this opportunity to turn to another continent for excitement and adventure.

He looked upon all things un-European as rather more than less impossible, still he was not at all averse to enjoying the novelty of unaccustomed places, and making the most of strangers indigenous thereto, however unspeakable they might have seemed to him at home. In manner he was suave and courteous to all—if possible a trifle more punctilious toward those he considered of meaner clay than toward the few he mentally admitted to equality.

Nature had favored him with a splendid physique and a handsome face, and also with sufficient good judgment to appreciate that while he might enjoy the contemplation of his superiority to the masses, there was little likelihood of the masses being equally entranced by the same cause. And so he easily maintained the reputation of being a most democratic and likeable fellow, and indeed he was likable. Just a shade of his egotism was occasionally apparent—never sufficient to become a burden to his associates. And this, briefly, was the Hon. Morison Baynes of luxurious European civilization. What would be the Hon. Morison Baynes of central Africa it were difficult to guess.

Meriem, at first, was shy and reserved in the presence of the strangers. Her benefactors had seen fit to ignore mention of her strange past, and so she passed as their ward whose antecedents not having been mentioned were not to be inquired into. The guests found her sweet and unassuming, laughing, vivacious and a never exhausted storehouse of quaint and interesting jungle lore.

She had ridden much during her year with Bwana and My Dear. She knew each favorite clump of concealing reeds along the river that the buffalo loved best. She knew a dozen places where lions laired, and every drinking hole in the drier country twenty-five miles back from the river. With unerring precision that was almost uncanny she could track the largest or the smallest beast to his hiding place. But the thing that baffled them all was her instant consciousness of the presence of carnivora that others, exerting their faculties to the utmost, could neither see nor hear.

The Hon. Morison Baynes found Meriem a most beautiful and charming companion. He was delighted with her from the first. Particularly so, it is possible, because he had not thought to find companionship of this sort upon the African estate of his London friends. They were together a great deal as they were the only unmarried couple in the little company. Meriem, entirely unaccustomed to the companionship of such as Baynes, was fascinated by him. His tales of the great, gay cities with which he was familiar filled her with admiration and with wonder. If the Hon. Morison always shone to advantage in these narratives Meriem saw in that fact but a most natural consequence to his presence upon the scene of his story—wherever Morison might be he must be a hero; so thought the girl.

With the actual presence and companionship of the young Englishman the image of Korak became less real. Where before it had been an actuality to her she now realized that Korak was but a memory. To that memory she still was loyal; but what weight has a memory in the presence of a fascinating reality?

Meriem had never accompanied the men upon a hunt since the arrival of the guests. She never had cared particularly for the sport of killing. The tracking she enjoyed; but the mere killing for the sake of killing she could not find pleasure in—little savage that she had been, and still, to some measure, was. When Bwana had gone forth to shoot for meat she had always been his enthusiastic companion; but with the coming of the London guests the hunting had deteriorated into mere killing. Slaughter the host would not permit; yet the purpose of the hunts were for heads and skins and not for food. So Meriem remained behind and spent her days either with My Dear upon the shaded verandah, or riding her favorite pony across the plains or to the forest edge. Here she would leave him untethered while she took to the trees for the moment's unalloyed pleasures of a return to the wild, free existence of her earlier childhood.

Then would come again visions of Korak, and, tired at last of leaping and swinging through the trees, she would stretch herself comfortably upon a branch and dream. And presently, as today, she found the features of Korak slowly dissolve and merge into those of another, and the figure of a tanned, half-naked Tarmangani become a khaki clothed Englishman astride a hunting pony.

And while she dreamed there came to her ears from a distance, faintly, the terrified bleating of a kid. Meriem was instantly alert. You or I, even had we been able to hear the pitiful wail at so great distance, could not have interpreted it; but to Meriem it meant a species of terror that afflicts the ruminant when a carnivore is near and escape impossible.

It had been both a pleasure and a sport of Korak's to rob Numa of his prey whenever possible, and Meriem too had often enjoyed in the thrill of snatching some dainty morsel almost from the very jaws of the king of beasts. Now, at the sound of the kid's bleat, all the well remembered thrills recurred. Instantly she was all excitement to play again the game of hide-and-seek with death.

Quickly she loosened her riding skirt and tossed it aside—it was a heavy handicap to successful travel in the trees. Her boots and stockings followed the skirt, for the bare sole of the human foot does not slip upon dry or even wet bark as does the hard leather of a boot. She would have liked to discard her riding breeches also, but the motherly admonitions of My Dear had convinced Meriem that it was not good form to go naked through the world.

At her hip hung a hunting knife. Her rifle was still in its boot at her pony's withers. Her revolver she had not brought.

The kid was still bleating as Meriem started rapidly in its direction, which she knew was straight toward a certain water hole which had once been famous as a rendezvous for lions. Of late there had been no evidence of carnivora in the neighborhood of this drinking place; but Meriem was positive that the bleating of the kid was due to the presence of either lion or panther.

But she would soon know, for she was rapidly approaching the terrified animal. She wondered as she hastened onward that the sounds continued to come from the same point. Why did the kid not run away? And then she came in sight of the little animal and knew. The kid was tethered to a stake beside the water hole.

Meriem paused in the branches of a nearby tree and scanned the surrounding clearing with quick, penetrating eyes. Where was the hunter? Bwana and his people did not hunt thus. Who could have tethered this poor little beast as a lure to Numa? Bwana never countenanced such acts in his country and his word was law among those who hunted within a radius of many miles of his estate.

Some wandering savages, doubtless, thought Meriem; but where were they? Not even her keen eyes could discover them. And where was Numa? Why had he not long since sprung upon this delicious and defenseless morsel? That he was close by was attested by the pitiful crying of the kid. Ah! Now she saw him. He was lying close in a clump of brush a few yards to her right. The kid was down wind from him and getting the full benefit of his terrorizing scent, which did not reach Meriem.

To circle to the opposite side of the clearing where the trees approached closer to the kid. To leap quickly to the little animal's side and cut the tether that held him would be the work of but a moment. In that moment Numa might charge, and then there would be scarce time to regain the safety of the trees, yet it might be done. Meriem had escaped from closer quarters than that many times before.

The doubt that gave her momentary pause was caused by fear of the unseen hunters more than by fear of Numa. If they were stranger blacks the spears that they held in readiness for Numa might as readily be loosed upon whomever dared release their bait as upon the prey they sought thus to trap. Again the kid struggled to be free. Again his piteous wail touched the tender heartstrings of the girl. Tossing discretion aside, she commenced to circle the clearing. Only from Numa did she attempt to conceal her presence. At last she reached the opposite trees. An instant she paused to look toward the great lion, and at the same moment she saw the huge beast rise slowly to his full height. A low roar betokened that he was ready.

Meriem loosened her knife and leaped to the ground. A quick run brought her to the side of the kid. Numa saw her. He lashed his tail against his tawny sides. He roared terribly; but, for an instant, he remained where he stood—surprised into inaction, doubtless, by the strange apparition that had sprung so unexpectedly from the jungle.

Other eyes were upon Meriem, too—eyes in which were no less surprise than that reflected in the yellow-green orbs of the carnivore. A white man, hiding in a thorn *boma*, half rose as the young girl leaped into the clearing and dashed toward the kid. He saw Numa hesitate. He raised his rifle and covered the beast's breast. The girl reached the kid's side. Her knife flashed, and the little prisoner was free. With a parting bleat it dashed off into the jungle. Then the girl turned to retreat toward the safety of the tree from which she had dropped so suddenly and unexpectedly into the surprised view of the lion, the kid and the man.

As she turned the girl's face was turned toward the hunter. His eyes went wide as he saw her features. He gave a little gasp of surprise; but now the lion demanded all his attention—the baffled, angry beast was charging. His breast was still covered by the motionless rifle. The man could have fired and stopped the charge at once; but for some reason, since he had seen the girl's face, he hesitated. Could it be that he did not care to save her? Or, did he prefer, if possible, to remain unseen by her? It must have been the latter cause which kept the trigger finger of the steady hand from exerting the little pressure that would have brought the great beast to at least a temporary pause.

Like an eagle the man watched the race for life the girl was making. A second or two measured the time which the whole exciting event consumed from the moment that the lion broke into his charge. Nor once did the rifle sights fail to cover the broad beast or the tawny sire as the lion's course took him a little to the man's left. Once, at the very last moment, when escape seemed impossible, the hunter's finger tightened ever so little upon the trigger, but almost coincidentally the girl leaped for an over hanging branch and seized it. The lion leaped too; but the nimble Meriem had swung herself beyond his reach without a second or an inch to spare.

The man breathed a sigh of relief as he lowered his rifle. He saw the girl fling a grimace at the angry, roaring, maneater beneath her, and then, laughing, speed away into the forest. For an hour the lion remained about the water hole. A hundred times could the hunter have bagged his prey. Why did he fail to do so? Was he afraid that the shot might attract the girl and cause her to return?

At last Numa, still roaring angrily, strode majestically into the jungle. The hunter crawled from his *boma*, and half an hour later was entering a little camp snugly hidden in the forest. A handful of black followers greeted his return with sullen indifference. He was a great bearded man, a huge, yellow-bearded giant, when he entered his tent. Half an hour later he emerged smooth shaven.

His blacks looked at him in astonishment.

"Would you know me?" he asked.

"The hyena that bore you would not know you, Bwana," replied one.

The man aimed a heavy fist at the black's face; but long experience in dodging similar blows saved the presumptuous one.

17

MERIEM RETURNED SLOWLY toward the tree in which she had left her skirt, her shoes and her stockings. She was singing blithely; but her song came to a sudden stop when she came within sight of the tree, for there, disporting themselves with glee and pulling and hauling upon her belongings, were a number of baboons. When they saw her they showed no signs of terror. Instead they bared their fangs and growled at her. What was there to fear in a single she-Tarmangani? Nothing, absolutely nothing.

In the open plain beyond the forest the hunters were returning from the day's sport. They were widely separated, hoping to raise a wandering lion on the homeward journey across the plain. The Hon. Morison Baynes rode closest to the forest. As his eyes wandered back and forth across the undulating, shrub sprinkled ground they fell upon the form of a creature close beside the thick jungle where it terminated abruptly at the plain's edge.

He reined his mount in the direction of his discovery. It was yet too far away for his untrained eyes to recognize it; but as he came closer he saw that it was a horse, and was about to resume the original direction of his way when he thought that he discerned a saddle upon the beast's back. He rode a little closer. Yes, the animal was saddled. The Hon. Morison approached yet nearer, and as he did so his eyes expressed a pleasurable emotion of anticipation, for they had now recognized the pony as the special favorite of Meriem.

He galloped to the animal's side. Meriem must be within the wood. The man shuddered a little at the thought of an unprotected girl alone in the jungle that was still, to him, a fearful place of terrors and stealthily stalking death. He dismounted and left his horse beside Meriem's. On foot he entered the jungle. He knew that she was probably safe enough and he wished to surprise her by coming suddenly upon her.

He had gone but a short distance into the wood when he heard a great jabbering in a nearby tree. Coming closer he saw a band of baboons snarling over something. Looking intently he saw that one of them held a woman's riding skirt and that others had boots and stockings. His heart almost ceased to beat as he quite naturally placed the most direful explanation upon the scene. The baboons had killed Meriem and stripped this clothing from her body. Morison shuddered.

He was about to call aloud in the hope that after all the girl still lived when he saw her in a tree close beside that was occupied by the baboons, and now he saw that they were snarling and jabbering at her. To his amazement he saw the girl swing, ape-like, into the tree below the huge beasts. He saw her pause upon a branch a few feet from the nearest baboon. He was about to raise his rifle and put a bullet through the hideous creature that seemed about to leap upon her when he heard the girl speak. He almost dropped his rifle from surprise as a strange jabbering, identical with that of the apes, broke from Meriem's lips.

The baboons stopped their snarling and listened. It was quite evident that they were as much surprised as the Hon. Morison Baynes. Slowly and one by one they approached the girl. She gave not the slightest evidence of fear of them. They quite surrounded her now so that Baynes could not have fired without endangering the girl's life; but he no longer desired to fire. He was consumed with curiosity.

For several minutes the girl carried on what could be nothing less than a conversation with the baboons, and then with seeming alacrity every article of her apparel in their possession was handed over to her. The baboons still crowded eagerly about her as she

donned them. They chattered to her and she chattered back. The
Hon. Morison Baynes sat down at the foot of a tree and mopped
his perspiring brow. Then he rose and made his way back to his
mount.

When Meriem emerged from the forest a few minutes later she
found him there, and he eyed her with wide eyes in which were
both wonder and a sort of terror.

"I saw your horse here," he explained, "and thought that I
would wait and ride home with you—you do not mind?"

"Of course not," she replied. "It will be lovely."

As they made their way stirrup to stirrup across the plain the
Hon. Morison caught himself many times watching the girl's
regular profile and wondering if his eyes had deceived him or if, in
truth, he really had seen this lovely creature consorting with
grotesque baboons and conversing with them as fluently as she
conversed with him. The thing was uncanny—impossible; yet he
had seen it with his own eyes.

And as he watched her another thought persisted in obtruding
itself into his mind. She was most beautiful and very desirable; but
what did he know of her? Was she not altogether impossible? Was
the scene that he had but just witnessed not sufficient proof of her
impossibility? A woman who climbed trees and conversed with
the baboons of the jungle! It was quite horrible!

Again the Hon. Morison mopped his brow. Meriem glanced
toward him.

"You are warm," she said. "Now that the sun is setting I find it
quite cool. Why do you perspire now?"

He had not intended to let her know that he had seen her with
the baboons; but quite suddenly, before he realized what he was
saying, he had blurted it out.

"I perspire from emotion," he said. "I went into the jungle when
I discovered your pony. I wanted to surprise you; but it was I who
was surprised. I saw you in the trees with the baboons."

"Yes?" she said quite unemotionally, as though it was a matter
of little moment that a young girl should be upon intimate terms
with savage jungle beasts.

"It was horrible!" ejaculated the Hon. Morison.

"Horrible?" repeated Meriem, puckering her brows in bewilderment. "What was horrible about it? They are my friends. Is it
horrible to talk with one's friends?"

"You were really talking with them, then?" cried the Hon.
Morison. "You understood them and they understood you?"

"Certainly."

"But they are hideous creatures—degraded beasts of a lower order. How could you speak the language of beasts?"

"They are not hideous, and they are not degraded," replied Meriem. "Friends are never that. I lived among them for years before Bwana found me and brought me here. I scarce knew any other tongue than that of the Mangani. Should I refuse to know them now simply because I happen, for the present, to live among humans?"

"For the present!" ejaculated the Hon. Morison. "You cannot mean that you expect to return to live among them? Come, come, what foolishness are we talking! The very idea! You are spoofing me, Miss Meriem. You have been kind to these baboons here and they know you and do not molest you; but that you once lived among them—no, that is preposterous."

"But I did, though," insisted the girl, seeing the real horror that the man felt in the presence of such an idea reflected in his tone and manner, and rather enjoying baiting him still further. "Yes, I lived, almost naked, among the great apes and the lesser apes. I dwelt among the branches of the trees. I pounced upon the smaller prey and devoured it—raw. With Korak and A'ht I hunted the antelope and the boar, and I sat upon a tree limb and made faces at Numa, the lion, and threw sticks at him and annoyed him until he roared so terribly in his rage that the earth shook.

"And Korak built me a lair high among the branches of a mighty tree. He brought me fruits and flesh. He fought for me and was kind to me—until I came to Bwana and My Dear I do not recall that any other than Korak was ever kind to me." There was a wistful note in the girl's voice now and she had forgotten that she was bantering the Hon. Morison. She was thinking of Korak. She had not thought of him a great deal of late.

For a time both were silently absorbed in their own reflections as they rode on toward the bungalow of their host. The girl was thinking of a god-like figure, a leopard skin half concealing his smooth, brown hide as he leaped nimbly through the trees to lay an offering of food before her on his return from a successful hunt. Behind him, shaggy and powerful, swung a huge anthropoid ape, while she, Meriem, laughing and shouting her welcome, swung upon a swaying limb before the entrance to her sylvan bower. It was a pretty picture as she recalled it. The other side seldom obtruded itself upon her memory—the long, black nights—the chill, terrible jungle nights—the cold and damp and discomfort of the rainy season—the hideous mouthings of the savage carnivora as they prowled through the Stygian darkness beneath—the constant menace of Sheeta, the panther, and Histah, the snake—the stinging insects—the loathsome vermin. For, in truth, all these had been outweighed by the happiness of the sunny days, the freedom of it all, and, most, the companionship of Korak.

The man's thoughts were rather jumbled. He had suddenly realized that he had come mighty near falling in love with this girl of whom he had known nothing up to the previous moment when she had voluntarily revealed a portion of her past to him. The more he thought upon the matter the more evident it became to him that he had given her his love—that he had been upon the verge of offering her his honorable name. He trembled a little at the narrowness of his escape. Yet, he still loved her. There was no objection to that according to the ethics of the Hon. Morison Baynes and his kind. She was a meaner clay than he. He could no more have taken her in marriage than he could have taken one of her baboon friends, nor would she, of course, expect such an offer from him. To have his love would be sufficient honor for her—his name he would, naturally, bestow upon one in his own elevated social sphere.

A girl who had consorted with apes, who, according to her own admission, had lived almost naked among them, could have no considerable sense of the finer qualities of virtue. The love that he would offer her, then, would, far from offending her, probably cover all that she might desire or expect.

The more the Hon. Morison Baynes thought upon the subject the more fully convinced he became that he was contemplating a most chivalrous and unselfish act. Europeans will better understand his point of view than Americans, poor, benighted provincials, who are denied a true appreciation of caste and of the fact that "the king can do no wrong." He did not even have to argue the point that she would be much happier amidst the luxuries of a London apartment, fortified as she would be by both his love and his bank account, than lawfully wed to such a one as her social position warranted. There was one question however, which he wished to have definitely answered before he committed himself even to the program he was considering.

"Who were Korak and A'ht?" he asked.

"A'ht was a Mangani," replied Meriem, "and Korak a Tarmangani."

"And what, pray, might a Mangani be, and a Tarmangani?"

The girl laughed.

"You are a Tarmangani," she replied. "The Mangani are covered with hair—you would call them apes."

"Then Korak was a white man?" he asked.

"Yes."

"And he was—ah—your—er—your—?" He paused, for he found it rather difficult to go on with that line of questioning while the girl's clear, beautiful eyes were looking straight into his.

"My what?" insisted Meriem, far too unsophisticated in her unspoiled innocence to guess what the Hon. Morison was driving at.

"Why—ah—your brother?" he stumbled.

"No, Korak was not my brother," she replied.

"Was he your husband, then?" he finally blurted.

Far from taking offense, Meriem broke into a merry laugh.

"My husband!" she cried. "Why how old do you think I am? I am too young to have a husband. I had never thought of such a thing. Korak was—why—" and now she hesitated, too, for she never before had attempted to analyze the relationship that existed between herself and Korak— "why, Korak was just Korak," and again she broke into a gay laugh as she realized the illuminating quality of her description.

Looking at her and listening to her the man beside her could not believe that depravity of any sort or degree entered into the girl's nature, yet he wanted to believe that she had not been virtuous, for otherwise his task was less a sinecure—the Hon. Morison was not entirely without conscience.

For several days the Hon. Morison made no appreciable progress toward the consummation of his scheme. Sometimes he almost abandoned it for he found himself time and again wondering how slight might be the provocation necessary to trick him into making a bona fide offer of marriage to Meriem if he permitted himself to fall more deeply in love with her, and it was difficult to see her daily and not love her. There was a quality about her which, all unknown to the Hon. Morison, was making his task an extremely difficult one—it was that quality of innate goodness and cleanness which is a good girl's stoutest bulwark and protection—an impregnable barrier that only degeneracy has the affrontery to assail. The Hon. Morison Baynes would never be considered a degenerate.

He was sitting with Meriem upon the verandah one evening after the others had retired. Earlier they had been playing tennis— a game in which the Hon. Morison shone to advantage, as, in truth, he did in most all manly sports. He was telling Meriem stories of London and Paris, of balls and banquets, of the wonderful women and their wonderful gowns, of the pleasures and pastimes of the rich and powerful. The Hon. Morison was a past master in the art of insidious boasting. His egotism was never flagrant or tiresome—he was never crude in it, for crudeness was a plebeianism that the Hon. Morison studiously avoided, yet the impression derived by a listener to the Hon. Morison was one that was not at all calculated to detract from the glory of the house of Baynes, or from that of its representative.

Meriem was entranced. His tales were like fairy stories to this little jungle maid. The Hon. Morison loomed large and wonderful and magnificent in her mind's eye. He fascinated her, and when he drew closer to her after a short silence and took her hand she thrilled as one might thrill beneath the touch of a deity—a thrill of exaltation not unmixed with fear.

He bent his lips close to her ear.

"Meriem!" he whispered. "My little Meriem! May I hope to have the right to call you 'my little Meriem'?"

The girl turned wide eyes upward to his face; but it was in shadow. She trembled but she did not draw away. The man put an arm about her and drew her closer.

"I love you!" he whispered.

She did not reply. She did not know what to say. She knew nothing of love. She had never given it a thought; but she did know that it was very nice to be loved, whatever it meant. It was nice to have people kind to one. She had known so little of kindness or affection.

"Tell me," he said, "that you return my love."

His lips came steadily closer to hers. They had almost touched when a vision of Korak sprang like a miracle before her eyes. She saw Korak's face close to hers, she felt his lips hot against hers, and then for the first time in her life she guessed what love meant. She drew away, gently.

"I am not sure," she said, "that I love you. Let us wait. There is plenty of time. I am too young to marry yet, and I am not sure that I should be happy in London or Paris—they rather frighten me."

How easily and naturally she had connected his avowal of love with the idea of marriage! The Hon. Morison was perfectly sure that he had not mentioned marriage—he had been particularly careful not to do so. And then she was not sure that she loved him! That, too, came rather in the nature of a shock to his vanity. It seemed incredible that this little barbarian should have any doubts whatever as to the desirability of the Hon. Morison Baynes.

The first flush of passion cooled, the Hon. Morison was enabled to reason more logically. The start had been all wrong. It would be better now to wait and prepare her mind gradually for the only proposition which his exalted estate would permit him to offer her. He would go slow. He glanced down at the girl's profile. It was bathed in the silvery light of the great tropic moon. The Hon. Morison Baynes wondered if it were to be so easy a matter to "go slow." She was most alluring.

Meriem rose. The vision of Korak was still before her.

"Good night," she said. "It is almost too beautiful to leave." She waved her hand in a comprehensive gesture which took in the starry heavens, the great moon, the broad, silvered plain, and the dense shadows in the distance, that marked the jungle. "Oh, how I love it!"

"You would love London more," he said earnestly. "And London would love you. You would be a famous beauty in any capital of Europe. You would have the world at your feet, Meriem."

"Good night!" she repeated, and left him.

The Hon. Morison selected a cigarette from his crested case, lighted it, blew a thin line of blue smoke toward the moon, and smiled.

18

MERIEM AND BWANA were sitting on the verandah together the following day when a horseman appeared in the distance riding across the plain toward the bungalow. Bwana shaded his eyes with his hand and gazed out toward the oncoming rider. He was puzzled. Strangers were few in central Africa. Even the blacks for a distance of many miles in every direction were well known to him. No white man came within a hundred miles that word of his coming did not reach Bwana long before the stranger.

His every move was reported to the big Bwana—just what animals he killed and how many of each species, how he killed them, too, for Bwana would not permit the use of prussic acid or strychnine; and how he treated his "boys."

Several European sportsmen had been turned back to the coast by the big Englishman's orders because of unwarranted cruelty to their black followers, and one, whose name had long been heralded in civilized communities as that of a great sportsman, was driven from Africa with orders never to return when Bwana found that his big bag of fourteen lions had been made by the diligent use of poisoned bait.

The result was that all good sportsmen and all the natives loved and respected him. His word was law where there had never been law before. There was scarce a head man from coast to coast who would not heed the big Bwana's commands in preference to those of the hunters who employed them, and so it was easy to turn back any undesirable stranger—Bwana had simply to threaten to order his boys to desert him.

But there was evidently one who had slipped into the country unheralded. Bwana could not imagine who the approaching horseman might be. After the manner of frontier hospitality the globe round he met the newcomer at the gate, welcoming him even before he had dismounted. He saw a tall, well-knit man of thirty or over, blonde of hair and smooth shaven. There was a tantalizing familiarity about him that convinced Bwana that he should be able to call the visitor by name, yet he was unable to do so. The newcomer was evidently of Scandinavian origin—both his appearance and accent denoted that. His manner was rough but open. He made a good impression upon the Englishman, who was wont to accept strangers in this wild and savage country at their own valuation, asking no questions and assuming the best of them until they proved themselves undeserving of his friendship and hospitality.

"It is rather unusual that a white man comes unheralded," he said, as they walked together toward the field into which he had suggested that the traveler might turn his pony. "My friends, the natives, keep us rather well-posted."

"It is probably due to the fact that I came from the south," explained the stranger, "that you did not hear of my coming. I have seen no village for several marches."

"No, there are none to the south of us for many miles," replied Bwana. "Since Kovudoo deserted his country I rather doubt that one could find a native in that direction under two or three hundred miles."

Bwana was wondering how a lone white man could have made his way through the savage, unhospitable miles that lay toward the south. As though guessing what must be passing through the other's mind, the stranger vouchsafed an explanation.

"I came down from the north to do a little trading and hunting," he said, "and got way off the beaten track. My head man, who was the only member of the *safari* who had ever before been in the country, took sick and died. We could find no natives to guide us, and so I simply swung back straight north. We have been living on the fruits of our guns for over a month. Didn't have an idea there was a white man within a thousand miles of us when we camped last night by a water hole at the edge of the plain. This morning I started out to hunt and saw the smoke from your chimney, so I sent my gun bearer back to camp with the good news and rode straight over here myself. Of course I've heard of you—everybody who comes into central Africa does—and I'd be mighty glad of permission to rest up and hunt around here for a couple of weeks."

"Certainly," replied Bwana. "Move your camp up close to the river below my boys' camp and make yourself at home."

They had reached the verandah now and Bwana was introducing the stranger to Meriem and My Dear, who had just come from the bungalow's interior.

"This is Mr. Hanson," he said, using the name the man had given him. "He is a trader who has lost his way in the jungle to the south."

My Dear and Meriem bowed their acknowledgments of the introduction. The man seemed rather ill at ease in their presence. His host attributed this to the fact that his guest was unaccustomed to the society of cultured women, and so found a pretext to quickly extricate him from his seemingly unpleasant position and lead him away to his study and the brandy and soda which were evidently much less embarrassing to Mr. Hanson.

When the two had left them Meriem turned toward My Dear.

"It is odd," she said, "but I could almost swear that I had known Mr. Hanson in the past. It is odd, but quite impossible," and she gave the matter no further thought.

Hanson did not accept Bwana's invitation to move his camp closer to the bungalow. He said his boys were inclined to be quarrelsome, and so were better off at a distance; and he, himself, was around but little, and then always avoided coming into contact with the ladies. A fact which naturally aroused only laughing comment on the rough trader's bashfulness. He accompanied the men on several hunting trips where they found him perfectly at home and well versed in all the finer points of big game hunting. Of an evening he often spent much time with the white foreman of the big farm, evidently finding in the society of this rougher man more common interests than the cultured guests of Bwana possessed for him. So it came that his was a familiar figure about the premises by night. He came and went as he saw fit, often wandering along in the great flower garden that was the especial pride and joy of My Dear and Meriem. The first time that he had been surprised there he apologized gruffly, explaining that he had always been fond of the good old blooms of northern Europe which My Dear had so successfully transplanted in African soil.

Was it, though, the ever beautiful blossoms of hollyhocks and phlox that drew him to the perfumed air of the garden, or that other infinitely more beautiful flower who wandered often among the blooms beneath the great moon—the black-haired, sun-tanned Meriem?

For three weeks Hanson had remained. During this time he said that his boys were resting and gaining strength after their terrible ordeals in the untracked jungle to the south; but he had not been as idle as he appeared to have been. He divided his small following into two parties, entrusting the leadership of each to men whom he believed that he could trust. To them he explained his plans and the rich reward that they would win from him if they carried his designs to a successful conclusion. One party he moved very slowly northward along the trail that connects with the great caravan routes entering the Sahara from the south. The other he ordered straight westward with orders to halt and go into permanent camp just beyond the great river which marks the natural boundary of the country that the big Bwana rightfully considers almost his own.

To his host he explained that he was moving his *safari* slowly toward the north—he said nothing of the party moving westward. Then, one day, he announced that half his boys had deserted, for a hunting party from the bungalow had come across his northerly camp and he feared that they might have noticed the reduced numbers of his following.

And thus matters stood when, one hot night, Meriem, unable to sleep, rose and wandered out into the garden. The Hon. Morison had been urging his suit once more that evening, and the girl's mind was in such a turmoil that she had been unable to sleep.

The wide heavens about her seemed to promise a greater freedom from doubt and questioning. Baynes had urged her to tell him that she loved him. A dozen times she thought that she might honestly give him the answer that he demanded. Korak fast was becoming but a memory. That he was dead she had come to believe, since otherwise he would have sought her out. She did not know that he had even better reason to believe her dead, and that it was because of that belief he had made no effort to find her after his raid upon the village of Kovudoo.

Behind a great flowering shrub Hanson lay gazing at the stars and waiting. He had lain thus and there many nights before. For what was he waiting, or for whom? He heard the girl approaching, and half raised himself to his elbow. A dozen paces away, the reins looped over a fence post, stood his pony.

Meriem, walking slowly, approached the bush behind which the waiter lay. Hanson drew a large bandanna handkerchief from his pocket and rose stealthily to his knees. A pony neighed down at the corrals. Far out across the plain a lion roared. Hanson changed his position until he squatted upon both feet, ready to come erect quickly.

Again the pony neighed—this time closer. There was the sound of his body brushing against shrubbery. Hanson heard and wondered how the animal had gotten from the corral, for it was evident that he was already in the garden. The man turned his head in the direction of the beast. What he saw sent him to the ground, huddled close beneath the shrubbery—a man was coming, leading two ponies.

Meriem heard now and stopped to look and listen. A moment later the Hon. Morison Baynes drew near, the two saddled mounts at his heels.

Meriem looked up at him in surprise. The Hon. Morison grinned sheepishly.

"I couldn't sleep," he explained, "and was going for a bit of a ride when I chanced to see you out here, and I thought you'd like to join me. Ripping good sport, you know, night riding. Come on."

Meriem laughed. The adventure appealed to her.

"All right," she said.

Hanson swore beneath his breath. The two led their horses from the garden to the gate and through it. There they discovered Hanson's mount.

"Why here's the trader's pony," remarked Baynes.

"He's probably down visiting with the foreman," said Meriem.

"Pretty late for him, isn't it?" remarked the Hon. Morison. "I'd hate to have to ride back through that jungle at night to his camp."

As though to give weight to his apprehensions the distant lion roared again. The Hon. Morison shivered and glanced at the girl to note the effect of the uncanny sound upon her. She appeared not to have noticed it.

A moment later the two had mounted and were moving slowly across the moon-bathed plain. The girl turned her pony's head straight toward the jungle. It was in the direction of the roaring of the hungry lion.

"Hadn't we better steer clear of that fellow?" suggested the Hon. Morison. "I guess you didn't hear him."

"Yes, I heard him," laughed Meriem. "Let's ride over and call on him."

The Hon. Morison laughed uneasily. He didn't care to appear at a disadvantage before this girl, nor did he care, either, to approach a hungry lion too closely at night. He carried his rifle in his saddle boot; but moonlight is an uncertain light to shoot by, nor ever had he faced a lion alone—even by day. The thought gave him a distinct nausea. The beast ceased his roaring now. They heard him no more and the Hon. Morison gained courage accordingly. They were riding down wind toward the jungle. The lion lay in a little swale to their right. He was old. For two nights he had not fed, for no longer was his charge as swift or his spring as mighty as in the days of his prime when he spread terror among the creatures of his wild domain. For two nights and days he had gone empty, and for long time before that he had fed only upon carrion. He was old; but he was yet a terrible engine of destruction.

At the edge of the forest the Hon. Morison drew rein. He had no desire to go further. Numa, silent upon his padded feet, crept into the jungle beyond them. The wind, now, was blowing gently between him and his intended prey. He had come a long way in search of man, for even in his youth he had tasted human flesh and while it was poor stuff by comparison with eland and zebra it was less difficult to kill. In Numa's estimation man was a slow-witted, slow-footed creature which commanded no respect unless accompanied by the acrid odor which spelled to the monarch's sensitive nostrils the great noise and the blinding flash of an express rifle.

He caught the dangerous scent tonight; but he was ravenous to madness. He would face a dozen rifles, if necessary, to fill his empty belly. He circled about into the forest that he might again be down wind from his victims, for should they get his scent he could not hope to overtake them. Numa was famished; but he was old and crafty.

Deep in the jungle another caught faintly the scent of man and of Numa both. He raised his head and sniffed. He cocked it upon one side and listened.

"Come on," said Meriem, "let's ride in a way—the forest is wonderful at night. It is open enough to permit us to ride."

The Hon. Morison hesitated. He shrank from revealing his fear in the presence of the girl. A braver man, sure of his own position, would have had the courage to have refused uselessly to expose the girl to danger. He would not have thought of himself at all; but the egotism of the Hon. Morison required that he think always of self first. He had planned the ride to get Meriem away from the bungalow. He wanted to talk to her alone and far enough away so should she take offense at his purposed suggestion he would have time in which to attempt to right himself in her eyes before they reached home. He had little doubt, of course, but that he should succeed; but it is to his credit that he did have some slight doubts.

"You needn't be afraid of the lion," said Meriem, noting his slight hesitancy. "There hasn't been a maneater around here for two years, Bwana says, and the game is so plentiful that there is no necessity to drive Numa to human flesh. Then, he has been so often hunted that he rather keeps out of man's way."

"Oh, I'm not afraid of lions," replied the Hon. Morison. "I was just thinking what a beastly uncomfortable place a forest is to ride in. What with the underbrush and the low branches and all that, you know, it's not exactly cut out for pleasure riding."

"Let's go a-foot then," suggested Meriem, and started to dismount.

"Oh, no," cried the Hon. Morison, aghast at this suggestion. "Let's ride," and he reined his pony into the dark shadows of the wood. Behind him came Meriem and in front, prowling ahead waiting a favorable opportunity, skulked Numa, the lion.

Out upon the plain a lone horseman muttered a low curse as he saw the two disappear from sight. It was Hanson. He had followed them from the bungalow. Their way led in the direction of his camp, so he had a ready and plausible excuse should they discover him; but they had not seen him for they had not turned their eyes behind.

Now he turned directly toward the spot at which they had entered the jungle. He no longer cared whether he was observed or not. There were two reasons for his indifference. The first was that he saw in Baynes' act a counterpart of his own planned abduction of the girl. In some way he might turn the thing to his own purposes. At least he would keep in touch with them and make sure that Baynes did not get her. His other reason was based on his knowledge of an event that had transpired at his camp the previous night—an event which he had not mentioned at the bungalow for fear of drawing undesired attention to his movements and bringing the blacks of the big Bwana into dangerous intercourse with his own boys. He had told at the bungalow that half his men had deserted. That story might be quickly disproved should his boys and Bwana's grow confidential.

The event that he had failed to mention and which now urged him hurriedly after the girl and her escort had occurred during his absence early the preceding evening. His men had been sitting around their camp fire, entirely encircled by a high, thorn *boma*, when, without the slightest warning, a huge lion had leaped amongst them and seized one of their number. It had been solely due to the loyalty and courage of his comrades that his life had been saved, and then only after a battle royal with the hunger-enraged beast had they been able to drive him off with burning brands, spears, and rifles.

From this Hanson knew that a maneater had wandered into the district or been developed by the aging of one of the many lions who ranged the plains and hills by night, or lay up in the cool wood by day. He had heard the roaring of a hungry lion not half an hour before, and there was little doubt in his mind but that the maneater was stalking Meriem and Baynes. He cursed the Englishman for a fool, and spurred rapidly after them.

Meriem and Baynes had drawn up in a small, natural clearing. A hundred yards beyond them Numa lay crouching in the underbrush, his yellow-green eyes fixed upon his prey, the tip of his sinuous tail jerking spasmodically. He was measuring the distance between him and them. He was wondering if he dared venture a charge, or should he wait yet a little longer in the hope that they might ride straight into his jaws. He was very hungry; but also was he very crafty. He could not chance losing his meat by a hasty and ill-considered rush. Had he waited the night before until the blacks slept he would not have been forced to go hungry for another twenty-four hours.

Behind him the other that had caught his scent and that of man together came to a sitting posture upon the branch of a tree in which he had reposed himself for slumber. Beneath him a lumbering gray hulk swayed to and fro in the darkness. The beast in the tree uttered a low guttural and dropped to the back of the gray mass. He whispered a word in one of the great ears and Tantor, the elephant, raised his trunk aloft, swinging it high and low to catch the scent that the word had warned him of. There was another whispered word—was it a command?—and the lumbering beast wheeled into an awkward, yet silent shuffle, in the direction of Numa, the lion, and the stranger Tarmangani his rider had scented.

Onward they went, the scent of the lion and his prey becoming stronger and stronger. Numa was becoming impatient. How much longer must he wait for his meat to come his way? He lashed his tail viciously now. He almost growled. All unconscious of their danger the man and the girl sat talking in the little clearing.

Their horses were pressed side by side. Baynes had found Meriem's hand and was pressing it as he poured words of love into her ear, and Meriem was listening.

"Come to London with me," urged the Hon. Morison. "I can gather a *safari* and we can be a whole day upon the way to the coast before they guess that we have gone."

"Why must we go that way?" asked the girl. "Bwana and My Dear would not object to our marriage."

"I cannot marry you just yet," explained the Hon. Morison, "there are some formalities to be attended to first—you do not understand. It will be all right. We will go to London. I cannot wait. If you love me you will come. What of the apes you lived with? Did they bother about marriage? They love as we love. Had you stayed among them you would have mated as they mate. It is the law of nature—no man-made law can abrogate the laws of God. What difference does it make if we love one another? What do we care for anyone in the world besides ourselves? I would give my life for you—will you give nothing for me?"

"You love me?" she said. "You will marry me when we have reached London?"

"I swear it," he cried.

"I will go with you," she whispered, "though I do not understand why it is necessary." She leaned toward him and he took her in his arms and bent to press his lips to hers.

At the same instant the head of a huge tusker poked through the trees that fringed the clearing. The Hon. Morison and Meriem, with eyes and ears for one another alone, did not see or hear; but Numa did. The man upon Tantor's broad head saw the girl in the man's arms. It was Korak; but in the trim figure of the neatly garbed girl he did not recognize his Meriem. He only saw a Tarmangani with his she. And then Numa charged.

With a frightful roar, fearful lest Tantor had come to frighten away his prey, the great beast leaped from his hiding place. The earth trembled to his mighty voice. The ponies stood for an instant transfixed with terror. The Hon. Morison Baynes went white and cold. The lion was charging toward them full in the brilliant light of the magnificent moon. The muscles of the Hon. Morison no longer obeyed his will—they flexed to the urge of a greater power—the power of Nature's first law. They drove his spurred heels deep into his pony's flanks, they bore the rein against the brute's neck that wheeled him with an impetuous drive toward the plain and safety.

The girl's pony, squealing in terror, reared and plunged upon the heels of his mate. The lion was close upon him. Only the girl was cool—the girl and the half-naked savage who bestrode the neck of his mighty mount and grinned at the exciting spectacle chance had staked for his enjoyment.

To Korak here were but two strange Tarmangani pursued by Numa, who was empty. It was Numa's right to prey; but one was a she. Korak felt an intuitive urge to rush to her protection. Why, he could not guess. All Tarmangani were enemies now. He had lived too long a beast to feel strongly the humanitarian impulses that were inherent in him—yet feel them he did, for the girl at least.

He urged Tantor forward. He raised his heavy spear and hurled it at the flying target of the lion's body. The girl's pony had reached the trees upon the opposite side of the clearing. Here he would become easy prey to the swiftly moving lion; but Numa, infuriated, preferred the woman upon his back. It was for her he leaped.

Korak gave an exclamation of astonishment and approval as Numa landed upon the pony's rump and at the same instant the girl swung free of her mount to the branches of a tree above her.

Korak's spear struck Numa in the shoulder, knocking him from his precarious hold upon the frantically plunging horse. Freed of the weight of both girl and lion the pony raced ahead toward safety. Numa tore and struck at the missile in his shoulder but could not dislodge it. Then he resumed the chase.

Korak guided Tantor into the seclusion of the jungle. He did not wish to be seen, nor had he.

Hanson had almost reached the wood when he heard the lion's terrific roars, and knew that the charge had come. An instant later the Hon. Morison broke upon his vision, racing like mad for safety. The man lay flat upon his pony's back hugging the animal's neck tightly with both arms and digging the spurs into his sides. An instant later the second pony appeared—riderless.

Hanson groaned as he guessed what had happened out of sight in the jungle. With an oath he spurred on in the hope of driving the lion from his prey—his rifle was ready in his hand. And then the lion came into view behind the girl's pony. Hanson could not understand. He knew that if Numa had succeeded in seizing the girl he would not have continued in pursuit of the others.

He drew in his own mount, took quick aim and fired. The lion stopped in his tracks, turned and bit at his side, then rolled over dead. Hanson rode on into the forest, calling aloud to the girl.

"Here I am," came a quick response from the foliage of the trees just ahead. "Did you hit him?"

"Yes," replied Hanson. "Where are you? You had a mighty narrow escape. It will teach you to keep out of the jungle at night."

Together they returned to the plain where they found the Hon. Morison riding slowly back toward them. He explained that his pony had bolted and that he had had hard work stopping him at all. Hanson grinned, for he recalled the pounding heels that he had seen driving sharp spurs into the flanks of Baynes' mount; but he said nothing of what he had seen. He took Meriem up behind him and the three rode in silence toward the bungalow.

19

Behind them Korak emerged from the jungle and recovered his spear from Numa's side. He still was smiling. He had enjoyed the spectacle exceedingly. There was one thing that troubled him—the agility with which the she had clambered from her pony's back into the safety of the tree *above* her. That was more like Mangani—more like his lost Meriem. He sighed. His lost

Meriem! His little, dead Meriem! He wondered if this she stranger resembled his Meriem in other ways. A great longing to see her overwhelmed him. He looked after the three figures moving steadily across the plain. He wondered where might lie their destination. A desire to follow them came over him, but he only stood there watching until they had disappeared in the distance. The sight of the civilized girl and the dapper, khaki clad Englishman had aroused in Korak memories long dormant.

Once he had dreamed of returning to the world of such as these; but with the death of Meriem, hope and ambition seemed to have deserted him. He cared now only to pass the remainder of his life in solitude, as far from man as possible. With a sigh he turned slowly back into the jungle.

Tantor, nervous by nature, had been far from reassured by close proximity to the three strange whites, and with the report of Hanson's rifle had turned and ambled away at his long, swinging shuffle. He was nowhere in sight when Korak returned to look for him. The ape-man, however, was little concerned by the absence of his friend. Tantor had a habit of wandering off unexpectedly. For a month they might not see one another, for Korak seldom took the trouble to follow the great pachyderm, nor did he upon this occasion. Instead he found a comfortable perch in a large tree and was soon asleep.

At the bungalow Bwana had met the returning adventurers on the verandah. In a moment of wakefulness he had heard the report of Hanson's rifle far out across the plain, and wondered what it might mean. Presently it had occurred to him that the man whom he considered in the light of a guest might have met with an accident on his way back to camp, so he had arisen and gone to his foreman's quarters where he had learned that Hanson had been there earlier in the evening but had departed several hours before. Returning from the foreman's quarters Bwana had noticed that the corral gate was open and further investigation revealed the fact that Meriem's pony was gone and also the one most often used by Baynes. Instantly Bwana assumed that the shot had been fired by Hon. Morison, and had again aroused his foreman and was making preparations to set forth in investigation when he had seen the party approaching across the plain.

Explanations on the part of the Englishman met a rather chilly reception from his host. Meriem was silent. She saw that Bwana was angry with her. It was the first time and she was heartbroken.

"Go to your room, Meriem," he said, "and Baynes, if you will step into my study, I'd like to have a word with you in a moment."

He stepped toward Hanson as the others turned to obey him. There was something about Bwana even in his gentlest moods that commanded instant obedience.

"How did you happen to be with them, Hanson?" he asked.

"I'd been sitting in the garden," replied the trader, "after leaving Jervis' quarters. I have a habit of doing that as your lady probably knows. Tonight I fell asleep behind a bush, and was awakened by them two spooning. I couldn't hear what they said, but presently Baynes brings two ponies and they ride off. I didn't like to interfere for it wasn't any of my business, but I knew they hadn't ought to be ridin' about that time of night, leastways not the girl—it wasn't right and it wasn't safe. So I follows them and it's just as well I did. Baynes was gettin' away from the lion as fast as he could, leavin' the girl to take care of herself, when I got a lucky shot into the beast's shoulder that fixed him."

Hanson paused. Both men were silent for a time. Presently the trader coughed in an embarrassed manner as though there was something on his mind he felt in duty bound to say, but hated to.

"What is it, Hanson?" asked Bwana. "You were about to say something weren't you?"

"Well, you see it's like this," ventured Hanson. "Bein' around here evenings a good deal I've seen them two together a lot, and, beggin' your pardon, sir, but I don't think Mr. Baynes means the girl any good. I've overheard enough to make me think he's tryin' to get her to run off with him." Hanson, to fit his own ends, hit nearer the truth than he knew. He was afraid that Baynes would interfere with his own plans, and he had hit upon a scheme to both utilize the young Englishman and get rid of him at the same time.

"And I thought," continued the trader, "that inasmuch as I'm about due to move you might like to suggest to Mr. Baynes that he go with me. I'd be willin' to take him north to the caravan trails as a favor to you, sir."

Bwana stood in deep thought for a moment. Presently he looked up.

"Of course, Hanson, Mr. Baynes is my guest," he said, a grim twinkle in his eye. "Really I cannot accuse him of planning to run away with Meriem on the evidence that we have, and as he is my guest I should hate to be so discourteous as to ask him to leave; but, if I recall his words correctly, it seems to me that he has spoken of returning home, and I am sure that nothing would delight him more than going north with you—you say you start tomorrow? I think Mr. Baynes will accompany you. Drop over in the morning, if you please, and now good night, and thank you for keeping a watchful eye on Meriem."

Hanson hid a grin as he turned and sought his saddle. Bwana stepped from the verandah to his study, where he found the Hon. Morison pacing back and forth, evidently very ill at ease.

"Baynes," said Bwana, coming directly to the point, "Hanson is leaving for the north tomorrow. He has taken a great fancy to you, and just asked me to say to you that he'd be glad to have you accompany him. Good night, Baynes."

At Bwana's suggestion Meriem kept to her room the following morning until after the Hon. Morison Baynes had departed. Hanson had come for him early—in fact he had remained all night with the foreman, Jervis, that they might get an early start.

The farewell exchanges between the Hon. Morison and his host were of the most formal type, and when at last the guest rode away Bwana breathed a sigh of relief. It had been an unpleasant duty and he was glad that it was over; but he did not regret his action. He had not been blind to Baynes' infatuation for Meriem, and knowing the young man's pride in caste he had never for a moment believed that his guest would offer his name to this nameless Arab girl, for, extremely light in color though she was for a full blood Arab, Bwana believed her to be such.

He did not mention the subject again to Meriem, and in this he made a mistake, for the young girl, while realizing the debt of gratitude she owed Bwana and My Dear, was both proud and sensitive, so that Bwana's action in sending Baynes away and giving her no opportunity to explain or defend hurt and mortified her. Also it did much toward making a martyr of Baynes in her eyes and arousing in her breast a keen feeling of loyalty toward him.

What she had half-mistaken for love before, she now wholly mistook for love. Bwana and My Dear might have told her much of the social barriers that they only too well knew Baynes must feel existed between Meriem and himself, but they hesitated to wound her. It would have been better had they inflicted this lesser sorrow, and saved the child the misery that was to follow because of her ignorance.

As Hanson and Baynes rode toward the former's camp the Englishman maintained a morose silence. The other was attempting to formulate an opening that would lead naturally to the proposition he had in mind. He rode a neck behind his companion, grinning as he noted the sullen scowl upon the other's patrician face.

"Rather rough on you, wasn't he?" he ventured at last, jerking his head back in the direction of the bungalow as Baynes turned his eyes upon him at the remark. "He thinks a lot of the girl," continued Hanson, "and don't want nobody to marry her and take her away; but it looks to me as though he was doin' her more harm than good in sendin' you away. She ought to marry some time, and she couldn't do better than a fine young gentleman like you."

Baynes, who had at first felt inclined to take offense at the mention of his private affairs by this common fellow, was mollified by Hanson's final remark, and immediately commenced to see in him a man of fine discrimination.

"He's a darned bounder," grumbled the Hon. Morison, "but I'll get even with him. He may be the whole thing in central Africa but I'm as big as he is in London, and he'll find it out when he comes home."

"If I was you," said Hanson, "I wouldn't let any man keep me from gettin' the girl I want. Between you and me I ain't got no use for him either, and if I can help you any way just call on me."

"It's mighty good of you, Hanson," replied Baynes, warming up a bit, "but what can a fellow do here in this God-forsaken hole?"

"I know what I'd do," said Hanson. "I'd take the girl along with me. If she loves you she'll go, all right."

"It can't be done," said Baynes. "He bosses this whole blooming country for miles around. He'd be sure to catch us."

"No, he wouldn't, not with me running things," said Hanson. "I've been trading and hunting here for ten years and I know as much about the country as he does. If you want to take the girl along I'll help you, and I'll guarantee that there won't nobody catch up with us before we reach the coast. I'll tell you what, you write her a note and I'll get it to her by my head man. Ask her to meet you to say good-bye—she won't refuse that. In the meantime we can be movin' camp a little further north all the time and you can make arrangements with her to be all ready on a certain night. Tell her I'll meet her then while you wait for us in camp. That'll be better for I know the country well and can cover it quicker than you. You can take care of the *safari* and be movin' along slow toward the north and the girl and I'll catch up to you."

"But suppose she won't come?" suggested Baynes.

"Then make another date for a last good-bye," said Hanson, "and instead of you I'll be there and I'll bring her along anyway. She'll have to come, and after it's all over she won't feel so bad about it—especially after livin' with you for two months while we're makin' the coast."

A shocked and angry protest rose to Baynes' lips; but he did not utter it, for almost simultaneously came the realization that this was practically the same thing he had been planning upon himself. It had sounded brutal and criminal from the lips of the rough trader; but nevertheless the young Englishman saw that with Hanson's help and his knowledge of African travel the possibilities of success would be much greater than as though the Hon. Morison were to attempt the thing single handed. And so he nodded a glum assent.

The balance of the long ride to Hanson's northerly camp was made in silence, for both men were occupied with their own thoughts, most of which were far from being either complimentary or loyal to the other. As they rode through the wood the sounds of their careless passage came to the ears of another jungle wayfarer. The Killer had determined to come back to the place where he had seen the white girl who took to the trees with the ability of long habitude. There was a compelling something in the recollection of her that drew him irresistibly toward her. He wished to see her by the light of day, to see her features, to see the color of her eyes and hair. It seemed to him that she must bear a strong resemblance to his lost Meriem, and yet he knew that the chances were that she did not. The fleeting glimpse that he had had of her in the moonlight as she swung from the back of her plunging pony into the branches of the tree above her had shown him a girl of about the same height as his Meriem; but of a more rounded and developed femininity.

Now he was moving lazily back in the direction of the spot where he had seen the girl when the sounds of the approaching horsemen came to his sharp ears. He moved stealthily through the branches until he came within sight of the riders. The younger man he instantly recognized as the same he had seen with his arms about the girl in the moonlit glade just the instant before Numa charged. The other he did not recognize though there was a familiarity about his carriage and figure that puzzled Korak.

The ape-man decided that to find the girl again he would but have to keep in touch with the young Englishman, and so he fell in behind the pair, following them to Hanson's camp. Here the Hon. Morison penned a brief note, which Hanson gave into the keeping of one of his boys who started off forthwith toward the south.

Korak remained in the vicinity of the camp, keeping a careful watch upon the Englishman. He had half expected to find the girl at the destination of the two riders and had been disappointed when no sign of her materialized about the camp.

Baynes was restless, pacing back and forth beneath the trees when he should have been resting against the forced marches of the coming flight. Hanson lay in his hammock and smoked. They spoke but little. Korak lay stretched upon a branch among the dense foliage above them. Thus passed the balance of the afternoon. Korak became hungry and thirsty. He doubted that either of the men would leave camp now before morning, so he withdrew, but toward the south, for there it seemed most likely the girl still was.

In the garden beside the bungalow Meriem wandered thoughtfully in the moonlight. She still smarted from Bwana's, to her, unjust treatment of the Hon. Morison Baynes. Nothing had been explained to her, for both Bwana and My Dear had wished to spare her the mortification and sorrow of the true explanation of Baynes' proposal. They knew, as Meriem did not, that the man had had no intention of marrying her, else he would have come directly to Bwana, knowing full well that no objection would be interposed if Meriem really cared for him.

Meriem loved them both and was grateful to them for all that they had done for her; but deep in her little heart surged the savage love of liberty that her years of untrammeled freedom in the jungle had made part and parcel of her being. Now, for the first time since she had come to them, Meriem felt like a prisoner in the bungalow of Bwana and My Dear.

Like a caged tigress the girl paced the length of the enclosure. Once she paused near the outer fence, her head upon one side— listening. What was it she had heard? The pad of naked human feet just beyond the garden. She listened for a moment. The sound was not repeated. Then she resumed her restless walking. Down to the opposite end of the garden she passed, turned and retraced her steps toward the upper end. Upon the sward near the bushes that hid the fence, full in the glare of the moonlight, lay a white envelope that had not been there when she had turned almost upon the very spot a moment before.

Meriem stopped short in her tracks, listening again, and sniffing—more than ever the tigress; alert, ready. Beyond the bushes a naked black runner squatted, peering through the foliage. He saw her take a step closer to the letter. She had seen it. He rose quietly and following the shadows of the bushes that ran down to the corral was soon gone from sight.

Meriem's trained ears heard his every move. She made no attempt to seek closer knowledge of his identity. Already she had guessed that he was a messenger from the Hon. Morison. She stooped and picked up the envelope. Tearing it open she easily read the contents by the moon's brilliant light. It was, as she had guessed, from Baynes.

"I cannot go without seeing you again," it read. "Come to the clearing early tomorrow morning and say good-bye to me. Come alone."

There was a little more—words that made her heart beat faster and a happy flush mount her cheek.

20

I T WAS STILL dark when the Hon. Morison Baynes set forth for the trysting place. He insisted upon having a guide, saying that he was not sure that he could find his way back to the little clearing. As a matter of fact the thought of that lonely ride through the darkness before the sun rose had been too much for his courage, and he craved company. A black, therefore, preceded him on foot. Behind and above him came Korak, whom the noise in the camp had awakened.

It was nine o'clock before Baynes drew rein in the clearing. Meriem had not yet arrived. The black lay down to rest. Baynes lolled in his saddle. Korak stretched himself comfortably upon a lofty limb, where he could watch those beneath him without being seen.

An hour passed. Baynes gave evidence of nervousness. Korak had already guessed that the young Englishman had come here to meet another, nor was he at all in doubt as to the identity of that other. The Killer was perfectly satisfied that he was soon again to see the nimble she who had so forcefully reminded him of Meriem.

Presently the sound of an approaching horse came to Korak's

ears. She was coming! She had almost reached the clearing before Baynes became aware of her presence, and then as he looked up, the foliage parted to the head and shoulders of her mount and Meriem rode into view. Baynes spurred to meet her. Korak looked searchingly down upon her, mentally anathematizing the broad-brimmed hat that hid her features from his eyes. She was abreast the Englishman now. Korak saw the man take both her hands and draw her close to his breast. He saw the man's face concealed for a moment beneath the same broad brim that hid the girl's. He could imagine their lips meeting, and a twinge of sorrow and sweet recollection combined to close his eyes for an instant in that involuntary muscular act with which we attempt to shut out from the mind's eye harrowing reflections.

When he looked again they had drawn apart and were conversing earnestly. Korak could see the man urging something. It was equally evident that the girl was holding back. There were many of her gestures, and the way in which she tossed her head up and to the right, tip-tilting her chin, that reminded Korak still more strongly of Meriem. And then the conversation was over and the man took the girl in his arms again to kiss her good-bye. She turned and rode toward the point from which she had come. The man sat on his horse watching her. At the edge of the jungle she turned to wave him a final farewell.

"Tonight!" she cried, throwing back her head as she called the words to him across the little distance which separated them— throwing back her head and revealing her face for the first time to the eyes of The Killer in the tree above. Korak started as though pierced through the heart with an arrow. He trembled and shook like a leaf. He closed his eyes, pressing his palms across them, and then he opened them again and looked but the girl was gone— only the waving foliage of the jungle's rim marked where she had disappeared. It was impossible! It could not be true! And yet, with his own eyes he had seen his Meriem—older a little, with figure more rounded by nearer maturity, and subtly changed in other ways; more beautiful than ever, yet still his little Meriem. Yes, he had seen the dead alive again; he had seen his Meriem in the flesh. She lived! She had not died! He had seen her—he had seen his Meriem—*in the arms of another man*! And that man sat below him now, within easy reach. Korak, The Killer, fondled his heavy spear. He played with the grass rope dangling from his gee-string. He stroked the hunting knife at his hip. And the man beneath him called to his drowsy guide, bent the rein to his pony's neck and moved off toward the north. Still sat Korak, The Killer, alone among the trees. Now his hands hung idly at his sides. His weapons and what he had intended were forgotten for the moment. Korak was thinking. He had noted that subtle change in Meriem. When last he had seen her she had been his little, half-naked Mangani—wild, savage, and uncouth. She had not seemed uncouth to him then; but now, in the change that had come over her, he knew that such she had been; yet no more uncouth than he, and he was still uncouth.

In her had taken place the change. In her he had just seen a sweet and lovely flower of refinement and civilization, and he shuddered as he recalled the fate that he himself had planned for her—to be the mate of an ape-man, his mate, in the savage jungle. Then he had seen no wrong in it, for he had loved her, and the way he had planned had been the way of the jungle which they two had chosen as their home; but now, after having seen the Meriem of civilized attire, he realized the hideousness of his once cherished plan, and he thanked God that chance and the blacks of Kovudoo had thwarted him.

Yet he still loved her, and jealousy seared his soul as he recalled the sight of her in the arms of the dapper young Englishman. What were his intentions toward her? Did he really love her? How could one not love her? And she loved him, of that Korak had had ample proof. Had she not loved him she would not have accepted his kisses. His Meriem loved another! For a long time he let that awful truth sink deep, and from it he tried to reason out his future plan of action. In his heart was a great desire to follow the man and slay him; but ever there rose in his consciousness the thought: She loves him. Could he slay the creature Meriem loved? Sadly he shook his head. No, he could not. Then came a partial decision to follow Meriem and speak with her. He half started, and then glanced down at his nakedness and was ashamed. He, the son of a British peer, had thus thrown away his life, had thus degraded himself to the level of a beast that he was ashamed to go to the woman he loved and lay his love at her feet. He was ashamed to go to the little Arab maid who had been his jungle playmate, for what had he to offer her?

For years circumstances had prevented a return to his father and mother, and at last pride had stepped in and expunged from his mind the last vestige of any intention to return. In a spirit of boyish adventure he had cast his lot with the jungle ape. The killing of the crook in the coast inn had filled his childish mind with terror of the law, and driven him deeper into the wilds. The rebuffs that he had met at the hands of men, both black and white, had had their effect upon his mind while yet it was in a formative state, and easily influenced.

He had come to believe that the hand of man was against him, and then he had found in Meriem the only human association he required or craved. When she had been snatched from him his sorrow had been so deep that the thought of ever mingling again with human beings grew still more unutterably distasteful. Finally and for all time, he thought, the die was cast. Of his own volition he had become a beast, a beast he had lived, a beast he would die.

Now that it was too late, he regretted it. For now Meriem, still living, had been revealed to him in a guise of progress and advancement that had carried her completely out of his life. Death itself could not have further removed her from him. In her new world she loved a man of her own kind. And Korak knew that it was right. She was not for him—not for the naked, savage ape. No, she was not for him; but he still was hers. If he could not have her and happiness, he would at least do all that lay in his power to assure happiness to her. He would follow the young Englishman. In the first place he would know that he meant Meriem no harm, and after that, though jealously wrenched his heart, he would watch over the man Meriem loved, for Meriem's sake; but God help that man if he thought to wrong her!

Slowly he aroused himself. He stood erect and stretched his great frame, the muscles of his arms gliding sinuously beneath his tanned skin as he bent his clenched fists behind his head. A movement on the ground beneath caught his eye. An antelope was entering the clearing. Immediately Korak became aware that he was empty—again he was a beast. For a moment love had lifted him to sublime heights of honor and renunciation.

The antelope was crossing the clearing. Korak dropped to the ground upon the opposite side of the tree, and so lightly that not even the sensitive ears of the antelope apprehended his presence. He uncoiled his grass rope—it was the latest addition to his armament, yet he was proficient with it. Often he traveled with nothing more than his knife and his rope—they were light and easy to carry. His spear and bow and arrows were cumbersome and he usually kept one or all of them hidden away in a private cache.

Now he held a single coil of the long rope in his right hand, and the balance in his left. The antelope was but a few paces from him. Silently Korak leaped from his hiding place swinging the rope free from the entangling shrubbery. The antelope sprang away almost instantly; but instantly, too, the coiled rope, with its sliding noose, flew through the air above him. With unerring precision it settled

about the creature's neck. There was a quick wrist movement of
the thrower, the noose tightened. The Killer braced himself with
the rope across his hip, and as the antelope tautened the singing
strands in a last frantic bound for liberty he was thrown over upon
his back.

Then, instead of approaching the fallen animal as a roper of the
western plains might do, Korak dragged his captive to himself,
pulling him in hand over hand, and when he was within reach
leaping upon him even as Sheeta the panther might have done, and
burying his teeth in the animal's neck while he found its heart with
the point of his hunting knife. Recoiling his rope, he cut a few generous strips from his kill and took to the trees again, where he ate
in peace. Later he swung off in the direction of a nearby water
hole, and then he slept.

In his mind, of course, was the suggestion of another meeting
between Meriem and the young Englishman that had been borne
to him by the girl's parting: "Tonight!"

He had not followed Meriem because he knew from the direction from which she had come and in which she returned that
wheresoever she had found an asylum it lay out across the plains
and not wishing to be discovered by the girl he had not cared to
venture into the open after her. It would do as well to keep in touch
with the young man, and that was precisely what he intended
doing.

To you or me the possibility of locating the Hon. Morison in the
jungle after having permitted him to get such a considerable start
might have seemed remote; but to Korak it was not at all so. He
guessed that the white man would return to his camp; but should
he have done otherwise it would be a simple matter to The Killer
to trail a mounted man accompanied by another on foot. Days
might pass and still such a spoor would be sufficiently plain to
lead Korak unfalteringly to its end; while a matter of a few hours
only left it as clear to him as though the makers themselves were
still in plain sight.

And so it came that a few minutes after the Hon. Morison
Baynes entered the camp to be greeted by Hanson, Korak slipped
noiselessly into a nearby tree. There he lay until late afternoon and
still the young Englishman made no move to leave camp. Korak
wondered if Meriem were coming there. A little later Hanson and
one of his black boys rode out of camp. Korak merely noted the
fact. He was not particularly interested in what any other member
of the company than the young Englishman did.

Darkness came and still the young man remained. He ate his

evening meal, afterward smoking numerous cigarettes. Presently he began to pace back and forth before his tent. He kept his boy busy replenishing the fire. A lion coughed and he went into his tent to reappear with an express rifle. Again he admonished the boy to throw more brush upon the fire. Korak saw that he was nervous and afraid, and his lip curled in a sneer of contempt.

Was this the creature who had supplanted him in the heart of his Meriem? Was this a man, who trembled when Numa coughed? How could such as he protect Meriem from the countless dangers of the jungle? Ah, but he would not have to. They would live in the safety of European civilization, where men in uniforms were hired to protect them. What need had a European of prowess to protect his mate? Again the sneer curled Korak's lip.

Hanson and his boy had ridden directly to the clearing. It was already dark when they arrived. Leaving the boy there Hanson rode to the edge of the plain, leading the boy's horse. There he waited. It was nine o'clock before he saw a solitary figure galloping toward him from the direction of the bungalow. A few moments later Meriem drew in her mount beside him. She was nervous and flushed. When she recognized Hanson she drew back, startled.

"Mr. Baynes' horse fell on him and sprained his ankle," Hanson hastened to explain. "He couldn't very well come so he sent me to meet you and bring you to camp."

The girl could not see in the darkness the gloating, triumphant expression on the speaker's face.

"We had better hurry," continued Hanson, "for we'll have to move along pretty fast if we don't want to be overtaken."

"Is he hurt badly?" asked Meriem.

"Only a little sprain," replied Hanson. "He can ride all right; but we both thought he'd better lie up tonight, and rest, for he'll have plenty hard riding in the next few weeks."

"Yes," agreed the girl.

Hanson swung his pony about and Meriem followed him. They rode north along the edge of the jungle for a mile and then turned straight into it toward the west. Meriem, following, payed little attention to directions. She did not know exactly where Hanson's camp lay and so she did not guess that he was not leading her toward it. All night they rode, straight toward the west. When morning came, Hanson permitted a short halt for breakfast, which he had provided in well-filled saddle bags before leaving his camp. Then they pushed on again, nor did they halt a second time until in the heat of the day he stopped and motioned the girl to dismount.

"We will sleep here for a time and let the ponies graze," he said.

"I had no idea the camp was so far away," said Meriem.

"I left orders that they were to move on at day break," explained the trader, "so that we could get a good start. I knew that you and I could easily overtake a laden *safari*. It may not be until tomorrow that we'll catch up with them."

But though they traveled part of the night and all the following day no sign of the *safari* appeared ahead of them. Meriem, an adept in jungle craft, knew that none had passed ahead of them for many days. Occasionally she saw indications of an old spoor, a very old spoor, of many men. For the most part they followed this well-marked trail along elephant paths and through park-like groves. It was an ideal trail for rapid traveling.

Meriem at last became suspicious. Gradually the attitude of the man at her side had begun to change. Often she surprised him devouring her with his eyes. Steadily the former sensation of previous acquaintanceship urged itself upon her. Somewhere, sometime before she had known this man. It was evident that he had not shaved for several days. A blonde stubble had commenced to cover his neck and cheeks and chin, and with it the assurance that he was no stranger continued to grow upon the girl.

It was not until the second day, however, that Meriem rebelled. She drew in her pony at last and voiced her doubts. Hanson assured her that the camp was but a few miles further on.

"We should have overtaken them yesterday," he said. "They must have marched much faster than I had believed possible."

"They have not marched here at all," said Meriem. "The spoor that we have been following is weeks old."

Hanson laughed.

"Oh, that's it, is it?" he cried. "Why didn't you say so before? I could have easily explained. We are not coming by the same route; but we'll pick up their trail sometime today, even if we don't overtake them."

Now, at last, Meriem knew the man was lying to her. What a fool he must be to think that anyone could believe such a ridiculous explanation? Who was so stupid as to believe that they could have expected to overtake another party, and he had certainly assured her that momentarily he expected to do so, when that party's route was not to meet theirs for several miles yet?

She kept her own counsel however, planning to escape at the first opportunity when she might have a sufficient start of her captor, as she now considered him, to give her some assurance of outdistancing him. She watched his face continually when she could without being observed. Tantalizingly the placing of his familiar features persisted in eluding her. Where had she known him? Under what conditions had they met before she had seen him about the farm of Bwana? She ran over in her mind all the few white men she ever had known. There were some who had come to her father's *douar* in the jungle. Few it is true, but there had been some. Ah, now she had it! She had seen him there! She almost seized upon his identity and then, in an instant, it had slipped from her again.

It was mid afternoon when they suddenly broke out of the jungle upon the banks of a broad and placid river. Beyond, upon the opposite store, Meriem described a camp surrounded by a high, thorn *boma*.

"Here we are at last," said Hanson. He drew his revolver and fired in the air. Instantly the camp across the river was astir. Black men ran down the river's bank. Hanson hailed them. But there was no sign of the Hon. Morison Baynes.

In accordance with their master's instructions the blacks manned a canoe and rowed across. Hanson placed Meriem in the little craft and entered it himself, leaving two boys to watch the horses, which the canoe was to return for and swim across to the camp side of the river.

Once in the camp Meriem asked for Baynes. For the moment her fears had been allayed by the sight of the camp, which she had come to look upon as more or less a myth. Hanson pointed toward the single tent that stood in the center of the enclosure.

"There," he said, and preceded her toward it. At the entrance he held the flap aside and motioned her within. Meriem entered and looked about. The tent was empty. She turned toward Hanson. There was a broad grin on his face.

"Where is Mr. Baynes?" she demanded.

"He ain't here," replied Hanson. "Leastwise I don't see him, do you? But I'm here, and I'm a damned sight better man than that thing ever was. You don't need him no more—you got me," and he laughed uproariously and reached for her.

Meriem struggled to free herself. Hanson encircled her arms and body in his powerful grip and bore her slowly backward toward the pile of blankets at the far end of the tent. His face was bent close to hers. His eyes were narrowed to two slits of heat and passion and desire. Meriem was looking full into his face as she fought for freedom when there came over her a sudden recollection of a similar scene in which she had been a participant and with it full recognition of her assailant. He was the Swede Malbihn who had attacked her once before, who had shot his companion who would have saved her, and from whom she had been rescued by Bwana. His smooth face had deceived her; but now with the growing beard and the similarity of conditions recognition came swift and sure.

But today there would be no Bwana to save her.

21

THE BLACK BOY whom Malbihn had left awaiting him in the clearing with instructions to remain until he returned sat crouched at the foot of a tree for an hour when he was suddenly startled by the coughing grunt of a lion behind him. With celerity born of the fear of death the boy clambered into the branches of the tree, and a moment later the king of beasts entered the clearing and approached the carcass of an antelope which, until now, the boy had not seen.

Until daylight the beast fed, while the black clung, sleepless, to his perch, wondering what had become of his master and the two ponies. He had been with Malbihn for a year, and so was fairly conversant with the character of the white. His knowledge presently led him to believe that he had been purposely abandoned. Like the balance of Malbihn's followers, this boy hated his master cordially—fear being the only bond that held him to the white man. His present uncomfortable predicament but added fuel to the fires of his hatred.

As the sun rose the lion withdrew into the jungle and the black descended from his tree and started upon his long journey back to camp. In his primitive brain revolved various fiendish plans for a revenge that he would not have the courage to put into effect when the test came and he stood face to face with one of the dominant race.

A mile from the clearing he came upon the spoor of two ponies crossing his path at right angles. A cunning look entered the black's eyes. He laughed uproariously and slapped his thighs.

Negroes are tireless gossipers, which, of course, is but a round-about way of saying that they are human. Malbihn's boys had been no exception to the rule and as many of them had been with him at various times during the past ten years there was little about his acts and life in the African wilds that was not known directly or by hearsay to them all.

And so, knowing his master and many of his past deeds, knowing, too, a great deal about the plans of Malbihn and Baynes that had been overheard by himself, or other servants; and knowing well from the gossip of the head men that half of Malbihn's party lay in camp by the great river far to the west, it was not difficult for the boy to put two and two together and arrive at four as the sum—the four being represented by a firm conviction that his master had deceived the other white man and taken the latter's woman to his western camp, leaving the other to suffer capture and punishment at the hands of the Big Bwana whom all feared. Again the boy bared his rows of big, white teeth and laughed aloud. Then he resumed his northward way, traveling at a dogged trot that ate up the miles with marvelous rapidity.

In the Swede's camp the Hon. Morison had spent an almost sleepless night of nervous apprehension and doubts and fears. Toward morning he had slept, utterly exhausted. It was the head man who awoke him shortly after sun rise to remind him that they must at once take up their northward journey. Baynes hung back. He wanted to wait for "Hanson" and Meriem. The head man urged upon him the danger that lay in loitering. The fellow knew his master's plans sufficiently well to understand that he had done something to arouse the ire of the Big Bwana and that it would fare ill with them all if they were overtaken in Big Bwana's country. At the suggestion Baynes took alarm.

What if the Big Bwana, as the head man called him, had surprised "Hanson" in his nefarious work. Would he not guess the truth and possibly be already on the march to overtake and punish him? Baynes had heard much of his host's summary method of dealing out punishment to malefactors great and small who transgressed the laws or customs of his savage little world which lay beyond the outer ramparts of what men are pleased to call frontiers. In this savage world where there was no law the Big Bwana was law unto himself and all who dwelt about him. It was even rumored that he had extracted the death penalty from a white man who had maltreated a native girl.

Baynes shuddered at the recollection of this piece of gossip as he wondered what his host would exact of the man who had attempted to steal his young, white ward. The thought brought him to his feet.

"Yes," he said, nervously, "we must get away from here at once. Do you know the trail to the north?"

The head man did, and he lost no time in getting the *safari* upon the march.

It was noon when a tired and sweat-covered runner overtook the trudging little column. The man was greeted with shouts of welcome from his fellows, to whom he imparted all that he knew and guessed of the actions of their master, so that the entire *safari* was aware of matters before Baynes, who marched close to the head of the column, was reached and acquainted with the facts and the imaginings of the black boy whom Malbihn had deserted in the clearing the night before.

When the Hon. Morison had listened to all that the boy had to say and realized that the trader had used him as a tool whereby he himself might get Meriem into his possession, his blood ran hot with rage and he trembled with apprehension for the girl's safety.

That another contemplated no worse a deed than he had contemplated in no way palliated the hideousness of the other's offense. At first it did not occur to him that he would have wronged Meriem no less than he believed "Hanson" contemplated wronging her. Now his rage was more the rage of a man beaten at his own game and robbed of the prize that he had thought already his.

"Do you know where your master has gone?" he asked the black.

"Yes, Bwana," replied the boy. "He has gone to the other camp beside the big *afi* that flows far toward the setting sun."

"Can you take me to him?" demanded Baynes.

The boy nodded affirmatively. Here he saw a method of revenging himself upon his hated Bwana and at the same time of escaping the wrath of the Big Bwana whom all were positive would first follow after the northerly *safari*.

"Can you and I, alone, reach his camp?" asked the Hon. Morison.

"Yes, Bwana," assured the black.

Baynes turned toward the head man. He was conversant with "Hanson's" plans now. He understood why he had wished to move the northern camp as far as possible toward the northern boundary of the Big Bwana's country—it would give him far more time to make his escape toward the West Coast while the Big Bwana was chasing the northern contingent. Well, he would utilize the man's plans to his own end. He, too, must keep out of the clutches of his host.

"You may take the men north as fast as possible," he said to the head man. "I shall return and attempt to lead the Big Bwana to the west."

The Negro assented with a grunt. He had no desire to follow this strange white man who was afraid at night; he had less to remain at the tender mercies of the Big Bwana's lusty warriors, between whom and his people there was long-standing blood feud; and he was more than delighted, into the bargain, for a legitimate excuse for deserting his much hated Swede master. He knew a way to the north and his own country that the white men did not know—a short cut across an arid plateau where lay water holes of which the white hunters and explorers that had passed from time to time the fringe of the dry country had never dreamed. He might even elude the Big Bwana should he follow them, and with this thought uppermost in his mind he gathered the remnants of Malbihn's *safari* into a semblance of order and moved off toward the north. And toward the southwest the black boy led the Hon. Morison Baynes into the jungles.

Korak had waited about the camp, watching the Hon. Morison until the *safari* had started north. Then, assured that the young Englishman was going in the wrong direction to meet Meriem he had abandoned him and returned slowly to the point where he had seen the girl, for whom his heart yearned, in the arms of another.

So great had been his happiness at seeing Meriem alive that, for the instant, no thought of jealousy had entered his mind. Later these thoughts had come—dark, bloody thoughts that would have made the flesh of the Hon. Morison creep could he have guessed that they were revolving in the brain of a savage creature creeping stealthily among the branches of the forest giant beneath which he waited the coming of "Hanson" and the girl.

And with passing of the hours had come subdued reflection in which he had weighed himself against the trimly clad English gentleman and—found that he was wanting. What had he to offer her by comparison with that which the other might offer? What was his "mess of pottage" to the birthright that the other had preserved? How could he dare go, naked and unkempt, to that fair thing who had once been his jungle-fellow and propose the thing that had been in his mind when first the realization of his love had swept over him? He shuddered as he thought of the irreparable wrong that his love would have done the innocent child but for the chance that had snatched her from him before it was too late. Doubtless she knew now the horror that had been in his mind. Doubtless she hated and loathed him as he hated and loathed himself when he let his mind dwell upon it. He had lost her. No more surely had she been lost when he thought her dead than she was in reality now that he had seen her living—living in the guise of a refinement that had transfigured and sanctified her.

He had loved her before, now he worshipped her. He knew that he might never possess her now, but at last he might see her. From a distance he might look upon her. Perhaps he might serve her; but never must she guess that he had found her or that he lived.

He wondered if she ever thought of him—if the happy days that they had spent together never recurred to her mind. It seemed unbelievable that such could be the case, and yet, too, it seemed almost equally unbelievable that this beautiful girl was the same disheveled, half naked, little sprite who skipped nimbly among the branches of the trees as they ran and played in the lazy, happy days of the past. It could not be that her memory held more of the past than did her new appearance.

It was a sad Korak who ranged the jungle near the plain's edge waiting for the coming of his Meriem—the Meriem who never came.

But there came another—a tall, broad-shouldered man in khaki at the head of a swarthy crew of ebon warriors. The man's face was set in hard, stern lines and the marks of sorrow were writ deep about his mouth and eyes—so deep that the set expression of rage upon his features could not obliterate them.

Korak saw the man pass beneath him where he hid in the great tree that had harbored him before upon the edge of that fateful little clearing. He saw him come and he set rigid and frozen and suffering above him. He saw him search the ground with his keen eyes, and he only sat there watching with eyes that glazed from the intensity of his gaze. He saw him sign to his men that he had come upon that which he sought and he saw him pass out of sight toward the north, and still Korak sat like a graven image, with a heart that bled in dumb misery. An hour later Korak moved slowly away, back into the jungle toward the west. He went listlessly, with bent head and stooped shoulders, like an old man who bore upon his back the weight of a great sorrow.

Baynes, following his black guide, battled his way through the dense underbrush, riding stooped low over his horse's neck, or often he dismounted where the low branches swept too close to earth to permit him to remain in the saddle. The black was taking him the shortest way, which was no way at all for a horseman, and after the first day's march the young Englishman was forced to abandon his mount, and follow his nimble guide entirely on foot.

During the long hours of marching the Hon. Morison had much time to devote to thought, and as he pictured the probable fate of Meriem at the hands of the Swede his rage against the man became the greater. But presently there came to him a realization of the fact that his own base plans had led the girl into this terrible predicament, and that even had she escaped "Hanson" she would have found but little better desserts awaiting her with him.

There came too, the realization that Meriem was infinitely more precious to him than he had imagined. For the first time he commenced to compare her with other women of his acquaintance—women of birth and position—and almost to his surprise—he discovered that the young Arab girl suffered less than they by the comparison. And then from hating "Hanson" he came to look upon himself with hate and loathing—to see himself and his perfidious act in all their contemptible hideousness.

Thus, in the crucible of shame amidst the white heat of naked truths, the passion that the man had felt for the girl he had considered his social inferior was transmuted into love. And as he staggered on there burned within him beside his newborn love another great passion—the passion of hate urging him on to the consummation of revenge.

A creature of ease and luxury, he had never been subjected to the hardships and tortures which now were his constant companionship, yet, his clothing torn, his flesh scratched and bleeding, he urged the black to greater speed, though with every dozen steps he himself fell from exhaustion.

It was revenge which kept him going—that and a feeling that in his suffering he was partially expiating the great wrong he had done the girl he loved—for hope of saving her from the fate into which he had trapped her had never existed. "Too late! Too late!" was the dismal accompaniment of thought to which he marched. "Too late! Too late to save; but not too late to avenge!" That kept him up.

Only when it became too dark to see would he permit of a halt.

A dozen times in the afternoon he had threatened the black with instant death when the tired guide insisted upon resting. The fellow was terrified. He could not understand the remarkable change that had so suddenly come over the white man who had been afraid in the dark the night before. He would have deserted this terrifying master had he had the opportunity; but Baynes guessed that some such thought might be in the other's mind, and so gave the fellow none. He kept close to him by day and slept touching him at night in the rude thorn *boma* they constructed as a slight protection against prowling carnivora.

That the Hon. Morison could sleep at all in the midst of the savage jungle was sufficient indication that he had changed considerably in the past twenty-four hours, and that he could lie close beside a none-too-fragrant black man spoke of possibilities for democracy within him yet all undreamed of.

Morning found him stiff and lame and sore, but none the less determined to push on in pursuit of "Hanson" as rapidly as possible. With his rifle he brought down a buck at a ford in a small stream shortly after they broke camp, breakfastless. Begrudgingly he permitted a halt while they cooked and ate, and then on again through the wilderness of trees and vines and underbrush.

And in the meantime Korak wandered slowly westward, coming upon the trail of Tantor, the elephant, whom he overtook browsing in the deep shade of the jungle. The ape-man, lonely and sorrowing, was glad of the companionship of his huge friend. Affectionately the sinuous trunk encircled him, and he was swung to the mighty back where so often before he had lolled and dreamed the long afternoon away.

Far to the north the Big Bwana and his black warriors clung tenaciously to the trail of the fleeing *safari* that was luring them further and further from the girl they sought to save, while back at the bungalow the woman who had loved Meriem as though she had been her own waited impatiently and in sorrow for the return of the rescuing party and the girl she was positive her invincible lord and master would bring back with him.

22

As Meriem struggled with Malbihn, her hands pinioned to her sides by his brawny grip, hope died within her. She did not utter a sound for she knew that there was none to come to her assistance, and, too, the jungle training of her earlier life had taught her the futility of appeals for succor in the savage world of her upbringing.

But as she fought to free herself one hand came in contact with the butt of Malbihn's revolver where it rested in the holster at his hip. Slowly he was dragging her toward the blankets, and slowly her fingers encircled the coveted prize and drew it from its resting place.

Then, as Malbihn stood at the edge of the disordered pile of blankets, Meriem suddenly ceased to draw away from him, and as quickly hurled her weight against him with the result that he was thrown backward, his feet stumbled against the bedding and he was hurled to his back. Instinctively his hands flew out to save himself and at the same instant Meriem leveled the revolver at his breast and pulled the trigger.

But the hammer fell futilely upon an empty shell, and Malbihn was again upon his feet clutching at her. For a moment she eluded him, and ran toward the entrance to the tent, but at the very doorway his heavy hand fell upon her shoulder and dragged her back. Wheeling upon him with the fury of a wounded lioness Meriem grasped the long revolver by the barrel, swung it high above her head and crashed it down full in Malbihn's face.

With an oath of pain and rage the man staggered backward, releasing his hold upon her and then sank unconscious to the ground. Without a backward look Meriem turned and fled into the open. Several of the blacks saw her and tried to intercept her flight, but the menace of the empty weapon kept them at a distance. And so she won beyond the encircling *boma* and disappeared into the jungle to the south.

Straight into the branches of a tree she went, true to the arboreal instincts of the little Mangani she had been, and here she stripped off her riding skirt, her shoes and her stockings, for she knew that she had before her a journey and a flight which would not brook the burden of these garments. Her riding breeches and jacket would have to serve as protection from cold and thorns, nor would they hamper her over much; but a skirt and shoes were impossible among the trees.

She had not gone far before she commenced to realize how slight were her chances for survival without means of defense or a weapon to bring down meat. Why had she not thought to strip the cartridge belt from Malbihn's waist before she had left his tent! With cartridges for the revolver she might hope to bag small game, and to protect herself from all but the most ferocious of the enemies that would beset her way back to the beloved hearthstone of Bwana and My Dear.

With the thought came determination to return and obtain the coveted ammunition. She realized that she was taking great chances of recapture; but without means of defense and of obtaining meat she felt that she could never hope to reach safety. And so she turned her face back toward the camp from which she had but just escaped.

She thought Malbihn dead, so terrific a blow had she dealt him, and she hoped to find an opportunity after dark to enter the camp and search his tent for the cartridge belt; but scarcely had she found a hiding place in a great tree at the edge of the *boma* where she could watch without danger of being discovered, then she saw the Swede emerge from his tent, wiping blood from his face, and hurling a volley of oaths and questions at his terrified followers.

Shortly after the entire camp set forth in search of her and when Meriem was positive that all were gone she descended from her hiding place and ran quickly across the clearing to Malbihn's tent. A hasty survey of the interior revealed no ammunition; but in one corner was a box in which were packed the Swede's personal belongings that he had sent along by his head man to this westerly camp.

Meriem seized the receptacle as the possible container of extra ammunition. Quickly she loosed the cords that held the canvas covering about the box, and a moment later had raised the lid and was rummaging through the heterogeneous accumulation of odds and ends within. There were letters and papers and cuttings from old newspapers, and among other things the photograph of a little girl upon the back of which was pasted a cutting from a Paris daily—a cutting that she could not read, yellowed and dimmed by age and handling—but something about the photograph of the little girl which was also reproduced in the newspaper cutting held her attention. Where had she seen that picture before? And then, quite suddenly, it came to her that this was a picture of herself as she had been years and years before.

Where had it been taken? How had it come into the possession of this man? Why had it been reproduced in a newspaper? What was the story that the faded type told of it?

Meriem was baffled by the puzzle that her search for ammunition had revealed. She stood gazing at the faded photograph for a time and then bethought herself of the ammunition for which she had come. Turning again to the box she rummaged to the bottom and there in a corner she came upon a little box of cartridges. A single glance assured her that they were intended for the weapon she had thrust inside the band of her riding breeches, and slipping them into her pocket she turned once more for an examination of the baffling likeness of herself that she held in her hand.

As she stood thus in vain endeavor to fathom this inexplicable mystery the sound of voices broke upon her ears. Instantly she was all alert. They were coming closer! A second later she recognized the lurid profanity of the Swede. Malbihn, her persecutor, was returning! Meriem ran quickly to the opening of the tent and looked out. It was too late! She was fairly cornered! The white man and three of his black henchmen were coming straight across the clearing toward the tent. What was she to do? She slipped the photograph into her waist. Quickly she slipped a cartridge into each of the chambers of the revolver. Then she backed toward the end of the tent, keeping the entrance covered by her weapon. The man stopped outside, and Meriem could hear Malbihn profanely issuing instructions. He was a long time about it, and while he talked in his bellowing, brutish voice, the girl sought some avenue of escape. Stooping, she raised the bottom of the canvas and looked beneath and beyond. There was no one in sight upon that side. Throwing herself upon her stomach she wormed beneath the tent wall just as Malbihn, with a final word to his men, entered the tent.

Meriem heard him cross the floor, and then she rose and, stooping low, ran to a native hut directly behind. Once inside this she turned and glanced back. There was no one in sight. She had not been seen. And now from Malbihn's tent she heard a great cursing. The Swede had discovered the rifling of his box. He was shouting to his men, and as she heard them reply Meriem darted from the hut and ran toward the edge of the *boma* furthest from Malbihn's tent. Overhanging the *boma* at this point was a tree that had been too large, in the eyes of the rest-loving blacks, to cut down. So they had terminated the *boma* just short of it. Meriem was thankful for whatever circumstance had resulted in the leaving of that particular tree where it was, since it gave her the much needed avenue of escape which she might not otherwise have had.

From her hiding place she saw Malbihn again enter the jungle, this time leaving a guard of three of his boys in the camp. He went toward the south, and after he had disappeared, Meriem skirted the outside of the enclosure and made her way to the river. Here lay the canoes that had been used in bringing the party from the opposite shore. They were unwieldy things for a lone girl to handle, but there was no other way and she must cross the river.

The landing place was in full view of the guard at the camp. To risk the crossing under their eyes would have meant undoubted capture. Her only hope lay in waiting until darkness had fallen, unless some fortuitous circumstance should arise before. For an hour she lay watching the guard, one of whom seemed always in a position where he would immediately discover her should she attempt to launch one of the canoes.

Presently Malbihn appeared, coming out of the jungle, hot and puffing. He ran immediately to the river where the canoes lay and counted them. It was evident that it had suddenly occurred to him that the girl must cross here if she wished to return to her protectors. The expression of relief on his face when he found that none of the canoes was gone was ample evidence of what was passing in his mind. He turned and spoke hurriedly to the head man who had followed him out of the jungle and with whom were several other blacks.

Following Malbihn's instructions they launched all the canoes but one. Malbihn called to the guards in the camp and a moment later the entire party had entered the boats and were paddling up stream.

Meriem watched them until a bend in the river directly above the camp hid them from her sight. They were gone! She was alone, and they had left a canoe in which lay a paddle! She could scarce believe the good fortune that had come to her. To delay now would be suicidal to her hopes. Quickly she ran from her hiding place and dropped to the ground. A dozen yards lay between her and the canoe.

Upstream, beyond the bend, Malbihn ordered his canoes in to shore. He landed with his head man and crossed the little point slowly in search of a spot where he might watch the canoe he had left at the landing place. He was smiling in anticipation of the almost certain success of his stratagem—sooner or later the girl would come back and attempt to cross the river in one of their canoes. It might be that the idea would not occur to her for some time. They might have to wait a day, or two days; but that she would come if she lived or was not captured by the men he had scouting the jungle for her Malbihn was sure. That she would come so soon, however, he had not guessed, and so when he topped the point and came again within sight of the river he saw that which drew an angry oath from his lips—his quarry already was half way across the river.

Turning, he ran rapidly back to his boats, the head man at his heels. Throwing themselves in Malbihn urged his paddlers to their most powerful efforts. The canoes shot out into the stream and down with the current toward the fleeing quarry. She had almost completed the crossing when they came in sight of her. At the same instant she saw them, and redoubled her efforts to reach the opposite shore before they should overtake her. Two minutes' start of them was all Meriem cared for. Once in the trees she knew that she could outdistance and elude them. Her hopes were high—they could not overtake her now—she had had too good a start of them.

Malbihn, urging his men onward with a stream of hideous oaths and blows from his fists, realized that the girl was again slipping from his clutches. The leading canoe, in the bow of which he stood, was yet a hundred yards behind the fleeing Meriem when she ran the point of her craft beneath the overhanging trees on the shore of safety.

Malbihn screamed to her to halt. He seemed to have gone mad with rage at the realization that he could not overtake her, and then he threw his rifle to his shoulder, aimed carefully at the slim figure scrambling into the trees, and fired.

Malbihn was an excellent shot. His misses at so short a distance were practically non-existent, nor would he have missed this time but for an accident occurring at the very instant that his finger tightened upon the trigger—an accident to which Meriem owed her life—the providential presence of a water-logged tree trunk, one end of which was embedded in the mud of the river bottom and the other end of which floated just beneath the surface where the prow of Malbihn's canoe ran upon it as he fired. The slight deviation of the boat's direction was sufficient to throw the muzzle of the rifle out of aim. The bullet whizzed harmlessly by Meriem's head and an instant later she had disappeared into the foliage of the tree.

There was a smile on her lips as she dropped to the ground to cross a little clearing where once had stood a native village surrounded by its fields. The ruined huts still stood in crumbling decay. The rank vegetation of the jungle overgrew the cultivated ground. Small trees already had sprung up in what had been the village street; but desolation and loneliness hung like a pall above the scene. To Meriem, however, it presented but a place denuded of large trees which she must cross quickly to regain the jungle upon the opposite side before Malbihn should have landed.

The deserted huts were, to her, all the better because they were deserted—she did not see the keen eyes watching her from a dozen points, from tumbling doorways, from behind tottering granaries. In utter unconsciousness of impending danger she started up the village street because it offered the clearest pathway to the jungle.

A mile away toward the east, fighting his way through the jungle along the trail taken by Malbihn when he had brought Meriem to his camp, a man in torn khaki—filthy, haggard, unkempt—came to a sudden stop as the report of Malbihn's rifle resounded faintly through the tangled forest. The black man just ahead of him stopped, too.

"We are almost there, Bwana," he said. There was awe and respect in his tone and manner.

The white man nodded and motioned his ebon guide forward once more. It was the Hon. Morison Baynes—the fastidious—the exquisite. His face and hands were scratched and smeared with dried blood from the wounds he had come by in thorn and thicket. His clothes were tatters. But through the blood and the dirt and the rags a new Baynes shone forth—a handsomer Baynes than the dandy and the fop of yore.

In the heart and soul of every son of woman lies the germ of manhood and honor. Remorse for a scurvy act, and an honorable desire to right the wrong he had done the woman he now knew he really loved had excited these germs to rapid growth in Morison Baynes—and the metamorphosis had taken place.

Onward the two stumbled toward the point from which the single rifle shot had come. The black was unarmed—Baynes, fearing his loyalty had not dared trust him even to carry the rifle which the white man would have been glad to be relieved of many times upon the long march; but now that they were approaching their goal, and knowing as he did that hatred of Malbihn burned hot in the black man's brain, Baynes handed him the rifle, for he guessed that there would be fighting—he intended that there should, for he had come to avenge. Himself, an excellent revolver shot, would depend upon the smaller weapon at his side.

As the two forged ahead toward their goal they were startled by a volley of shots ahead of them. Then came a few scattering reports, some savage yells, and silence. Baynes was frantic in his endeavors to advance more rapidly, but there the jungle seemed a thousand times more tangled than before. A dozen times he tripped and fell. Twice the black followed a blind trail and they were forced to retract their steps; but at last they came out into a little clearing near the big *afi*—a clearing that once held a thriving village, but lay somber and desolate in decay and ruin.

In the jungle vegetation that overgrew what had once been the main village street lay the body of a black man, pierced through the heart with a bullet, and still warm. Baynes and his companion looked about in all directions; but no sign of living being could they discover. They stood in silence listening intently.

What was that! Voices and the dip of paddles out upon the river?

Baynes ran across the dead village toward the fringe of jungle upon the river's brim. The black was at his side. Together they forced their way through the screening foliage until they could obtain a view of the river, and there, almost to the other shore, they saw Malbihn's canoes making rapidly for camp. The black recognized his companions immediately.

"How can we cross?" asked Baynes.

The black shook his head. There was no canoe and the crocodiles made it equivalent to suicide to enter the water in an attempt to swim across. Just then the fellow chanced to glance downward. Beneath him, wedged among the branches of a tree, lay the canoe in which Meriem had escaped. The Negro grasped Baynes' arm and pointed toward his find. The Hon. Morison could scarce repress a shout of exultation. Quickly the two slid down the drooping branches into the boat. The black seized the paddle and Baynes shoved them out from beneath the tree. A second later the canoe shot out upon the bosom of the river and headed toward the opposite shore and the camp of the Swede. Baynes squatted in the bow, straining his eyes after the men pulling the other canoes upon the bank across from him. He saw Malbihn step from the bow of the foremost of the little craft. He saw him turn and glance back across the river. He could see his start of surprise as his eyes fell upon the pursuing canoe, and called the attention of his followers to it.

Then he stood waiting, for there was but one canoe and two men—little danger to him and his followers in that. Malbihn was puzzled. Who was this white man? He did not recognize him though Baynes' canoe was now in midstream and the features of both its occupants plainly discernible to those on shore. One of Malbihn's blacks it was who first recognized his fellow black in the person of Baynes' companion. Then Malbihn guessed who the white man must be, though he could scarce believe his own reasoning. It seemed beyond the pale of wildest conjecture to suppose that the Hon. Morison Baynes had followed him through the jungle with but a single companion—and yet it was true. Beneath the dirt and dishevelment he recognized him at last, and in the necessity of admitting that it was he, Malbihn was forced to recognize the incentive that had driven Baynes, the weakling and coward, through the savage jungle upon his trail.

The man had come to demand an accounting and to avenge. It seemed incredible, and yet there could be no other explanation. Malbihn shrugged. Well, others had sought Malbihn for similar reasons in the course of a long and checkered career. He fingered his rifle, and waited.

Now the canoe was within easy speaking distance of the shore.

"What do you want?" yelled Malbihn, raising his weapon threateningly.

The Hon. Morison Baynes leaped to his feet.

"You, damn you!" he shouted, whipping out his revolver and firing almost simultaneously with the Swede.

As the two reports rang out Malbihn dropped his rifle, clutched frantically at his breast, staggered, fell first to his knees and then lunged upon his face. Baynes stiffened. His head flew back spasmodically. For an instant he stood thus, and then crumpled very gently into the bottom of the boat.

The black paddler was at a loss as to what to do. If Malbihn really were dead he could continue on to join his fellows without fear; but should the Swede only be wounded he would be safer upon the far shore. Therefore he hesitated, holding the canoe in mid stream. He had come to have considerable respect for his new master and was not unmoved by his death. As he sat gazing at the crumpled body in the bow of the boat he saw it move. Very feebly the man essayed to turn over. He still lived. The black moved forward and lifted him to a sitting position. He was standing in front of him, his paddle in one hand, asking Baynes where he was hit when there was another shot from shore and the Negro pitched head long overboard, his paddle still clutched in his dead fingers—shot through the forehead.

Baynes turned weakly in the direction of the shore to see Malbihn drawn up upon his elbows leveling his rifle at him. The Englishman slid to the bottom of the canoe as a bullet whizzed above him. Malbihn, sore hit, took longer in aiming, nor was his aim as sure as formerly. With difficulty Baynes turned himself over on his belly and grasping his revolver in his right hand drew himself up until he could look over the edge of the canoe.

Malbihn saw him instantly and fired; but Baynes did not flinch or duck. With painstaking care he aimed at the target upon the shore from which he now was drifting with the current. His finger closed upon the trigger—there was a flash and a report, and Malbihn's giant frame jerked to the impact of another bullet.

But he was not yet dead. Again he aimed and fired, the bullet splintering the gunwale of the canoe close by Baynes's face. Baynes fired again as his canoe drifted further down stream and Malbihn answered from the shore where he lay in a pool of his own blood. And thus, doggedly, the two wounded men continued to carry on their weird duel until the winding African river had carried the Hon. Morison Baynes out of sight around a wooded point.

23

MERIEM HAD TRAVERSED half the length of the village street when a score of white-robed Negroes and half-castes leaped out upon her from the dark interiors of surrounding huts. She turned to flee, but heavy hands seized her, and when she turned at last to plead with them her eyes fell upon the face of a tall, grim, old man glaring down upon her from beneath the folds of his burnous.

At sight of him she staggered back in shocked and terrified surprise. It was The Sheik!

Instantly all the old fears and terrors of her childhood returned upon her. She stood trembling before this horrible old man, as a murderer before the judge about to pass sentence of death upon him. She knew that The Sheik recognized her. The years and the changed raiment had not altered her so much but what one who had known her features so well in childhood would know her now.

"So you have come back to your people, eh?" snarled The Sheik. "Come back begging for food and protection, eh?"

"Let me go," cried the girl. "I ask nothing of you, but that you let me go back to the Big Bwana."

"The Big Bwana?" almost screamed The Sheik, and then followed a stream of profane, Arabic invective against the white man whom all the transgressors of the jungle feared and hated. "You would go back to the Big Bwana, would you? So that is where you have been since you ran away from me, is it? And who comes now across the river after you—the Big Bwana?"

"The Swede whom you once chased away from your country when he and his companion conspired with Nbeeda to steal me from you," replied Meriem.

The Shiek's eyes blazed, and he called his men to approach the shore and hide among the bushes that they might ambush and annihilate Malbihn and his party; but Malbihn already had landed and crawling through the fringe of jungle was at that very moment looking with wide and incredulous eyes upon the scene being enacted in the street of the deserted village. He recognized The Sheik the moment his eyes fell upon him. There were two men in the world that Malbihn feared as he feared the devil. One was the Big Bwana and the other The Sheik. A single glance he took at that gaunt, familiar figure and then he turned tail and scurried back to his canoe calling his followers after him. And so it happened that the party was well out in the stream before The Sheik reached the shore, and after a volley and a few parting shots that were returned from the canoes the Arab called his men off and securing his prisoner set off toward the South.

One of the bullets from Malbihn's force had struck a black standing in the village street where he had been left with another to guard Meriem, and his companions had left him where he had fallen, after appropriating his apparel and belongings. His was the body that Baynes had discovered when he had entered the village.

The Sheik and his party had been marching southward along the river when one of them, dropping out of line to fetch water, had seen Meriem paddling desperately from the opposite shore. The fellow had called The Sheik's attention to the strange sight— a white woman alone in central Africa and the old Arab had hidden his men in the deserted village to capture her when she landed, for thoughts of ransom were always in the mind of The Sheik. More than once before had glittering gold filtered through his fingers from a similar source. It was easy money and The Sheik had none too much easy money since the Big Bwana had so circumscribed the limits of his ancient domain that he dared not even steal ivory from natives within two hundred miles of the Big Bwana's *douar*. And when at last the woman had walked into the trap he had set for her and he had recognized her as the same little girl he had brutalized and maltreated years before his gratification had been huge. Now he lost no time in establishing the old relations of father and daughter that had existed between them in the past. At the first opportunity he struck her a heavy blow across the face. He forced her to walk when he might have dismounted one of his men instead, or had her carried on a horse's rump. He seemed to revel in the discovery of new methods for torturing or humiliating her, and among all his followers she found no single one to offer her sympathy, or who dared defend her, even had they had the desire to do so.

A two days' march brought them at last to the familiar scenes of her childhood, and the first face upon which she set her eyes as she was driven through the gates into the strong stockade was that of the toothless, hideous Mabunu, her one time nurse. It was as though all the years that had intervened were but a dream. Had it not been for her clothing and the fact that she had grown in stature she might well have believed it so. All was there as she had left it—the new faces which supplanted some of the old were of the same bestial, degraded type. There were a few young Arabs who had joined The Sheik since she had been away. Otherwise all was the same—all but one. Geeka was not there, and she found herself missing Geeka as though the ivory-headed one had been a flesh and blood intimate and friend. She missed her ragged little confidante, into whose deaf ears she had been wont to pour her many miseries and her occasional joys—Geeka, of the splinter limbs and the ratskin torso—Geeka the disreputable—Geeka the beloved.

For a time the inhabitants of The Sheik's village who had not been upon the march with him amused themselves by inspecting the strangely clad white girl, whom some of them had known as a little child. Mabunu pretended great joy at her return, baring her toothless gums in a hideous grimace that was intended to be indicative of rejoicing. But Meriem could but shudder as she recalled the cruelties of this terrible old hag in the years gone by.

Among the Arabs who had come in her absence was a tall young fellow of twenty—a handsome, sinister looking youth—who stared at her in open admiration until The Sheik came and ordered him away, and Abdul Kamak went, scowling.

At last, their curiosity satisfied, Meriem was alone. As of old, she was permitted the freedom of the village, for the stockade was high and strong and the only gates were well-guarded by day and by night; but as of old she cared not for the companionship of the cruel Arabs and the degraded blacks who formed the following of The Sheik, and so, as had been her wont in the sad days of her childhood, she slunk down to an unfrequented corner of the enclosure where she had often played at housekeeping with her beloved Geeka beneath the spreading branches of the great tree that had overhung the palisade; but now the tree was gone, and Meriem guessed the reason. It was from this tree that Korak had descended and struck down The Sheik the day that he had rescued her from the life of misery and torture that had been her lot for so long that she could remember no other.

There were low bushes growing within the stockade, however, and in the shade of these Meriem sat down to think. A little glow of happiness warmed her heart as she recalled her first meeting with Korak and then the long years that he had cared for and protected her with the solicitude and purity of an elder brother. For months Korak had not so occupied her thoughts as he did today. He seemed closer and dearer now than ever he had before, and she wondered that her heart had drifted so far from loyalty to his memory. And then came the image of the Hon. Morison, the exquisite, and Meriem was troubled. Did she really love the flawless young Englishman? She thought of the glories of London, of which he had told her in such glowing language. She tried to picture herself admired and honored in the midst of the gayest society of the great capital. The pictures she drew were the pictures that the Hon. Morison had drawn for her. They were alluring pictures, but through them all the brawny, half-naked figure of the giant Adonis of the jungle persisted in obtruding itself.

Meriem pressed her hand above her heart as she stifled a sigh, and as she did so she felt the hard outlines of the photograph she had hidden there as she slunk from Malbihn's tent. Now she drew it forth and commenced to re-examine it more carefully than she had had time to do before. She was sure that the baby face was hers. She studied every detail of the picture. Half hidden in the lace of the dainty dress rested a chain and locket. Meriem puckered her brows. What tantalizing half-memories it awakened! Could this flower of evident civilization be the little Arab Meriem, daughter of The Sheik? It was impossible, and yet that locket? Meriem knew it. She could not refute the conviction of her memory. She had seen that locket before and it had been hers. What strange mystery lay buried in her past?

As she sat gazing at the picture she suddenly became aware that she was not alone—that someone was standing close behind her—someone who had approached her noiselessly. Guiltily she thrust the picture back into her waist. A hand fell upon her shoulder. She was sure that it was The Sheik and she awaited in dumb terror the blow that she knew would follow.

No blow came and she looked upward over her shoulder—into the eyes of Abdul Kamak, the young Arab.

"I saw," he said, "the picture that you have just hidden. It is you when you were a child—a very young child. May I see it again?"

Meriem drew away from him.

"I will give it back," he said. "I have heard of you and I know that you have no love for The Sheik, your father. Neither have I. I will not betray you. Let me see the picture."

Friendless among cruel enemies, Meriem clutched at the straw that Abdul Kamak held out to her. Perhaps in him she might find the friend she needed. Anyway he had seen the picture and if he was not a friend he could tell The Sheik about it and it would be taken away from her. So she might as well grant his request and hope that he had spoken fairly, and would deal fairly. She drew the photograph from its hiding place and handed it to him.

Abdul Kamak examined it carefully, comparing it, feature by feature with the girl sitting on the ground looking up into his face. Slowly he nodded his head.

"Yes," he said, "it is you, but where was it taken? How does it happen that The Sheik's daughter is clothed in the garments of the unbeliever?"

"I do not know," replied Meriem. "I never saw the picture until a couple of days ago, when I found it in the tent of the Swede, Malbihn."

Abdul Kamak raised his eyebrows. He turned the picture over

and as his eyes fell upon the old newspaper cutting they went wide. He could read French, with difficulty, it is true; but he could read it. He had been to Paris. He had spent six months there with a troupe of his desert fellows, upon exhibition, and he had improved his time, learning many of the customs, some of the language, and most of the vices of his conquerors. Now he put his learning to use. Slowly, laboriously he read the yellowed cutting. His eyes were no longer wide. Instead they narrowed to two slits of cunning. When he had done he looked at the girl.

"You have read this?" he asked.

"It is French," she replied, "and I do not read French."

Abdul Kamak stood long in silence looking at the girl. She was very beautiful. He desired her, as had many other men who had seen her. At last he dropped to one knee beside her.

A wonderful idea had sprung to Abdul Kamak's mind. It was an idea that might be furthered if the girl were kept in ignorance of the contents of that newspaper cutting. It would certainly be doomed should she learn its contents.

"Meriem," he whispered, "never until today have my eyes beheld you, yet at once they told my heart that it must ever be your servant. You do not know me, but I ask that you trust me. I can help you. You hate The Sheik—so do I. Let me take you away from him. Come with me, and we will go back to the great desert where my father is a sheik mightier than is yours. Will you come?"

Meriem sat in silence. She hated to wound the only one who had offered her protection and friendship; but she did not want Abdul Kamak's love. Deceived by her silence the man seized her and strained her to him; but Meriem struggled to free herself.

"I do not love you," she cried. "Oh, please do not make me hate you. You are the only one who has shown kindness toward me, and I want to like you, but I cannot love you."

Abdul Kamak drew himself to his full height.

"You will learn to love me," he said, "for I shall take you whether you will or no. You hate The Sheik and so you will not tell him, for if you do I will tell him of the picture. I hate The Sheik, and—"

"You hate The Sheik?" came a grim voice from behind them.

Both turned to see The Sheik standing a few paces from them. Abdul still held the picture in his hand. Now he thrust it within his burnous.

"Yes," he said, "I hate The Sheik," and as he spoke he sprang toward the older man, felled him with a blow and dashed on across the village to the line where his horse was picketed, saddled and ready, for Abdul Kamak had been about to ride forth to hunt when he had seen the stranger girl alone by the bushes.

Leaping into the saddle Abdul Kamak dashed for the village gates. The Sheik, momentarily stunned by the blow that had felled him, now staggered to his feet, shouting lustily to his followers to stop the escaped Arab. A dozen blacks leaped forward to intercept the horseman, only to be ridden down or brushed aside by the muzzle of Abdul Kamak's long musket, which he lashed from side to side about him as he spurred on toward the gate. But here he must surely be intercepted. Already the two blacks stationed there were pushing the unwieldly portals to. Up flew the barrel of the fugitive's weapon. With reins flying loose and his horse at a mad gallop the son of the desert fired once—twice; and both the keepers of the gate dropped in their tracks. With a wild whoop of exultation, twirling his musket high above his head and turning in his saddle to laugh back into the faces of his pursuers, Abdul Kamak dashed out of the village of The Sheik and was swallowed up by the jungle.

Foaming with rage The Sheik ordered immediate pursuit, and then strode rapidly back to where Meriem sat huddled by the bushes where he had left her.

"The picture!" he cried. "What picture did the dog speak of? Where is it? Give it to me at once!"

"He took it," replied Meriem, dully.

"What was it?" again demanded The Sheik, seizing the girl roughly by the hair and dragging her to her feet, where he shook her venomously. "What was it a picture of?"

"Of me," said Meriem, "when I was a little girl. I stole it from Malbihn, the Swede—it had printing on the back cut from an old newspaper."

The Sheik went white with rage.

"What said the printing?" he asked in a voice so low that she but barely caught his words.

"I do not know. It was in French and I cannot read French."

The Sheik seemed relieved. He almost smiled, nor did he again strike Meriem before he turned and strode away with the parting admonition that she speak never again to any other than Mabunu and himself. And along the caravan trail galloped Abdul Kamak toward the north.

As his canoe drifted out of sight and range of the wounded Swede the Hon. Morison sank weakly to its bottom where he lay for long hours in partial stupor.

It was night before he fully regained consciousness. And then he lay for a long time looking up at the stars and trying to recollect where he was, what accounted for the gently rocking motion of the thing upon which he lay, and why the position of the stars changed so rapidly and miraculously. For a while he thought he was dreaming, but when he would have moved to shake sleep from him the pain of his wound recalled to him the events that had led up to his present position. Then it was that he realized that he was floating down a great African river in a native canoe—alone, wounded, and lost.

Painfully he dragged himself to a sitting position. He noticed that the wound pained him less than he had imagined it would. He felt of it gingerly—it had ceased to bleed. Possibly it was but a flesh wound after all, and nothing serious. If it totally incapacitated him even for a few days it would mean death, for by that time he would be too weakened by hunger and pain to provide food for himself.

From his own troubles his mind turned to Meriem's. That she had been with the Swede at the time he had attempted to reach the fellow's camp he naturally believed; but he wondered what would become of her now. Even if Hanson died of his wounds would Meriem be any better off? She was in the power of equally villainous men—brutal savages of the lowest order. Baynes buried his face in his hands and rocked back and forth as the hideous picture of her fate burned itself into his consciousness. And it was he who had brought this fate upon her! His wicked desire had snatched a pure and innocent girl from the protection of those who loved her to hurl her into the clutches of the bestial Swede and his outcast following! And not until it had become too late had he realized the magnitude of the crime he himself had planned and contemplated. Not until it had become too late had he realized that greater than his desire, greater than his lust, greater than any passion he had ever felt before was the newborn love that burned within his breast for the girl he would have ruined.

The Hon. Morison Baynes did not fully realize the change that had taken place within him. Had one suggested that he ever had been aught than the soul of honor and chivalry he would have taken umbrage forthwith. He knew that he had done a vile thing when he had plotted to carry Meriem away to London, yet he excused it on the ground of his great passion for the girl having temporarily warped his moral standards by the intensity of its heat. But, as a matter of fact, a new Baynes had been born. Never again could this man be bent to dishonor by the intensity of a desire. His moral fiber had been strengthened by the mental suffering he had endured. His mind and his soul had been purged by sorrow and remorse.

His one thought now was to atone—win to Meriem's side and lay down his life, if necessary, in her protection. His eyes sought the length of the canoe in search of the paddle, for a determination had galvanized him to immediate action despite his weakness and his wound. But the paddle was gone. He turned his eyes toward the shore. Dimly through the darkness of a moonless night he saw the awful blackness of the jungle, yet it touched no responsive chord of terror within him now as it had done in the past. He did not even wonder that he was unafraid, for his mind was entirely occupied with thoughts of another's danger.

Drawing himself to his knees he leaned over the edge of the canoe and commenced to paddle vigorously with his open palm. Though it tired and hurt him he kept assiduously at his self imposed labor for hours. Little by little the drifting canoe moved nearer and nearer the shore. The Hon. Morison could hear a lion roaring directly opposite him and so close that he felt he must be almost to the shore. He drew his rifle closer to his side; but he did not cease to paddle.

After what seemed to the tired man an eternity of time he felt the brush of branches against the canoe and heard the swirl of the water about them. A moment later he reached out and clutched a leafy limb. Again the lion roared—very near it seemed now, and Baynes wondered if the brute could have been following along the shore waiting for him to land.

He tested the strength of the limb to which he clung. It seemed strong enough to support a dozen men. Then he reached down and lifted his rifle from the bottom of the canoe, slipping the sling over his shoulder. Again he tested the branch, and then reaching upward as far as he could for a safe hold he drew himself painfully and slowly upward until his feet swung clear of the canoe, which, released, floated silently from beneath him to be lost forever in the blackness of the dark shadows down stream.

He had burned his bridges behind him. He must either climb aloft or drop back into the river; but there had been no other way. He struggled to raise one leg over the limb, but found himself scarce equal to the effort, for he was very weak. For a time he hung there feeling his strength ebbing. He knew that he must gain the branch above at once or it would be too late.

Suddenly the lion roared almost in his ear. Baynes glanced up.

He saw two spots of flame a short distance from and above him. The lion was standing on the bank of the river glaring at him, and—waiting for him. Well, thought the Hon. Morison, let him wait. Lions can't climb trees, and if I get into this one I shall be safe enough for him.

The young Englishman's feet hung almost to the surface of the water—closer than he knew, for all was pitch dark below as above him. Presently he heard a slight commotion in the river beneath him and something banged against one of his feet, followed almost instantly by a sound that he felt he could not have mistaken—the click of great jaws snapping together.

"By George!" exclaimed the Hon. Morison, aloud. "The beggar nearly got me," and immediately he struggled again to climb higher and to comparative safety; but with that final effort he knew that it was futile. Hope that had survived persistently until now began to wane. He felt his tired, numbed fingers slipping from their hold—he was dropping back into the river—into the jaws of the frightful death that awaited him there.

And then he heard the leaves above him rustle to the movement of a creature among them. The branch to which he clung bent beneath an added weight—and no light weight, from the way it sagged; but still Baynes clung desperately—he would not give up voluntarily either to the death above or the death below.

He felt a soft, warm pad upon the fingers of one of his hands where they circled the branch to which he clung, and then something reached down out of the blackness above and dragged him up among the branches of the tree.

24

SOMETIMES LOLLING UPON Tantor's back, sometimes roaming the jungle in solitude, Korak made his way slowly toward the West and South. He made but a few miles a day, for he had a whole lifetime before him and no place in particular to go. Possibly he would have moved more rapidly but for the thought which continually haunted him that each mile he traversed carried him further and further away from Meriem—no longer his Meriem, as of yore, it is true! but still as dear to him as ever.

Thus he came upon the trail of The Sheik's band as it traveled down river from the point where The Sheik had captured Meriem to his own stockaded village. Korak pretty well knew who it was that had passed, for there were few in the great jungle with whom he was not familiar, though it had been years since he had come this far north. He had no particular business, however, with the old Sheik and so he did not propose following him—the further from men he could stay the better pleased he would be—he wished that he might never see a human face again. Men always brought him sorrow and misery.

The river suggested fishing and so he waddled upon its shores, catching fish after a fashion of his own devising and eating them raw. When night came he curled up in a great tree beside the stream—the one from which he had been fishing during the afternoon—and was soon asleep. Numa, roaring beneath him, awoke him. He was about to call out in anger to his noisy neighbor when something else caught his attention. He listened. Was there something in the tree beside himself? Yes, he heard the noise of something below him trying to clamber upward. Presently he heard the click of a crocodile's jaws in the waters beneath, and then, low but distinct: "By George! The beggar nearly got me." The voice was familiar.

Korak glanced downward toward the speaker. Outlined against the faint luminosity of the water he saw the figure of a man clinging to a lower branch of the tree. Silently and swiftly the ape-man clambered downward. He felt a hand beneath his foot. He reached down and clutched the figure beneath him and dragged it up among the branches. It struggled weakly and struck at him; but Korak paid no more attention than Tantor to an ant. He lugged his burden to the higher safety and greater comfort of a broad crotch, and there he propped it in a sitting position against the bole of the tree. Numa still was roaring beneath them, doubtless in anger that he had been robbed of his prey. Korak shouted down at him, calling him, in the language of the great apes, "Old green-eyed eater of carrion," "Brother of Dango," the hyena, and other choice appellations of jungle approbrium.

The Hon. Morison Baynes, listening, felt assured that a gorilla had seized upon him. He felt for his revolver, and as he was drawing it stealthily from its holster a voice asked in perfectly good English, "Who are you?"

Baynes started so that he nearly fell from the branch.

"My God!" he exclaimed. "Are you a man?"

"What did you think I was?" asked Korak.

"A gorilla," replied Baynes, honestly.

Korak laughed.

"Who are you?" he repeated.

"I'm an Englishman by the name of Baynes; but who the devil are you?" asked the Hon. Morison.

"They call me The Killer," replied Korak, giving the English translation of the name that Akut had given him. And then after a pause during which the Hon. Morison attempted to pierce the darkness and catch a glimpse of the features of the strange being into whose hands he had fallen, "You are the same whom I saw kissing the girl at the edge of the great plain to the East, that time that the lion charged you?"

"Yes," replied Baynes.

"What are you doing here?"

"The girl was stolen—I am trying to rescue her."

"Stolen!" The word was shot out like a bullet from a gun. "Who stole her?"

"The Swede trader, Hanson," replied Baynes.

"Where is he?"

Baynes related to Korak all that has transpired since he had come upon Hanson's camp. Before he was done the first gray dawn had relieved the darkness. Korak made the Englishman comfortable in the trees. He filled his canteen from the river and fetched him fruits to eat. Then he bid him good-bye.

"I am going to the Swede's camp," he announced. "I will bring the girl back to you here."

"I shall go, too, then," insisted Baynes. "It is my right and my duty, for she was to have become my wife."

Korak winced. "You are wounded. You could not make the trip," he said. "I can go much faster alone."

"Go, then," replied Baynes, "but I shall follow. It is my right and duty."

"As you will," replied Korak, with a shrug. If the man wanted to be killed it was none of his affair. He wanted to kill him himself, but for Meriem's sake he would not. If she loved him then he must do what he could to preserve him, but he could not prevent his following him, more than to advise him against it, and this he did, earnestly.

And so Korak set out rapidly toward the North, and limping slowly and painfully along, soon far to the rear, came the tired and wounded Baynes. Korak had reached the river bank opposite Malbihn's camp before Baynes had covered two miles. Late in the afternoon the Englishman was still plodding wearily along, forced a stop often for rest when he heard the sound of the galloping feet of a horse behind him. Instinctively he drew into the concealing foliage of the underbrush and a moment later a white-robed Arab dashed by. Baynes did not hail the rider. He had heard of the nature of the Arabs who penetrate thus far to the South, and what he had heard had convinced him that a snake or a panther would as quickly befriend him as one of these villainous renegades from the Northland.

When Abdul Kamak had passed out of sight toward the North Baynes resumed his weary march. A half hour later he was again surprised by the unmistakable sound of galloping horses. This time there were many. Once more he sought a hiding place; but it chanced that he was crossing a clearing which offered little opportunity for concealment. He broke into a slow trot—the best that he could do in his weakened condition; but it did not suffice to carry him to safety and before he reached the opposite side of the clearing a band of white-robed horsemen dashed into view behind him.

At sight of him they shouted in Arabic, which, of course, he could not understand, and then they closed about him, threatening and angry. Their questions were unintelligible to him, and no more could they interpret his English. At last, evidently out of patience, the leader ordered two of his men to seize him, which they lost no time in doing. They disarmed him and ordered him to climb to the rump of one of the horses, and then the two who had been detailed to guard him turned and rode back toward the South, while the others continued their pursuit of Abdul Kamak.

As Korak came out upon the bank of the river across from which he could see the camp of Malbihn he was at a loss as to how he was to cross. He could see men moving about among the huts inside the *boma*—evidently Hanson was still there. Korak did not know the true identity of Meriem's abductor.

How was he to cross? Not even he would dare the perils of the river—almost certain death. For a moment he thought, then wheeled and sped away into the jungle, uttering a peculiar cry, shrill and piercing. Now and again he would halt to listen as though for an answer to his weird call, then on again, deeper and deeper into the wood.

At last his listening ears were rewarded by the sound they craved—the trumpeting of a bull elephant, and a few moments later Korak broke through the trees into the presence of Tantor, standing with upraised trunk, waving his great ears.

"Quick, Tantor!" shouted the ape-man, and the beast swung him to his head. "Hurry!" and the mighty pachyderm lumbered off through the jungle, guided by kicking of naked heels against the sides of his head.

Toward the northwest Korak guided his huge mount, until they came out upon the river a mile or more above the Swede's camp, at a point where Korak knew that there was an elephant ford. Never pausing the ape-man urged the beast into the river, and with trunk held high Tantor forged steadily toward the opposite bank. Once an unwary crocodile attacked him but the sinuous trunk dove beneath the surface and grasping the amphibian about the middle dragged it to light and hurled it a hundred feet down stream. And so, in safety, they made the opposite shore, Korak perched high and dry above the turgid flood.

Then back toward the South Tantor moved, steadily, relentlessly, and with a swinging gait which took no heed of any obstacle other than the larger jungle trees. At times Korak was forced to abandon the broad head and take to the trees above, so close the branches raked the back of the elephant; but at last they came to the edge of the clearing where lay the camp of the renegade Swede, nor even then did they hesitate or halt. The gate lay upon the east side of the camp, facing the river. Tantor and Korak approached from the north. There was no gate there; but what cared Tantor or Korak for gates.

At a word from the ape-man and raising his tender trunk high above the thorns Tantor breasted the *boma*, walking through it as though it had not existed. A dozen blacks squatted before their huts looked up at the noise of his approach. With sudden howls of terror and amazement they leaped to their feet and fled for the open gates. Tantor would have pursued. He hated man, and he though that Korak had come to hunt these; but the ape-man held him back, guiding him toward a large, canvas tent that rose in the center of the clearing—there should be the girl and her abductor.

Malbihn lay in a hammock beneath canopy before his tent. His wounds were painful and he had lost much blood. He was very weak. He looked up in surprise as he heard the screams of his men and saw them running toward the gate. And then from around the corner of his tent loomed a huge bulk, and Tantor, the great tusker, towered above him. Malbihn's boy, feeling neither affection nor loyalty for his master, broke and ran at the first glimpse of the beast, and Malbihn was left alone and helpless.

The elephant stopped a couple of paces from the wounded man's hammock. Malbihn cowered, moaning. He was too weak to escape. He could only lie there with staring eyes gazing in horror into the blood rimmed, angry little orbs fixed upon him, and await his death.

Then, to his astonishment, a man slid to the ground from the elephant's back. Almost at once Malbihn recognized the strange figure as that of the creature who consorted with apes and baboons—the white warrior of the jungle who had freed the king baboon and led the whole angry horde of hairy devils upon him and Jenssen. Malbihn cowered still lower.

"Where is the girl?" demanded Korak, in English.

"What girl?" asked Malbihn. "There is no girl here—only the women of my boys. Is it one of them you want?"

"The white girl," replied Korak. "Do not lie to me—you lured her from her friends. You have her. Where is she?"

"It was not I," cried Malbihn. "It was an Englishman who hired me to steal her. He wished to take her to London with him. She was willing to go. His name is Baynes. Go to him, if you want to know where the girl is."

"I have just come from him," said Korak. "He sent me to you. The girl is not with him. Now stop your lying and tell me the truth. Where is she?" Korak took a threatening step toward the Swede.

Malbihn shrank from the anger in the other's face.

"I will tell you," he cried. "Do not harm me and I will tell you all that I know. I had the girl here; but it was Baynes who persuaded her to leave her friends—he had promised to marry her. He does not know who she is; but I do, and I know that there is a great reward for whoever takes her back to her people. It was only the reward I wanted. But she escaped and crossed the river in one of my canoes. I followed her, but The Sheik was there, God knows how, and he captured her and attacked me and drove me back. Then came Baynes, angry because he had lost the girl, and shot me. If you want her, go to The Sheik and ask him for her—she has passed as his daughter since childhood."

"She is not The Sheik's daughter?" asked Korak.

"She is not," replied Malbihn.

"Who is she then?" asked Korak.

Here Malbihn saw his chance. Possibly he could make use of his knowledge after all—it might even buy back his life for him. He was not so credulous as to believe that this savage ape-man would have any compunctions about slaying him.

"When you find her I will tell you," he said, "if you will promise to spare my life and divide the reward with me. If you kill me you will never know, for only The Sheik knows and he will never tell. The girl herself is ignorant of her origin."

"If you have told me the truth I will spare you," said Korak. "I shall go now to The Sheik's village and if the girl is not there I shall return and slay you. As for the other information you have, if the girl wants it when we have found her we will find a way to purchase it from you."

The look in The Killer's eyes and his emphasis of the word "purchase" were none too reassuring to Malbihn. Evidently, unless he found means to escape, this devil would have both his secret and his life before he was done with him. He wished he would be gone and take his evil-eyed companion away with him. The swaying bulk towering high above him, and the ugly little eyes of the elephant watching his every move made Malbihn nervous.

Korak stepped into the Swede's tent to assure himself that Meriem was not hid there. As he disappeared from view Tantor, his eyes still fixed upon Malbihn, took a step nearer the man. An elephant's eyesight is none too good; but the great tusker evidently had harbored suspicions of this yellow-bearded white man from the first. Now he advanced his snake-like trunk toward the Swede, who shrank still deeper into his hammock.

The sensitive member felt and smelled back and forth along the body of the terrified Malbihn. Tantor uttered a low, rumbling sound. His little eyes blazed. At last he had recognized the creature who had killed his mate long years before. Tantor, the elephant, never forgets and never forgives. Malbihn saw in the demoniacal visage above him the murderous purpose of the beast. He shrieked aloud to Korak. "Help! Help! The devil is going to kill me!"

Korak ran from the tent just in time to see the enraged elephant's trunk encircle the beast's victim, and then hammock, canopy and man were swung high over Tantor's head. Korak leaped before the animal, commanding him to put down his prey unharmed; but as well might he have ordered the eternal river to reverse its course. Tantor wheeled around like a cat, hurled Malbihn to the earth and kneeled upon him with the quickness of a cat. Then he gored the prostrate thing through and through with his mighty tusks, trumpeting and roaring in his rage, and at last, convinced that no slightest spark of life remained in the crushed and lacerated flesh, he lifted the shapeless clay that had been Sven Malbihn far aloft and hurled the bloody mass, still entangled in canopy and hammock, over the *boma* and out into the jungle.

Korak stood looking sorrowfully on at the tragedy he gladly would have averted. He had no love for the Swede, in fact only hatred; but he would have preserved the man for the sake of the secret he possessed. Now that secret was gone forever unless The Sheik could be made to divulge it; but in that possibility Korak placed little faith.

The ape-man, as unafraid of the mighty Tantor as though he had not just witnessed his shocking murder of a human being, signaled the beast to approach and lift him to its head, and Tantor came as he was bid, docile as a kitten, and hoisted The Killer tenderly aloft.

From the safety of their hiding places in the jungle Malbihn's boys had witnessed the killing of their master, and now, with wide, frightened eyes, they saw the strange white warrior, mounted upon the head of his ferocious charger, disappear into the jungle at the point from which he had emerged upon their terrified vision.

25

THE SHEIK GLOWERED at the prisoner which his two men brought back to him from the North. He had sent the party after Abdul Kamak, and he was wroth that instead of his erstwhile lieutenant they had sent back a wounded and useless Englishman. Why had they not dispatched him where they had found him? He was some penniless beggar of a trader who had wandered from his own district and became lost. He was worthless. The Sheik scowled terribly upon him.

"Who are you?" he asked in French.

"I am the Hon. Morison Baynes of London," replied his prisoner.

The title sounded promising, and at once the wily old robber had visions of ransom. His intentions, if not his attitude toward the prisoner underwent a change—he would investigate further.

"What were you doing poaching in my country?" growled he.

"I was not aware that you owned Africa," replied the Hon. Morison. "I was searching for a young woman who had been abducted from the home of a friend. The abductor wounded me and I drifted down river in a canoe—I was on my way back to his camp when your men seized me."

"A young woman?" asked The Sheik. "Is that she?" and he pointed to his left over toward a clump of bushes near the stockade.

Baynes looked in the direction indicated and his eyes went wide, for there, sitting cross-legged upon the ground, her back toward them, was Meriem.

"Meriem!" he shouted, starting toward her; but one of his guards grasped his arm and jerked him back. The girl leaped to her feet and turned toward him as she heard her name.

"Morison!" she cried.

"Be still, and stay where you are," snapped The Sheik, and then to Baynes, "So you are the dog of a Christian who stole my daughter from me?"

"Your daughter?" ejaculated Baynes. "She is your daughter?"

"She is my daughter," growled the Arab, "and she is not for any unbeliever. You have earned death, Englishman, but if you can pay for your life I will give it to you."

Baynes's eyes were still wide at the unexpected sight of Meriem here in the camp of the Arab when he had thought her in Hanson's power. What had happened? How had she escaped the Swede? Had the Arab taken her by force from him, or had she escaped and come voluntarily back to the protection of the man who called her "daughter"? He would have given much for a word with her. If she was safe here he might only harm her by antagonizing the Arab in an attempt to take her away and return her to her English friends. No longer did the Hon. Morison harbor thoughts of luring the girl to London.

"Well?" asked The Sheik.

"Oh," exclaimed Baynes, "I beg your pardon—I was thinking of something else. Why yes, of course, glad to pay, I'm sure. How much do you think I'm worth?"

The Sheik named a sum that was rather less exorbitant than the Hon. Morison had anticipated. The latter nodded his head in token of his entire willingness to pay. He would have promised a sum far beyond his resources just as readily, for he had no intention of paying anything—his one reason for seemingly to comply with The Sheik's demands was that the wait for the coming of the ransom money would give him the time and the opportunity to free Meriem if he found that she wished to be freed. The Arab's statement that he was her father naturally raised the question in the Hon. Morison's mind as to precisely what the girl's attitude toward escape might be. It seemed, of course, preposterous that this fair and beautiful young woman should prefer to remain in the filthy *douar* of an illiterate old Arab rather than return to the comforts, luxuries, and congenial associations of the hospitable African bungalow from which the Hon. Morison had tricked her. The man flushed at the thought of his duplicity which these recollections aroused—thoughts which were interrupted by The Sheik, who instructed the Hon. Morison to write a letter to the British consul at Algiers, dictating the exact phraseology of it with a fluency that indicated to his captive that this was not the first time the old rascal had had occasion to negotiate with English relatives for

the ransom of a kinsman. Baynes demurred when he saw that the
letter was addressed to the consul at Algiers, saying that it would
require the better part of a year to get the money back to him; but
The Sheik would not listen to Baynes' plan to send a messenger
directly to the nearest coast town, and from there communicate
with the nearest cable state, sending the Hon. Morison's request
for funds straight to his own solicitors. No, The Sheik was cautious and wary. He knew his own plan had worked well in the past.
In the other were too many untried elements. He was in no hurry
for the money—he could wait a year, or two years if necessary;
but it should not require over six months. He turned to one of the
Arabs who had been standing behind him and gave the fellow
instructions in relation to the prisoner.

Baynes could not understand the words, spoken in Arabic, but
the jerk of the thumb toward him showed that he was the subject
of conversation. The Arab addressed by The Sheik bowed to his
master and beckoned Baynes to follow him. The Englishman
looked toward The Sheik for confirmation. The latter nodded
impatiently, and the Hon. Morison rose and followed his guide
toward a native hut which lay close beside one of the outside
goatskin tents. In the dark, stifling interior his guard led him, then
stepped to the doorway and called to a couple of black boys squatting before their own huts. They came promptly and in accordance
with the Arab's instructions bound Baynes' wrists and ankles
securely. The Englishman objected strenuously; but as neither the
blacks nor the Arab could understand a word he said his pleas
were wasted. Having bound him they left the hut. The Hon.
Morison lay for a long time contemplating the frightful future
which awaited him during the long months which must intervene
before his friends learned of his predicament and could get succor
to him. Now he hoped that they would send the ransom—he
would gladly pay all that he was worth to be out of this hole. At
first it had been his intention to cable his solicitors to send no
money but to communicate with the British West African author-
ities and have an expedition sent to his aid.

His patrician nose wrinkled in disgust as his nostrils were
assailed by the awful stench of the hut. The nasty grasses upon
which he lay exuded the effluvium of sweaty bodies, of decayed
animal matter and of offal. But worse was yet to come. He had lain
in the uncomfortable position in which they had thrown him but
for a few minutes when he became distinctly conscious of an acute
itching sensation upon his hands, his neck and scalp. He wriggled
to a sitting posture horrified and disgusted. The itching rapidly

extended to other parts of his body—it was torture, and his hands were bound securely at his back!

He tugged and pulled at his bonds until he was exhausted; but not entirely without hope, for he was sure that he was working enough slack out of the knot to eventually permit of his withdrawing one of his hands. Night came. They brought him neither food nor drink. He wondered if they expected him to live on nothing for a year. The bites of the vermin grew less annoying though not less numerous. The Hon. Morison saw a ray of hope in this indication of future immunity through inoculation. He still worked weakly at his bonds, and then the rats came. If the vermin were disgusting the rats were terrifying. They scurried over his body, squealing and fighting. Finally one commenced to chew at one of his ears. With an oath, the Hon. Morison struggled to a sitting posture. The rats retreated. He worked his legs beneath him and came to his knees, and then, by superhuman effort, rose to his feet. There he stood, reeling drunkenly, dripping with cold sweat.

"God!" he muttered, "what have I done to deserve—" He paused. What had he done? He thought of the girl in another tent in that accursed village. He was getting his deserts. He set his jaws firmly with the realization. He would never complain again! At that moment he became aware of voices raised angrily in the goatskin tent close beside the hut in which he lay. One of them was a woman's. Could it be Meriem's? The language was probably Arabic—he could not understand a word of it; but the tones were hers.

He tried to think of some way of attracting her attention to his near presence. If she could remove his bonds they might escape together—if she wished to escape. That thought bothered him. He was not sure of her status in the village. If she were the petted child of the powerful Sheik then she would probably not care to escape. He must know, definitely.

At the bungalow he had often heard Meriem sing God Save the King, as My Dear accompanied her on the piano. Raising his voice he now hummed the tune. Immediately he heard Meriem's voice from the tent. She spoke rapidly.

"Good-bye, Morison," she cried. "If God is good I shall be dead before morning, for if I still live I shall be worse than dead after tonight."

Then he heard an angry exclamation in a man's voice, followed by the sounds of a scuffle. Baynes went white with horror. He struggled frantically again with his bonds. They were giving. A moment later one hand was free. It was but the work of an instant then to loose the other. Stooping, he untied the rope from his ankles, then he straighted and started for the hut doorway bent on reaching Meriem's side. As he stepped out into the night the figure of a huge black rose and barred his progress.

When speed was required of him Korak depended upon no other muscles than his own, and so it was that the moment Tantor had landed him safely upon the same side of the river as lay the village of The Sheik, the ape-man deserted his bulky comrade and took to the trees in a rapid race toward the south and the spot where the Swede had told him Meriem might be. It was dark when he came to the palisade, strengthened considerably since the day that he had rescued Meriem from her pitiful life within its cruel confines. No longer did the giant tree spread its branches above the wooden rampart; but ordinary man-made defenses were scarce considered obstacles by Korak. Loosening the rope at his waist he tossed the noose over one of the sharpened posts that composed the palisade. A moment later his eyes were above the level of the obstacle taking in all within their range beyond. There was no one in sight close by, and Korak drew himself to the top and dropped lightly to the ground within the enclosure.

Then he commenced his stealthy search of the village. First toward the Arab tents he made his way, sniffing and listening. He passed behind them searching for some sign of Meriem. Not even the wild Arab curs heard his passage, so silently he went—a shadow passing through shadows. The odor of tobacco told him that the Arabs were smoking before their tents. The sound of laughter fell upon his ears, and then from the opposite side of the village came the notes of a once familiar tune: God Save the King. Korak halted in perplexity. Who might it be—the tones were those of a man. He recalled the young Englishman he had left on the river trail and who had disappeared before he returned. A moment later there came to him a woman's voice in reply—it was Meriem's, and The Killer, quickened into action, slunk rapidly in the direction of these two voices.

The evening meal over Meriem had gone to her pallet in the women's quarters of The Sheik's tent, a little corner screened off in the rear by a couple of priceless Persian rugs to form a partition. In these quarters she had dwelt with Mabunu alone, for The Sheik had no wives. Nor were conditions altered now after the years of her absence—she and Mabunu were alone in the women's quarters.

Presently The Sheik came and parted the rugs. He glared through the dim light of the interior.

"Meriem!" he called. "Come hither."

The girl arose and came into the front of the tent. There the light of a fire illuminated the interior. She saw Ali ben Kadin, The Sheik's half brother, squatted upon a rug, smoking. The Sheik was standing. The Sheik and Ali ben Kadin had had the same father, but Ali ben Kadin's mother had been a slave—a West Coast Negress. Ali ben Kadin was old and hideous and almost black. His nose and part of one cheek were eaten away by disease. He looked up and grinned as Meriem entered.

The Sheik jerked his thumb toward Ali ben Kadin and addressed Meriem.

"I am getting old," he said, "I shall not live much longer. 1 fore I have given you to Ali ben Kadin, my brother."

That was all. Ali ben Kadin rose and came toward her. Meriem shrank back, horrified. The man seized her wrist.

"Come!" he commanded, and dragged her from The Sheik's tent and to his own.

After they had gone The Sheik chuckled. "When I send her north in a few months," he soliloquized, "they will know the reward for slaying the son of the sister of Amor ben Khatour."

And in Ali ben Kadin's tent Meriem pleaded and threatened, but all to no avail. The hideous old half-caste spoke soft words at first, but when Meriem loosed upon him the vials of her horror and loathing he became enraged, and rushing upon her seized her in his arms. Twice she tore away from him, and in one of the intervals during which she managed to elude him she heard Baynes' voice humming the tune that she knew was meant for her ears. At her reply Ali ben Kadin rushed upon her once again. This time he dragged her back into the rear apartment of his tent where three Negresses looked up in stolid indifference to the tragedy being enacted before them.

As the Hon. Morison saw his way blocked by the huge frame of the giant black his disappointment and rage filled him with a bestial fury that transformed him into a savage beast. With an oath he leaped upon the man before him, the momentum of his body hurling the black to the ground. There they fought, the black to draw his knife, the white to choke the life from the black.

Baynes' fingers shut off the cry for help that the other would have been glad to voice; but presently the Negro succeeded in drawing his weapon and an instant later Baynes felt the sharp steel in his shoulder. Again and again the weapon fell. The white man removed one hand from its choking grip upon the black throat. He felt around upon the ground beside him searching for some missile, and at last his fingers touched a stone and closed upon it. Raising it above his antagonist's head the Hon. Morison drove home a terrific blow. Instantly the black relaxed—stunned. Twice more Baynes struck him. Then he leaped to his feet and ran for the goatskin tent from which he had heard the voice of Meriem in distress.

But before him was another. Naked but for his leopard skin and his loin cloth, Korak, The Killer, slunk into the shadows at the back of Ali ben Kadin's tent. The half-caste had just dragged Meriem into the rear chamber as Korak's sharp knife slit a six foot opening in the tent wall, and Korak, tall and mighty, sprang through upon the astonished visions of the inmates.

Meriem saw and recognized him the instant that he entered the apartment. Her heart leaped in pride and joy at the sight of the noble figure for which it had hungered for so long.

"Korak!" she cried.

"Meriem!" He uttered the single word as he hurled himself upon the astonished Ali ben Kadin. The three Negresses leaped from their sleeping mats, screaming. Meriem tried to prevent them from escaping; but before she could succeed the terrified blacks had darted through the hole in the tent wall made by Korak's knife, and were gone screaming through the village.

The Killer's fingers closed once upon the throat of the hideous Ali. Once his knife plunged into the putrid heart—and Ali ben Kadin lay dead upon the floor of his tent. Korak turned toward Meriem and at the same moment a bloody and disheveled apparition leaped into the apartment.

"Morison!" cried the girl.

Korak turned and looked at the newcomer. He had been about to take Meriem in his arms, forgetful of all that might have transpired since last he had seen her. Then the coming of the young Englishman recalled the scene he had witnessed in the little clearing, and a wave of misery swept over the ape-man.

Already from without came the sounds of the alarm that the three Negresses had started. Men were running toward the tent of Ali ben Kadin. There was no time to be lost.

"Quick!" cried Korak, turning toward Baynes, who had scarce yet realized whether he was facing a friend or foe. "Take her to the palisade, following the rear of the tents. Here is my rope. With it you can scale the wall and make your escape."

"But you, Korak?" cried Meriem.

"I will remain," replied the ape-man. "I have business with The Sheik."

Meriem would have demurred, but The Killer seized them both by the shoulders and hustled them through the slit wall and out into the shadows beyond.

"Now run for it," he admonished, and turned to meet and hold those who were pouring into the tent from the front.

The ape-man fought well—fought as he had never fought before; but the odds were too great for victory, though he won that which he most craved—time for the Englishman to escape with Meriem. Then he was overwhelmed by numbers, and a few minutes later, bound and guarded, he was carried to The Sheik's tent.

The old men eyed him in silence for a long time. He was trying to fix in his own mind some form of torture that would gratify his rage and hatred toward this creature who twice had been the means of his losing possession of Meriem. The killing of Ali ben Kadin caused him little anger—always had he hated the hideous son of his father's hideous slave. The blow that this naked white warrior had once struck him added fuel to his rage. He could think of nothing adequate to the creature's offense.

And as he sat there looking upon Korak the silence was broken by the trumpeting of an elephant in the jungle beyond the palisade. A half smile touched Korak's lips. He turned his head a trifle in the direction from which the sound had come and then there broke from his lips a low, weird call. One of the blacks guarding him struck him across the mouth with the haft of his spear; but none there knew the significance of his cry.

In the jungle Tantor cocked his ears as the sound of Korak's voice fell upon them. He approached the palisade and lifting his trunk above it, sniffed. Then he placed his head against the wooden logs and pushed; but the palisade was strong and only gave a little to the pressure.

In The Sheik's tent The Sheik rose at last, and, pointing toward the bound captive, turned to one of his lieutenants.

"Burn him," he commanded. "At once. The stake is set."

The guard pushed Korak from The Sheik's presence. They dragged him to the open space in the center of the village, where a high stake was set in the ground. It had not been intended for burnings, but offered a convenient place to tie up refractory slaves that they might be beaten—ofttimes until death relieved their agonies.

To this stake they bound Korak. Then they brought brush and piled about him, and The Sheik came and stood by that he might watch the agonies of his victim. But Korak did not wince even after they had fetched a brand and the flames had shot up among the dry tinder.

Once, then, he raised his voice in the low call that he had given in The Sheik's tent, and now, from beyond the palisade, came again the trumpeting of an elephant.

Old Tantor had been pushing at the palisade in vain. The sound of Korak's voice calling him, and the scent of man, his enemy, filled the great beast with rage and resentment against the dumb barrier that held him back. He wheeled and shuffled back a dozen paces, then he turned, lifted his trunk and gave voice to a mighty roaring, trumpet-call of anger, lowered his head and charged like a huge battering ram of flesh and bone and muscle straight for the mighty barrier.

The palisade sagged and splintered to the impact, and through the breach rushed the infuriated bull. Korak heard the sounds that the others heard, and he interpreted them as the others did not. The flames were creeping closer to him when one of the blacks, hearing a noise behind him turned to see the enormous bulk of Tantor lumbering toward them. The man screamed and fled, and then the bull elephant was among them tossing Negroes and Arabs to right and left as he tore through the flames he feared to the side of the comrade he loved.

The Sheik, calling orders to his followers, ran to his tent to get his rifle. Tantor wrapped his trunk about the body of Korak and the stake to which it was bound, and tore it from the ground. The flames were searing his sensitive hide—sensitive for all its thickness—so that in his frenzy to both rescue his friend and escape the hated fire he had all but crushed the life from the ape-man.

Lifting his burden high above his head the giant beast wheeled and raced for the breach that he had just made in the palisade. The Sheik, rifle in hand, rushed from his tent directly into the path of the maddened brute. He raised his weapon and fired once, the bullet missed its mark, and Tantor was upon him, crushing him beneath those gigantic feet as he raced over him as you and I might crush out the life of an ant that chanced to be in our pathway.

And then, bearing his burden carefully, Tantor, the elephant, entered the blackness of the jungle.

26

Meriem, dazed by the unexpected sight of Korak whom she had long given up as dead, permitted herself to be led away by Baynes. Among the tents he guided her safely to the palisade, and there, following Korak's instructions, the Englishman pitched a noose over the top of one of the upright logs that formed the barrier. With difficulty he reached the top and then lowered his hand to assist Meriem to his side.

"Come!" he whispered. "We must hurry." And then, as though she had awakened from a sleep, Meriem came to herself. Back there, fighting her enemies, alone, was Korak—her Korak. Her place was by his side, fighting with him and for him. She glanced up at Baynes.

"Go!" she called. "Make your way back to Bwana and bring help. My place is here. You can do no good remaining. Get away while you can and bring the Big Bwana back with you."

Silently the Hon. Morison Baynes slid to the ground inside the palisade to Meriem's side.

"It was only for you that I left him," he said, nodding toward the tents they had just left. "I knew that he could hold them longer than I and give you a chance to escape that I might not be able to have given you. It was I though who should have remained. I heard you call him Korak and so I know now who he is. He befriended you. I would have wronged you. No—don't interrupt. I'm going to tell you the truth now and let you know just what a beast I have been. I planned to take you to London, as you know; but I did not plan to marry you. Yes, shrink from me—I deserve it. I deserve your contempt and loathing; but I didn't know then what love was. Since I have learned that I have learned something

359

else—what a cad and what a coward I have been all my life. I looked down upon those whom I considered my social inferiors. I did not think you good enough to bear my name. Since Hanson tricked me and took you for himself I have been through hell; but it has made a man of me, though too late. Now I can come to you with an offer of honest love, which will realize the honor of having such as you share my name with me."

For a moment Meriem was silent, buried in thought. Her first question seemed irrelevant.

"How did you happen to be in this village?" she asked.

He told her all that had transpired since the black had told him of Hanson's duplicity.

"You say that you are a coward," she said, "and yet you have done all this to save me? The courage that it must have taken to tell me the things that you told me but a moment since, while courage of a different sort, proves that you are no moral coward, and the other proves that you are not a physical coward. I could not love a coward."

"You mean that you love me?" he gasped in astonishment, taking a step toward her as though to gather her into his arms; but she placed her hand against him and pushed him gently away, as much as to say, not yet. What she did mean she scarcely knew. She thought that she loved him, of that there can be no question; nor did she think that love for this young Englishman was disloyalty to Korak, for her love for Korak was undiminished—the love of a sister for an indulgent brother. As they stood there for the moment of their conversation the sounds of tumult in the village subsided.

"They have killed him," whispered Meriem.

The statement brought Baynes to a realization of the cause of their return.

"Wait here," he said. "I will go and see. If he is dead we can do him no good. If he lives I will do my best to free him."

"We will go together," replied Meriem. "Come!" And she led the way back toward the tent in which they last had seen Korak. As they went they were often forced to throw themselves to the ground in the shadow of a tent or hut, for people were passing hurriedly to and fro now—the whole village was aroused and moving about. The return to the tent of Ali ben Kadin took much longer than had their swift flight to the palisade. Cautiously they crept to the slit that Korak's knife had made in the rear wall. Meriem peered within—the rear apartment was empty. She crawled through the aperture, Baynes at her heels, and then silently crossed the space to the rugs that partitioned the tent into two rooms. Parting the hangings Meriem looked into the front room. It, too, was deserted. She crossed to the door of the tent and looked out. Then she gave a little gasp of horror. Baynes at her shoulder looked past her to the sight that had startled her, and he, too, exclaimed; but his was an oath of anger.

A hundred feet away they saw Korak bound to a stake—the brush piled about him already alight. The Englishman pushed Meriem to one side and started to run for the doomed man. What he could do in the face of scores of hostile blacks and Arabs he did not stop to consider. At the same instant Tantor broke through the palisade and charged the group. In the face of the maddened beast the crowd turned and fled, carrying Baynes backward with them. In a moment it was all over, and the elephant had disappeared with his prize; but pandemonium reigned throughout the village. Men, women and children ran helter skelter for safety. Curs fled, yelping. The horses and camels and donkeys, terrorized by the trumpeting of the pachyderm, kicked and pulled at their tethers. A dozen or more broke loose, and it was the galloping of these past him that brought a sudden idea into Baynes' head. He turned to search for Meriem only to find her at his elbow.

"The horses!" he cried. "If we can get a couple of them!"

Filled with the idea Meriem led him to the far end of the village.

"Loosen two of them," she said, "and lead them back into the shadows behind those huts. I know where there are saddles. I will bring them and the bridles," and before he could stop her she was gone.

Baynes quickly untied two of the restive animals and led them to the point designated by Meriem. Here he waited impatiently for what seemed an hour; but was, in reality, but a few minutes. Then he saw the girl approaching beneath the burden of two saddles. Quickly they placed these upon the horses. They could see by the light of the torture fire that still burned that the blacks and Arabs were recovering from their panic. Men were running about gathering in the loose stock, and two or three were already leading their captives back to the end of the village where Meriem and Baynes were busy with the trappings of their mounts.

Now the girl flung herself into the saddle.

"Hurry!" she whispered. "We shall have to run for it. Ride through the gap that Tantor made," and as she saw Baynes swing his leg over the back of his horse, she shook the reins free over her mount's neck. With a lunge, the nervous beast leaped forward. The shortest path led straight through the center of the village, and this Meriem took. Baynes was close behind her, their horses running at full speed.

So sudden and impetuous was their dash for escape that it carried them half-way across the village before the surprised inhabitants were aware of what was happening. Then an Arab recognized them, and, with a cry of alarm, raised his rifle and fired. The shot was a signal for a volley, and amid the rattle of musketry Meriem and Baynes leaped their flying mounts through the breach in the palisade and were gone up the well-worn trail toward the north.

And Korak?

Tantor carried him deep into the jungle, nor paused until no sound from the distant village reached his keen ears. Then he laid his burden gently down. Korak struggled to free himself from his bonds, but even his great strength was unable to cope with the many strands of hard-knotted cord that bound him. While he lay there, working and resting by turns, the elephant stood guard above him, nor was there jungle enemy with the hardihood to tempt the sudden death that lay in that mighty bulk.

Dawn came, and still Korak was no nearer freedom than before. He commenced to believe that he should die there of thirst and starvation with plenty all about him, for he knew that Tantor could not unloose the knots that held him.

And while he struggled through the night with his bonds, Baynes and Meriem were riding rapidly northward along the river. The girl had assured Baynes that Korak was safe in the jungle with Tantor. It had not occurred to her that the ape-man might not be able to burst his bonds. Baynes had been wounded by a shot from the rifle of one of the Arabs, and the girl wanted to get him back to Bwana's home, where he could be properly cared for.

"Then," she said, "I shall get Bwana to come with me and search for Korak. He must come and live with us."

All night they rode, and the day was still young when they came suddenly upon a party hurrying southward. It was Bwana himself and his sleek, black warriors. At sight of Baynes the big Englishman's brows contracted in a scowl; but he waited to hear Meriem's story before giving vent to the long anger in his breast. When she had finished he seemed to have forgotten Baynes. His thoughts were occupied with another subject.

"You say that you found Korak?" he asked. "You really saw him?"

"Yes," replied Meriem, "as plainly as I see you, and I want you to come with me, Bwana, and help me find him again."

"Did you see him?" He turned toward the Hon. Morison.

"Yes, sir," replied Baynes, "very plainly."

"What sort of appearing man is he?" continued Bwana. "About how old, should you say?"

"I should say he was an Englishman, about my own age," replied Baynes, "though he might be older. He is remarkably muscled, and exceedingly tanned."

"His eyes and hair, did you notice them?" Bwana spoke rapidly, almost excitedly. It was Meriem who answered him.

"Korak's hair is black and his eyes are gray," she said.

Bwana turned to his head man.

"Take Miss Meriem and Mr. Baynes home," he said. "I am going into the jungle."

"Let me go with you, Bwana," cried Meriem. "You are going to search for Korak. Let me go, too."

Bwana turned sadly but firmly upon the girl.

"Your place," he said, "is beside the man you love."

Then he motioned to his head man to take his horse and commence the return journey to the farm. Meriem slowly mounted the tired Arab that had brought her from the village of The Sheik. A litter was rigged for the now feverish Baynes, and the little cavalcade was soon slowly winding off along the river trail.

Bwana stood watching them until they were out of sight. Not once had Meriem turned her eyes backward. She rode with bowed head and drooping shoulders. Bwana sighed. He loved the little Arab girl as he might have loved an own daughter. He realized that Baynes had redeemed himself, and so he could interpose no objections now if Meriem really loved the man; but, somehow, some way, Bwana could not convince himself that the Hon. Morison was worthy of his little Meriem. Slowly he turned toward a nearby tree. Leaping upward he caught a lower branch and drew himself up among the branches. His movements were cat-like and agile. High into the tree he made his way and there commenced to divest himself of his clothing. From the game bag slung across one shoulder he drew a long strip of doeskin, a neatly coiled rope, and a wicked looking knife. The doeskin he fashioned into a loincloth, the rope he looped over one shoulder, and the knife he thrust into the belt formed by his gee string.

When he stood erect, his head thrown back and his great chest expanded a grim smile touched his lips for a moment. His nostrils dilated as he sniffed the jungle odors. His gray eyes narrowed. He crouched and leaped to a lower limb and was away through the trees toward the southeast, bearing away from the river. He moved swiftly, stopping only occasionally to raise his voice in a weird and piercing scream, and to listen for a moment after for a reply.

He had traveled thus for several hours when, ahead of him and a little to his left, he heard, far off in the jungle, a faint response—the cry of a bull ape answering his cry. His nerves tingled and his eyes lighted as the sound fell upon his ears. Again he voiced his hideous call, and sped forward in the new direction.

Korak, finally becoming convinced that he must die if he remained where he was, waiting for the succor that could not come, spoke to Tantor in the strange tongue that the great beast understood. He commanded the elephant to lift him and carry him toward the northeast. There, recently, Korak had seen both white men and black. If he could come upon one of the latter it would be a simple matter to command Tantor to capture the fellow, and then Korak could get him to release him from the stake. It was worth trying at least—better than lying there in the jungle until he died. As Tantor bore him along through the forest Korak called aloud now and then in the hope of attracting Akut's band of anthropoids, whose wanderings often brought them into their neighborhood. Akut, he thought, might possibly be able to negotiate the knots—he had done so upon that other occasion when the Russian had bound Korak years before; and Akut, to the south of him, heard his calls faintly, and came. There was another who heard them, too.

After Bwana had left his party, sending them back toward the farm, Meriem had ridden for a short distance with bowed head. What thoughts passed through that active brain who may say? Presently she seemed to come to a decision. She called the head man to her side.

"I am going back with Bwana," she announced.

The black shook his head. "No!" he announced. "Bwana says I take you home. So I take you home."

"You refuse to let me go?" asked the girl.

The black nodded, and fell to the rear where he might better watch her. Meriem half smiled. Presently her horse passed beneath a low-hanging branch, and the black head man found himself gazing at the girl's empty saddle. He ran forward to the tree into which she had disappeared. He could see nothing of her. He called; but there was no response, unless it might have been a low, taunting laugh far to the right. He sent his men into the jungle to search for her; but they came back empty handed. After a while he resumed his march toward the farm, for Baynes, by this time, was delirious with fever.

Meriem raced straight back toward the point she imagined

Tantor would make for—a point where she knew the elephants often gathered deep in the forest due east of The Sheik's village. She moved silently and swiftly. From her mind she had expunged all thoughts other than that she must reach Korak and bring him back with her. It was her place to do that. Then, too, had come the tantalizing fear that all might not be well with him. She upbraided herself for not thinking of that before—of letting her desire to get the wounded Morison back to the bungalow blind her to the possibilities of Korak's need for her. She had been traveling rapidly for several hours without rest when she heard ahead of her the familiar cry of a great ape calling to his kind.

She did not reply, only increased her speed until she almost flew. Now there came to her sensitive nostrils the scent of Tantor and she knew that she was on the right trail and close to him she sought. She did not call out because she wished to surprise him, and presently she did, breaking into sight of them as the great elephant shuffled ahead balancing the man and the heavy stake upon his head, holding them there with his upcurled trunk.

"Korak!" cried Meriem from the foliage above him.

Instantly the bull swung about, lowered his burden to the ground and, trumpeting savagely, prepared to defend his comrade. The ape-man, recognizing the girl's voice, felt a sudden lump in his throat.

"Meriem!" he called back to her.

Happily the girl clambered to the ground and ran forward to release Korak; but Tantor lowered his head ominously and trumpeted a warning.

"Go back! Go back!" cried Korak. "He will kill you."

Meriem paused. "Tantor!" she called to the huge brute. "Don't you remember me? I am little Meriem. I used to ride on your broad back," but the bull only rumbled in his throat and shook his tusks in angry defiance. Then Korak tried to placate him. Tried to order him away, that the girl might approach and release him; but Tantor would not go. He saw in every human being other than Korak an enemy. He thought the girl bent upon harming his friend and he would take no chances. For an hour the girl and the man tried to find some means whereby they might circumvent the beast's ill directed guardianship, but all to no avail; Tantor stood his ground in grim determination to let no one approach Korak.

Presently the man hit upon a scheme. "Pretend to go away," he called to the girl. "Keep down wind from us so that Tantor won't get your scent, then follow us. After a while I'll have him put me down, and find some pretext for sending him away. While he is gone you can slip up and cut my bonds—have you a knife?"

"Yes, I have a knife," she replied. "I'll go now—I think we may be able to fool him; but don't be too sure—Tantor invented cunning."

Korak smiled, for he knew that the girl was right. Presently she had disappeared. The elephant listened, and raised his trunk to catch her scent. Korak commanded him to raise him to his head once more and proceed upon their way. After a moment's hesitation he did as he was bid. It was then that Korak heard the distant call of an ape.

"Akut!" he thought. "Good! Tantor knew Akut well. He would let him approach." Raising his voice Korak replied to the call of the ape; but he let Tantor move off with him through the jungle; it would do no harm to try the other plan. They had come to a clearing and plainly Korak smelled water. Here was a good place and a good excuse. He ordered Tantor to lay him down, and go and fetch him water in his trunk. The big beast deposited him upon the grass in the center of the clearing, then he stood with cocked ears and attentive trunk, searching for the slightest indication of danger—there seemed to be none and he moved away in the direction of the little brook that Korak knew was some two or three hundred yards away. The ape-man could scarce help smiling as he thought how cleverly he had tricked his friend; but well as he knew Tantor he little guessed the guile of his cunning brain. The animal ambled off across the clearing and disappeared in the jungle beyond in the direction of the stream; but scarce had his great bulk been screened by the dense foliage than he wheeled about and came cautiously back to the edge of the clearing where he could see without being seen. Tantor, by nature, is suspicious. Now he still feared the return of the she Tarmangani who had attempted to attack his Korak. He would just stand there for a moment and assure himself that all was well before he continued on toward the water. Ah! It was well that he did! There she was now dropping from the branches of a tree across the clearing and running swiftly toward the ape-man. Tantor waited. He would let her reach Korak before he charged—that would ensure that she had no chance of escape. His little eyes blazed savagely. His tail was elevated stiffly. He could scarce restrain a desire to trumpet forth his rage to the world. Meriem was almost at Korak's side when Tantor saw the long knife in her hand, and then he broke forth from the jungle, bellowing horribly, and charged down upon the frail girl.

27

KORAK SCREAMED COMMANDS to his huge protector, in an effort to halt him; but all to no avail. Meriem raced toward the bordering trees with all the speed that lay in her swift, little feet; but Tantor, for all his huge bulk, drove down upon her with the rapidity of an express train.

Korak lay where he could see the whole frightful tragedy. The cold sweat broke out upon his body. His heart seemed to have stopped its beating. Meriem might reach the trees before Tantor overtook her, but even her agility would not carry her beyond the reach of that relentless trunk—she would be dragged down and tossed. Korak could picture the whole frightful scene. Then Tantor would follow her up, goring the frail, little body with his relentless tusks, or trampling it into an unrecognizable mass beneath his ponderous feet.

He was almost upon her now. Korak wanted to close his eyes, but could not. His throat was dry and parched. Never in all his savage existence had he suffered such blighting terror—never before had he known what terror meant. A dozen more strides and the brute would seize her. What was that? Korak's eyes started from their sockets. A strange figure had leaped from the tree the shade of which Meriem already had reached—leaped beyond the girl straight into the path of the charging elephant. It was a naked white giant. Across his shoulder a coil of rope was looped. In the band of his gee string was a hunting knife. Otherwise he was unarmed. With naked hands he faced the maddening Tantor. A sharp command broke from the stranger's lips—the great beast halted in his tracks—and Meriem swung herself upward into the tree to safety. Korak breathed a sigh of relief not unmixed with wonder. He fastened his eyes upon the face of Meriem's deliverer and as recognition slowly filtered into his understanding they went wide in incredulity and surprise.

Tantor, still rumbling angrily, stood swaying to and fro close before the giant white man. Then the latter stepped straight beneath the upraised trunk and spoke a low word of command. The great beast ceased his muttering. The savage light died from his eyes, and as the stranger stepped forward toward Korak. Tantor trailed docilely at his heels.

Meriem was watching, too, and wondering. Suddenly the man turned toward her as though recollecting her presence after a moment of forgetfulness. "Come! Meriem," he called, and then she recognized him with a startled: "Bwana!" Quickly the girl dropped from the tree and ran to his side. Tantor cocked a questioning eye at the white giant, but receiving a warning word let Meriem approach. Together the two walked to where Korak lay, his eyes wide with wonder and filled with a pathetic appeal for forgiveness, and, mayhap, a glad thankfulness for the miracle that had brought these two of all others to his side.

"Jack!" cried the white giant, kneeling at the ape-man's side.

"Father!" came chokingly from The Killer's lips. "Thank God that it was you. No one else in all the jungle could have stopped Tantor."

Quickly the man cut the bonds that held Korak, and as the youth leaped to his feet and threw his arms about his father, the older man turned toward Meriem.

"I thought," he said, sternly, "that I told you to return to the farm."

Korak was looking at them wonderingly. In his heart was a great yearning to take the girl in his arms; but in time he remembered the other—the dapper young English gentleman—and that he was but a savage, uncouth ape-man.

Meriem looked up pleadingly into Bwana's eyes.

"You told me," she said, in a very small voice, "that my place was beside the man I loved," and she turned her eyes toward Korak all filled with the wonderful light that no other man had yet seen in them, and that none other ever would.

The Killer started toward her with outstretched arms; but suddenly he fell upon one knee before her, instead, and lifting her hand to his lips kissed it more reverently than he could have kissed the hand of his country's queen.

A rumble from Tantor brought the three, all jungle bred, to instant alertness. Tantor was looking toward the trees behind them, and as their eyes followed his gaze the head and shoulders of a great ape appeared amidst the foliage. For a moment the creature eyed them, and then from its throat rose a loud scream of recognition and of joy, and a moment later the beast had leaped to the ground, followed by a score of bulls like himself, and was waddling toward them, shouting in the primordial tongue of the anthropoid:

"Tarzan has returned! Tarzan, Lord of the Jungle!"

It was Akut, and instantly he commenced leaping and bounding about the trio, uttering hideous shrieks and mouthings that to any other human beings might have indicated the most ferocious rage; but these three knew that the king of the apes was doing homage to a king greater than himself. In his wake leaped his shaggy bulls, vying with one another as to which could spring the highest and which utter the most uncanny sounds.

Korak laid his hand affectionately upon his father's shoulder. "There is but one Tarzan," he said. "There can never be another."

Two days later the three dropped from the trees on the edge of the plain across which they could see the smoke rising from the bungalow and the cook house chimneys. Tarzan of the Apes had regained his civilized clothing from the tree where he had hidden it, and as Korak refused to enter the presence of his mother in the savage half-raiment that he had worn so long and as Meriem would not leave him, for fear, as she explained, that he would change his mind and run off into the jungle again, the father went on ahead to the bungalow for horses and clothes.

My Dear met him at the gate, her eyes filled with questioning and sorrow, for she saw that Meriem was not with him.

"Where is she?" she asked, her voice trembling. "Muviri told me that she disobeyed your instructions and ran off into the jungle after you had left them. Oh, John, I cannot bear to lose her, too!" And Lady Greystoke broke down and wept, as she pillowed her head upon the broad breast where so often before she had found comfort in the great tragedies of her life.

Lord Greystoke raised her head and looked down into her eyes, his own smiling and filled with the light of happiness.

"What is it, John?" she cried. "You have good news—do not keep me waiting for it."

"I want to be quite sure that you can stand hearing the best news that ever came to either of us," he said.

"Joy never kills," she cried. "You have found—her?" She could not bring herself to hope for the impossible.

"Yes, Jane," he said, and his voice was husky with emotion; "I have found her, and—*him*!"

"Where is he? Where are they?" she demanded.

"Out there at the edge of the jungle. He wouldn't come to you in his savage leopard skin and his nakedness—he sent me to fetch him civilized clothing."

She clapped her hands in ecstasy, and turned to run toward the bungalow. "Wait!" she cried over her shoulder. "I have all his little suits—I have saved them all. I will bring one to you."

Tarzan laughed and called to her to stop.

"The only clothing on the place that will fit him," he said, "is mine—if it isn't too small for him—your little boy has grown, Jane."

She laughed, too; she felt like laughing at everything, or at nothing. The world was all love and happiness and joy once more—the world that had been shrouded in the gloom of her great sorrow for so many years. So great was her joy that for the moment she forgot the sad message that awaited Meriem. She called to Tarzan after he had ridden away to prepare her for it, but he did not hear and rode on without knowing himself what the event was to which his wife referred.

And so, an hour later, Korak, The Killer, rode home to his mother—the mother whose image had never faded in his boyish heart—and found in her arms and her eyes the love and forgiveness that he plead for.

And then the mother turned toward Meriem, an expression of pitying sorrow erasing the happiness from her eyes.

"My little girl," she said, "in the midst of our happiness a great sorrow awaits you—Mr. Baynes did not survive his wound."

The expression of sorrow in Meriem's eyes expressed only what she sincerely felt; but it was not the sorrow of a woman bereft of her best beloved.

"I am sorry," she said, quite simply. "He would have done me a great wrong; but he amply atoned before he died. Once I thought that I loved him. At first it was only fascination for a type that was new to me—then it was respect for a brave man who had the moral courage to admit a sin and the physical courage to face death to right the wrong he had committed. But it was not love. I did not know what love was until I knew that Korak lived," and she turned toward The Killer with a smile.

Lady Greystoke looked quickly up into the eyes of her son—

the son who one day would be Lord Greystoke. No thought of the difference in the stations of the girl and her boy entered her mind. To her Meriem was fit for a king. She only wanted to know that Jack loved the little Arab waif. The look in his eyes answered the question in her heart, and she threw her arms about them both and kissed them each a dozen times.

"Now," she cried, "I shall really have a daughter!"

It was several weary marches to the nearest mission; but they only waited at the farm a few days for rest and preparation for the great event before setting out upon the journey, and after the marriage ceremony had been performed they kept on to the coast to take passage for England. Those days were the most wonderful of Meriem's life. She had not dreamed even vaguely of the marvels that civilization held in store for her. The great ocean and the commodious steamship filled her with awe. The noise, and bustle and confusion of the English railway station frightened her.

"If there was a good-sized tree at hand," she confided to Korak, "I know that I should run to the very top of it in terror of my life."

"And make faces and throw twigs at the engine?" he laughed back.

"Poor old Numa," sighed the girl. "What will he do without us?"

"Oh, there are others to tease him, my little Mangani," assured Korak.

The Greystoke town house quite took Meriem's breath away; but when strangers were about none might guess that she had not been to the manner born.

They had been home but a week when Lord Greystoke received a message from his friend of many years, D'Arnot.

It was in the form of a letter of introduction brought by one General Armand Jacot. Lord Greystoke recalled the name, as who familiar with modern French history would not, for Jacot was in reality the Prince de Cadrenet—that intense republican who refused to use, even by courtesy, a title that had belonged to his family for four hundred years.

"There is no place for princes in a republic," he was wont to say.

Lord Greystoke received the hawk-nosed, gray mustached soldier in his library, and after a dozen words the two men had formed a mutual esteem that was to endure through life.

"I have come to you," explained General Jacot, "because our dear Admiral tells me that there is no one in all the world who is more intimately acquainted with central Africa than you.

"Let me tell you my story from the beginning. Many years ago my little daughter was stolen, presumably by Arabs, while I was serving with the Foreign Legion in Algeria. We did all that love and money and even government resources could do to discover her; but all to no avail. Her picture was published in the leading papers of every large city in the world, yet never did we find a man or woman who ever had seen her since the day she mysteriously disappeared.

"A week since there came to me in Paris a swarthy Arab, who called himself Abdul Kamak. He said that he had found my daughter and could lead me to her. I took him at once to Admiral D'Arnot, whom I knew had traveled some in central Africa. The man's story led the Admiral to believe that the place where the white girl the Arab supposed to be my daughter was held in captivity was not far from your African estates, and he advised that I come at once and call upon you—that you would know if such a girl were in your neighborhood."

"What proof did the Arab bring that she was your daughter?" asked Lord Greystoke.

"None," replied the other. "That is why we thought best to consult you before organizing an expedition. The fellow had only an old photograph of her on the back of which was pasted a newspaper cutting describing her and offering a reward. We feared that having found this somewhere it had aroused his cupidity and led him to believe that in some way he could obtain the reward, possibly by foisting upon us a white girl on the chance that so many years had elapsed that we would not be able to recognize an imposter as such."

"Have you the photograph with you?" asked Lord Greystoke.

The General drew an envelope from his pocket, took a yellowed photograph from it and handed it to the Englishman.

Tears dimmed the old warrior's eyes as they fell again upon the pictured features of his lost daughter.

Lord Greystoke examined the photograph for a moment. A queer expression entered his eyes. He touched a bell at his elbow, and an instant later a footman entered.

"Ask my son's wife if she will be so good as to come to the library," he directed.

The two men sat in silence. General Jacot was too well bred to show in any way the chagrin and disappointment he felt in the summary manner in which Lord Greystoke had dismissed the subject of his call. As soon as the young lady had come and he had been presented he would make his departure. A moment later Meriem entered.

Lord Greystoke and General Jacot rose and faced her. The Englishman spoke no word of introduction—he wanted to mark the effect of the first sight of the girl's face on the Frenchman, for he had a theory—a heaven-born theory that had leaped into his mind the moment his eyes had rested on the baby face of Jeanne Jacot.

General Jacot took one look at Meriem, then he turned toward Lord Greystoke.

"How long have you known it?" he asked, a trifle accusingly.

"Since you showed me that photograph a moment ago," replied the Englishman.

"It is she," said Jacot, shaking with suppressed emotion; "but she does not recognize me—of course she could not." Then he turned to Meriem. "My child," he said, "I am your—"

But she interrupted him with a quick, glad cry, as she ran toward him with outstretched arms.

"I know you! I know you!" she cried. "Oh, now I remember," and the old man folded her in his arms.

Jack Clayton and his mother were summoned, and when the story had been told them they were only glad that little Meriem had found a father and a mother.

"And really you didn't marry an Arab waif after all," said Meriem. "Isn't it fine!"

"You are fine," replied The Killer. "I married my little Meriem, and I don't care, for my part, whether she is an Arab, or just a little Tarmangani."

"She is neither, my son," said General Armand Jacot. "She is a princess in her own right."

A NOTE TO ERB ENTHUSIASTS

For readers interested in learning more about the life and work of
Edgar Rice Burroughs, Del Rey suggests the following list of ERB
fan clubs and their magazines. Write to the addresses below for
information on memberships and subscriptions.

British Edgar Rice Burroughs Society
77 Pembroke Road
Seven Kings
Ilford, Essex
IG3 8PQ England

Burroughs Bibliophiles
Burroughs Memorial Collection
University of Louisville
Louisville, Kentucky 40292

Erbania
8001 Fernview Lane
Tampa, Florida 33615

ERB Collector
7315 Livingston Road
Oxon Hill, Maryland 20745

ERB-Fan
Eschenweg 5
8070 Ingolstadt
Germany

ERB News Dateline
1990 Pine Grove Drive
Jenison, Michigan 49428

Tarzine
914 Country Club Drive
Midland, Texas 79701

DEL REY ONLINE!

The Del Rey Internet Newsletter...
A monthly electronic publication, posted on the Internet, GEnie, CompuServe, BIX, various BBSs, and the Panix gopher (gopher.panix.com). It features hype-free descriptions of books that are new in the stores, a list of our upcoming books, special announcements, a signing/reading/convention-attendance schedule for Del Rey authors, "In Depth" essays in which professionals in the field (authors, artists, designers, sales people, etc.) talk about their jobs in science fiction, a question-and-answer section, behind-the-scenes looks at sf publishing, and more!

Online editorial presence: Many of the Del Rey editors are online, on the Internet, GEnie, CompuServe, America Online, and Delphi. There is a Del Rey topic on GEnie and a Del Rey folder on America Online.

Our official e-mail address for Del Rey Books is delrey@randomhouse.com

Internet information source!
A lot of Del Rey material is available to the Internet on a gopher server: all back issues and the current issue of the Del Rey Internet Newsletter, a description of the DRIN and summaries of all the issues' contents, sample chapters of upcoming or current books (readable or downloadable for free), submission requirements, mail-order information, and much more. We will be adding more items of all sorts (mostly new DRINs and sample chapters) regularly. The address of the gopher is gopher.panix.com

Why? We at Del Rey realize that the networks are the medium of the future. That's where you'll find us promoting our books, socializing with others in the sf field, and—most importantly—making contact and sharing information with sf readers.

For more information, e-mail delrey@randomhouse.com